Praise for the Rhona MacLeod series

'Lin Anderson is one of Scotland's national treasures . . . her writing is unique, bringing warmth and depth to even the seediest parts of Glasgow. Rhona MacLeod is a complex and compelling heroine who just gets better with every outing'
Stuart MacBride

'From Glasgow's real underbelly, Lin Anderson will have you biting your nails and wondering why you ever bought a telly. Inventive, compelling, genuinely scary and beautifully written, as always'
Denzil Meyrick

'Hugely imaginative and exciting'
James Grieve (Emeritus Professor of Forensic Pathology)

'Vivid and atmospheric . . . enthralling'
Guardian

'Shades of *The Wicker Man*, with a touch of Agatha Christie. Superb'
Daily Mail

'The bleak landscape is beautifully described, giving this popular series a new lease of life'
Sunday Times

'Greenock-born Anderson's work is sharper than a pathologist's scalpel. One of the best Scottish crime series since Rebus'
Daily Record

'Guaranteed to grip the reader's imagination. Lin Anderson writes at a cracking pace . . . Very readable. Every last word'
Sunday Herald

Follow the Dead

Lin Anderson is a Scottish author and screenwriter known for her bestselling crime series featuring forensic scientist Dr Rhona MacLeod. Four of her novels have been longlisted for the Scottish Crime Book of the Year, with *Follow the Dead* being a 2018 finalist. Her short film *River Child* won both a Scottish BAFTA for Best Fiction and the Celtic Film Festival's Best Drama award and has now been viewed more than one million times on YouTube. Lin is also the co-founder of the international crime writing festival Bloody Scotland, which takes place annually in Stirling.

By Lin Anderson

Driftnet
Torch
Deadly Code
Dark Flight
Easy Kill
Final Cut
The Reborn
Picture Her Dead
Paths of the Dead
The Special Dead
None but the Dead
Follow the Dead
Sins of the Dead
Time for the Dead

NOVELLA
Blood Red Roses

Follow the Dead

LIN ANDERSON

PAN BOOKS

First published 2017 by Macmillan

This edition first published 2019 by Pan Books
an imprint of Pan Macmillan
The Smithson, 6 Briset Street, London EC1M 5NR
Associated companies throughout the world
www.panmacmillan.com

ISBN 978-1-5290-0071-9

3 5 7 9 8 6 4 2

A CIP catalogue record for this book is available from the British Library.

Map artwork by Hemesh Alles
Typeset by Palimpsest Book Production Limited, Falkirk, Stirlingshire
Printed and bound by CPI Group (UK) Ltd, Croydon, CR0 4YY

Visit **www.panmacmillan.com** to read more about all our books
and to buy them. You will also find features, author interviews and
news of any author events, and you can sign up for e-newsletters
so that you're always first to hear about our new releases.

For The Cairngorm Mountain Rescue Team

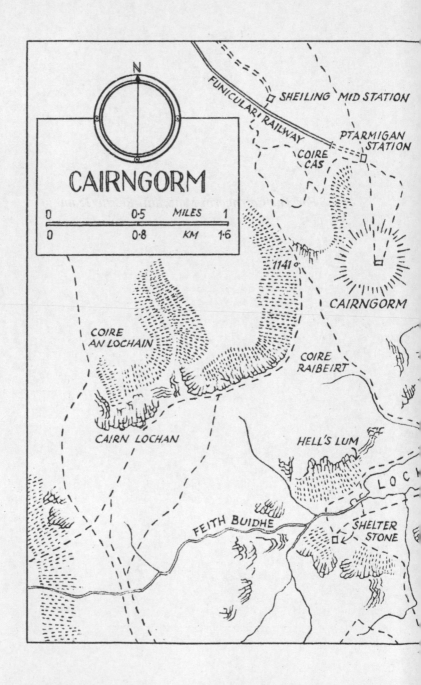

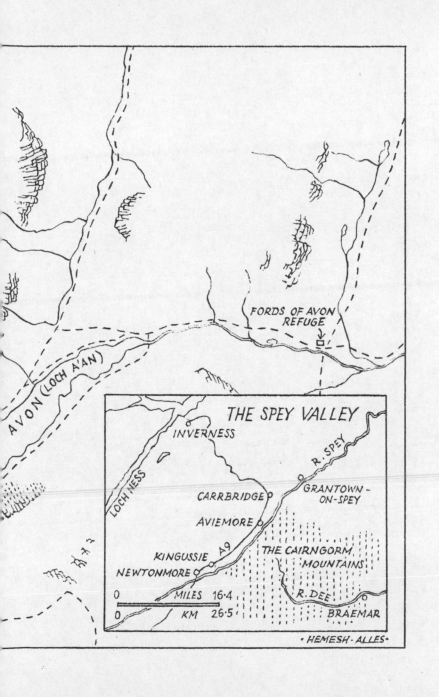

FORDS OF AVON
REFUGE

AVON (LOCH A'AN)

THE SPEY VALLEY

INVERNESS

R. SPEY

LOCH NESS

CARRBRIDGE

GRANTOWN-
ON-SPEY

AVIEMORE

A9

KINGUSSIE

THE CAIRNGORM
MOUNTAINS

NEWTONMORE

0   MILES 16·4

R. DEE

0   KM 26·5

BRAEMAR

· HEMESH · ALLES ·

They were holding hands, reminding him of Hansel and Gretel, or babes in the wood, although this place was barren of all vegetation. Come spring, the cold, hard ground would awaken allowing the tundra to burst into life. Not so for these two.

And yet . . . in their frozen perfection, you might imagine it possible that with a little warmth and perhaps a kiss on the cheek, the ice might melt and free them from their prison, just like Snow White in her glass case.

The boy was the smaller of the two. Perhaps five or six years old. He imagined her to be ten, maybe eleven. Even as he asked himself what they were doing there, on the border between Russia and his country, he knew the answer.

In the near distance, a herd of reindeer nosed the snow, looking for the sustenance which lay beneath, their thick coats rustling in the encroaching wind. Had they not wandered this way with their herdsman, the children's bodies would never have been found.

He glanced up, noting the heavy snow clouds moving swiftly across the pale blue heavens. Instinct and the Sami herdsman's motion skywards told him they would have to leave now with the bodies if they wanted to get out at all.

1

'Round three. Famous characters – fictional or otherwise.'

Gavin winked at Isla as he handed round the Post-its, which she took as a hint that she could probably guess who he would choose – a character out of *Star Wars* or his current hero, Rick Grimes from *The Walking Dead*.

Isla wrote down her character's name and passed it on. As did the others. Then they set about sticking the Post-it they'd received on their foreheads. The purpose of the game was simple. To ask questions which might lead you to correctly guess the character whose name was stuck to your brow, and more importantly, cause as much merriment as possible during the process.

Huddled together for warmth, a blizzard raging outside their stone refuge, laughter was helping to keep their temperature and their spirits up.

I was right, she thought as she spotted Rick Grimes across from her. The chance of Lucy guessing her given character was close to zero, the tale of a walking-dead apocalypse not being on her radar. No wonder Gavin was grinning. As to what Isla had on her own brow, that was causing Malcolm some merriment, which probably meant he'd want her to go first.

Gavin took pity on her. 'I'll go,' he offered.

3

LIN ANDERSON

Isla smiled back at him. After all, he was wearing the
character that she'd chosen.

'Female?' Gavin began.

A chorus of *No*.

'Fictional?'

That particular question had the other three looking at
one another in consternation. Should 'The Big Grey Man of
Ben Macdui' be regarded as fact or fiction? There were
plenty of stories about his ghostly presence on Cairngorm.
He was the unseen walker you heard behind you, whose
appearance brought such an indescribable sense of terror
and dread that well-seasoned climbers had been known to
flee the hill quicker than they thought possible.

Gavin was examining their expressions. 'Well?'

At that moment, the howl of the wind round the Shelter
Stone increased in volume, whipping snow through the
cracks and crevices of the makeshift walls. The fire brick
they'd found in the cave and lit, spluttered and for a moment
Isla thought it might have been blown out.

Sensing their discomfort, Gavin tried to get them back on
track. 'Fact or fiction?' he demanded.

Malcolm obliged with a hand signal that seemed to indicate it could be either way.

Gavin went studiously quiet. Isla could almost hear his
brain working.

The jammy bastard's going to get it.

Gavin gave them a triumphant smile before saying, 'The
Big Grey Man?'

'How did you know that?' Lucy said in disbelief.

'Wasn't that him howling outside?' Gavin said, all innocence.

4

His joke fell flat as the high-pitched howl sounded again. This time the fire brick did go out.

Head torches were now the only light in the gloom.

'Shall we pack up and go to bed?' Lucy said, her voice a little strained.

'I agree,' Isla backed her up.

Their best bet was to get some sleep. After all, they had to try to get off the mountain tomorrow, assuming the conditions improved.

Their intention hadn't been to spend the evening on Cairngorm, but at Macdui's inn in Aviemore. The ascent of the deep gully known as Hell's Lum had been challenging, but sheltered. Emerging out of the deep cornice at the top, they'd only then realized the full strength of the wind bearing down on them from the north – making their planned walk back in that direction impossible. Hence Gavin's sensible decision that they should drop back down the gully and bivouac at the Shelter Stone for yet another night.

Isla couldn't help but imagine the scene in the valley below. Macdui's would be heaving with partygoers, live music and drink. A blizzard raging on Cairngorm was of no significance to them. Tomorrow was Hogmanay and the resort was packed with holidaymakers wanting to bring in the New Year in the Highlands of Scotland. She contemplated the comfortable room and bed where she had hoped to spend the night and, catching Gavin's glance, decided he was sharing the same thought.

Gavin produced his hip flask. 'We'll have a dram, then head for bed.'

The whisky went down a treat. Isla felt its warmth spread. And a double sleeping bag was almost as good as a bed once the lights were out, especially since Gavin radiated heat whatever the temperature.

As they settled down, Gavin removed her forgotten Post-it. 'Give us a kiss, Princess Leia.'

Isla woke at two, knowing she would have to go outside, despite the weather. No one, but no one, went to the toilet inside the refuge, whatever the circumstances. Isla wished now that she hadn't had that final whisky.

There was nothing for it but to go.

Unzipping the sleeping bag, she pulled herself reluctantly out, realizing almost immediately that the temperature had dropped further since they'd gone to bed.

It must be easily minus fifteen.

She pulled on her outer garments, then eased her way past the second sleeping bag and crawled out of the crevice entrance. On exit, an ice-cold wind met her head-on, snow immediately gathering on her lashes and mouth.

She would have to be quick.

She realized then that the blizzard had momentarily eased and the powder snow that met her face was being whipped from the surface. Above her, the clouds parted, exposing a half-moon and accompanying stars. To the west, its beams had magically found the long strip of a frozen Loch A'an. For a moment she took in this wonder, then need drove her to locate a sheltered spot via her head torch where she might undress enough to relieve herself.

The snow began falling again as she rearranged her clothing, the wind returning with a force that suggested it had only paused long enough to allow her to go to the toilet. In moments she was surrounded by a swirling snowstorm, fierce and disorientating. Only yards from the cave, Isla was no longer certain of its exact direction. The huge slab of rock that formed the Shelter Stone had disappeared, as had the loch and surrounding mountains.

The force of a sudden gust thrust her to her knees and her head met a nearby rock. Dazed by the impact, she looked up to discover a tall figure beside her as though formed by snow. A gloved hand caught her arm. She thought it must be Gavin come to look for her, then registered that it wasn't.

'You okay?' a male voice said.

She nodded. 'I came out to—' She halted, realizing she had no need to explain.

'You have companions?'

'Yes, at the Shelter Stone.'

He helped her up, the bulk of his white-suited body shielding her from the wind, and pointed the way. She wanted to ask him who he was and where he had come from, but that would have to wait until they got to the cave. Around her the air crackled as though charged with electricity and behind her the crunch of her companion's footsteps seemed unnaturally loud and spaced out as though she was being followed by a giant.

The Big Grey Man of Ben Macdui.

She anticipated introducing him as such to the others and their imagined reaction brought a smile to Isla's frozen lips.

Then, as the curtain of snow briefly parted, she suddenly saw what lay before her. They were going in the wrong direction, heading down the boulder scree towards the loch, rather than upwards to the stone. She turned to tell him this and her head torch picked out his face staring down at her.

As the wind swallowed her words – 'We're going the

wrong way' – Isla began scrambling back, her numb hands trying desperately to grip the snow-covered boulders.

Finding her feet again, she rose to face him. And in that moment she knew.

He has no intention of helping me.

His gloved hand met her chest with a force that knocked the air from her lungs. She staggered, losing her foothold on the jumble of snow-crusted rocks. Thrust backwards by the impact, she tried to find her centre of gravity again, but couldn't right herself before the second punch arrived, this time in her stomach. She crumpled under the impact, bile rising in her throat.

He had chosen the spot well. Behind her was nothing but a steep boulder-strewn slope that even the snow couldn't soften. He was on his knees now, peering down at her, determined to finish the job this time. Isla made one last desperate grab for her attacker.

I'll take the bastard with me.

Her grasping hand found his face and she dug her nails in hard. His muffled shriek told her she had hit home.

Then the short fight was over. The third and final impact achieved its aim. As she tumbled backwards, crashing against rocks, rolling, her mouth open in a silent scream, the tall figure melted into the blanketing snow.

2

Glasgow, Hogmanay
'So, decided yet?'

DS Michael McNab had been going through the book of tattoos for the last fifteen minutes, and had yet to make up his mind.

'Can I show you what I want covered? Maybe you could suggest something?' he said.

Mannie looked intrigued.

'Come on through.'

He held aside a curtain behind which were a series of open booths. Three were occupied. McNab was shown into the fourth, where he stripped off his top half and turned round to let Mannie view his back.

'Jesus.' The tenor of his reaction suggested he was quite impressed. 'You took a bullet?'

McNab nodded.

'Don't see bullet wounds often except for a few squaddies lucky enough to return from Afghanistan.'

'I want it covered.'

'Can I ask why?'

'I'm fed up answering questions about it,' McNab said.

Mannie raised his eyebrows, which now disappeared into his forehead tattoos. 'They'll ask about the tattoo.'

'I prefer that. So what do you suggest?'

9

'Something Viking?' Mannie said. 'They're popular, since the TV programme starring Ragnar Lodbrok.'

McNab definitely didn't want a fucking Viking on his back and said so.

Mannie smiled. 'What about a skull then? We could mask the bullet hole in an eye socket.'

'That'll do,' McNab said, bored now at having to make a choice.

Mannie pointed to a sample on the wall. 'It's a lot of ink, but I think it'll work.'

'Go ahead.'

'How old's the scar exactly?'

'Why?'

'If it's less than a couple of years old it's not recommended.'

'It's fine,' McNab insisted.

'Okay. You're the boss, Detective Sergeant.'

Mannie pressed a call bell and moments later a young woman appeared. Dark-haired, slim, the body skin on show a walking advertisement for her chosen profession.

'This is Ellie. She'll be the one to work on you. Skulls are her thing.' Mannie waited for a moment, expecting McNab to argue. When he didn't, Mannie departed.

As Ellie set to work, McNab made it plain he had no desire for conversation. Instead he concentrated on the varying degrees of pain the selection of needles offered.

'You should ideally have something on the other shoulder. Balance things up a bit,' Ellie said when they took a break. 'I wouldn't recommend it today, but you could come back when this heals.'

'I wasn't planning on getting shot in the other shoulder,' McNab said, easing himself up.

McNab had seen that look before. The *I'm dying to ask you who, where and why, but not sure how you'll react* look.

'It was a woman I cheated on,' he lied. 'I'm lucky she didn't shoot a hole through my prick.'

She gave him a smile. 'We tattoo penises too.'

'No shit?' The thought made McNab wince.

Ellie, seeing his look of disbelief, rummaged through a box of photographs, extracted one and handed it to him. The penis on show was coloured like a snake. It was also considerably longer than Mr Average.

'Of course, it takes balls to have something like that done,' Ellie told him.

McNab met her challenging look. 'And I bet you do balls too?'

She smiled. 'Just inked a guy's testicles with the words "I'm nuts about you".'

McNab laughed and, holding up his hand, said, 'Okay, you win.'

'I always do,' she assured him.

At this she ordered him back into position so that she might complete her artwork. As the needle pierced his skin, McNab tried hard not to imagine it engaging with a more precious part of his anatomy, a thought which bizarrely made him hard.

'Okay,' he said. 'Let's talk. Keep my mind off that photograph.'

'You talk. I'll listen,' she said.

This'll be a first, McNab thought.

An hour later, he had made a return appointment for the other shoulder, and Ellie had promised to have a drink with him. He decided he was rather satisfied with the morning's proceedings. A fleeting memory of his last love interest suddenly presented itself. A PhD student at Glasgow University,

Freya had had a keen interest in witchcraft, and for a while, him. Until he'd been dumped. *A kindness on her part*, was McNab's final thought on that topic.

Emerging from the tattoo parlour, he found the rain had turned to sleet, the pavement now covered in slush. He slithered his way across to his parked car. Forgetting momentarily where he'd just been and what he'd had done, he threw himself inside, where his newly inked back collided with the driver's seat. The result reminded him of the months after he'd been shot. Sleeping on his front, dosed up with painkillers, if he slept at all.

Give over, you big pussy.

He recalled Ellie's bare arms and their riot of colour. God knows where else she'd had inked and he couldn't imagine she was one to complain about pain.

As he fired up the engine, his mobile buzzed an incoming message. McNab's pleasure at its contents made him momentarily forget his discomfort.

It seemed the Hogmanay special was on.

3

Aviemore, Hogmanay

'Not bad, eh?'

Sean, on one elbow, gazed down at her.

'Are we talking about you, the hotel or the weather?' Rhona said.

'What do you think?' He placed a kiss on her lips. 'What further delights do you have planned for this morning?'

'It'll soon be lunchtime,' Rhona informed him.

'So we start with lunch and go on from there.'

He rose naked to look out of the window. 'Snow's on again. Maybe we should just order room service and stay put?' His grin suggested he meant it.

'Don't you have to set up for tonight?'

'I do, but not until later.' Trying to interpret her expression, he offered, 'What say we go for a drive around then have something to eat?'

'Sounds good.'

Rhona threw back the duvet and padded to the shower.

The village has grown considerably, Rhona decided, as they took a brief tour round Aviemore. The number of newly built houses stretching up the hill on the northern side of the nearby A9 surprised her, as did the development of Scandinavian-style holiday apartments to the south-east. They'd arrived last night

13

in the dark from Glasgow, so there'd been no chance to see the changes since she'd previously been here.

This part of Scotland was a first for Sean and he was obviously seriously impressed by the surrounding scenery, in particular the view of the Cairngorms.

'Fancy a run up the funicular?' he said as they completed their short tour of the village.

'Okay, but we should check the weather first. My memory of coming here as a teenager was that it could be okay in the valley, and a howling gale up top.'

They decided to take a chance and headed for the Coylumbridge road that led to the ski slopes. The road was black, evidence that the plough had been along, but snow blanketed the surrounding countryside, the branches of the Scots pines stooped low with its weight.

Rhona recalled their trip through Drumochter Pass the previous evening, where they'd been part of a cavalcade of cars following a snowplough in what at times had been a white-out. Sean had done the driving and by the expression on his face had relished the experience.

'It's quite magical,' Sean said of the view.

'If you're well wrapped up.'

'You used to ski?'

'I did.'

'But not any more?'

'Maybe, on a sunny day in the Alps. A howling gale on the summit of Cairngorm, with horizontal ice biting my face, doesn't offer the same attraction.'

'And here's me thinking you were up for anything.' Sean smiled round at her.

I made the right decision to tag along, Rhona thought. She'd initially turned down Sean's invitation to accompany him to his Hogmanay gig in the Highlands. Sean rarely played outside the jazz club, or Glasgow for that matter, except for his occasional visits to his beloved Paris. She'd visited that city with him back in the early days of their up-and-down relationship. Rhona smiled a little at the memory of Sean's determination to entice her there. How she'd eventually succumbed to his Irish charm. *But here was different.* Aviemore was a trip down a different memory lane, not one Rhona relished taking. She had come here with Edward, her former lover and father of her son, Liam, in the days when she was young and thought she was in love.

A lifetime ago.

Besides, she rarely took time off from her work as a forensic scientist. And it was Hogmanay after all.

To her right Loch Morlich lay unmoving, its surface covered by a film of ice. Beyond stretched the Forest of Rothiemurchus and the towering massif that was Cairngorm.

'The road's closed,' Sean read the digital sign. 'Due to high winds and snow.'

Rhona had expected as much.

'Let's take a walk along the head of the loch instead,' she suggested.

Sean followed her directions into the car park, which had been free once, but was no longer. They parked up and set off through the ancient pines, where a few hardy souls were camped out in a mix of tents, camper vans and the occasional caravan.

'They must be mad,' Sean ventured as he pulled his woolly hat down over his ears.

'It's not that bad,' Rhona told him. 'With survival clothing and a good sleeping bag.'

'You'd rather we'd stayed here than at the hotel?' Sean slipped his arm about her shoulders.

'Definitely not,' she said, grateful for his warm embrace.

Ice puddles cracked underfoot and a couple of dogs slithered on the frozen ripples that edged the sand.

'We should come back in the summer,' Sean offered. 'I bet it's beautiful then.'

Rhona didn't respond. Planned holidays were not her thing, especially with Sean.

Reaching the far side of the loch, they located the path that followed a burn. Other walkers had paved the way for them, their footsteps visible in the powder snow. The swift-moving river was ice free, except in the stiller waters close to the edge. As they walked, the silence of the forest was broken by the sound of a helicopter. Glancing upwards, Rhona spotted the distinctive red and white shape of a Bristow patrol. With a headquarters in Inverness, Bristow, she knew, had taken over Search and Rescue from the RAF.

'Trouble?' Sean said.

'Probably just monitoring the road.'

As the chopper disappeared into thickening grey clouds, large flakes of snow started fluttering down. In moments the light began to fail, apart from a thin bright streak at the treeline.

'We should head back,' Rhona said. 'Before this gets any worse.'

The car park was empty of all but their own vehicle. It seemed the other visitors had already assumed the weather was about to deteriorate.

On the return journey, the thickening snow forced Sean down to a crawl as the drivers in front took fright at the sudden lack of visibility. Then the roundabout at the entrance to Aviemore came into view. Across the road the bright Christmas lights in the windows of La Taverna Italian restaurant offered a vision of checked tablecloths, warmth and food.

'Fancy an Italian, in preparation for the long night of celebration ahead?' Sean suggested.

A quick nod from Rhona saw them tackle the roundabout, then take the exit that led into the restaurant's car park.

4

Cairngorm, Hogmanay

Hearing the distinctive sound of chopper blades, he looked skywards.

Had someone seen and reported the wreckage?

The white-out had protected him until now, but the appearance of a search team would restrict his movements and make it more difficult for him to locate the girl.

She has to be dead, he told himself once again. His blow had sent her flying. It was a rocky area.

But yet I can't locate the body.

As soon as dawn had broken, he'd emerged from the Shelter Stone cave and made for the place she'd gone over. Heavy overnight snow had covered the boulder slope and he couldn't see a body anywhere, although there was evidence of a small localized avalanche which might have buried it. Buried bodies, he knew, were rarely discovered before spring when the snow melted.

And yet. It would be better to make sure.

The red-and-white chopper was back, circling the hill above him, obviously fighting the increasing wind gusts. The weather was worsening. Whatever the reason for the presence of the helicopter, it would have to abandon the hill soon. His clothing wasn't the bright colours usually sported by climbers but there was still a chance they might spot him.

He dipped behind the nearest rock and waited for the beat of the blades to pass.

Did the helicopter's appearance have something to do with the climbers in the cave or the wreckage on the loch? Or were they simply monitoring the ski road for trapped cars?

Then another thought took shape. One he liked least of all.

What if the girl had survived? What if she'd managed to raise the alarm?

As the chopper headed away, he extracted himself from his hiding place and, checking his compass and position, considered which route he should take out. The most obvious would be to head up Coire Raibert to the ski slopes. Then again if a mountain rescue team did appear, it would likely come from that direction. There was of course another route. Longer, maybe twenty miles, and it would take him back towards the wreckage. Alternatively, he could dig himself a snow hole, and sit it out for a few days. He had both the equipment and supplies, and if he stayed close by, he could monitor what happened.

With an eye on the sky, he made his decision.

5

Glasgow, Hogmanay

'So, what's up?' Chrissy McInsh gave McNab a penetrating look.

When he didn't answer, she said, 'You scored last night?'

McNab chose not to respond.

'You've plans to score tonight?' she tried.

That was one way to describe it.

McNab headed for the coffee machine. Chrissy's coffee wasn't strong enough for his taste, but it was a caffeine fix.

'Well, are you going to tell me why you're here?' she demanded.

'Just visiting my favourite forensic people,' McNab said with studied nonchalance.

'Rhona's not here,' Chrissy told him.

McNab tried to prevent his face falling, but couldn't.

'She's in Aviemore,' Chrissy paused for emphasis, 'with Sean.'

McNab was stuck for a response to that piece of news, so he changed the subject. 'You have plans for Hogmanay?'

'Of course. Don't you?' she said, with a glint in her eye.

'I'm working,' he said mysteriously.

Chrissy was studying him in a manner McNab knew too

well. *She should be the detective*, he thought, and not for the first time.

'Really, on what exactly?' she prodded.

McNab assumed his *can't say* expression.

'Piss off, McNab, I've more important things to do than massage your ego.'

'I might be free after midnight,' he offered, 'if there's a party on?' He assumed a pleading look.

Chrissy laughed. 'You need my help with your social life?'

'Always,' he admitted truthfully.

Chrissy relented. 'Text me when you're finished, I'll let you know where we are.'

McNab retreated then. He would have loved to tell Chrissy what the job was. It had been in the planning long enough, but Rhona's forensic assistant, with her army of spies, would be one of the first to know once it went down.

Emerging from the building, he found darkness had descended and the snow had come back on. Plus the temperature had dropped considerably, freezing the slush. McNab watched as unsuspecting fellow pedestrians found their feet going out from under them.

A&E will be busy tonight.

Reaching the car, he eased his way out onto the black road which now glistened as the surface water started to freeze. Nearing rush hour, the traffic was nose to tail. McNab took his place in the queue.

Half an hour later he was at his flat. He ordered pizza before heading up the stairs. His plan was to free himself of the cling film he'd been wrapped in (having waited the obligatory two hours), and have a shower. Ellie had been pretty insistent as to the need to keep the inked area clean and had given him a sheet of paper with instructions on it.

In the bathroom, McNab stripped off and stood naked at the full-length mirror, trying not to recall the photograph of the tattooed penis. Gingerly unwrapping the cling film, he stepped under the running shower. Ellie had told him to wash the tattoo three times a day and wear cling film for at least three days, and that included overnight. In fact she'd gone so far as to suggest they wait for thirty-six hours before sharing that drink. McNab had chosen to take that as an indication that she might like to see him naked, before he had the other side done.

Then again maybe she was into cling film.

The sound of the buzzer as he stepped out of the shower suggested that his pepperoni pizza had arrived. McNab quickly secured a towel round his middle and went to answer it. Gus, his usual delivery boy, turned out tonight to be Sandi, a girl. McNab had been looking forward to show-ing off his tattoo to the person who'd recommended the Ink Parlour in the first place.

'Sorry,' he said. 'I assumed it would be Gus.' McNab hoped his dripping hair and body would prove that he *had* just got out of the shower, and wasn't the weirdo suggested by the look on her face.

Sandi didn't respond, but merely handed over the pizza and waited to be paid.

'I have an account,' McNab explained.

'I'm new,' she countered. 'I was told to get the money.'

McNab went to retrieve his wallet and felt her eyes on his back. On his return, she said, 'Cool tattoo,' with what he interpreted as an admiring smile.

McNab quickly paid her, conscious that a pretty girl's

admiration coupled with his own nakedness was having an effect. The door firmly shut, he perched on the edge of the settee, clicked on the TV and set about the pizza. In exactly three hours' time, his Hogmanay party would begin.

6

'Four climbers from Glasgow, all experienced. Two men, two women, mid-twenties.'

Owen Drummond, leader of the Cairngorm Mountain Rescue team, glanced at the window where the wind was fashioning the driving snow into an intricate paisley pattern on the glass.

His long-time fellow team member and local piper, Kyle Dunn, continued: 'They set off two days ago from Glenmore Lodge. The warden said their plan was to bivouac at the Shelter Stone and make an early start on Hell's Lum yesterday morning and be back down that night in preparation for Hogmanay.'

The Shelter Stone, the huge slab of rock that had fallen from the crag above forming a natural cavity in the jumble of boulders and granite slabs of the lower slopes, was regularly used as a mountain refuge and bivouac for climbers. Hell's Lum, which had been the group's goal, was a deep chimney cleft on the face of a neighbouring crag, its apocalyptic-sounding name incorporating the Scots word for chimney. A serious place full of pitfalls for the inexperienced, and a long way from help if an accident occurred.

'No communication?' Owen said.

24

Kyle shook his head. 'The weather came in pretty quickly from the north.'

Had the climbers emerged from Hell's Lum to find a strong north snow-laden wind hitting them head-on, it would have made sense to retreat rather than try to make for the Coire Cas car park.

'You think they'll have headed back to the Shelter Stone?' Owen said.

'Or made for one of the snow holes along Feith Buidhe.' If they were experienced, that would be what to expect.

A sudden gust brought his attention back to the window. Owen watched as the powder snow birled in mad pirouettes around the Land Rover, the wheels of which were already half buried.

'Looks like we might be here for the duration ourselves,' he said.

The centre was well equipped with plenty of food and a warm bed for the night. So they were a great deal better off than anyone out on the hill. Still, experienced climbers knew what to expect and wouldn't have ventured onto Cairngorm in winter unless they enjoyed a challenge.

'I'm planning to bring in the New Year at Macdui's,' Kyle said.

'With Annieska?'

Kyle nodded. 'She's working behind the bar.'

'Better get moving then,' Owen urged him.

'What about you?'

'I'll maybe catch you later.'

When Kyle had set out like an Arctic explorer into the blizzard, Owen made himself a mug of coffee and settled down with a book. He'd already made up his mind to stay where he was. He didn't mind bringing in the New Year alone here. Since Shona had moved out, he'd found himself avoiding spending much time at home. Too many memories and few of them good. In fact crossing the threshold of the Aviemore flat they'd shared felt like re-entering a crime scene.

Where I was the perpetrator.

Thirty minutes later, he laid the book down. The shriek of the wind had increased, the driving snow now blocking any view of the yard and the surrounding trees. He hoped Kyle had made it into Aviemore with the vehicle. If he had got stuck, he would no doubt have walked the rest. He could take the shortcut by the railway and reach the village that way.

Owen rose and, abandoning his book and cold coffee, went walkabout, intent on checking that all was secure against the storm. A former Free Church of Scotland place of worship, the building had stood among the ancient Rothiemurchus pines since 1895, the solid stone surviving numerous severe winters and wild storms such as this one.

Owned now by the team, it had been transformed into the Rescue Centre. Designed like many churches in the form of an upturned boat, the big doors that had once welcomed in the faithful now led into a well-equipped kitchen. The room where they'd worshipped had been split in two and housed a small lecture theatre and the place where the team gathered prior to a rescue.

Owen stood for a moment in the lecture theatre. The pulpit had gone but the arch of wood above it had been retained, maintaining the excellent acoustics enjoyed by the minister as he'd given his sermons in both Gaelic and English. Owen found it easy to imagine the call and recall of Gaelic psalms resonating in this room. Below were the shelves which housed their extensive library of mountaineering books, dedicated to a former team member.

Satisfied that all was well and that the leaded windows with the four-inch squares of glass were resolute against the onslaught, Owen walked through the tidy assembly area and from there back into the control room. When a rescue was in full swing this room would house three team members coordinating twenty or more members of the search team and of course the police.

But no rescue tonight.

He found himself almost wishing there was. At least it would keep him busy and prevent him from thinking about what an arse he'd been with Shona.

Owen checked the time to find he was half an hour away from the New Year. He imagined Kyle at Macdui's, no doubt enjoying a pint, and felt a little sorry for himself.

I should have gone with him. Too late now.

He decided he would have a dram to welcome in the New Year, then bunk down in one of the four small bedrooms, each named after one of the Cairngorm peaks: Macdui, Cairngorm, Braeriach and Cairn Toul. Tonight he would sleep in Macdui, minus the party.

7

The dog's eyes met his own, its panting forming a balloon of mist in the cold air. Straining at the handler's leash, it was exhibiting the same excitement that McNab was experiencing. Behind him three officers awaited his instructions. From beyond the thick door came the heavy beat of music. By the locked door and the noise, it looked like the Delta Club was hosting a private party.

All the better for us.

McNab waved the Enforcer forward. Close to two feet long and weighing thirty-five pounds, with an impact of almost three tons, in the hands of a trained officer the 'big key' would open any door. McNab's shouts demanding entry were swallowed in the thumping beat. Even the sound of the door being broken down went unheeded.

McNab, first in, led the way swiftly down the dimly lit corridor, the sniffer dog at his heels, its squeals of pleasure suggesting it could already scent its prey. By the far end, the sound was deafening, and McNab had to rely on hand signals. Having got this far, he didn't want a screw-up now.

As he threw open the door, the red laser spots of his armed colleagues were lost in a mad dance of sweeping laser beams that played in tandem with the pulsating music. Before him was what could only be described as a real clusterfuck – a writhing mass of naked bodies intertwined on a large plastic mat laid down for the purpose. The smell of male sweat and other bodily fluids hit McNab with force. The same sight and scent drove the dog mad and it started to bark. McNab tried to shout his own order but no one indulging in the orgy as yet appeared to notice they had visitors, or simply didn't care.

McNab's hand signals conveyed that someone should cut the sound system and that the dog be let loose. Maybe a German shepherd bounding into their midst could break up the orgy where armed police had failed.

As the dog plunged into the melee, the music and accompanying laser show abruptly ended to be replaced by stark electric light and a cacophony of shrieks and curses. Now the scene was revealed in all its true and hideous form. At a quick butt count, there were six males and four females. As the men finally realized who had arrived to spoil their fun, there was a mad scramble to flee with the women being thrown roughly aside, and at least one of them trampled underfoot.

Then McNab spotted his prize. Brodie had apparently been observing the proceedings rather than taking part in them. The only man in the room fully clothed, he was shoving his way through the turmoil, heading, it seemed, for a door in the wall behind the bar. McNab lunged after him, barging his way through the scrabble of naked flesh.

'Stop, police!' he shouted.

Brodie ignored him and, easily vaulting the counter, sent glasses flying to shatter on the floor. In moments he was through the open door and had shut it behind him.

Got you, you bastard.

There was, as far as McNab was aware, only one other way out of here, and they had that covered.

Gun at the ready, he cautiously opened the door to discover the real reason for the raid on the club.

Happy New Year!

Even as he mouthed this, he heard a crack as a bullet passed his ear. McNab dived for the floor as a second bullet brushed his arm and embedded itself in the wall behind. He heard excited barks as the dog entered, having found its target. A room full of cocaine, packaged and ready for distribution.

The dog jumped onto the table, scattering the kilo packs which, pierced by the gunshots, now blew up a dust cloud concealing what lay beyond the counter. McNab heard a door being wrenched open, and a blast of cold air found its way into the room to feed the swirling white cloud.

The bastard's getting away.

As he launched himself through the cloud, McNab felt the taste of cocaine on his lips and in his nostrils. He wiped his mouth then spat, aware that with so much coke in the air he'd already ingested it.

I'll be high whatever I do.

Outside, an icy wind whipping down the alley met him straight on. McNab checked both ways, wondering what had happened to the officer he'd stationed round the back. Then he saw a dark shadow to the right which was surely a fallen body in the snow. McNab headed in that direction.

A quick check for a pulse found one, and steady. Help would be here soon enough and he didn't want to lose his assailant.

McNab rose and, quickly exiting the alleyway, searched for his prey among the ebullient Hogmanay partygoers who thronged the inner-city streets. The cocaine, he realized now, had reached his bloodstream and was coursing through it, making his heart pound even faster and spiking the colour in the crowds that surrounded him.

'Hey, mate, are you okay?'

A hand caught his arm. McNab flung it off and a splatter of blood found the white of the crusted snow by his feet.

'I'm a police officer. Did a man run past you?'

'A big bald bloke?' the guy said, looking frightened.

A wave of nausea accompanied McNab's nod.

'He went in there.' He pointed at an open door from where came the sound of pounding music, which seemed to match McNab's own rapid heartbeat.

McNab leaned a hand on the wall in an attempt to quell his stomach's reaction to the rush of cocaine, as the entrance to the nightclub pulsated before him.

Fucking hell.

The jowelled face of an angry bouncer was shoved in his own.

'No drunks allowed.'

McNab marshalled himself and retrieved his ID.

'Call 999. Tell them Detective Sergeant McNab told you to. Tell them I'm in pursuit of a suspect. Give them the name of this place.'

Without waiting for a response, McNab shoved his way past the burly figure to enter a busy lobby. His senses on high alert, he scanned the faces of the males hanging about there, all too young to be his man. Music poured through a set of open doors like a rushing tide. More rapid in beat than at the clusterfuck, but with the same laser light show sweeping over the jerking, but thankfully clothed bodies.

McNab entered and, ignoring the dancers, began checking out those crowded round a nearby bar, as a female voice shouted something in his ear.

When he looked down he found a blonde female with a concerned look on her face. Interpreting her mouth movements, he heard, 'You're hurt, sir.'

Her use of the title *sir* confused him. He took a closer look.

'PC Alison Watt, sir,' she said in a voice that suggested he would know the name.

Perplexed by this development, McNab tried to examine her face a bit more closely.

'You don't recognize me, sir?' she said.

McNab didn't, but decided to pretend he did.

'I can show you my ID?' she offered.

McNab shook his head. He didn't want such an exchange on view, having just spotted his prey taking up a spot behind a pillar.

The bastard has no idea he was followed in here.

Which suited McNab very well. Meanwhile, his newly discovered PC was offering her services in whatever he was doing.

'Do you think you could keep an eye on that bald bloke by the pillar?'

'Will do, sir.' She drew herself up and assumed a determined smile.

'Be careful. He may be armed,' McNab warned.

She nodded.

McNab made for the lobby to find the bouncer deep in conversation with another man who he took to be the manager. As the effects of the cocaine rush began to ebb, McNab suddenly registered the pain in his arm and the fact that his heart was slowing down. Despite this, it seemed his feet still wanted to be on the move. He forced himself to control his desire to pace as the manager said, 'We don't want any trouble, officer. We always comply with the police, report drugs on the premises—'

McNab interrupted his frightened flow. 'We'll apprehend the suspect as quietly as we can, and you can continue with the party.'

Relief flooded the manager's face, then vanished as two armed police officers from the raid appeared.

McNab drew them to one side and explained how this would play out. When he mentioned PC Watt, one of the men indicated that he knew her.

'She'll be fine, sir,' he added as though reading McNab's worry.

There in the lobby, they were attracting less attention from the partygoers than expected. Maybe because it was no longer unusual to see armed police in Glasgow city centre.

Back in the dance area, McNab checked for his man. The pillar was still there, but Brodie was no longer against it. And where the hell was PC Watt? The officer who'd professed to know her was scanning the crowd, a worried expression on his face.

Then he saw her coming towards them, pushing her way through the dancers.

'He went to the Gents and hasn't come back out.' She pointed in the direction she'd come from.

McNab headed for the sign. The door opened on a short corridor. Two doors, first Ladies, then Gents. McNab banged on the Gents door, shouted, 'Police. Stand back,' and shouldered the door to find two guys at the urinals, scrabbling to put their dicks away, neither of them Brodie. There were six cubicles, two with closed doors.

McNab ordered whoever was inside them to come out. One answered crossly that he was taking a dump and wasn't finished yet. The other door opened and a young blood appeared with a frightened face and big pupils which, McNab suspected, matched his own.

'Now!' McNab told the other occupant.

The toilet was flushed and the door opened. It wasn't Brodie, but the occupant had pissed McNab off. He ordered one of the officers to take down his name and advise him about obstructing an officer in the line of duty.

'Fuck's sake,' the man said.

'And swearing at a police officer.'

'If you're looking for the big bald bloke, he took the fire exit just as I came in here,' his antagonist said, looking for a helpful way out of his situation.

Back in the corridor, McNab located the nearest exit, which looked closed but, on inspection, wasn't. Pushing the double doors open, he found himself in the ubiquitous back lane, which of course was empty except for snow and bins.

'Fuck.' McNab took a breath of the cold night air. Reality was back and with it the nagging pain in his arm and an increasingly light-headed feeling. Slowly retracing his steps, he tried to take some pleasure in what had just happened, despite their loss of Brodie. After all, they'd never expected him to be at the club, not on Hogmanay. And not at the same time as a cocaine consignment.

If only I hadn't lost the bastard.

Nailing Brodie had, McNab acknowledged, become his prime obsession since the completion of the Orkney case. The man had been on McNab's radar far longer than that, but with nothing concrete, it seemed he was the only one who thought that Brodie, identified as a low-key pimp and hard man, might just be the mastermind behind an international import and export business.

Okay, so I was right, but . . .

And they certainly hadn't anticipated an orgy. A memory of that scene came flooding back and it wasn't pretty. He imagined all those participants being taken to the station for questioning, hopefully clothed.

He'd gone there hoping to find cocaine. And from what he had seen, it was a big haul. Maybe even bigger than the half a million's worth a forensic team had taken a week to unearth in the hold of a foreign-owned tug they'd intercepted in the North Sea and brought into Aberdeen harbour. They had long suspected the east-coast port wasn't the only entry point and that shipments may have been moved to the western seaboard. With Scotland having the longest coastline in Europe after Norway and Greece, every remote west-coast bay and harbour could provide an ideal drop-off point for smuggled drugs.

And maybe smuggled humans?

McNab recalled the females he'd seen in that room. All of them young. He also had a fleeting memory of the words they'd shouted in their fear.

They weren't speaking English.

Back at the alley behind the Delta club, McNab noted that the injured officer had been removed and the area sealed off. Lifting the crime scene tape, he made for the exit he'd used in his pursuit. A white boiler suit met him just inside the door.

'Welcome to the party,' Chrissy said, her eyes accusing above the mask.

8

McNab was feeling decidedly groggy. Either blood loss, a cocaine hangover or a mixture of both being to blame, according to the nurse who was currently helping him off with his bulletproof vest, then his shirt. Up to a few seconds ago, he'd forgotten all about his cling-film undergarment which unfortunately was about to be revealed in all its glory.

Give the nurse her due, she did not make a caustic remark, although had he been in her place, he most certainly would have. McNab had a sudden flash memory of the tattooed penis, which begged the question . . . did you have to wear cling film on your nether regions as well?

He registered that the nurse had now spotted the reason for the wrap.

'Nice job,' she was saying, while stepping back for a better view. 'Where did you have it done?'

McNab told her.

'Don't get many septic ones from there.'

'Septic?' McNab muttered worriedly.

'The cling film will need to come off, I'm afraid, if I'm to clean and dress the arm wound. You can rewrap yourself once you get home.'

McNab wasn't sure when that would be, his plan being to head to the station and check out the participants in the

36

orgy. There had been money involved there, big money he suspected. The provision of such a party wouldn't come cheap, especially with a plentiful supply of cocaine on the side. Plus he thought he might have recognized at least one of the males taking part. His face, that was. Not the naked torso.

The nurse's cleansing of the wound and surrounding area now stood out against the dusting of cocaine that covered the remainder of his exposed skin.

'You'll need to shower this off,' the nurse was telling him.

'Think I'll save it for later,' McNab said. 'As an alternative to painkillers.'

Nurse Debby, according to her name badge, shot him a warning look from a pair of rather attractive hazel eyes.

'Just joking, nurse,' McNab said, although he wasn't sure he was.

Having cleaned the flesh wound, she began taping it. 'You were lucky. An inch to the right and you would have had another bullet hole.'

So she'd spotted the first one.

'I won't need an arm tattoo?'

'No,' she assured him. 'Although you might want to balance your back with one on the other side.'

'Are you on commission from the Ink Parlour?'

She gave him a wicked grin.

The dressing completed, she indicated he could sit back now. Instead, McNab swung his legs off the bed and stood up, to begin the laborious process of pulling on his shirt. The nurse looked as though she might argue, then helped him instead.

'Did the police bring anyone else here from the raid?'

'An officer with concussion and a young woman. Two

37

cubicles down,' she said helpfully. 'There's an officer sitting outside.'

If the raid had produced only one casualty from that stampede, they were lucky. Dressed now, he took his leave of Nurse Debby, who handed him a sheet of paper with instructions on how to look after his wound. McNab thanked her and shoved it in his pocket with the one on tattoos.

A variety of sounds emanated from the various cubicles as medical personnel dealt with the fallout from a snowy and no doubt alcohol-fuelled Hogmanay. As promised, two cubicles along sat a uniformed, bored-looking constable, who immediately jumped to attention when he spotted McNab.

'Constable Munro, sir.'

When asked if there was anyone with the young woman, he shook his head.

McNab pulled back the curtain and stepped inside. The face that lay against the pillows was young, ridiculously young it seemed to McNab. She was what his mother would have called 'a slip of a girl'. The hospital gown dwarfed her shoulders, one of which was bandaged, the matching arm in a sling. Above this, the brown neck and cheek were a mass of bruising in the shape of a footprint.

McNab was suddenly back in that room full of writhing flesh. The barking dog. The screams of the females ringing in his ears as the men disengaged and trampled over them in a determined effort to escape.

She must have been on the floor when it happened and some bastard stood on her.

He was so put out by that image he failed to register that her dark eyes had opened and she was regarding him fearfully. McNab sought to allay this with a reassuring smile. That worked briefly until he displayed his ID and introduced himself, then a spark of recognition suggested she remembered him from the melee that had brought her here. She pulled herself away from him as far as was possible.

'Do you speak English?'

She shook her head.

By eye and skin colour alone, she looked more Mediterranean than Eastern European, but McNab attempted the only expression he knew in Polish. 'Robi wy mówicie Język polski?'

She eyed him warily, but said nothing.

PC Munro drew back the curtain and offered, 'She might be Norwegian, sir. I heard her say, 'Han vil drepe meg.'

'And that means?'

'He'll kill me . . . I think.'

'You speak Norwegian?'

The constable shook his head. 'I watch Norwegian crime drama, sir. I've picked up a few words.'

'I thought all Norwegians spoke English, usually better than we do,' McNab said.

PC Munro thought about that then agreed. 'You're right, sir.'

McNab had watched the girl out of the corner of his eye during this conversation and was pretty sure she wasn't following it, which put his theory out of the window.

McNab pulled out his mobile and brought up a world map. Showing it to the girl, he pointed first to himself, then Scotland, then indicated that she might show him where she was from. She peered at the screen, eventually pointing to a large land mass east of Turkey.

Fucking Syria?

When he said, 'Syria?' out loud, she nodded.

McNab brought up the notepad and wrote down a number.

'Me,' he said, pointing to himself, then at the number on the screen. He handed her the mobile and, understanding his request, she did as asked.

Jesus Christ.

'She's thirteen,' he told PC Munro. 'She's only thirteen years old.'

A seminar he'd attended on human trafficking had indicated that those brought into the UK came principally from Nigeria and the Eastern Bloc. But then only recently he'd read about the unaccompanied refugee children from war-torn Syria disappearing in Europe in their thousands.

She was eyeing him anxiously. McNab gave her what he hoped was an encouraging smile.

'Michael,' he said, pointing to his chest. When he asked for her name, she hesitated then said shyly, 'Amena.'

But if she was from Syria, how come she spoke Norwegian?

The girl had turned her face away from him, but McNab noted that the hand that lay on the sheet was trembling. When he made his way round the foot of the bed, he found her eyes closed and the thick black lashes wet with tears.

'Her injuries are the result of being trampled on. Just as well they weren't wearing boots or high heels for that matter.' The doctor paused long enough to check his notes. 'Dislocated right shoulder, three broken ribs, extensive bruising to the face and neck, and –' he looked up – 'severe bruising and some lacerations to the vagina and anus.' The doctor shook his head. 'She's been very roughly treated sexually over a period of time.'

'How did you communicate with her?'

'By signs. She doesn't speak English.'

'I think she's Syrian, but my constable thought he heard her say something in Norwegian.'

'Really? That might be useful.'

'Why?'

'We have a junior doctor on A&E here who has connections to Norway. She might be able to help.'

'Is she available?'

'Being Hogmanay, we have a depleted staff. I'll check. If she's around, I'll send her to you.'

McNab thanked the doctor and made for the waiting room, which had calmed down since his own arrival. He found himself a quiet corner, then gave Chrissy a ring.

'Remind me to kill you when I see you,' she told him.

'It was you who packed me off to A&E, remember?'

'Only to prevent further blood loss inflicted by me. Are you still high?'

'Sadly no, but I have the hangover. How are things there?'

Chrissy told him that all six male participants had been taken to the station, along with three females. None of whom seemed to speak English. 'They're all in their teens by the look of it.'

'Anyone of any note among the men?'

'No idea.'

'What's the haul?'

Chrissy's response, 'Possibly bigger than Aberdeen,' made McNab smile.

'Worth missing a Hogmanay party for,' he said.

The sound he got in return suggested Chrissy remained to

be convinced. McNab rang off as a young woman in hospital garb approached.

'Detective Sergeant McNab?'

He nodded.

'Sylvia Reynold. I'm a junior doctor here. I spent a year in Norway as an au pair and can speak a little Norwegian.'

McNab thanked her for her help in advance and explained that he believed the girl was Syrian, but she appeared to speak some Norwegian. Back in the cubicle, Dr Reynold took a seat beside the bed and in a low and calm voice introduced herself and explained what McNab had just told her. By the expression on the girl's face she understood the rather halting Norwegian. Minutes later, the doctor gestured to McNab that they should go outside.

'Her name is Amena Tamar. She understands a little Norwegian because the man who brought her to this country was from there.'

'Do we have a name for the trafficker?'

'Stefan. That's all.'

'And the other women she was with?'

Dr Reynolds shook her head. 'We didn't get past "he will kill me" and her country of origin.'

McNab thanked her as her buzzer sounded and she was called away. The girl seemed to be asleep. Either that or she'd had enough questioning for the moment. McNab looked down on the child's battered face, trying not to think about the other injuries. He had no kids, or none he knew of. But if he had, wouldn't he try to get them out of a war zone?

Europe, the UK. The promised land. Like fuck it was.

He checked on Munro before he left. 'It could be worse,

42

you could be on duty on Hogmanay in Glasgow city centre,' he told him.

'Perish the thought, sir.'

'Look after her.'

'I will, sir.'

9

Macdui's, Aviemore, Hogmanay

Rhona wondered how many more people they could squash in here. Standing four deep at the bar, with all the tables filled, she was lucky to have a corner next to the stage, although how she would ever reach the Ladies if required was another matter. Now and again the front door would open and a few more snow-covered figures would arrive along with a blast of cold air. The snowstorm hadn't appeared to frighten folk away from their desire to party on Hogmanay.

At that moment Sean came back with their drinks. Having already played his first set, he was now relaxed and obviously enjoying himself. Other musicians had turned up, including an Irish guitarist whom he knew, and the second half promised to be a jamming session which he was clearly looking forward to. At midnight a piper had brought in the New Year with 'Auld Lang Syne' and Rhona had found herself crossing arms with a couple from London. After that the crowd settled down to enjoy the New Year with enthusiasm.

'I like a wee quiet night,' Sean said with a grin.

'When does this place close?'

'Who knows? Officially I finish at one. If you've had

enough by then, we have only to cross the road and we're home.'

Just as well, Rhona thought, judging by the build-up of snow outside. She felt the vibration of her mobile in her pocket as a text arrived, which proved to be from an irate Chrissy who, having wished her Happy New Year, then indicated that she wasn't having the Hogmanay she'd hoped for, due to McNab. Rhona couldn't resist replying what a great time she was having and illustrating it with suitable party emojis. She then added that due to a blizzard she was likely to be stuck here for days. As she was about to press the send button, she took pity on her forensic assistant and removed the threat that she might be marooned in Aviemore.

As Sean made his way back on stage, Rhona found herself staring up at the piper, who introduced himself as Kyle Dunn, then told her he was a member of the Cairngorm Mountain Rescue team along with a former colleague of hers, Charlie Robertson.

'Professor Robertson, the pathologist?' Rhona said, surprised.

'That's him, the Prof. He gets ribbed about that a lot.'

Rhona glanced around the room. 'Is Charlie here?'

'No. He's in Inverness but has a cottage here in Aviemore. He comes down most weekends. If there's a call-out, he joins us.'

Rhona remembered Charlie from a number of cases she'd dealt with in the north. Ebullient and entertaining, he'd once addressed the annual weekend conference of AAPT members – anatomical pathology technologists, or mortuary people, to the uninitiated. The conference itself was unremarkable; not so the riotous after-party, which she and

Charlie had eventually escaped by climbing over a five-bar gate.

'How did you know who I was?' she said, mystified.

'I told the Prof that Sean Maguire, the saxophonist, was playing here on Hogmanay. He said to look out for Dr Rhona MacLeod in case she came with him.'

'It's a small world,' Rhona said.

'It is that,' Kyle agreed. 'We also have a DI previously from Govan Major Investigation Team. Ruth Abernethy?'

'I know Ruth. She was a keen hillwalker.'

'She's based in Inverness MIT now.'

'So how many are in the rescue team?'

'Forty-four, but they're well spread out and, of course, most have jobs – doctors, police, teachers – so aren't always available. For a big rescue we can muster maybe twenty or so.'

'So no call-outs tonight?' As Rhona spoke the door blew open and another snow-dusted figure entered.

'Not yet, anyway,' Kyle said, 'although who knows what the night might bring.'

'You wouldn't go out in weather like this?' Rhona said, surprised.

'If we have a location we usually try, providing the wind speed's under 100mph. Over that and we'd be crawling, which makes for very slow progress,' he laughed.

'What about air support?'

'No chance of that in high winds or poor visibility. Most times we either walk folk out if they're able, or stretcher them out if they're hurt.'

'And the dead?'

'Bristow don't bring out dead bodies, unless our team would be putting themselves in danger by retrieving them.'

Rhona apologized for the ghoulish turn in the conversation. 'I'm always on the job,' she explained.

'As am I,' Kyle assured her. 'How long are you here for?'

'A couple of days.'

'If you fancy seeing the set-up, give me a call.' They exchanged cards. 'We're out on the ski road at Inverdruie.'

They parted company then as the band struck up, drowning any possibility of further conversation. Rhona put Kyle's number in her mobile, then took a selfie in the midst of the party and sent a copy to both Chrissy and McNab to prove she was definitely off-duty.

She abandoned the jamming session an hour later, assuring Sean she could find her way across the road to the hotel unaided. The powder snow was knee high, but it had stopped falling from the sky. The wind had dropped, although evidence of its former strength was all about her. Snowdrifts hid the lower windows of the pub and the vehicles in the hotel car park were indistinguishable one from the other in their white mantles.

The thick cloud formation of earlier had dispersed and a watery partial moon now outlined the glistening summit of Cairngorm against an inky sky. Rhona stopped for a moment to admire the view, before trudging across to the shining beacon which was her hotel. Music came from here too, indicating yet another party was in full swing.

She threaded her way through the crowd that had spilled from the bar, and made her way upstairs. Shutting the bedroom door on the sounds of the party, she undressed and got into bed. Minutes later she was asleep.

10

12 hours earlier

She opened her eyes to a thin beam of light coming from a hole high above her. The light reflected off the myriad icicles that hung from the underside of the roof of the snow cave. For a moment, she was pain free, then she was swamped again by its arrival. Gritting her teeth, she decided it was bearable, just, and probably because she had lost so much feeling in her frozen limbs.

It's stopped blowing. And snowing. They'll come looking for me now.

Gavin would waken and find her missing from the sleeping bag. At first he would assume she had gone outside to the toilet. Then when she didn't return, he would get concerned and come in search of her.

But how will he find me, here?

Snow had ceased to fall through the opening sometime during the night. The pile it had formed was gradually being dissolved by the hill burn that flowed alongside her. Once again she reminded herself how lucky she had been. The impact of her assailant's blows had sent her flying backwards down the rocky slope. Yet she'd avoided hitting her head against the numerous hidden boulders and landed in here.

I should be dead. But I'm not, she reminded herself. *Not yet anyway.*

Her mind went back to Gavin. He was persistent, too persistent she'd thought at times. He would not give up on her. She was sure of that. And now that the blizzard had ceased, he would get word out that she was missing. There was no mobile signal at the Shelter Stone. Lucy and Malcolm would make for the car park and sound the alarm, while Gavin continued to search for her. She would be rescued. And she would point the finger at her attacker.

In that terrible moment when she'd registered that the stranger on the mountain wasn't her saviour but the exact opposite, she'd determined to commit his face to memory. At least what she could see of it. And his voice. His distinctive voice. She replayed it again in her head. His English had been perfect, but he had no accent. It was as though the English had been stripped clean of any intonation that might place his origins. In the light from her head torch the stubble on his chin had been sandy. The eyes not covered by glasses, a pale blue. Dressed all in white, he'd reminded her of a skier in an old war movie set in the Alps.

Iceman.

Whether from fear or cold, a shiver suddenly shot through her body like a live current. Then came a thought. One she dared not contemplate. One which halted her desire to shout Gavin's name at the top of her lungs.

If her attacker wanted her dead, would he not check that he'd accomplished his aim?

Then a second thought. As terrifying as the first.

He'd asked if she had companions, and she'd told him.

At the Shelter Stone.

11

Sean was sound asleep beside her and in no danger of being wakened by the noise of an incoming text. Rhona considered ignoring it, but once her sleep had been broken she rarely fell back into slumber. Glancing at the screen, she expected to find Chrissy's name after her provocative selfie of the previous night.

It wasn't from Chrissy, but Kyle Dunn, her Hogmanay acquaintance.

> Team called out if want to observe the proceedings. Prof on his way with SAR helicopter.

Rhona checked on Sean, who was dead to the world and would be for a few hours yet. She decided in that moment that she would go, assuming she could make it as far as Inverdruie, by foot if necessary. She texted back her acceptance, then rising, headed for the shower. When she emerged, she found a second text from Kyle offering her a lift in the Rescue Land Rover.

> Outside Macdui's, if you're ready to go?

Rhona texted him back in the affirmative.

Minutes later she emerged from the hotel to find a winter

wonderland. Cars parked on either side of the road were buried in banks of snow, only their roofs on view. A snow-plough had been by earlier, clearing the main road through the village. The Rescue Centre's Land Rover stood opposite, Kyle at the wheel.

'I think we may be the only folk awake in Aviemore,' he said as she tossed her backpack into the passenger seat.

'Apart from the snowplough drivers.'

'And Cairngorm Mountain Rescue.'

'Of which you've become an honorary member. For today anyway.'

As Kyle guided the Land Rover between the banks of snow, he brought Rhona up to date.

'Four climbers set off to climb Hell's Lum three days ago. Their plan was to bivouac nearby for the night before the climb. All are said to be experienced, but that can often be a loose term. We know they didn't make it back last night to Glenmore Lodge, but there is a chance they might have chosen to sit out the storm at the Shelter Stone before walk-ing out today. Also,' Kyle continued, 'A climber reported a downed plane on frozen Loch A'an this morning. That's not official as yet. We've had no radar report of a missing plane, so he may have been mistaken.'

'What's the forecast?' Rhona asked as they passed the Italian restaurant of yesterday and headed up the Coylum-bridge road.

'Mostly clear skies. Light wind. Intermittent snow show-ers up top,' Kyle told her. 'Good conditions for a search, although the avalanche warning from SAIS, the Scottish Avalanche Information Service, for the northern Cairngorms is orange.'

'And that's bad?'

51

'Not as bad as red.'

Turning left into the Rescue Centre, they found a Bristow helicopter already landed.

'That'll be the Prof's ride,' Kyle told her.

The area around the former church had been cleared of snow and was a hive of activity between the helicopter and the two mountain rescue Land Rovers that matched the one she'd arrived in. Kyle led her inside, through a busy assembly area and into the control room.

'Rhona. Kyle said you might be coming along. It's good to see you.' Charlie Robertson, already kitted up in his CMR yellow jacket, came to greet her with a *Happy New Year* hug.

'So this is how you spend your free time,' Rhona said.

'Now you know why I was so adept at climbing that five-bar gate, the last time we met.' Charlie turned to Kyle and the other man in the room at this point. 'Dr MacLeod helped me escape fifty drunken mortuary assistants intent on making me sing karaoke and dance on tables.'

The other man introduced himself as Owen Drummond and shook her hand. 'I'm delighted you want to watch us in action.'

'You could stay in the control room with Owen,' Kyle said. 'Then again, if you'd like to, you could join me and the Prof on the helicopter?'

Rhona was surprised and delighted by the suggestion. 'I wouldn't be in the way?'

'Charlie says you're an ideal woman to have in an emergency. So no, you won't be in the way. You've flown in one before?'

'A few times.' Rhona decided not to own up to her general dislike of flying.

Follow the Dead

'We'll be checking out the possible crash site. If it turns out to be true, we'll land. Any accidents on Cairngorm are regarded by the police as crime scenes. And you're an expert at dealing with those.'

That was true enough.

'Okay. It only remains to get you kitted up and we can be off.'

As the helicopter rose, the three rescue vehicles headed out, sirens blasting, lights flashing. Rhona felt a surge of excitement that drowned out her discomfort at being in the air again. The noise was deafening but the view was spectacular. Under blue skies she was staring across miles of sparkling snow.

The helicopter would get them to their destination speedily. The remainder of the team would, according to Kyle, take at least three hours to reach the Shelter Stone if all went well. Their route would take them to the Cairngorm car park, followed by a climb to the height of 1,141 feet, then downwards via Coire Raibert, and from there to the western end of Loch A'an.

'So the call-outs are in the same area?' Rhona had asked.

'Yes. Although Loch A'an is almost three miles in length and the Shelter Stone lies at its western end.'

Loch Morlich now stretched out below them, backed by the deep green of the Rothiemurchus forest of pines. Rhona spotted the route she'd taken with Sean only yesterday, the tops of the camper vans among the trees, and the winding stream that met the south end of the loch. Then they were up and over the line of the funicular and the Day Lodge. Rhona momentarily forgot her fear of flying, or at least her disbelief in the physics of flying, although it seemed to her

53

that the whirling blades holding her up were more believable than aircraft wings.

Kyle touched her arm and indicated below. The ground had fallen away to the south, meeting the outline of what she presumed was a flat, frozen, snow-covered Loch A'an. Rhona scanned it, seeing nothing that suggested debris. The helicopter dipped lower and began to follow the line of the loch from north-east to south-west.

Then she spotted what had caught Kyle's attention. He turned and gave her the thumbs-up. There was a plane, and it looked, if not complete, then not a pile of debris. As they swung over the light aircraft below, she quickly took in the scene. Blue and white livery, and at first glance it was intact apart from the right wing and tail. Tipped back, nose in the air, it lay on the side with the broken wing. At their first swing over, she saw no sign of bodies outside the aircraft. But that didn't mean there weren't any inside it.

Their own pilot was turning, considering a suitable place to land. Rhona's immediate fear was that the ice wouldn't hold them. Kyle, sensing this, patted her hand to reassure her and mouthed something she thought was *one yard thick*. The noise as they descended filled her head. Powdery snow whipped up by the blades entered the open door and met her face and lips to melt there. For a sequence of moments the noise seemed deafening, then she felt a nudge as the feet met the surface, settled and were finally steady. The blades slowed, the whirring changing to a bearable level. Cold invaded the space, not blown in, but descending like a blanket about them.

Then she heard the words, 'It's minus twelve out there.'
I'm in the Arctic, she thought.

12

McNab emerged from the warmth of the hospital to discover more snow had visited Glasgow overnight. The low temperature that set his teeth chittering accounted for the frozen surface. Hugging himself against an icy wind that seemed to be blowing from the wide expanse of the Clyde, he tried to remember where he had left the car in the mammoth car park. Then he recalled that he hadn't arrived by car, but by ambulance, insisted upon by Chrissy since he was 'bleeding and high on cocaine'.

I probably wasn't the only one in that state last night.

He contemplated calling for a police vehicle to come get him, then changed his mind. It would be quicker taking a cab. That thought proved to be faulty. Being Ne'erday, cabs it seemed were in short supply. He did eventually commandeer one by flashing his ID as it deposited a passenger at the hospital entrance. The driver gave up on his *I'm already booked* line and waved him into the back.

'You on the job, Detective?'

'Always,' McNab said.

The rest of the journey passed in silence, apart from an incoming call asking why the cab hadn't turned up for its booking. The driver replied that he 'had the polis in the back' and was on his way to Govan police station, which was met with, 'You're fucking kidding me, right?'

LIN ANDERSON

The roads were quiet, with few pedestrians walking the snowy pavements. Govan was still sleeping off the excesses of its Hogmanay celebrations, or its residents couldn't face the biting wind the New Year had brought with it.

Entering the police station, he found the desk sergeant happy to bring him up to date with the fallout from the raid.

'The men were processed, statements given and released,' he told McNab. 'The TARA Project managed to find crisis accommodation for the females.'

McNab was pleased to hear that. 'And the debriefing?'

'Already started.' The desk sergeant looked sympathetic. 'I'd have some coffee first. They don't know you've been discharged yet. And by the way, you look like shite.'

McNab thanked him for the kind words and headed for the coffee machine. Two espressos later, he was ready for the fray.

As he tried to slip in unannounced at the back, silence fell and all eyes turned towards him, including the boss's. DI Wilson seemed to be waiting for him to speak, but in response to what exactly?

When it became apparent that McNab was at a loss, DI Wilson said, 'The injured girl?'

McNab came back immediately. 'She's thirteen, sir. A Syrian refugee, trafficked here by a Norwegian national called Stefan. We'll need an Arabic translator before we can get more.' He halted, puzzled by the atmosphere in the room.

'The girl's missing, Sergeant.'

McNab tried to process this perplexing news. 'I left an officer on duty outside her room,' he said.

'He went to the toilet. When he came back, the girl had gone.'

56

McNab's brain moved into overdrive; none of the thoughts swirling around in there were pleasant.

'Could she have left the hospital by herself?' the boss was saying.

McNab tried to imagine the injured girl, fearful and in pain, orchestrating her escape from the apparent safety of the hospital. *Why would she do that?*

'She's been taken so she won't talk,' he said, certain now that that was the explanation.

'She's not the only witness,' DI Wilson reminded him. 'We have three other females at the safe house.'

'Then we'd better make sure we keep them there.'

McNab slipped his key into the lock. He hadn't taken too kindly to being ordered home, but DI Wilson had been adamant, reminding him that he'd been without sleep for over twenty-four hours, had sustained a bullet wound and been subjected to cocaine ingestion. *Plus you look hellish.* For a man not prone to swearing, that was strong for the boss.

McNab had finally agreed, on the understanding that he would be kept informed on the missing girl.

Now he was here, the boss's order didn't seem such a bad idea after all. Under the shower, his injured arm stuck out to avoid the spray, he watched the remnants of the cocaine cloud disappear down the plughole. As it did so it seemed that the throbbing in his arm and the prickling of the tattoo on his back increased.

Once out of the shower he rummaged in the bathroom cabinet. Paracetamol had been a mainstay when he'd been on the whisky. A necessity every morning when he'd had to face the bloodshot eyes and thumping head. But he hadn't replenished his supply since he'd cut down on the booze.

The cabinet proved to be empty of anything resembling a painkiller, so he went through to the bedroom and tried the drawer next to his bed, where he was luckier – a silver strip with two pockets yet untouched. McNab released the tablets and, heading to the kitchen, ran a glass of water. As he swallowed them, his mobile rang.

'DS McNab,' he immediately answered.

There was a surprised silence before a female voice responded with, 'So you *are* a policeman? I could have sworn Mannie was having me on.'

'Do you still want to talk to me now that you know the truth?' McNab said.

'I've nothing against the police, and as far as I know, they have nothing on me,' Ellie told him. Without waiting for his response to her declaration, she said, 'Have you been taking care of my tattoo as per instructions?'

'I'm just about to rewrap myself,' McNab fibbed.

'Good.'

The pause that followed seemed ripe with possibilities. McNab, even in his present state of exhaustion, recognized that at least.

'What about that drink you promised?' he ventured.

'Okay,' she answered slowly. 'Why don't you come by the Ink Parlour later? I'll check my work, then we can go for that drink.'

McNab smiled to himself as he rang off, then headed for the kitchen and the cling film. Suitably wrapped, he turned the volume on his mobile to high and, setting the alarm for three hours hence, climbed gratefully into bed.

13

Despite Kyle's assurances, Rhona stepped gingerly out onto the frozen loch. The air crackled with cold, each footstep on the crunching snow loud and echoing. The chill gripped her nostrils and cheeks, causing her eyes to stream in sympathy. Brushing away the tears with her gloved hands, she stopped for a moment, stunned by the beauty that surrounded her, in spite of the circumstances.

The flatness of the frozen surface stretched out like a tendril behind them. To her right the mountain reared, rugged and menacing. Somewhere on that precipitous face was Hell's Lum, the steep funnel of rock the climbers had tackled. Rhona couldn't imagine what drove people to do such a thing, and in such temperatures.

The wreckage grew in size as they made their way across the ice. In its blanket of snow, only patches of blue livery peeked out. Given a further heavy fall it would have become invisible, Rhona realized, especially from above. The propeller hung with long glassy icicles, as did the wings and undercarriage. It resembled, she thought, a large bird frozen solid as it had come in to land.

Kyle led the way, Rhona following in his footsteps, with Charlie behind. The wreckage, they all suspected, would hold a body or bodies, dead or maybe alive? On reaching the plane, Kyle immediately pulled himself up onto the broken wing, which lay drunkenly to one side, and began clearing the snow from the Perspex cockpit, only to reveal an ice casing below.

'I can't see anything,' he shouted down to them.

Rhona watched as he attacked the glistening surface with his ice axe. Eventually a slab broke free and fell to the ground to shatter in the snow.

As the hood scraped back, Rhona prepared herself to be told there was one body at least. In that she was wrong.

'It's empty,' were Kyle's words. He sounded as surprised and relieved as Rhona felt. 'But there's blood on the instrument panel.'

He jumped down, his feet crunching the frozen surface. 'Before we do anything else, we need to record the scene,' he told Rhona. 'There's a camera in your rescue gear.'

'It's okay, I brought my own, and my forensic kit.' At Kyle's surprised expression, Rhona explained, 'I keep a bag in the boot of the car.'

'See what you can find out,' Kyle said, 'while we secure the scene and look for survivors.'

Rhona walked round the aircraft taking a series of photos from all angles, then a video. She was no expert on flying, but the care with which the plane had been landed seemed to suggest the pilot had been in control. What he couldn't have known was what would happen when he met the surface.

He must have worried about the thickness of the ice and whether it would hold him.

So why when he'd landed safely would he abandon the plane? Did he fear the wreckage might catch fire? Or that the ice wasn't thick enough to hold its weight for long? At least in the aircraft he would have been sheltered from the blizzard. To leave its relative safety and seek somewhere else to ride out the storm seemed to Rhona as dangerous as staying put.

But I wasn't here last night.

Having examined all that she could from the exterior of the aircraft, Rhona now donned a forensic suit over the winter gear, glad for once that one (giant) size fitted all, and climbed into the cockpit. Kyle was right. There was blood on the instrument panel, possibly from a head wound during landing. She worked her way over the front two seats, then moved into the back. There was nothing to suggest how many people had been on the plane when it came down. She wondered again about the plane's flight path and why it hadn't been reported missing. Then a thought occurred. If there was luggage stowed in the hold, it might give them a clue as to who had been on board.

Rhona climbed out of the cockpit and dropped down from the wing. There was no sign of Charlie although markers were obvious where he'd recorded the scattered debris for the benefit of the Air Accident Investigation Branch who would no doubt visit the scene soon. Rhona presumed he'd followed Kyle in his search for the plane's occupants. The helicopter had taken to the air and was circling above, looking for signs of life.

Shielding her eyes against the sun's glare on the pristine snow, she focused on the area below the hovering chopper, eventually catching sight of two yellow-clad figures, who appeared to be checking a heap of snow she assumed was the result of an avalanche, with long rods.

Rhona turned her attention westward. How far was it to the end of the loch? Could any survivors have headed in that direction? If they'd known about the existence of the Shelter Stone then that would have been a possible choice.

But first she would try to discover who they were looking for.

Circling the plane, she eventually found the opening to the hold, encased in ice like the cockpit. Following Kyle's lead, she used her ice axe and was surprised at how much effort it took on her part to break through. Eventually, though, it cracked and the next blow saw the sheet slide south. Prising entry was less difficult, because the hatch was already partially open. She pulled the door back fully to view an empty cavity. Her immediate thought was that whoever had escaped the plane had taken their belongings with them.

But was that probable?

More likely for them to take what they needed to face the weather and leave the rest. Walking out of here would have been difficult enough in a hundred-mile-an-hour gale without carrying baggage. As she prepared to abandon the hold something caught her eye. The gloved hand she'd used to check for contents now had a thin film of dust on the fingers. White dust. Rhona lifted the glove to her face, sniffed, licked it, then spat it out.

Cocaine?

Rhona rummaged around in her kit, looking for the cocaine wipes. Each swab was sensitive to trace amounts of residue; far less than could be collected for regular field testing. Breaking the hermetic seal, she extracted the swab and applied it, waiting for the colour change, pretty sure she was right by taste alone.

A definite blue.

When she used her radio, Kyle answered immediately.

'Found anything?'

Rhona told him what she suspected.

'That's what the plane was carrying?' he said, surprised.

'All it tells us is that cocaine has been in that hold. When exactly, we don't know.'

'Maybe that's why the flight was off-radar?'

'It's a possibility,' Rhona conceded. 'I'm going to start walking west. Whoever was in the plane has an injury. I suspect a head wound on impact. They may be concussed and disorientated.'

'Okay. We'll follow you. We've found no evidence of anyone being caught in the avalanche.'

Rhona set a course for the head of the loch, shading her eyes to look for signs that someone had trodden a path through the snow before her. As she walked, she realized that the resounding crunch of her footsteps, coupled with the sharpness of the air entering her lungs, was energizing.

Was this why people came up here? To feel alive? Or to experience danger?

On Sanday in Orkney during a previous investigation, looking out across the vast expanse of the North Sea, she'd felt as though she stood on the edge of the world. But she'd never felt endangered by the weather on Sanday, just grossly inconvenienced at times by it. Here, in what were surely Arctic conditions, the weather and environment might appear to be your friend in one moment, only to become your fiercest enemy in the next.

Rhona slowed as she discerned a shape in the distance. Was it a rock protruding from the loch or something lying on the surface? She upped her pace, more confident now of the solidity of what lay beneath her feet. Yards from the object, she came to an abrupt stop.

Blood on snow.

Blood, in all its patterns, was her business. It told a tale of injury and death, often pointing to who had inflicted the injuries, and the weapon used. Up to this point she'd discerned no blood trail, so had assumed that whatever the injury was, it hadn't been as serious as the trail now suggested.

Rhona hesitated, thinking to photograph the evidence, knowing that the weather might change abruptly and she wouldn't get another opportunity. But, aware there might be a chance that whoever had bled here could still be alive, she hurried on.

Steps away now, she noted that the figure was clothed in white, hence its ability to merge with the landscape. He, or she, lay face down, arms spread out like a supplicant's before the altar that was the imposing edifice of the neighbouring crag. On approach, she registered that the freezing temperature had obliterated the familiar scent of death, yet Rhona knew that death lay before her.

She knelt down and touched the bristled right cheek, finding it as frigid as the ice on which it lay. Below the head, the layer of snow had turned pink, like the frosting on a cake. Any forlorn hope that a pulse might beat in the creases of the neck was quickly abandoned. Her own breath condensing before her, she used the radio to alert Kyle to her discovery, then set about recording the scene.

Now, easing the body over, Rhona discovered the reason for the blood trail and stained snow. The right side of the face had a deep wound just above the eye and a long score mark down the cheek.

Was this the wound that had resulted in blood in the cockpit? There hadn't been copious amounts in the plane and she hadn't followed a blood trail here, but there was no other obvious evidence of injury. And the blizzard could have covered any trail there might have been.

Rhona recorded the body in detail, before checking for any means of identification. There had been none in the plane, and there was, as far as her search revealed, none on the body.

Looking up, she spotted Kyle and Charlie trudging towards her.

Her second radio message had alerted them to a body, and as part of a rescue team, that wouldn't be an unusual occurrence. Rhona stood up, assembling the words that might match the circumstances, but at the sight of the body Charlie became swiftly circumspect and knelt for a closer look. Kyle's expression was one of sadness. The mountains sometimes killed those who loved them. That was a given. But this man hadn't chosen such danger. Circumstances beyond his control had brought his plane down. Having survived that, either the cold or his wounds had taken his life.

'There's no ID on him and there was none in the plane.'

'Looks like the flight and its occupant was definitely off the radar,' Kyle said. 'Something for AAIB and Police Scotland to handle.'

A few flakes of snow began to fall, alerting them to the fact that the sky was no longer a pristine blue.

'We'll bag the body and stretcher it out,' Charlie said. 'Have you recorded it?'

Rhona indicated she had. As she and Charlie secured the remains, Kyle radioed the base to give them the latest.

Owen answered immediately. 'You're required at the Shelter Stone.' And then he told them why.

14

McNab woke to the repeated buzzing of the intercom. Insistent, like a bluebottle at his ear, it jerked him out of a deep slumber. Cursing, he realized that whoever was pressing the button wasn't likely to give up, so swung his legs out of bed.

'If it's another fucking Amazon delivery for that guy upstairs . . .' He grabbed the handset. 'What?'

'Detective Sergeant McNab?' a polite male voice answered.

'Who are you?' McNab retorted.

'Police Inspector Alvis Olsen of the Norwegian National Bureau of Investigation. May I come up?'

A mystified McNab clicked the door free, then, suddenly registering his lack of clothing, made a quick attempt to get decent. A few moments later as he struggled to fasten his shirt over the dressing and cling film, there was a soft knock at the door. McNab composed himself, then striding over, opened it.

The man facing him was tall, perhaps a couple of inches taller than McNab. Age-wise, McNab estimated mid-forties. The fair hair was cut close, the square jawline clean-shaven. McNab had the impression that below the padded black jacket was a muscled body.

His visitor, producing ID, re-introduced himself. Registering McNab's cautious expression, he said, 'I'd like to speak to you about the recent raid on the Delta Club.'

Whatever McNab had been expecting, it wasn't that.

'In what capacity?' he said, immediately on guard.

'We believe there may be a Norwegian connection.'

'*We* being?'

'KRIPOS.'

'KRIPOS,' McNab repeated, his brain racing at this development.

'The Norwegian National Criminal Investigation Service—'

'I know what KRIPOS is,' McNab interrupted him. 'But if Operation Delta has become a joint investigation with Norway, no one told me about it.'

His visitor, who didn't appear discomfited by McNab's sharp response, now said, 'I believe you were injured in the raid?' His eyes roamed over McNab as though looking for evidence of that. When McNab didn't respond, he posed yet another question. 'The girl taken to hospital. You interviewed her prior to her disappearance?'

McNab, irritated at what was fast resembling an interrogation, interrupted the request to know what had been said during that interview. 'Have you spoken to my commanding officer, Detective Inspector Wilson? Did he give you permission to come here?'

'KRIPOS has been in touch with senior officers at MIT.'

McNab decided that really wasn't an answer. To indicate this, he walked round his visitor and opened the door.

'I'll be at MIT in an hour, Inspector Olsen. If you have permission from my commanding officer, then I'd be happy to talk to you there.'

His visitor looked as though he was ripe for an argument, but wisely chose not to engage in one. As he strode past, a wave of annoyance was directed at McNab. Barely waiting for his visitor to leave, McNab shut the door.

Heading to the window, he watched Olsen's exit. Minutes later, his visitor emerged and immediately took out a mobile and made what looked like an irate call, before crossing the road and climbing into a car.

At that moment McNab's phone alarm went off, reminding him that his three-hour rest was at an end.

15

She woke to the sound of shattering ice. The icicle that had formed near the opening above her head had broken free and fallen like a knife blade towards her, missing her face by inches.

I shouldn't lie here. It's too dangerous.

But if she shifted to the right, she would immerse more than just her left foot in the moving water. The possibility of easing herself forward was equally dangerous. Close to her feet the stream pooled briefly before cascading over what she took to be a vertical drop.

She contemplated again the possibility of trying to climb out the way she'd come in. If she'd taken her ice axe with her on that fateful trip to the toilet, that might have been a possibility. After all, she had climbed Hell's Lum.

But that was before I hurt my ankle.

She didn't think she'd broken it, but her fall had definitely done something. Her foot felt twice its size inside her boot and putting any weight on it was agony.

She tried to drag herself into a sitting position. Fear of her attacker had diminished as her fear of dying of cold had increased. It would be dark again soon. Surely there were people out looking for her? If so, they wouldn't find her down here. And what about Gavin and the others? What if something had happened to them?

Rising to her knees, she let the pain wash over her.

I can do this, she muttered to herself.

Raising herself via her good leg to a standing position, and keeping the weight off her right foot, she balanced herself with her hands on the ice wall. She was now a foot and a half below the opening. She had turned off her head torch, keen to preserve the eight-hour battery. Turning it on now, she directed it at the hole, partially covered with a web of powdered snow. Another heavy shower and the crevice would be out of sight completely.

But if I make the hole bigger?

She plucked an icicle from the roof and, using it like a knife, she stretched upwards to poke at the opening. As she did so, she heard the muffled sound of what had to be the throb of a helicopter. If she could shine her light through the opening, would they see it?

It's like climbing the Lum, she told herself, as every muscle and sinew in her upper body sang with the effort. And she would have done it, but for balance. There were no crampons fixed in place to prevent a fall, no ice axe buried deep to hold her steady. No Gavin above her, ready to help.

She screamed in fury as much as fear as her one good leg gave way beneath her, the final stretch proving too much for her precarious balancing act. Breath burst from her lungs on impact, carrying a string of expletives with it. Stunned, she lay rigid and groaning, tears springing from her eyes, knowing that the jagged rock she'd landed on had met her spine like a sledgehammer.

16

Grey clouds had begun to form as they walked west. Owen's forecast from the Rescue Centre had warned of intermittent snow showers and a light breeze. The low temperatures would remain, dropping further as the sun went down. They had said nothing as the two men carried the stretcher and Rhona walked behind, Owen's news of what had been found by the other half of the team reducing them to a studied silence.

The Shelter Stone was, according to Kyle, a ten-minute walk from the most western end, where a mountain stream met the loch. The only sound that had accompanied them had been the crunch of their boots. Occasionally, patches of ice had been exposed by the wind and, as they'd reached the shallows, Rhona had made out silvery weeds through the ice, where it was made thinner by the burn water as it entered the loch.

Now, approaching the shoreline, she spotted the other members of the team in the distance, their bright yellow jackets highly visible against the snow cover and background of grey rock. She'd been warned about the size of the Shelter Stone, but was still taken aback when she caught sight of the huge flat boulder that had, at some time in the distant past, detached itself from the towering crag, and

Follow the Dead

rolled down, coming to rest in such a manner that it might offer a place of safety to those passing through.

But not this time.

On arrival, Kyle had a swift word with the others. By his gestures, Rhona realized he was detailing someone to carry out the body they'd brought there. The allotted stretcher bearers would retrace their own trail, climbing back up towards the car park, where a vehicle would transport the remains to the mortuary in Inverness.

'Okay, let's take a look,' Charlie said.

Markers had been placed a few yards back from the stone, the equivalent of crime scene tape in standard circumstances. Rhona had dealt with bodies, both buried and exposed, inside buildings and out in the open. She had, however, never dealt with a location such as the one she found herself entering now, on hands and knees. The space was just about big enough to accommodate the two sleeping bags that lay on the earthen floor.

Both bags were unzipped. The bag nearest to the entrance held two bodies. A male and a female. Its neighbour, although also a double, held only a single male. All were clothed in a base layer of thermal tops and long johns, with hats and gloves. According to Charlie, removing snowy outer garments before retiring for the night was the norm.

All three corpses were rigid, but not from rigor mortis.

In low temperatures of minus 15 to minus 20 degrees, bodies would freeze quickly after death, any variability in time dependent on the amount of body fat, which acted as a form of insulation. In this instance the bodies were of three people probably in their mid-twenties. As climbers of Hell's Lum they had no doubt been fit, with little extraneous fat.

73

Charlie, having given the bodies a cursory inspection, came back alongside her.

'It was around minus fifteen last night, but,' he glanced around at the walls built of a patchwork of smaller stones, semi-sealed by snow, 'they were sheltered from the blizzard. Their sleeping bags are dry and of winter quality.' He voiced his thoughts out loud. 'And two inside a sleeping bag is warmer than one.' He fell silent, thinking.

Hypothermia could be extremely subtle, so the circumstances were often key. It had certainly been cold enough, had the victims been exposed to the elements, but for all three to die together in similar circumstances?

'They should have survived?' Rhona said.

Charlie looked at her. 'Should? Maybe, but they didn't, and we won't know why until I get them on the table.'

'What about the second girl?'

'If she was suffering from hypothermia she might have become confused and gone wandering outside. Alternatively she realized something was wrong here and went for help.'

'There are only three sets of outer garments,' Rhona told him. 'She must have dressed before going out.'

'Which suggests she wasn't in a confused state.' He threw Rhona a questioning look. 'I'm assuming you would like to process the scene before we transport the bodies out?'

Rhona nodded. That was exactly what she wanted.

17

The safe house was a Victorian mansion whose grandeur was long gone. The garden out front had a neglected look with a patchy grassed area surrounded by an overgrown hedge. Yet he was pretty sure that to the women who found their way here, it must appear like heaven.

McNab pressed the entry button, gave his name and held up his ID for the camera. Seconds later he saw a shadow approach via the patterned half-glass of the door. When it clicked open he found himself face to face with Cheryl Lafferty.

'Detective Inspector McNab,' she said with a wide smile. 'Long time no see.'

'So long that I'm a detective sergeant again,' he said with a less than sorry face.

'Bloody hell, what did you do?'

McNab shrugged. 'You don't want to know.'

'I heard about your exploits last night.' Her face clouded over. 'Is the girl taken to the hospital okay?'

McNab gave her a brief résumé of what had happened since the fateful raid.

'You think she ran away or that some bastard took her?' Cheryl demanded.

'I suspect the latter, but I was hoping the other women might throw some light on that.'

She looked concerned. 'I'm not sure they'll agree to talk to you. They're all pretty frightened.'

'The missing girl's name's Amena Tamar,' McNab said. 'She's a Syrian refugee and she's thirteen years old.'

Cheryl gritted her teeth at that news. 'The others are from various countries in Eastern Europe. Poland, Lithuania, Romania.'

'Can they speak English?'

'They seem to understand it, although they haven't said much.'

McNab waited, aware that Cheryl's job was to protect the women brought to her, and that meant from the police as well if necessary. He was counting on her cooperation though, because of their own history. As a rookie cop he had seen at first-hand what a man like Cheryl's partner at the time was capable of. Torture was the only way to describe it. The scars on her hands, the broken finger bones. Cheryl had been on the front line, pimped out, abused and terrified. If anyone could appreciate how these women might be feeling this morning, it was her.

'Okay,' she said finally. 'I'll see if anyone's willing to talk to you.'

Ten minutes later a young woman appeared in the doorway. McNab didn't recognize her, his memory of last night's encounter being a jumble of naked bodies punctured by screams and a barking dog. She was tall, slim to thin, with her brown hair tied back. She had the look of someone recently scrubbed in the shower, and the mix-and-match clothes she wore had obviously come out of Cheryl's store. Having briefly met his eye, she looked away. McNab forced himself to remain silent until she entered, aware there was every chance she might change her mind and bolt.

'Detective Sergeant Michael McNab,' he offered. 'Thank you for agreeing to speak to me.'

She nodded and took the chair he indicated. McNab sat down opposite, a coffee table offering a safety barrier between them.

'May I ask your name?'

'Ursula . . . Gorecki.' The hesitation before she delivered the surname made him wonder if it was a substitute for her real one.

'From Poland?'

She nodded. A few further questions got answers he'd heard before from other trafficked females. She'd been recruited to work in the care home sector in the UK. When she'd arrived at Glasgow airport, she'd been met by a woman who'd taken her to a house in the city. At first she thought it was going to be all right. Then . . .

'And the other women at the Delta Club?'

'I met them for the first time last night.'

'You'd never met Amena Tamar before?'

'The little girl who got hurt? No. But . . .' She hesitated. 'A man brought her into the club. She was very frightened. He was rough with her.'

'Amena mentioned a Norwegian she called Stefan?'

'That might have been him, although he spoke English.'

'And he had nothing to do with bringing you here?'

'No. I was recruited by an agency. Everything seemed to be in order, until I got here and they took my passport.' She paused. 'Will I be allowed to stay in Scotland?'

McNab wondered why she would want to, after what had been done to her, but if she was a European citizen, she had every right to remain. Not so, Amena Tamar. Refugee children and unaccompanied minors who found themselves in a hostile Europe were ripe for trafficking. No passports. No redress. No hope.

Just at that moment, Cheryl appeared at the door, and Ursula grabbed her arrival as an opportunity to leave. She quickly rose and, giving McNab a nod as a goodbye, departed.

'Any luck?' Cheryl said when she'd disappeared up the staircase.

'She maintains she didn't know the girl or the man who delivered her to the Delta Club. Of course, she may be lying.' He looked to Cheryl for confirmation of that possibility.

'Give her and the others some time. Once we gain their trust, you may get more.'

McNab wasn't convinced of that. He was already questioning his interview with Ursula Gorecki. He'd been easy on her and he suspected that she'd played him. It could be that neither she nor the other women had been trafficked, but were in Scotland and at the orgy at the Delta Club by choice. Either that or she knew Stefan too and her denial of the supposed trafficker was merely self-preservation.

Cheryl showed him to the door. 'I'll give you a call if there are any developments,' she promised. 'A few nights free of fear and they often start to confide in me.'

'You still have my number?' McNab said, surprised.

Cheryl gave him a look that spoke volumes. 'You were my knight in shining armour. I won't forget that.'

McNab turned abruptly away, made uncomfortable by both her look and her words.

Stepping out into an icy wind made him think of Rhona somewhere in the frozen north. Where had Chrissy said she was? *Aviemore?* McNab fumbled for his mobile and brought up Rhona's selfie of last night. Her Hogmanay party had been decisively different from his own, he noted. But what was she doing now? He had a mental image of snow-clad mountains and daft folk slithering down them on skis and snowboards. *Is that what Rhona was up to?* If so it was yet another aspect of Dr Rhona MacLeod that he knew nothing about.

And what of Sean Maguire?

McNab couldn't imagine the Irishman bothering with such an activity. Sean was more of a townie like himself.

And that's not all we have in common, he thought, as an alternative occupation for Rhona entered his mind. One that featured Sean Maguire. One McNab did not relish. Blanking his mind of that image, McNab fastened his jacket against a flurry of snow and went in search of his parked car.

18

She could hear the occasional calls of the searchers, but no one came to disturb her. Conscious of the time, and the diminishing light, Rhona worked swiftly.

Her first thought on entering the cave had been that the three victims had succumbed to exposure. Now she checked for any physical evidence of that. She tackled the woman first. One possible indication of hypothermia was a pink, blotchy discoloration around the larger joints of knees and elbows. When Rhona pulled both sleeves up far enough to check the elbows, she found no such signs.

And the knees?

Rolling up the trousers, Rhona found both knees also free of discoloration.

Repeating her actions, she checked the two men and discovered the same. Her test by no means proved they hadn't died from exposure but other aspects of the situation didn't fit either. Paradoxically, as the brain chilled, victims often thought themselves too hot and stripped off in an attempt to cool down. In this case, the bags had been unzipped, but no attempt had been made to get out of them, except in the case of the fourth member of the group.

It was the uniformity of the scene in the cave that really puzzled her. For three people to become uniformly cold and die together?

There was perhaps another possible explanation. At the back of the cave she found what looked like a fire brick which had obviously been lit. She had once been called to a bothy where two dead hillwalkers had been found. Having brought a barbecue into such a confined space, they'd succumbed to carbon monoxide poisoning. But victims of CO poisoning developed cherry-pink postmortem lividity like cyanide poisoning and that wasn't the case here, and she couldn't believe that a single fire brick lit in a draughty environment could have caused three deaths.

Just then something caught her eye. Rhona picked up the yellow slip of paper, recognizing it as a Post-it. On it was the name *Rick Grimes*. Having spotted one discarded notelet, she now located another three, all with names on them, she thought, of fictional characters.

The Big Grey Man of Ben Macdui she knew as one of the local legends of the Cairngorms.

It appeared the four friends had been playing a game to pass the night away and – she spotted a leather-bound hip-flask – perhaps toasting the New Year before going to sleep.

Never to wake up?

At that moment an alternative explanation presented itself. One that seemed scarcely credible although in any other scenario would have to be considered.

Each of the three had a self-inflating pillow under their heads. The fourth pillow lay alongside, its owner missing somewhere on the hillside. Like hypothermia, suffocation could be extremely subtle, sometimes without any convincing features at all. It should however show signs of asphyxia. There were no obvious marks on the faces, no bruising or scratches, no discoloration around the nose, which might indicate pressure to stop the flow of oxygen.

Bearing in mind that any death on the mountain was regarded as a crime scene until proved otherwise, Rhona performed the same tasks on the bodies and surrounding area she would normally carry out at a suspicious death, paying special attention to the nose and mouth area. It was in the female's mouth she discovered the gravel. Fine particles lodged in the back of the throat.

How had the gravel found its way into her mouth?

Had the circumstances in the cave been different, displaying obvious evidence of the disorientation of three people with hypothermia, she could imagine one or more of them exhibiting strange behaviour.

Might she have eaten snow to cool down and the snow contained gravel?

The surrounding walls were made up of layered stones, the spaces between them packed with snow. Snowflakes had been constantly drifting in through crevices and the doorway as she'd worked. A handful would have been easy to come by, even inside the cave.

And snow packed into a mouth and nose could stop someone breathing.

Anyone who had dealt with avalanche victims knew that.

The thought took root and developed. The snow would melt, leaving only the residual gravel. With that in mind, Rhona took care to swab the back of the males' throats as well.

She then concentrated on the fourth pillow. If that, instead of snow, had been used to block the airways, trace evidence would indicate it.

'How's it going?' Charlie's face peered at her from the narrow crevice entrance.

'Almost finished.'

'Any further thoughts?'

'A few, but I'd rather wait for the PM. Will you be involved in that?' she said, aware that there were always two pathologists present.

He nodded. 'I'll make a point of being there.'

'No luck with finding the fourth member of the group?' Rhona asked.

Charlie shook his head.

'So no one's left to tell the tale?'

'It's beginning to look that way. And we have a media presence,' he added grimly.

'How?' Rhona said in disbelief.

'Overhead. A press helicopter. Apparently the story of a downed plane on frozen Loch A'an and four dead bodies is a scoop.'

Rhona understood the frustration in his voice. The truth of tragedies on the mountain was often replaced by sensationalist reporting. Bad for both the family members of the deceased and for the members of the team, who always tried to be as honest as possible, while protecting the innocent.

'How did they find out?' Rhona said.

'Once a call-out happens, a statement has to be made. And not everyone in police headquarters is above selling an interest story to the press.'

Crawling out of the cave minutes later, Rhona spotted the helicopter hovering above them with a bird's-eye view of the proceedings, which only a deterioration in the weather could prevent.

'Heavy snow's on the way, so if you're okay with us moving the remains, we should leave now.'

Even as Charlie said this, Rhona spotted the threatening bank of grey on the horizon.

'I'll walk out with the stretchers,' Charlie said. 'You need to catch a ride on the chopper before the weather grounds it.'

'What about the missing girl?'

Charlie's face clouded over. 'I wouldn't be being honest if I didn't tell you that if she's out in the open, she's likely dead already.'

19

McNab looked to the window where another shower was tossing large flakes to melt against the glass. When he'd arrived at the station, he'd expected to find the Norwegian detective with the boss. His trip to the safe house had taken more than an hour, and during the intervening time it seemed his future had been sealed.

Through the black cloud currently descending on his brain, he heard the boss's words.

'The Norwegian police believe that both cocaine and girls are being trafficked via Norway en route to the UK. The latest haul of cocaine off the coast of Aberdeen may have been part of that.'

'We have no reason to believe that's the case, sir. I've been hard on Brodie's tail since Orkney. He has no connections in Aberdeen.'

DI Wilson ignored the riposte. 'You will work with Police Inspector Olsen. Give him all the help and information you can, Sergeant.'

McNab remained silent and unconvinced. His own investigation which had led to the Delta Club pointed at the drug entering Scotland by sea via the remote west coast, and the conversation with Ursula suggested the women from last night may have arrived in the UK legally, although coerced into prostitution afterwards.

But not Amena Tamar, a small internal voice reminded him.

'Our priority is to find Brodie and the girl, sir.'

'Inspector Olsen may be able to help you do that.' Perhaps noting McNab's belligerent look, he added, 'This is as much a diplomatic mission between Norway and Scotland, Sergeant, as a joint investigation.'

And there it was. Police Scotland was under orders from the Scottish government to work with KRIPOS, which quickly brought another thought.

'The men detained last night, sir. Were any of them Norwegian?'

By the boss's expression, McNab suspected he might be right.

'Inspector Olsen is currently going through the men's details. I suggest you join him.'

And with that McNab was dismissed.

On exit he headed for the coffee machine, signalling to DS Janice Clark that it would be good if she came with him. He and Janice went back a long way, since her early days as a detective constable where he'd tried to lord it over her in his elevated position as DS. Then she'd been promoted, deservedly so, just as he, having climbed the ladder to DI, had very swiftly slid back down the snake. Now they were equals. McNab found that worked better, for him at least.

'You okay?' she said, a pucker between her brows. 'I heard you got shot . . . again,' she added, as though it was his fault.

'A scratch.' He shook his head in dismissal. 'Have you met the Norwegian bloke?'

'I have,' Janice said with a smile. 'He's charming and he speaks perfect English.'

McNab made a sound which might have been mistaken for a growl. At this Janice raised an eyebrow.

'What's up?'

'Do you have a list of the men we picked up last night?'

'Inspector Olsen's going through them now. You could join him.'

This, McNab thought, *is beginning to resemble a forced marriage, where I am the reluctant wife, about to be fucked.* 'I'd rather look at them alone, first.'

There was a pause as Janice considered his attitude. One that she was more than familiar with.

'Your pal in the Tech department is running background checks,' she finally offered.

Entering the Tech department was something McNab did only if it couldn't be avoided. Being surrounded by computer screens manned by what seemed ridiculously young men (and women on occasion) made him feel old, and worse, stupid. This was despite the fact that normal policing was now predominantly high-tech. In fact you didn't get more high-tech than the new Police Scotland headquarters at Gartcosh, with the most advanced forensic facilities in Europe.

True, McNab's recent encounter with policing outside the digital world, on a northern Scottish island where there had been no CCTV, an intermittent mobile signal and internet access as rare as his love for Old Firm games, had proved that his own policing methods did require digital input, however much he'd prefer that not to be the case.

That doesn't mean I have to like it.

It was the hum that freaked him. All those buzzing machines sounded to him like acute tinnitus. McNab searched the room for his only recognized ally. An impossibly young man who resembled an owl. How the hell had his mother known that when she'd decided on his name?

He's here.

McNab felt a surge of relief he didn't want to acknowledge as he marched towards his saviour.

'DS McNab!' The big eyes relinquished a screen filled, to McNab's understanding at least, with gobbledegook.

'Ollie. Good to see you.'

'You too, Sergeant.' Ollie waited, knowing McNab didn't visit him here unless under duress. Eventually he prompted, 'What can I do to help you, Sergeant?'

'The Delta raid. You're doing background checks on the participants?'

'I am. Want a look?' When McNab nodded, he added, 'Pull up a chair.'

Fleetingly remembered images of the tangle of naked bodies in that room sprang back into life. The scene had been ludicrous enough to cause sniggering among his team as the laser lights of the guns played on bare flesh and thrusting buttocks. For the most part the female bodies had been out of sight, covered as they had been by the men. McNab didn't think he would recognize any of the female faces, except that of the frightened little Amena, but he was wrong. As the collage of photographs appeared, he immediately spotted Ursula.

'That one.' McNab pointed at the screen.

Ollie brought up her details. 'Ursula Gorecki. From Kraków. Eighteen years old. A student nurse. She's not on any police database I've checked so far.'

So she had, on the surface at any rate, been telling the truth.

'And the missing girl?'

'Nothing on her at all.'

The remaining two women had yet to have their identities confirmed, so McNab now moved on to the men.

Six faces stared out at him. All, he estimated, were in their thirties or forties.

'Now it gets interesting,' Ollie said. 'That one.' He pointed to the first photograph. The man had short, well-groomed fair hair and enough growth to be called a beard. Ollie clicked on the thumbnail image. When the details were revealed, Ollie read them out.

'Jakob Svindal and Tobias Hansen work for Statoil and are based in Stavanger, Norway. The third Norwegian, Petter Lund, also works for Statoil but is based in Aberdeen.'

'And the other three fuckers?'

'James McVitie, an accountant from Bishopbriggs, Thomas Bellevue, a solicitor from Newton Mearns, and,' here Ollie paused, 'Blair Watson, a law advisor to the Scottish government.'

'Jesus, that won't go down well in parliament.'

Ollie brought up the three photographs side by side. Last night McNab had had the fleeting impression he may have recognized one of the male faces in the melee. Now, he knew, he'd been right. He pointed to the one in the middle.

'Him,' he said, trying not to recall the heavy wobbling mound of naked flesh that had been attached to that head.

'The accountant?'

'So that's his job now . . .' McNab smiled. 'And here's me thinking he was still in the money-laundering business.'

'He doesn't appear on the police database.'

'He's never been charged. Yet.' McNab paused. 'You have a recording of the orgy?'

Ollie looked surprised and a little disappointed, which suggested he'd been planning that revelation himself. 'How did you know there was one?'

'There were cameras everywhere and a big digital screen. That was what Brodie was glued to when we arrived.'

'You want to take a look?'

'The injured girl's thirteen years old. Anyone caught fucking her on camera can be done for having sex with a minor.'

'Then we have someone, Sergeant,' Ollie said with a smile.

20

It had taken him four hours to locate a suitable spot and dig the snow hole. Instinct had told him not to desert the field. His consignment was safe, at least until an eventual thaw. The girl on the hill had been problematic, but had she lived she would have told her friends about him. With both her and the others dispensed with, no one could possibly know that the plane had held more than just its pilot. Except of course for the pilot himself, which was no longer a possibility.

As usual, he'd had the sense to carry a basic survival pack with him, something which had proved useful on more than just this occasion. Unpacking his gear, he'd set up camp, estimating that he had the means to survive here for three days at least. Enough time for the mountain rescue team to remove the bodies from the cave and either give up on the girl or find her body and remove it too.

Then the plan could be resumed.

Unpacking the little stove, he lit it and put some supper on to heat.

Once the rescue team moves on, I might have another look, just to make sure.

Sitting in his burrow, he'd heard the muffled sound of a chopper and assumed it had brought in part of the search team. Dead bodies, he knew, weren't transported out that way, which meant four bodies, maybe five, he thought with a frisson of pleasure, would have to be carried out by stretcher. That meant upwards of ten members of the team absent from the field, which cut down the number left to search for the girl's remains. Then the persistent and nagging question surfaced yet again to trouble him.

What if she isn't dead?

He immediately consoled himself with the thought that were she alive, which was highly unlikely, she'd barely seen him anyway. At this point his hand rose instinctively to his cheek. The gouge left by her nails had crusted over. Without a mirror he had no way of telling how obvious it was.

But such a scratch could be easily explained, especially in this environment.

He turned his attention to the contents of the pot, now simmering, the aroma of which was reminding him how hungry he was. He ate straight from the pan, taking care to do so slowly, aware he would have to ration himself in case he needed to stay around for a while.

As he wiped the pot clean with snow, he heard the beat of blades again. Crawling along the entrance tunnel, he looked skywards. This time the chopper wasn't the red and white of the rescue service, but black. Jutting from the open door was a telephoto lens.

So the newsmen were on to it. Was it the downed plane that interested them? Or the bodies in the cave?

21

McNab left the station with a jaunty step. He'd decided not to immediately seek out Inspector Olsen, despite the boss's orders. Armed with the same information the Norwegian policeman had, McNab was inclined to pursue his own path regarding the characters on the clusterfuck list, although as far as he was concerned the main priority had to be to locate Brodie and the girl. In respect of that, he'd received a rather promising text message from an old friend, who on occasion had supplied him with useful information.

Davey Stevenson, McNab sometimes mused, was the man he would have liked to become himself, had he not entered the police force. In fact even now, on occasion, he wished he'd followed in his school pal's footsteps. If so, he might have owned a string of betting shops, have a big house overlooking a nice Glasgow park and be invited to social events on both sides of the Glasgow divide. Jesus, Davey was even known to grace tables in Edinburgh's New Town. For a Glasgow wide boy, that was a definite sign you'd made it into the upper echelons of Scottish society, in the central belt at least.

And Davey had bagged the looker they'd both hankered after at school. Mary Grant. From some wee highland village, she'd appeared in their fourth year of secondary school. McNab had been immediately stricken. She'd been cooler, *but occasionally accommodating.* McNab smiled at the memory.

Christ, I had the hots for her.

She'd eventually ditched him of course. Once she'd seen sense, and got to know Davey better. They'd got hitched while McNab was at Tulliallan police college, trying to become a police officer, showing off his knife skills to the better-educated recruits as a way to compensate for his own inadequacies.

As far as he knew, Davey and Mary were still together. Envy cut through McNab, but only briefly. They were well suited, and they had a common project: to get rich and enjoy life . . . together.

The lovely Mary would never have settled for a sad bastard DS living in a room-and-kitchen flat.

McNab checked the text again on the way to the car. Davey, ever mindful of prying eyes, hadn't made his reasons for a meeting plain, but McNab knew the man's humour and his intention.

Davey's betting shops weren't his only income stream. McNab was no longer certain how many businesses his old pal owned, but knew they included a health club, two bar restaurants and a posh hairdressing salon, which was definitely Mary's responsibility. McNab, despite his own lowly status, was secretly rather proud of his mate. He'd rather Davey owned half of Glasgow than some posh out-of-town bastards.

Davey had no need to tell him where they'd meet. It was always the same location; the hangout from their shared past. An old-fashioned boozer that neither Davey nor any other company had decided was worth a makeover. In truth, it didn't need it. It had wood panelling, brass finishings, a majestic mirror and a rail to put your foot on as you supped your chosen poison.

The clientele had changed a bit since their misspent youth and there was no fug of smoke any more. Now it was more likely to be the white stuff puffing up your nostrils. No background music, *thank God*, and no giant flat-screen TV pumping out a mix of sport and inane drivel. McNab always said a prayer on entry that it would stay this way.

He found Davey in the snug, the area that had in the past been kept for any women brave enough to venture inside a pub. In this new era, and at this time of the day, a few had. There was a group of four round a table with a couple of bottles of wine. Dressed up, they were definitely planning a night out. The sight of them in all their finery suddenly reminded McNab that he'd promised to go by the Ink Parlour about now. As he pulled out his mobile to text Ellie that he'd be a bit later than planned, Davey looked up and spotted him.

'Mikey!' He waved him over and stood up, asking him what he was having. 'The usual?'

McNab would have loved to say yes, but didn't. 'Black coffee. I'm still on duty and I've got the car.' Even as he said this, he made up his mind to ditch the vehicle before he met Ellie. If they were going for a drink together, he intended alcohol to be involved.

Davey threw him an understanding look and indicated his own glass, which was filled with what looked like water, ice and lemon.

'I had to buy the bottled stuff to keep them happy. Cost almost as much as a real bloody drink.'

When Davey headed to the bar, McNab checked his

phone to find no further message from Ellie. He quickly texted:

See you in half an hour?

Then laid the mobile where he could watch for a reply.

They settled into a familiar silence as McNab tasted his concoction. Lacking a kick of any sort, he wondered if there was caffeine involved at all.

'So,' Davey said. 'You took another bullet?'

'A graze,' McNab said in surprise. 'How the hell did you know about that?'

Davey made a bemused face. 'The nurse that treated you in A&E works out at my gym. She's a boxer. I bet you didn't know that.'

McNab shook his head in wonderment at the reach of Davey's empire.

'She said you were covered in cocaine and high as a kite.'

When McNab didn't respond, Davey continued, 'The wee lassie you brought in disappeared from the hospital.'

'You're the one should be the detective,' McNab told him.

A shadow crossed Davey's face. 'My places are clean, at least as clean as I can make them. I don't want scum like Brodie anywhere in my vicinity.'

'He's been trying?'

'Someone's always trying.' Davey met McNab's eye. 'And not all officers of the law are free from blame for that. Coppers are like spoons. The cheaper they are, the easier they bend.'

'You have names?'

'If they piss me off enough, I'll let you know.' Davey took

a sip of his expensive water and, lowering his voice, said, 'I heard tell Brodie is on his way to Aberdeen.'

'With the girl?'

'Sorry, mate, don't know that.'

'She was thirteen. Thirteen,' McNab repeated.

Davey threw him a sympathetic glance. 'You don't have to be a refugee to be pimped out at thirteen in Glasgow,' he reminded him.

Which McNab knew was true. Child exploitation wasn't necessarily a foreign affair.

Davey grued as he took another sip of his water. 'What have we come to? Drinking bloody coffee and water in a pub?'

McNab was inclined to agree. Now he came to the real reason for his visit. 'The name James McVitie mean anything to you?'

A rain cloud took up residence on Davey's brow. 'That fucker,' he hissed.

'So, not a pal then?'

'He tried to get in on the gym. Had boxing matches in mind. I told him to take a running fuck. But not before he'd set up a couple of the youngsters to fight underground. He preferred the lassies over the boys. Fancied pairing them, boy against girl. Seeing girls get hit appeared to turn him on.'

'You frightened him away?'

'I spoke sternly to him. Like our teacher in Primary 7. Remember Miss McGonigle?'

Davey was easing away from the subject, suggesting he had no wish to discuss McVitie any further at this juncture. McNab glanced round, wondering if someone, recently entered, was showing an interest in their conversation.

Just then, his mobile lit up with an incoming message. A glance at the screen told him it was from Ellie. A short, but sweet,

See you soon.

Bingo.

'I'll have to get going,' he said, draining the remainder of the coffee. 'Thanks for the tip-off on Brodie. And give my regards to Mary.'

Davey threw him a look that suggested he hadn't forgotten the history between the three of them.

'Maybe you could come eat with us one night? Mary would like that.'

McNab's first instinct was to make an excuse. 'Could do,' he offered as a holding plan.

'Mary's a great cook,' Davey said encouragingly.

From memory, Mary was great at everything, were the words McNab didn't say.

Eyeing McNab's mobile, Davey added, 'You could bring a date.'

McNab had a swift image of Ellie and him arriving at Davey's and rather liked it.

'Okay,' he said with a smile. 'Dinner it is. Text me some dates, and I'll try and fit you in.'

22

Kyle was on the radio. Rhona couldn't hear what was being said, but understood by his expression that it wasn't good news. They had begun their walk back to the lochside, in anticipation of the helicopter's arrival. The journey which had taken fifteen minutes earlier in the day had proved more challenging now. Mainly because of a rising wind, which, if this strong at ground level, would no doubt be causing problems in the air.

Rhona already knew before Kyle told her that a helicopter ride home was currently not a possibility. Which meant they either walked out or waited. Rhona was glad that she wouldn't be the one to decide which.

Kyle pulled a face as he gave her the bad news on her now non-existent ride.

'Okay,' she said. 'What do we do?'

'We take shelter and wait for things to calm down, or we start walking out now.'

'Which will it be?'

'I take it you're not an avid hill climber?' Kyle said.

'Digging up bodies is more my thing.'

'Then we sit it out. Owen thinks it might blow out overnight.'

'We'll sleep at the Shelter Stone?'

'That's one possibility. Or we might head for a snow hole

along Feith Buidhe. The search team reported a vacant one we could use. The route there's steep to begin with, but soon levels out.' He paused, awaiting her response.

'Let's go for the snow hole.' Rhona tried to cover her relief that there was an alternative to the Shelter Stone. She wasn't superstitious, but the thought of bedding down in what she still considered a crime scene locus did not appeal.

The light was fading fast, aided by a swift-moving grey blanket of snow clouds. Although the fall wasn't heavy as yet, its persistent light swirling motion made it difficult to see much past a yard in front of them, rendering progress slow although Kyle seemed certain of the way. For the first time that day, Rhona's thoughts went to Sean in Aviemore.

He'll be wondering where the hell I am.

She had left a note, explaining about the rescue, but Sean would surely be worried that he hadn't heard from her by now. She resolved to ask Kyle to contact the base and have Owen let Sean know she wouldn't be back tonight.

So much for his hopes of a romantic getaway.

Kyle had halted and was checking in with an update on their location, so Rhona took the opportunity to sit down on a nearby boulder. The snow here seemed softer than the knee-high crisp version she'd grown used to, suggesting the possibility that a nearby stream or boggy ground rather than rock lay beneath the snow cover.

The crackling sound of the radio came to an end and, through the moment's silence that followed, Rhona heard what sounded like a human voice calling. Her senses immediately on high alert, she strained to listen . . . and heard it again. Faint and high-pitched, but definitely there.

Kyle had put the radio away and was gesturing her to follow.

'Wait,' she said, not rising from her boulder.

He came swiftly towards her, concern in his voice. 'Are you feeling okay?'

'I heard something.'

Kyle immediately fell silent, listening as intently as Rhona. The wind, she knew, could mimic many sounds, human ones included. And yet . . .

'There,' she said, catching the sound again. 'Did you hear it?'

Kyle didn't hesitate. 'Yes,' he nodded. 'I did.'

He immediately cupped his hands and called out. 'Keep shouting. We'll find you.'

They stood, waiting, Rhona trying to convince herself that Kyle must have done this a hundred times when searching for those lost or hurt on Cairngorm. Surely he would be good at pinpointing direction, and definitely better than she would be?

Minutes later, Rhona began to think it must have been the wind after all. She said so.

But Kyle wasn't ready to give up. 'I definitely heard a voice. And I think it came from that direction.' He set off in the direction he'd indicated, urging Rhona to follow. The light had all but gone, rendering Kyle's figure a dark shadow before her, apart from the bouncing movement of his head torch.

In those moments, Rhona felt a flicker of fear as she imagined what it might feel like to be alone and hurt here, in what was an Arctic wilderness.

Kyle halted so suddenly, she almost collided with him. 'Listen,' he said.

And there it was. A high-pitched call of 'Help'.

It's a female. Maybe the missing member from the Shelter Stone.

The arc of Rhona's head lamp showed nothing but flat, pristine snow. Not even a boulder in sight.

'Where?' Rhona said, puzzled.

'It's coming from below us,' Kyle said.

Her immediate thought was that they were trekking through snow deposited by an avalanche, but Kyle swiftly put her straight.

'Look.' He guided her eyes to where a dark hole broke the snow cover. 'Follow me, exactly.'

Rhona had no desire to do anything else.

Kyle began to circle east of the dark patch, testing the snow carefully at each step. Then she heard it. Not the female voice again, but the sound of rushing water.

There's a stream under the snow.

As they approached the hole, Rhona noted that they were also nearing a sharp drop towards the valley floor. The sound of water was coming from a hill burn as it escaped its snow tunnel and cascaded into the corrie far below.

Her heart in her throat, Rhona watched Kyle lie flat and ease his way towards the narrow opening. Suddenly a light appeared from below, illuminating his face, followed by a cry of relief and delight.

'I'm with Cairngorm Mountain Rescue. How are you doing down there?'

23

As he walked to the car, McNab put in a call to the station to tell them Brodie was rumoured to be on his way to Aberdeen. The A90 was well patrolled, mainly because of the drugs traffic that was known to make its way up and down the main route between Edinburgh and the oil capital, but spotting Brodie wouldn't be easy, especially now he was aware he was being looked for. And if he did have the girl, she certainly wouldn't be in plain view.

Up to this point McNab had been pretty certain Brodie wasn't connected to the Aberdeen set-up. The Turkish tug carrying 3.2 tons of cocaine off Aberdeen had been the biggest haul in Scotland to date, but that area of coast could be patrolled, if you had the manpower. The myriad sea lochs and islands of the west coast were another matter. Much like Norway.

Maybe he and Inspector Olsen had something in common after all.

He ditched the car as soon as possible and jumped on the underground, which was busy. Offering the last available seat in the carriage to a young woman, he accepted her thanks and took up a stance next to the door, imagining how Ellie might be impressed by that.

Sad bastard that I am.

Fifteen minutes later he stood outside the Ink Parlour,

perturbed that the door was shut and apparently locked. Pulling out his mobile again, he called Ellie's number and she answered immediately.

'Wait there,' she told him.

McNab, relieved, did as instructed. Moments later the door was opened and Ellie ushered him inside.

'I'm sorry I'm late,' he began.

'It doesn't matter. I've just finished anyway. The last one was tricky and took longer than expected.'

'Not another set of balls?'

She smiled. 'No, but it did feature the groin area.'

McNab flinched, despite himself.

'So,' she said, indicating a booth. 'Let's take a look at you.'

McNab wondered if he should warn her of what was to come. He had no wish to admit to having been shot again, but if she asked what had happened to his arm, he would need an answer.

Facing his back, she didn't appear to register the arm dressing at first.

'Can I unwrap you?'

'Feel free.'

He flinched a little as her movements to do so collided with his more recent injury, alerting her to it.

'What happened to your arm?'

In that split second, McNab had to decide between the truth or a lie. As it was, he avoided both.

'It's nothing.' He changed the subject. 'How's the tattoo looking?'

A pregnant pause, then, 'Okay, but you need to be more careful with the wrapping.'

Suddenly McNab realized he desperately wanted to make

a move. Whether it would be rejected or accepted, he had no idea.

'I'll rewrap you, if you want?'

He did want.

He expected her to move away, to fetch the film. She didn't. There was a moment's stillness, then came the light tracing of a fingertip, as though she was exploring the outline of the skull she'd painted on his back.

The feeling was electric. He wondered if she knew just how much. Her next move confirmed that she did. The tongue's touch was lighter, and both warm and moist. She might as well have applied a vibrator to his balls. McNab reacted accordingly.

Her hands circled his waist now and met in his crotch. If he'd had any doubt as to what she was intimating, he had them no longer. Reluctant to interrupt her decided movements, McNab waited as she deftly unzipped his trousers and lifted him free.

Then she was round and facing him, a teasing smile on her face. 'You did say I could unwrap you?'

From past experience, the drink usually came first, followed by the sex. It seemed, for Ellie, it was the other way round. Stone-cold sober without even a recent caffeine hit, McNab hoped he'd made a decent job of it. Surreptitiously viewing Ellie as she dressed, he decided she looked cheerful enough. Having examined her naked body in some detail, he now knew where the tattoos were. It was a memory journey he suspected he would replay in her absence.

'So,' she said. 'One more thing to know about me, before we get that drink together.'

'And that is?' McNab said, suddenly worried she was

about to announce herself to be the daughter of a felon, or even worse, a felon herself. He should have had her checked out. The truth was he hadn't expected to get lucky quite so quickly.

'Don't look so worried. I told you the police know nothing about me. Except for you, of course.'

McNab tried to relax. Being suspicious about everyone was a feature of the job. Unfortunately it didn't help with relationships.

Ellie was heading for the door. 'You didn't bring your car, did you?'

McNab shook his head. 'Good,' she said, lifting a jacket from a peg near the door, and putting it on.

What the fuck? McNab almost said out loud. It seemed skulls were to Ellie's liking. And that included on leather jackets. A notion began to form in McNab's mind. One that both worried and enticed him.

'Good,' she said, holding open the door. 'Then I'll give you a ride.'

In his sudden nervousness, McNab almost said, *You just did*. Then they were outside and advancing on her mode of transport.

Ellie was regarding him. 'So, what d'you think?'

I've pulled a bloody biker chick.

McNab attempted to quell the words that would display what he really thought about the magnificent machine that stood before him, most of which were expletives of a decidedly sexual nature.

'My father was a speedway rider. I inherited his love of bikes, but women don't ride speedway, so . . .' She regarded the bike with a look more lustful than his own. 'Have you ridden bikes in the job?'

McNab had. In fact he'd loved it, as did many of his fellow officers. Even their last chief constable had been a bike man, who'd been known to turn up unannounced on his *very* powerful motorbike, to check on the workings of the lower orders. Something which had not been appreciated. You know that saying, if you need a big throbbing engine between your legs, you probably haven't got one of your own. McNab checked himself before uttering that thought.

'I have ridden a bike before, but not for a while.'

'Are you willing to sit behind me?' she asked with wide-eyed innocence.

'I could do.'

Now the helmets were produced. Ellie climbed aboard, an action that in itself brought him a frisson of pleasure.

'Now you,' she ordered.

McNab did as told.

'You can hold on to me if you like,' she offered.

Okay, this was way beyond pleasure now.

The roar when it came brought back a rush of memories. His brief internal question as to why the hell he'd chosen to be a detective and forsaken the bike was soon drowned in the excitement of being back on two wheels again.

Ten glorious minutes later, she brought them to a stylish halt in North Street, just down from the grandiose building that housed the famous Mitchell Library.

'My other day job,' she told him.

'You're a librarian?' McNab failed to mask his astonishment.

'No, but I do frequent the Mitchell quite a lot.' She indicated the building she actually meant.

'A Harley-Davidson shop?' McNab registered that his voice appeared to have risen half an octave in his surprise.

'No,' she corrected him. '*The* Harley-Davidson shop.'

McNab digested that as far as it was possible to do so. 'Where you . . . ?'

'Fix bikes. Well, I mostly add the extras people buy to make them look even cooler.'

This female is way beyond perfect. Why the fuck is she having anything to do with me?

She must have spotted that look. 'You're uncomfortable with that?'

McNab bounced back. 'Hey, are you comfortable with having a polis riding pillion?'

'I rather like it. Shall we park the bike back at the shop and look for somewhere to have that drink now?'

The snow came on as they meandered through Glasgow . . . to who knew where.

As far as McNab was concerned this woman could take him anywhere she wanted.

24

One wall of the snow cave was bare rock, the other three hard-packed snow and ice that sparkled like jewels in the beams from their head torches.

The burn, kept at zero degrees by gravity, occupied half the space. To the back, a miniature waterfall tumbled down a rock face as it entered the cave to swirl left of the injured climber. Merely a yard from her feet, the burn exited to plunge noisily to the loch below.

'Don't drop anything,' Kyle told her. 'It'll be over there in a second.'

The young woman lay flat on a rock, her right boot in the running water. She was shivering, a shudder running through her every few seconds. Despite this, her face glistened with sweat.

After Kyle had climbed in and surveyed the scene, he'd urged Rhona to join him. A radio report had already been sent and he expected a contingent of searchers from the Shelter Stone to arrive soon.

'Okay, where does it hurt?' he now asked the girl.

When she didn't answer, Kyle repeated the question. The girl was, Rhona suspected, stunned from her fall into the cave, or experiencing the onset of hypothermia, and with it, confusion. Eventually Kyle got a reply.

'My back and my ankle.'

Rhona manoeuvred round Kyle to take a look. The swelling was obvious, but possibly less than it might have been if the girl hadn't had the good sense to keep it in the running water, which had acted like an ice pack. If it was broken, much better to leave the boot in place until they got to the hospital. Rhona said as much. The girl's back was another matter. That would require support on the stretcher.

'Right, let's deal with the pain, then get you warm and comfortable,' Kyle said. 'There's Entonox in the gear,' he told Rhona. 'Can you reach it without getting soaked?'

It was virtually impossible to move around in the cave while avoiding the spray from the waterfall at the rear, but Rhona did her best.

As Kyle fixed the mask in place, he explained the need to take a big breath to open the valve and let the analgesic through.

By her expression, the first couple of attempts didn't do the trick.

'When the pain comes, breathe in deeply,' Rhona urged her. 'It's like being in labour. Although you probably don't know about that yet.' Her quip brought a faint smile to the girl's lips.

'We'll use the vacmat,' Kyle said. 'Then get her warmed up.'

He spread the vacuum mattress out on the stretcher. Minutes later they had her on board and in both a sleeping bag and a survival bag. While Kyle secured her neck with a brace, Rhona tucked a heat bag next to her body.

Kyle now proceeded to check her pulse and breathing. When he'd finished, he quietly told Rhona the result. 'Her blood pressure's down and she's close to hypothermic. Try to keep her conscious, while I find out how soon the others can get here.'

Rhona moved alongside the ashen-faced girl, registering the purple bruising round her eyes and the badly cut lip. As the analgesic began to ease the pain, the girl's eyes flickered shut in relief, so Rhona strove to keep her talking by asking her name.

'Isla,' came the faint reply.

'So, Isla. How did you get here from the Shelter Stone?'

The eyes re-opened and she looked briefly puzzled by the question, then fear swept in. 'Oh my God. Where's Gavin? And my friends? Are they okay?'

Rhona glanced across at Kyle, who mouthed a silent *no*. The girl was in a bad way and they needed her to stay strong enough to get her off the mountain.

'There are searchers over there now,' Rhona said, hating her prevarication, yet knowing that it was the lesser of two evils.

'What about the man?' the girl said, as though suddenly remembering.

'What man?' Rhona said.

'The Big Grey Man of Ben Macdui.'

The girl was mumbling now, something about Gavin. Then, staring into whatever dream or reality she was reliving, she added, 'I scratched his face.'

'Why?' Rhona asked.

'Because he tried to kill me.'

'Who did?' Rhona said, confused.

'The big grey man. But he wasn't grey, he was white.'

Rhona eased her backpack over beside her and said quietly to Kyle, 'I'm going to take a sample from under her nails.'

'She's delirious,' he responded with a puzzled expression. 'The big grey man's a mountain myth. A figment of climbers' imagination.'

'I know. But if she did scratch someone, I'd like to know who it was.'

Isla was sleeping now, and peacefully. No wonder, after what she'd endured over the last forty-eight hours. Rhona was tired herself and planning shortly to retire to the overnight stay hospital bed they'd kindly offered her. She would seriously have liked to be back in the hotel in Aviemore with Sean, but that had proved impossible. Anyway, she wanted to be here tomorrow at the mortuary, when the postmortem was performed on the climbers' bodies.

The girl's cheeks, which had been so pale in the ice cave, were now a little pinker. The pain etching the face had gone, the bruising round the eyes already turning yellow. Pumped full of drugs now, Isla was still unaware of the full horror that had ended her climbing trip to Hell's Lum.

It had taken an hour after the team had arrived to rescue Isla from the cave, the opening proving too narrow for the stretcher. As night had approached, the temperature had plummeted, turning the surrounds of the escape hole to thick ice. Kyle had climbed up, and suspended by the team above, had hacked his way through to create a big enough gap. As ice pieces had hurtled down on his head, his language had been enough to colour the cave purple and had even brought a smile to Isla's wan face behind the mesh basket they'd fixed over her head to protect her from falling debris.

Once out, Rhona had heard a shout of 'Let's kick ass', and the stretcher bearers, plus herself and Kyle, had begun their walk back down to the frozen loch, in anticipation of the chopper's arrival, the fall in temperature having thankfully been accompanied by a lessening in wind strength.

Settling down on the frozen loch on only one wheel, the pilot had skilfully tilted the chopper to allow them to avoid the rotors, and soon she and Kyle had risen swiftly into the cold night air, their casualty safely aboard.

Moonlight had bathed Loch Morlich below, suggesting a benign landscape, contradicting everything Rhona had experienced up to now. They'd remained silent as the pilot flew them north, travelling the route of the A9, empty of vehicles, the snow gates having been closed further south at Drumochter. Then they were over the final hill and looking down on the lights of Inverness, and the shining waters of the Moray Firth.

They'd landed on the six inches of snow that encircled Raigmore Hospital.

'Okay,' said Kyle as they'd touched down, 'we're here.'

Sean answered almost immediately.

'Where are you?'

'Raigmore Hospital in Inverness. They've given me a bed for the night.'

'I was worried.'

Rhona registered the hesitancy in Sean's voice. He knew she didn't like a fuss, so such an admission went against the grain.

'I'm fine,' she assured him. 'I'll stay here for the postmortem on the climbers.'

'They've promised the A9 will be open tomorrow.'

'Then go home. I'll follow.'

There was a short silence as Sean digested her news.

Rhona almost said, 'I'm sorry,' but didn't. 'How did tonight go?' she said instead.

'Good,' Sean conceded. 'I like Aviemore. I'll come again.' He didn't say, *I hope you'll come with me*, but Rhona heard those words anyway.

'I'll see you back in Glasgow,' she answered.

'What about your suitcase?'

'Take it with you.'

'Okay. Ring me,' Sean said.

He's playing the part I cast him in, Rhona thought. *Lover but not partner.* She rang off then, before any more need be said. Coming up here wasn't meant to cement or change their relationship, and it hadn't.

Rhona lay down, wondering if she would or could sleep with all that had happened. In the darkness, she heard the muffled sounds of a Highland hospital in action. The arrival of another helicopter, the swift trundle of a trolley, a woman's sobs, a man's quiet assurances. Eventually all merged with the remembered sounds and images of the snow cave. The young woman's pain and distress, Kyle's reassuring and steady voice, her own response. And through it all, the whispering of the burn alongside, before it plunged to the valley floor below.

25

The chopper's distinct sound had wakened him. Disorientated in the darkness, he couldn't for a moment remember where he was. The knock he'd taken as the plane had landed on the frozen loch had, he acknowledged, given him a mild concussion. Concentration on eliminating the danger to both himself and the job had kept him focused up to now.

I've grown careless in sleep.

He'd felt his way towards the entrance tunnel and crawled along it, the exit lit by moonlight on the white blanket of snow. Emerging, but keeping low, he'd scanned the sky and spotted the beams of the chopper over towards the loch.

Why were they back there now?

There would of course have to be an investigation into the crash, but it would hardly begin in the middle of the night. No, that hadn't been the reason for the helicopter's return. The rescue team had returned to provide their prime function . . . to rescue someone. And the service did not transport the dead. Which meant there was a live casualty.

With that, the nagging doubt had returned. Of course, it was highly likely that other climbers had been caught out by the swift onset of bad weather over the holiday period. There was bound to be more than one rescue required.

But it might be the girl.

LIN ANDERSON

That thought had brought him out of the snow hole. If they had found the girl, then there had to be a team nearby. And where there were searchers, there were lights. It hadn't taken him long to spot them. A line of head torches had been bound eastwards to meet the chopper. A larger group were headed towards the summit and the ski lodge, their job done.

Packed up now, he forsook the snow hole. Despite the freezing temperatures, he saw no further reason to remain there. The sky was clear, the moon bright, the wind no longer a threat. Convinced that the girl had been rescued, he wanted to know what her story was. And the best place to find that out was on the valley floor.

26

Stavanger, Norway, 31 December

Police Inspector Alvis Olsen departed his apartment on Kirkegata and set out towards the Commissariat de Polis on Lagårdsveien. The twenty-minute walk to work was, he thought, always a pleasant one, even at this time of year. The steep cobbled streets of Stavanger's old town glistened underfoot, a light fall of snow having occurred overnight. At this hour, most of the shops hadn't yet opened. Once they did, such snow as there was would quickly disappear under the footfall of the inhabitants.

Earlier, enjoying his morning coffee on the balcony at the top of the apartment building, Alvis had noted the arrival of yet another giant cruise ship, now tethered in the guest harbour, the upper decks of which reared even above Valbergtårnet, the old stone fire watchtower that crowned the highest point of the wooden-built town. Stavanger, as well as being the oil capital of Norway, was also a big tourist draw and no doubt this latest arrival was bound for Lysefjorden, the most famous fjord in the Stavanger region, as stunning in winter as it was in summer.

Now, reaching the park at Breiavatnet, he left the road to walk the western edge of the shallow lake, which according to local legend contained few if any fish, although home to swans and ducks. The park that surrounded the small expanse of water with its central fountain was deserted apart from himself, although ahead, at its southern end, the railway and bus stations were already busy with travellers, despite the early hour.

Having left the car-free area behind, he made for the pedestrian crossing at the foot of Lagård Gravlund, intent on spending five minutes in the company of his wife. Summer saw the graveyard green and blossoming. Midwinter was a different experience, one he enjoyed as much, although not on the all-too-frequent rainy days. Today, a crisp cold sun sparkled on the grey gravestones, some of which were as old as the town itself.

Entering the gate, Olsen turned left, to follow the path to the rear of the cemetery, immediately leaving the sound of traffic on the main road behind. Coming to the bench which was his usual resting place, he took a seat opposite the grave he had come to visit. As always, his eyes were drawn to the neighbouring stone, erected after Marita's. He found the message on it strangely comforting, although it featured an image of a baby boy who had died at nine months old. Marita had longed for children in life, and it seemed to Olsen, morosely perhaps, that she now had the companionship of at least one, in death.

Turning his attention to her own simple gravestone, he closed his eyes and brought his wife's face to mind, just as it had been two years ago, the last time he had seen her alive. It would be always thus, he realized. Marita forever young and vivacious, even as he grew old, wrinkled and worn.

As usual, he silently relayed what was on his mind and as before, when alive, Marita, in his head at least, listened with that quizzical look she would adopt as she tried to assimilate the suspicious workings of a police brain, so far removed from her own. The product of a Scottish mother and a Norwegian father, Marita had, to Olsen's mind, featured the best qualities of both nationalities, whereas he was purely Norwegian.

Talking silently to his wife always seemed to make things clearer, though it never worked half as well elsewhere, such as at home or in his office in the Commissariat. In this instance, the tale itself involved a child, or more correctly children, although not as young as her nearby companion in death. And it was not a pretty story.

As he completed his conversation, Olsen felt the light touch of snowflakes on his cheek and looked up to discover the bright morning sky now clouded over. Rising, he said a silent goodbye, then made his way back to the gate and the noisy world outside.

There were difficulties, as he'd explained to Marita. He had no option but to acknowledge that fact.

His visit to the north and the subsequent discovery of the dead children had altered his perception of the investigation.

Having returned, he was now required to alter the view of others involved in it. Plus there might well be the problem of international relations and diplomacy. Something he wasn't interested in, and which he believed shouldn't affect the investigation, but of course he was wrong in that respect, and probably naive. There was the law. And then there were those who believed themselves to be above and beyond it.

The walk alongside Lagård Gravlund complete, Olsen waited at the junction. Across the main road, the strange shop of many and unusual artefacts was advertising a sale with fifty per cent off, although wasn't yet open to allow buyers to take advantage of the offer. On his side, the imposing white-fronted edifice that was the Commissariat de Polis now came into view, and by the comings and goings around its entrance was definitely open for business.

A couple of young women stood hesitant under the awning, either taking momentary shelter from the thickening snow or else wondering about entering. Both were ill-dressed for the wintery weather and, listening to their murmured words as he approached, Olsen registered that they weren't Norwegian. The Politidistrikt Sør-Vest, which incorporated Stavanger, was home to more than one hundred different nationalities. Schengen offered European citizens such as these young women the freedom to work and make their home in Norway, despite the fact that the country wasn't a member of the European Union.

Realizing a police officer wished to enter, they swiftly stepped aside to allow him passage. Olsen contemplated asking them if they wanted to speak with someone, but noting the consternation with which they'd viewed his approach, decided to send a female officer out instead.

A wave of welcome warmth met him on entering the large reception area. A few people sat on the long padded benches that lined the left-hand wall, a few stood before the glassed enquiry desks. Olsen waited until one was free, then related his wish for a female member of staff to approach the young women, after which he made his way to the security door at the rear, which led upstairs to the functioning heart of the Commissariat.

The strategy meeting was scheduled to begin in ten minutes, where he would report his findings and suggest what might be their next move. Releasing the double security doors, Olsen entered to be greeted by the two women currently on duty on the switchboards.

'Someone ordered *pannekaken* for your meeting,' Birgitt informed him with a smile. 'Maybe you're having an important visitor?'

'Or maybe we're expected to be in there for some time,' Olsen countered as he made for the conference room.

Major organized crime in Norway was mainly centred on drug trafficking, THB and, increasingly, cybercrime, a problem recently prioritized in their move to a new sixteen-district model of policing. Trafficking in human beings was what Olsen had been investigating and what had taken him to the northernmost part of the country and their non-Schengen border with Russia.

What he'd found there wasn't what he'd expected. In fact the trail that he'd followed had proved illusionary, apart from those two small bodies in the snow. If there had been an increase in trafficking via Russia, it had now dwindled, as the local forces had been at pains to point out. Like all districts, they suffered from itinerant prostitution, often involving trafficked women from Eastern Europe or Nigeria.

Such offences were difficult to monitor and manage, the officer in charge had reminded him, the participants staying for only short periods of time before moving to another district. Even if a suspect was picked up, there was often no prosecution, the trafficked women being too afraid to testify for fear of reprisals on their families at home. Any DNA samples taken then had to be removed from the database, often to be re-entered again via another district, sometimes as little as a week later.

A cat-and-mouse game with little reward.

But not this time, Olsen told himself as he completed his

submission. The other three men sitting round the table had listened intently to what he'd had to say. Politiinspektør Harald Hjerngaard, Jonas Silvertsen and Oskar Gerhard, as part of the Criminal Investigation Department, respectively represented Forensics, Organized Crime and Child Sexual Abuse. All were aware of the various organized crime gangs working in Norway and in Politidistrikt Sør-Vest in particular.

Up to now, Olsen hadn't dismissed the possibility that one or more of the local criminal motorcycle gangs might be the prime instigators. With chapters all over Europe and beyond, they certainly had the reach, and prostitution and drug smuggling were their preferred occupations. Then there were the ethnic gangs from Lithuania, Poland, Romania, Chechnya and Albania, equally on his radar, particularly with the influx of unaccompanied minors flowing into Europe from war zones such as Syria and northern Africa. Minors who, he'd come to suspect, were being shipped between Norway and their near neighbour, Scotland. The news in the early hours of the morning from Glasgow had convinced him he was on the right track.

'So, when do you plan to go?' Harald said as the others nodded their agreement.

'As soon as possible,' Olsen told them, satisfied with the outcome of the meeting. 'Anything back from the coastguard?'

It was Silvertsen who answered. 'No sightings of the vessel you're interested in as yet, but there's a hundred square miles of open sea to search,' he said.

'And air traffic control?'

'They're checking all private flights that took off from Sola during the previous three days as requested.'

As he returned to the flat to finish packing, the snow came on in earnest. Snow wasn't a feature of Stavanger. Like

Aberdeen, its Scottish counterpart, it experienced mostly a wet winter, and often a wet summer too. Olsen had a momentary concern that worsening weather might delay or even prevent his flight, but decided if it did, he would reschedule for the following morning. Meanwhile, he would make contact with MIT Glasgow and inform them of his imminent visit.

Before he'd left the office he'd secured more information regarding the Delta project and the officers involved. Olsen didn't doubt that cooperation with the Scottish contingent would happen. Being part of mainland Europe, members of KRIPOS were used to dealing internationally, and Scotland and Norway were close neighbours. Both lay on the northernmost reaches of Europe. They shared many words and ancestry in common, something that Marita had often reminded him of. But in the end, it would all come down to the personnel involved, himself included.

The colourful playground constructed with discarded materials from the oil industry was busy with scrambling, excited children, reminding Olsen that it was in fact the school holidays. Holidays were something he rarely took now. Summer hillwalking and winter climbing had been two pastimes he'd enjoyed with Marita. In fact it had been she who'd organized all their holidays. She'd also been in charge of his social life, *which is why I no longer have one*, Olsen acknowledged, not for the first time.

Turning from the harbour into Kirkegata, he registered that the guest jetty had a superyacht tied up alongside, the *Mariusud*. A yacht Olsen recognized because the owner was one of the biggest shipping magnates in Norway. He would have liked to take a closer look at the sleek yacht, but glancing

LIN ANDERSON

at his watch, he abandoned that thought. If it was there when he returned . . .

Directly across from it, on the other side of the harbour, the World War Two ship, painted white with its red cross markings, lay in its permanent position, a reminder that Norway and its neighbours had oft times been at war.

We're still at war, Olsen thought, glancing again at the *Mariusud. It's just the enemy that's changed.*

27

McNab's eyes flickered open. Not recognizing the landscape, he wondered for a moment where he was, then a sudden memory brought his head round to discover the place beside him in the bed was empty. *Shit*. He looked at his mobile with trepidation. He'd heard no morning alarm and was worried he may have slept through it. But no, it had yet to go off. He rose and went to check he was alone in the flat.

A quick glance into the main room suggested he was. Added to which there was no sound from the shower. *She's gone*. At what time, he had no idea. McNab tested himself as to how he felt about that. It all depended on her reason for the early exit. Perhaps he'd pissed her off, or disappointed her, and she didn't fancy an early-morning repeat performance. Then again, if that were the case, surely she would have asked him to leave last night? McNab decided to assume that explanation, mainly because it was better for his ego.

Re-entering the bedroom, he now spotted a piece of paper, nestling where Ellie's head had been. The words were written in real ink and by an elegant hand. The note also sported a drawing of a small skull that looked like a miniature version of the one she'd inked on his back. Reading it, he smiled.

Morning. Feel free to use the shower and eat any food you're lucky enough to find in the kitchen. Remember the cling film. I left it in the bathroom for you. Ellie.

So he hadn't been a disappointment after all.

Under the shower and following Ellie's washing instructions to the letter, he heard his mobile ring. Jumping out, he got to it, dripping, but just in time.

'McNab.'

It was Janice. 'There's a strategy meeting at eleven.'

'I know,' he lied. 'I'll be there in half an hour.'

'We'd better talk first. I'll see you at the coffee machine.'

She hung up so quickly that McNab didn't have time to question the necessity of such a meeting. Her tone had been edgy, he acknowledged to himself, but then again, DS Clark was inclined to worry unduly, unlike him. Swiftly drying himself, he reached for his shirt, then remembered he still had to don the cling film.

No time, he thought, checking his watch, offering a silent apology to Ellie while already working on his excuse, should she find out.

A passing glance in the mirror reminded him of what he had done to his back. Arm tattoos were common enough on the force among both men and women. But a skull on your back, a biker tattoo, was tantamount to being seen as an arse.

What the hell would his work colleagues say if they saw it?

An image of DI Wilson's possible expression came to mind.

Maybe I could offer to go undercover among the biker gangs to make up for my stupidity?

He may have made a mistake getting inked, but Ellie's

painted body had, he decided, been beautiful. He'd never really reckoned tattoos much. Probably because of the men he'd seen sporting them. At the last European Football Championships, he'd viewed a rioter with an oversized belly emblazoned with a tattoo of Fred Flintstone, for chrissakes.

Who the hell would have Fred Flintstone inked on his belly?

Who the hell would choose to have a skull inked on his back?

And I can't even blame the drink.

McNab pulled the front door shut and set off down the stairs. His car was parked some way away, and demanded a swift walk.

There had been a thaw overnight and grey slush had now replaced the white stuff. The wind was a Glasgow special: damp and raw, biting at his cheeks and ears. *At least I'm not on Cairngorm.* That thought made McNab check his mobile, hoping for some indication that Rhona might be back in town, but there was nothing.

And why should there be?

Finally back at his car, he started her up and, glancing at his watch, decided on both the route and speed through the morning traffic that would allow him to turn up at the coffee machine at the allotted time.

28

All mortuaries are alike, Rhona thought. Same smell, temperature and shining steel, their difference lying mainly in their capacity. The mortuary at the new Queen Elizabeth Hospital in Glasgow could hold up to 200 bodies. This one, situated at the back of the main building of the Highland hospital, considerably fewer.

Looking through the intervening glass, Rhona could see the three climbers lying side by side, with the pilot of the light aircraft lying a little away from them. Rhona suspected that all four bodies probably hadn't thawed enough yet to allow for a postmortem investigation. Mortuary refrigerators, like those in a domestic kitchen, were maintained at plus four degrees centigrade. A temperature adequate for short-term preservation over a few days, and which kept the body 'workable'.

Climbers who died in the high Alps and on Everest might remain frozen for years. Ötzi the Iceman, whose body had been found between Austria and Italy, had been preserved in the ice for almost five and a half millennia. Cairngorm wasn't as high or cold as the Upper Alps or Mount Everest, but the temperature on the plateau had been low enough to freeze all four bodies solid.

Charlie came in as she contemplated the scene, and Rhona knew by his expression that something was wrong.

'I'm afraid we're not going ahead with any of the post-mortems.'

'They're too frozen?' Rhona said.

'They are, but that's not the reason.' His forehead creased in annoyance. 'The powers that be are transferring the bodies to Glasgow.'

'Why?' Rhona said in surprise. 'I thought you processed climbing deaths here.'

'We do, usually, although occasionally they're sent to Aberdeen.'

'So why are they going to Glasgow?' Rhona asked, already having a glimmer of what might be his answer.

'Because they have a bigger mortuary? Because they think we're not up to the job? Because of creeping central-ization?'

Rhona was aware there had been muted suggestions that all bodies should be transferred to a central point at the Queen Elizabeth. Colleagues in Aberdeen forensic pathology had already voiced a similar concern. It wasn't only criminal gangs that had turf wars. Academics in every field were known to indulge in them too. And bodies were business. Take them away and the expertise left with them.

'Do you want to take a look before they're prepared for transport?'

Rhona did. In the confines of the mountain refuge, the casualties still clothed, with the only light coming from her head torch, it had been impossible to fully establish the state of the bodies.

Now, gowned like Charlie, she could finally examine them in the full glare required.

'Their clothes have been bagged for forensic examination,' Charlie told her. 'All three climbers were wearing vests and leggings as you know, undergarments and hats and gloves. There was a fourth pair of gloves, I assume belonging to Isla.'

The bodies were gradually defrosting. Rhona could both see and feel the difference in the texture of the skin. She checked Gavin first. In the cave she hadn't registered scratches. Not somewhere visible, anyway. Naked now, she found a group on his chest. Not deep, but enough to draw blood.

'They all have scratches,' Charlie said, seeing her interest. 'Climbing places like Hell's Lum, it's inevitable. Like bruises. Around the wrists, shins, ankles, anywhere that engages with the rock face.'

'Isla, in her delirium, claimed she scratched a man who, she said, was trying to kill her.' Rhona repeated the garbled story, which had mixed up Gavin's name with that of the Big Grey Man.

'Hypothermia will do that. But even experienced climbers with no signs of hypothermia have claimed to see or hear the phantom of Ben Macdui. And that includes me. It's a trick of light and sound, which is yet to be explained scientifically.'

'What about what we found in the cave?'

'The circumstances were odd,' he agreed. 'But not without precedence.'

'And the grit I collected from the female's mouth?'

'Climbers melt snow for drinking water. It has grit in it.'

Rhona nodded; everything Charlie had said was reasonable, and as both a pathologist and part of CMR, he knew what he was talking about, but without a postmortem, they were still in the dark.

She moved now to the man they presumed to be the pilot of the light aircraft, although they had no real proof that was the case. Naked, he was muscular, healthy-looking and at a guess in his thirties. Both upper arms bore tattoos, Viking in nature, as did his chest, on which the words *Uten Frykt* were written in script form.

'Scandinavian?' Charlie tried. 'Or he's a fan of that TV programme *Vikings*.'

'*Frykt* looks like fright or fear,' Rhona said, fishing for her mobile to check online. 'Without fear,' she said, 'and it's Norwegian.'

'Perhaps the plane came from there?' Charlie said. 'Owen said AAIB plan to airlift the wreckage out today, if the weather keeps good.'

Rhona followed Charlie into the changing room and began to degown.

'You'll head south now?' he asked.

Rhona nodded. 'When the girl wakens up?'

'I'll let you know the story,' Charlie promised.

She caught the first flight to Glasgow. After having told Sean she would follow him, it seemed instead that she would be there before him. Waiting to board the plane, she'd watched the news on the TV screen. Under a blue sky, the footage of the A9 through Drumochter Pass showed it now open, although evidence of the blockage was obvious in a string of abandoned vehicles, whose occupants had had to be rescued at the height of the blizzard.

Then followed the images taken from the media helicopter. She even caught a glimpse of herself at the Shelter Stone with Charlie. The voice-over spoke of the horrifying death of three climbers 'which required the presence of forensic scientist, Dr Rhona MacLeod' – *how the hell did they know about me?* – and the subsequent 'intrepid' rescue of a fourth from an ice cave inches from a perilous drop. After which came the story of a 'mystery plane' that had crash-landed on Loch A'an. No one, according to the report, 'knew where this plane had come from, or what it had been carrying'. *That was true enough.* 'And,' the voice-over continued, 'its pilot was also found dead some distance from the wreckage in suspicious circumstances'.

At that point her flight had been called and she'd had to depart the screen. Now she understood Kyle and Owen's reticence about giving out information on rescues to the press. No matter what they said, the press would find their own story. Except in this case, the press had got it pretty well right and with a large measure of detail, including her own presence and profession. There were over twenty rescuers that day, Rhona recalled, all of whom would have friends and families. Someone among either the rescuers or the police had identified a juicy aspect to the story and handed it to the press.

Once the plane had landed at Glasgow airport, and they were given the go-ahead to turn on 'digital devices', the normal world returned with a vengeance in a flurry of missed calls, text messages and emails. One of which reported the real reason that the pilot's body had been ordered south.

29

The bus that had brought him down from the hill and deposited him in the village centre had been buzzing with stories of the blizzard. He'd tuned in, and when the guy beside him had asked what his own tale was, he'd said he'd dug a snow hole and left it at that.

For those who'd taken refuge in the ski lodge, and had access to TV reports, the talk was all about the three climbers found dead from exposure at the Shelter Stone, plus a fourth member of the party who'd been rescued and flown out by helicopter to Raigmore. At this point, he'd feigned sorrow at the deaths, and asked if anyone knew how badly hurt the survivor was. No one could tell him.

Now, alighting from the bus, he found somewhere to eat, which had Wi-Fi, and brought himself up to date via his mobile. The footage from a press helicopter concerned him. He didn't think he'd been caught on camera, but there was no guarantee of that. The snippet he did see of rescuers at the Shelter Stone, together with the report of a forensic scientist at the scene, worried him the most.

How the fuck did that happen?

Mountain rescue teams had all manner of people in them, but a forensic scientist from Glasgow? As he pondered this, the waitress came over with his meal. Catching a trace of his accent, she introduced herself as Annieska and told him she was Polish and from Kraków. He thanked her but didn't respond with his own nationality, which she seemed disappointed by.

'Were you on the hill last night?' she said.

He merely nodded, not wishing to engage in conversation.

'My boyfriend's in Cairngorm Mountain Rescue. It was Kyle and the forensic woman, Dr MacLeod, who rescued the casualty and transported her to Raigmore,' she told him proudly.

Now he *was* interested. 'I hope the girl was okay?'

'They found her in a snow cave over a burn, close to death.'

So that's why he couldn't find her body.

'But she didn't die?'

'Oh no. They think she'll be able to tell them what happened when she comes round.' She paused. 'Then they'll have to tell her that her boyfriend and the other couple are dead. How awful is that?'

'Awful,' he chimed in.

As he quickly ate, he determined to exit the valley as swiftly as possible. By the atmosphere in Macdui's, it was obvious that, like all small communities, nothing and nobody went past them, including strangers like himself. The question was whether he should head for Inverness to finish the job. And that all depended on whether she might recognize him.

He drank the remainder of his coffee. *No loose ends.* There was little chance that she could identify him, and he would take a risk by disposing of her in the hospital. If she should die back home in Glasgow, then no one would link her demise to what had happened on the mountain.

Checking his mobile, he discovered that the next train south, albeit with a change in Perth, would place him in the city by late afternoon. He had almost settled on catching it when a further thought occurred.

He gestured Annieska over with a smile. The climbing party would likely have a vehicle, still in the vicinity. And the mountain rescue people would know where it was.

30

McNab braced himself for the onslaught. DS Janice Clark had a tongue that could cut paper, when she chose to use it. She also had an ability to remind him of a disappointed parent. In his case, there was only one. His mother. And a look from her had usually been enough.

To his surprise, the room with the coffee machine was empty. McNab decided he would help himself to a double espresso then make a quick getaway, before DS Clark turned up. Then he could say, in a pious fashion, that he'd been there at the allotted time, but she hadn't.

His plan was thwarted as he waited for the machine to dispense his second shot. When the door opened, expecting Janice, and with his opening salvo prepared, he found himself instead facing the Norwegian detective.

The bitch set me up.

By the expression on Olsen's face, McNab briefly thought that he'd voiced his thoughts out loud. Then the officer was moving towards him with his hand outstretched.

Jesus, he wants to shake hands.

Nonplussed, McNab feigned pain in his injured arm and nodded his greeting instead. 'Inspector Olsen.'

'Can we talk, Detective Sergeant?'

As McNab considered his response, the Norwegian added, 'I've okayed it with DI Wilson this time.'

The conciliatory tone caught McNab off guard. Their first meeting had been bristly, caused as much by Olsen's manner as his own. But if this was to be a joint investigation . . .

'Okay,' he nodded.

'Somewhere private?' Olsen added.

'There's no privacy here, except in a cell or an interview room.'

'Either would do.'

'Let's go, then.' McNab finished his espresso and tossed the empty cup in the bin.

Olsen watched his Scottish counterpart's expression slowly move from distrust to curiosity. *He's suspicious of me. A necessary requirement for a detective. Everyone is guilty until proven innocent.*

They were seated across an interview desk, but on this occasion the tape wasn't running. With no view of the outside world, the room, Olsen thought, might have been in any western police headquarters, including Stavanger.

'I spoke with Amena only briefly,' McNab told him. 'She'd been injured in the exodus from the orgy, her face, ribs, shoulder. The doctor who dealt with her in A&E said she'd also been roughly treated sexually over a sustained period of time.' A shadow crossed McNab's face. 'We established she came from Syria and that her handler, known as Stefan, spoke Norwegian.'

'Did she indicate that she'd been in Norway?'

'No. And she only understood a little Norwegian, according to the doctor who spoke to her.' McNab hesitated, his face troubled. 'She's thirteen years old, and we have footage of at least one man raping her. A Norwegian national.'

Olsen met his challenging look. 'My investigation suggests that refugee minors like Amena Tamar are being trafficked from Norway to Scotland.'

'Via Aberdeen?' The Scottish detective sounded wary.

'Perhaps.' Olsen waited, sensing a reluctant response from McNab might be forthcoming. He was right.

'One of my sources suggests Amena may be en route to Aberdeen with Neil Brodie, the Delta Club's owner,' McNab said. 'If she's still alive.'

Olsen's heart lifted, then fell again, as he realized what that might mean.

'What is it?' McNab said.

'I think they will keep her alive,' Olsen assured him. 'Until . . .' He hesitated, unsure whether this was the point at which he should reveal the next horror.

'Until what?' McNab demanded.

When he told him, DS McNab's expression was, Olsen suspected, much like his own when this information had been revealed to him. He went on swiftly, not waiting for the angry vocal reaction which would undoubtedly follow. 'If the minor becomes difficult, or a danger to the operation . . .'

McNab's face was a tumult of emotions through which anger blazed. 'Where the fuck does this happen?'

'We suspect on board a ship currently lying somewhere between Scotland and Norway.'

McNab swallowed hard. He'd expected to talk cocaine shipments, which is what Operation Delta had been all about. The discovery of trafficked women and a young girl at the Delta Club hadn't been anticipated. Nor the Norwegian connection. For a moment he wished he was back there, prior to the raid, as ignorant of what lay ahead as he had been then. Glancing at Olsen, he found the inspector's countenance to be much as he imagined his own.

So that was to be little Amena's fate.

31

Rhona paused in her delivery as a ripple of response ran round the room.

The strategy meeting had been running for a little under half an hour, during which she'd outlined the Cairngorm Mountain Rescue team's response to the report of the downed plane and the discovery of the crash site. The image of the crippled plane festooned with icicles as thick as a man's arm had brought a surprised reaction from the assembled officers, much like her own had been when she'd first viewed it.

Olsen had listened closely to her report, in particular the result of the cocaine wipe of the hold, although she'd noted that the Norwegian inspector hadn't appeared particularly surprised by that discovery.

Now Rhona came to the images she'd recorded of the dead pilot in situ.

This was the first time a casualty had been displayed on the screen. A scene of death, regardless of how often it happened, always had an impact on an audience. In this case the startling juxtaposition of fresh blood on virgin snow, plus the frozen nature of the body heightened this reaction. Rhona explained about the severe conditions which had produced such a result.

A couple of related questions followed, regarding the

thickness of the ice and whether there was a possibility that a cocaine cargo might have been hidden beneath it. Something Rhona had considered at the time.

'The ice is at least a yard thick in the centre, or so I was assured as the helicopter landed,' she added, her expression at this point causing a ripple of laughter. 'Breaking through is possible. We broke through a thick film of ice on the cockpit of the plane with an axe. But there are numerous and easier places ashore to hide a cargo, provided you pinpoint the location, and bear in mind that the next snowfall could vastly change the landscape.'

Rhona continued, 'The PM as you know was delayed for the body to be brought to Glasgow. However, I did have a chance to examine it in the mortuary prior to its departure.'

She brought up the images she'd taken of the body markings. At this point she asked Inspector Olsen for his thoughts on the tattoos.

'The inscription is Norwegian and means "without fear",' Olsen confirmed. 'Although the Viking tattoos are universally popular.' He came to the front now, summoned by DI Wilson.

Taking his place beside Bill, Olsen listened quietly to his introduction, a small smile playing the corner of his mouth as though he thought it too complimentary. Bill explained that they were working with KRIPOS on this case and that the Delta raid, they believed, had thrown up connections between what Inspector Olsen was about to say and their own investigation into cocaine shipments entering Scotland.

Rhona glanced along the row at McNab, whose demeanour made her wonder whether he resented having his

LIN ANDERSON

project hijacked by outside forces. When he turned, sensing her gaze, Rhona silently messaged him that they needed to talk. He gave a vague nod, then refocused his attention on Olsen.

Something's up, Rhona thought. *Something I don't know about yet.*

'The plane,' Olsen was saying, 'is a Robin DR400/180 which took off, we believe, from a private airstrip near Stavanger. Stavanger to Aberdeen is approximately 312 miles and that particular aircraft has a range of 683 miles. We have no idea if it was in fact destined for Aberdeen or elsewhere. The bad weather is likely to have sent it off course.'

He continued, 'It's a four-seater model, with a gross capacity of 2,425 pounds. Dr MacLeod's discovery that it had housed cocaine in its hold may mean it had already delivered its cargo and was on its return journey when it came down on Loch A'an. Alternatively, the cargo may have been removed and hidden somewhere in the vicinity after the crash landing.'

At this point he looked to Rhona for a response.

'The deceased lay some hundred yards from the plane in the direction of the western head of the loch,' she said. 'There was no indication that he'd reached the shoreline in any direction, and a thorough search of the area for other survivors didn't produce luggage or cargo.'

'So, you don't think there was any?' Olsen asked.

Rhona hesitated. *How to put this?*

'We're assuming the deceased was the pilot,' she said, 'but that can't be confirmed until we match his blood to that found on the instrument panel.' Pausing here, she added, 'Assuming he was the one flying the plane, I don't think, given his injuries and the severity of the weather, he could have carried a cargo any distance.'

Olsen contemplated her answer for a moment.

'Was there anything at the scene that gave you reason to believe there may have been someone else on the plane?' he asked.

There was, but how could she explain why she thought so?

'No,' she said.

Olsen was studying her intently. 'Yet you suspect it?'

Now would be the time to say something about Isla's possible or imagined attacker, but she would have to qualify it with details of the girl's delirium. Rhona decided to hold back on that, for the moment.

'I think there *may* have been,' she conceded.

Olsen's sharp blue gaze flared. Rhona wasn't sure if it was because she'd failed to commit, or because he admired the fact that she hadn't.

McNab had mysteriously disappeared before they could have their conversation, and Bill had been called away as soon as the three of them had entered his office. He'd apologized to Inspector Olsen, and had thrown Rhona a look that had asked her to stick around.

In truth, Rhona couldn't deny Bill Wilson, her mentor for many years, anything, so she'd smiled in agreement, despite the fact she'd been keen to get back to her lab and the forensic evidence she'd brought with her from Cairngorm.

Rhona poured the inspector a coffee from the tray, and indicated he should take Bill's favourite swivel seat, which had survived a number of office refurbishments. 'It girns a bit,' she warned him. 'DI Wilson refuses to oil it. I'm not sure why.'

LIN ANDERSON

Olsen immediately tried it out. '*Girn*. A good Scots word that my wife Marita used. Often when referring to the sounds *I* made,' he smiled.

'You're married to a Scot?' Rhona said with interest.

'Was,' he corrected her. 'My wife died in an accident two years ago.'

His reply killed the jokey response Rhona had been planning.

Perhaps sensing this, Olsen apologized. 'I shouldn't have sprung that on you. I'm still getting used to saying those words out loud.'

A short silence followed, before Rhona asked, 'Where was your wife from?'

'Gartocharn, near Loch Lomond,' he said. 'Although there's no family there now. She was an only child,' he explained. 'So,' he changed the subject, 'I hear you've been to Stavanger?'

'I have,' Rhona told him. 'I attended a forensic conference there a couple of years back.'

'Where you met Harald Hjerngaard, our forensic specialist?'

Rhona smiled at the memory of Harald and the time they'd spent together. 'He and I drank a few beers together in a place by the harbour called Sørensens?'

Olsen nodded. 'With a fine view across the bay to the World War Two ship with the red cross symbol.'

'I remember. It looked like something out of a Hollywood movie.'

'Probably because it's featured in a few,' Olsen told her.

'There was a tattoo convention on that weekend. Harald and I were tempted to visit, after the beer-drinking session.

144

Luckily we didn't,' she laughed. 'Otherwise I'd have more than a memory and a few photos to remind me of my trip.'

'You might have ended up with a Viking tattoo or a Norwegian slogan like our mysterious pilot,' Olsen said.

Rhona acknowledged the inspector's skilful return to what he really wanted to discuss. 'I had the impression in the meeting that *you* believe someone else was on the plane,' she said. 'And you were keen for me to back that up.'

'But you didn't. Or couldn't?' Olsen offered, by way of encouragement.

Rhona had been hoping news from Charlie would clarify things before she admitted this, but there had been nothing so far from Inverness. She decided to tell him what little there was, anyway.

'The casualty was all in white,' she said. 'It made him difficult to spot in the terrain.'

'And this is important how?'

'The girl we rescued from the ice cave said a man in white pushed her off the hill.' Seeing Olsen's interest aroused, she qualified her statement. 'However, the girl did show signs of delirium. When she comes round, she may have a totally different explanation for her fall.'

'She said someone tried to kill her?' Olsen said.

'She was confused and afraid. She even mentioned Am Fear Liath Mòr, the local legend of the Big Grey Man who haunts the mountain.'

'You didn't take her seriously?'

'I extracted skin and blood samples from under her nails,' Rhona said.

'Which might have come from an attacker?'

'Or her dead boyfriend,' she countered. 'He had scratches on his chest.'

Olsen's expression suggested he was unaware of this further death, so Rhona explained about the three young climbers at the Shelter Stone, whose bodies she'd examined. 'It was a busy night for the Cairngorm rescue team.'

A shadow crossed Olsen's face. 'The winter mountains claim their victims in Norway, too,' he said. 'How far was this Shelter Stone from the crash site?'

'A twenty-minute walk, on a decent day,' Rhona told him.

'And these climbers, how did they die?'

'Most likely exposure. The temperature dropped below minus fifteen and the Shelter Stone is barely a cave, just a big boulder sat on top of other rocks. The postmortems of all four deaths will take place later today.'

'I'd like to be there,' Olsen said.

Just then, Rhona's mobile rang. Seeing McNab's name on the screen, she stepped out of earshot to answer.

'I thought you should know that Ruth Abernethy just called from Inverness MIT. Isla Crawford was interviewed prior to her discharge,' McNab said. 'There was no mention of an assailant. She said she went out to the toilet in the middle of the storm, lost her footing and fell, ending up in the snow cave.'

'So no Am Fear Liath Mòr, then?' Rhona said.

'Is that like *uisge-beatha*?' McNab came back at her.

Rhona laughed. 'You drink whisky better than you pronounce it.'

'Not any more,' McNab reminded her of his current sobriety. 'Are you with the Viking?' he added cautiously.

'I am?'

'Then we'll talk later,' McNab said before ringing off.

'That was Detective McNab,' she told Olsen. 'Isla Crawford

has given Inverness police a statement. It looks like she simply fell that night. So no bogeyman.'

'Or killer?' Olsen's look suggested he thought otherwise.

32

The dark-blue van with the climbing logo sat in the Coire Cas car park, just as Annieska had said. Her concern for Isla Crawford and how she would feel about retrieving the vehicle minus her companions, had told him all he needed to know.

'Her friends are all dead. It's terrible. Kyle says it just highlights how dangerous it is up there, even for experienced climbers.'

'The reports say they died of cold?' he'd asked.

'Yeah, although Kyle thinks it odd that she survived in an ice cave, with a burn running through it, so close to a sheer drop.'

He'd made suitably sympathetic noises at that point about the strange vagaries of the human condition, paid his bill and left. The car he'd hired had brought him back up the hill, disgorging him in front of the Day Lodge.

Sitting in the cafe now, surrounded by chatting skiers and the noisy crunch of ski boots on the wet floor, he could see the van in its parked position, yards away. According to TV reports, the girl, whom he now knew as Isla Crawford, had been discharged from hospital in Inverness earlier today, after giving a statement to the police. What had been said in that statement, he had no idea, although the tone of the TV report suggested the death of the climbers had been just another mountain tragedy. Common at this time of year.

Should the postmortem decide otherwise . . .

The best outcome would be to silence the girl permanently, then make for the landing site at Feshiebridge as in the prior arrangement, before the pilot had lost control of the plane.

Weather. It could screw up everything.

His thoughts shifted eastwards. Blizzards weren't an issue on the North Sea, but high winds and rough seas were.

The arrival of an Aviemore taxi halted that train of thought and drew his attention back to the car park. He watched as the slight figure of a girl got out and paid the driver, then hobbled towards the blue van.

It's her.

From here he couldn't make out the face, although he was almost certain he would recognize it close up. He recalled her wide-eyed stare that night when she'd realized what was about to happen. Then the flaring anger as she'd fought back.

The tail lights flashed as she unlocked the vehicle, then pulled herself up in a determined fashion. No wonder she hadn't been easy to dispose of. She might be small and slight, but she was no easy target.

Minutes later she emerged with a bag and began her slow walk towards the cafe.

She's coming in.

He arranged himself so that he might view the door without being seen himself, his mind racing as to how he might play the situation to his advantage. He bore no resemblance to the figure she'd seen on the hill. Clean-shaven now, no longer dressed in white, but his height and the scratch on his cheek, although not significant, might spark interest.

She'd entered now, and her eyes roamed the room looking

for a place to sit. She eventually chose a table some yards away. From where he was, he could see the bruising round her eyes.

She retrieved a mobile from the bag and made a call. He was too far away to hear what was being said. *Was she arranging for someone to come for her?* Her face crumpled as she spoke and he realized she was crying.

He turned away, not because her tears upset him, but because they changed his irritation to anger. How could she be so weak, yet thwart his attempts to get rid of her? She was like an annoying fly perpetually buzzing round your head. So, like the fly, she had to be disposed of.

It was just a matter of time.

33

'You've got to give me something,' McNab pleaded.

'You're talking about over a hundred square miles of open water, and at this time of year high seas. Plus I don't have the equipment. You should be talking to the Norwegian detective. According to my research, every Chief of Police is a leader of the Search and Rescue service within their district. And Stavanger police district, Politidistrikt Sør-Vest, is responsible for that part of the continental shelf,' Ollie told him.

'And on our side?' McNab demanded.

'Scotland's Border Policing Command would liaise with Border Force UK. Problem is, UK isn't big on patrol vessels any more. There's no fleet of Maritime Patrol Aircraft and the replacement P-8 Poseidons aren't due until 2020. If we were searching for a prowling Russian sub, then we'd ask our NATO allies to deploy aircraft via Lossiemouth. But to muster forces to look for a possible ship which *may* be doing something illegal between here and Norway . . .'

'So we've no chance of locating the boat Olsen referred to?'

'If your inspector knows the vessel's identity, and it's using an Automatic Identification System, it could be tracked via satellite. And intercepted with Norwegian input.'

McNab had known the answer before he'd asked the

question. Olsen had been clear that the evidence he had for the movement of trafficked children by sea between the two countries was unconfirmed. The Stavanger force were willing to put their considerable resources into what was little more than a good detective's hunch. Like McNab, Olsen had been sceptical whether the same would be true for Scotland. Had it been a hold full of cocaine, like the tug off Aberdeen, things would, he suspected, have been different.

McNab thanked Ollie for his help, although it'd consisted of nothing more than confirmation of what he'd already suspected. His usual bribe of a filled roll and coffee lay untouched, so McNab reminded Ollie to eat up, or he'd do so himself. His threat was greeted by a grin and an announcement, designed he thought to cheer him up.

'I've been looking through CCTV tapes,' Ollie began.

'As folk like you do, for fun . . .' McNab said.

Ollie, as well as being a digital geek, was also one of a new breed of super-recognizers, a group of operatives who could clearly recall a face, however brief an appearance or however poor an image they might be presented with.

'I was pretty sure I'd seen one of the Norwegian trio before, so I went looking for him.' Ollie busied himself bringing up the image.

When it arrived on screen, McNab stared at it in consternation. He prided himself on being able to spot a known criminal on a Glasgow street or in a busy bar, and often from CCTV footage. But as far as he could see, there wasn't enough face to recognize here.

'Which one d'you think it is?' he asked, perturbed.

Ollie obliged by bringing up photos of the possibilities alongside the CCTV image – three of the participants in the clusterfuck at the Delta Club – Jakob Svindal, Petter Lund and Tobias Hansen. It didn't make a blind bit of difference to McNab. There was no way he could link any of the three with the partial face on that CCTV screen. He turned to Ollie, his own expression a question mark.

'Okay. Who do you think it is?'

'Petter Lund,' Ollie said.

Even now he'd been told, McNab still couldn't see the resemblance.

'You're certain?'

'One hundred per cent,' Ollie declared.

'Where was this taken?'

'Aberdeen docks.'

'Why were we interested?'

'Watching for deliveries of cocaine.'

McNab fell silent. A link between Petter Lund and the Aberdeen harbour drug trade would add to what they had on him for having sex with an underage girl. But then, Amena was no longer around to testify, and it would be easy for Lund to deny, without further evidence, that it was him in the harbour image, even though Ollie had proved himself to be accurate ninety-seven per cent of the time.

'Find out all you can for me on Lund and the others we picked up. And I mean *everything*.'

When McNab exited the alternative digital universe, he made straight for DI Wilson's office, only to find it empty.

'Dr MacLeod and Inspector Olsen have gone to the post-mortems,' Janice informed him.

'And the boss?'

Her face clouded over. 'There was a call from the hospital.'

Janice didn't need to tell him what that was about. The

boss's wife, Margaret, his partner for thirty years, had defeated cancer only to have it return with a vengeance.

'He should be on compassionate leave,' McNab muttered, nonplussed by this not-so-unexpected development.

'I think he will be now.'

'It's that bad?' McNab blurted out.

'It's not good.'

McNab had intended to declare that he was bound for the postmortems, but using the word mortuary and its associated phrases seemed tactless at this point. So he said nothing.

'When will you be back?' Janice asked.

'You can get me on my mobile.'

Outside, the snow had gone, although the pavements were shiny with patches of ice. Frozen slush, he decided, at least warned you of the possibility of your feet going from under you. This did not. McNab was one of the *stride out* variety, which seemed preferable to *mincing out* in fear of falling. If you were destined to go down, that was your hard luck, or your hard fall.

Thankfully, he reached his car in an upright position. The main road was better, the constant movement of cars having melted any ice that might have had the temerity to form. Approaching mid-afternoon, it was already growing dark with the insistence of a foul mood.

McNab headed for the hospital, wishing more than once that the mortuary was still in the East End near the High Court where it belonged.

34

Dr Sissons studied their entry from above his mask. The eminent pathologist's thoroughness was legendary, his sarcasm even more so. Rhona waited for the remark that was bound to follow, but it was Charlie who spoke first.

'Ah, Dr MacLeod, delighted you could make it. Detective Sergeant McNab I recognize and . . .'

'This is Inspector Olsen of KRIPOS.' Rhona provided the introduction.

'Our Nordic cousins.' Sissons' eyes flashed with interest. 'And KRIPOS, no less. I'm assuming then that at least one of these four bodies has an international flavour? Perhaps the one associated with the downed plane?'

When Olsen replied in the affirmative, Sissons said, 'Then let's begin with him.'

Rhona was aware that McNab wasn't a keen observer of the process of dismemberment. He, like many police officers, found the sights and sounds associated with it difficult. Attending a crime scene, however violent and bloody, wasn't the same as witnessing an assault on a body in the mortuary. The high whine of a saw as it cut through bone tended to stay with you long after the event.

Despite this, McNab had come. Both she and Olsen had been already kitted up and on the point of entering when he'd arrived. The looks exchanged between the men suggested that, although acquainted, they weren't necessarily on friendly terms.

'Charlie Robertson's the second pathologist,' she'd told McNab. 'He got a helicopter ride down especially for it.'

When McNab had looked puzzled, Rhona had reminded him, 'Charlie was with me when we found the bodies.'

McNab's abstract air and Olsen's studied blank expression further enhanced her feeling that something was being left unsaid, and whatever it was, it might also involve Olsen. Rhona decided she would try to corner McNab after the PM and demand to know what was going on.

'Note the pattern in the stomach lining, known as leopard-skin stomach.' Dr Sissons glanced at McNab, whose colour suggested his own stomach wasn't happy at his being asked to take a look. 'You okay, Detective Sergeant?' Sissons said in a dry tone.

McNab didn't satisfy him with an answer. Rhona wasn't sure if that was because he daren't open his mouth for fear something other than words would emerge.

Sissons went on. 'Such mucosal haemorrhaging suggests our pilot was alive when he succumbed to hypothermia.'

'So the frontal blow wasn't fatal?' Rhona said.

'As you know, we think of injuries as necessarily or potentially fatal. In this case, prior to a specialist neuro-pathologist examining the brain, I would settle for potentially fatal.'

'And the deep wound above the eye?' Rhona said.

'Most likely been made by a sharp implement such as a knife, or alternatively, considering the environment in which he was found, an ice axe.'

'There was blood on the instrument panel,' she said.

Sissons admonished her. 'You and I both know the difference between blunt-force trauma and an injury such as this, Dr MacLeod.'

'So he was attacked?' Olsen came in.

'The facial score mark I would say was a product of the same weapon,' Sissons said. 'Perhaps an earlier blow which he partially avoided.'

They'd emerged after the first postmortem, Rhona to be revived by some coffee, Olsen because his question regarding the pilot's death had been answered. McNab, she suspected, could cope with one body being cut up, but not four.

'I'll stay for at least one of the climbers,' Rhona told them.

'You think their deaths are suspicious?' McNab asked.

'I think I still don't know how they died,' Rhona said.

'But the girl took back her statement about an assailant,' McNab said, puzzled.

'Perhaps *she* was the assailant?' Olsen was reading Rhona's mind.

'I'd like to know for certain how they died,' Rhona repeated.

'And you need to stand through three PMs to do that?' McNab sounded horrified by the prospect.

'I've asked Sissons to begin with the boyfriend. That will answer one question at least.'

McNab, degowned, threw his suit in the bin provided. 'We need to talk,' he muttered under his breath.

Olsen, catching McNab's tone, if not his words, offered to wait for him in the lobby.

McNab held his fire until the door closed. 'It's about the boss.'

Rhona listened in silence to his news, her heart sinking with each word.

'He's at the hospital?'

McNab nodded. 'Will you speak to him?'

'Of course.' She touched his arm, realizing how cut up McNab was. Bill, as well as being McNab's superior officer, had been a father figure to him. McNab would never have survived in the force without him. And, she also knew, because Bill had told her often enough, that he would never have survived the life of a detective without Margaret by his side.

'This is it,' McNab said with a degree of finality.

'You don't know that,' Rhona stressed.

'I do. And so do you.' McNab made a face. 'And now I have to share a car with the fucking Viking.'

'That's what you call Professor Pirie.' She reminded him of his bête noire, the Orcadian criminal profiler.

McNab shrugged, 'Okay, Ragnar Lodbrok, then.'

'Since when did you learn about Viking warriors?' Rhona said in surprise.

'From studying tattoos,' McNab informed her.

35

The postmortems complete, Rhona had immediately made for the main hospital building where reception had directed her to Margaret's ward. Walking along the corridor, she stopped a nurse to check which room.

Rhona waited by the door, which stood a little ajar. There was just one bed in the room, and Bill sat beside it, his back to her. Margaret was propped up on pillows, her eyes closed, an oxygen mask on, a tube running from her arm.

She watched as Bill lifted the mask and dampened her dry lips with a small sponge on a stick, then returned the sponge to the plastic cup of water he held in his hands.

To disturb him seems wrong, she thought. As she hesitated a tea trolley arrived and its attendant, a stout woman with a cheerful air, popped her head in to ask if Bill wanted a cup of tea. Turning, he answered in the affirmative, then spotting Rhona, promptly invited her in and ordered one for Dr MacLeod as well.

Indicating a wing-back chair across the bed from him, Bill urged her to take a seat.

'DS Clark told you I was here?' he asked.

'McNab,' she said.

Bill nodded. 'Margaret's comfortable and not in any pain. They've made sure of that. But she's having difficulty with her breathing.'

Margaret's journey to this point had been a protracted one. Her initial diagnosis had seen Bill taking compassionate leave during her chemotherapy. Margaret hadn't been pleased about that, having no wish to have her husband 'dreeping about' at home. When the illness returned, she'd insisted Bill stay at work. He had done so, until now.

'They've given me a bed if I need a sleep, but that chair is comfortable enough. And I prefer to stay with her.' He tested his tea, but decided it was too hot. 'Tell me what happened at the postmortems.'

Rhona did so in as much detail as she thought he would want to know.

'So,' he said thoughtfully, when she'd finished, 'it's down to considered opinion on the climbers.'

'And further tests.'

'And what do you think? Did Isla Crawford have anything to do with their deaths?'

'If she did, why not stick with her story about an assailant, who may then have gone on to kill her friends?' Rhona said. 'And I can't see someone so slight overpowering two strong young men, however fit and agile she was.'

'No evidence of toxic poisoning?' Bill asked. 'CO?'

'There was a single fire brick and although it's not strictly a cave, the roof's low and the sides were pretty well sealed by snow.' Rhona shook her head, as bemused by the outcome as Bill. 'Suffocation can be extremely subtle, sometimes without any convincing features at all, as can hypothermia,' she reminded him.

'There's a *but* left unsaid at the end of your sentence.'

'But,' she obliged him, 'someone was in the vicinity and that someone killed the pilot. And the Shelter Stone was the only refuge to get out of the storm. If the killer didn't want to share it with anyone.'

They fell silent, and Bill took a moment to dampen Margaret's lips again.

'How's McNab doing?' he asked.

'Acting secretive as usual. What's going on between him and Inspector Olsen?'

Bill gave a patient smile. 'He resents anyone messing in what he considers his case.'

'True,' Rhona said. 'But I get the feeling they're in cahoots about something, which wasn't revealed at the strategy meeting.'

'Then ask,' Bill said, turning his attention back to Margaret, whose eyes had flickered open for a moment. He took her hand and, stroking it, told her that he was here, beside her.

It was time to leave and Rhona did so, putting her own hand gently on Bill's shoulder on her way past.

'Keep me informed,' he said as she departed.

Darkness met her at the hospital entrance. The night sky was clear, the air crisp and clean. After the mugginess of the hospital, and the suffocating smell of the mortuary, it felt good to breathe it in. Checking her mobile as she walked to the car, she found three missed calls from Chrissy and a final text informing her that 'her forensic assistant' was going to the jazz club 'for a well-earned drink' and would expect to see her there.

Rhona's own plan had been to head for the lab, but realizing how late it was, she made the decision to do as Chrissy had demanded. Added to that, Sean apparently had her luggage in his office at the club, so she could pick it up – an added bonus.

The traffic was light through the Clyde tunnel, despite being the rush hour, reminding Rhona that the citizens of Glasgow were still on their extended Hogmanay holiday. Welcoming in the New Year was a serious occupation in Scotland.

Arriving at University Avenue, she managed to find a parking space, then cutting down the lane near the Archaeology Department, found herself under the strings of Christmas lights on Ashton Lane which was, despite the cold, thronged with people, including a queue for the art deco cinema.

Music floated up to her from the jazz club and a wave of warmth and voices met her as she descended the steps. She immediately decided to take a taxi home at the end of the night, or, if one wasn't available, walk back to the flat, leaving her luggage until tomorrow.

Chrissy was hugging the bar, sitting determinedly across two stools. Rhona tapped her on the shoulder.

'At last!' Chrissy exclaimed, and waved at the barman, who poured a large glass of chilled white wine and brought it across. 'I thought you'd never return from the frozen north.'

'Well, here I am,' Rhona said.

Chrissy was studying her with the intensity of a suspicious parent. 'The evidence from Cairngorm arrived. It's logged and stored.'

'I did plan to get to you earlier . . .'

'But you were attending *four* postmortems,' Chrissy finished for her. 'No wonder you need a drink,' she added as Rhona savoured a mouthful. 'How's Bill? McNab texted me.'

Rhona told her.

'Poor bugger.' Chrissy's words caught in her throat.

Silence fell as they both regained their composure.

'So, how was your romantic weekend?'

Since she never discussed her love life, with Chrissy or anyone else, Rhona remained silent. Expecting this, Chrissy announced triumphantly, 'McNab's got a new *lurve* interest.'

'Really?' Rhona wondered if that had been the secret he'd been keeping.

'Her name's Ellie something or other. And –' she paused for effect – 'she's a tattoo artist.' Chrissy watched for Rhona's reaction to this startling piece of news.

'So that's why he knew about Ragnar Lodbrok.' Rhona voiced her thoughts out loud.

Chrissy immediately pounced on her words. 'McNab's got a tattoo?' Her mouth fell open in amazement.

'No. Well, I don't think so.' Rhona explained the background to her declaration.

Chrissy's expression suggested she was considering the possibility that it might be true. 'If he has, it's a body one.' She looked to Rhona. 'Have you seen . . .'

'I haven't viewed McNab's body. Not recently, anyway.'

'Any chance—'

'No,' Rhona said firmly. 'Even to allay your suspicions.'

'Shame.' Chrissy shrugged.

'Use your army of spies,' Rhona suggested. 'You found out her name and what she does. I'm sure you can find out if she inked McNab.'

Chrissy smiled wickedly. 'Good idea. Leave it with me.'

Rhona slid from the chair. 'Keep my seat,' she ordered.

Checking with the barman, she learned that Sean was in his room and was due on stage shortly. Sean, who was a partner in the jazz club, as well as a performer, had a small room in the bowels of the building, which served as an office and an occasional place to sleep over. McNab had hidden out there for a while during a previous investigation.

'You made it back,' Sean said with a smile, when she entered.

'I got here before you. An early flight from Inverness. How was the road?'

'Less exciting on the return journey. Still plenty of snow though. We were driving through tunnels of it in convoy.' He gestured to her suitcase in the corner. 'If you're having a drink, I can drive you back later,' he offered.

'I'll grab a taxi,' she said.

He nodded, expecting that would be her answer. 'I saw the news. A shame about the climbers. I'm glad the girl survived.'

'So am I,' Rhona said.

The door opened and a female head popped round. 'Your audience awaits, boss,' she said, throwing Rhona a wary look.

'New staff?' Rhona asked when the girl had disappeared.

'Imogen's a post-graduate student of archaeology, working nights to help pay the rent,' Sean stated, meeting her eye, which, Rhona decided, didn't mean much in the long history of their relationship.

'I'll pick up my case later,' she said.

'Sure.'

On entering the bar, Sean made straight for the stage. Before Rhona had succeeded in threading her way back through the crowd, the notes of his saxophone were already filling the air.

The place had filled up since she'd left Chrissy at the bar, although her friend and forensic assistant was doggedly hanging on to the extra seat. Rhona almost stopped short when she realized who was standing next to her.

The Norwegian detective's head rose a full six inches above Chrissy's and most of those around her. The two were having an animated conversation.

Chrissy, Rhona thought, *can talk to anyone like a long-lost friend.*

With the air of a detective acutely aware of his surroundings, Olsen turned, sensing Rhona's approach. Noting her look of surprise at finding him there, he explained, 'I called the lab. Your assistant told me to come here. I understand you stayed for all four PMs.' He sounded impressed.

Rhona nodded, not sure where this was headed as Olsen stepped aside so that she might resume her seat.

'We were discussing McNab,' Chrissy said. 'I thought Alvis should know about him.'

'What about him, exactly?' Rhona said.

'That's he's a Byronic hero with all the faults,' Chrissy said with a straight face. 'And that he saved my unborn baby from a bullet.'

Rhona glanced at Olsen, wondering what on earth he must make of that pronouncement.

He told her. 'From the little time I've spent with Detective Sergeant McNab, I'm inclined to agree with Chrissy's description.'

'We think he's recently got himself a tattoo,' Chrissy told him, a twinkle in her eye.

'*You* think he has,' Rhona countered.

'I understood he was recently injured,' Olsen said. 'I assumed he was in pain from that . . . which is why he seemed to find the car seat uncomfortable.'

'He's had his back inked!' Chrissy beamed. 'God, I hope

LIN ANDERSON

he didn't have her name tattooed on it. His girlfriends never last long enough for that.'

Chrissy's mobile suddenly vibrated across the bar counter. She swiftly answered and after a few *yes* responses, hung up.

'That's me off. I want to see wee Michael before he goes to bed.' She turned to Olsen. 'Nice meeting you, Alvis. I'll leave you in Dr MacLeod's capable hands.' With that, Chrissy was off, leaving Rhona with the impression she had been set up. For what exactly, she had no idea.

36

A glance outside established just how late it was. The swiftly approaching darkness had rendered the car park full of shadows. The cafe, where he still sat, was verging on empty and there was little doubt that the staff were growing impatient at the stragglers, keen as they were to clean up and get home themselves.

The girl had sat on and on, sometimes on her mobile, sometimes, it seemed, just lost in thought. What she intended to do, he had no idea. Whatever it was, she would have to do it soon. Most of the vehicles had left the car park. Her van now stood alone on the left-hand flank overlooking the lower ski slopes, where the tows had ceased to run.

He'd remained as hidden as it was possible to be in the room, having no wish to leave before she did, because by now he would be in plain view as he made for the exit. He cursed a little under his breath. He should have gone outside earlier when the cafe had been busier. The warmth had made him stay, plus his need to watch her every move.

A number of scenarios had presented themselves as he'd waited. Now it was dark at least one of them had grown more attractive. In her injured state, it wouldn't be too difficult to intercept her as she walked to the van. The vehicle was isolated now, with very few people about. He felt his heart quicken in anticipation. Once he had her inside, he could simply drive off. Leaving the hired car here wouldn't be a problem. The details he'd given the company had been false, and it wasn't as if he'd stolen it.

She was getting to her feet. *At last.* He watched her hobble towards the door. *This was going to be easy.* He waited until she'd exited before he followed.

37

'We came to Scotland often,' Olsen was telling her. 'Marita was a keen walker and a better climber than me.'

'You've climbed on Cairngorm?' Rhona said.

He nodded. 'We used to bring the camper van across on the ferry from Stavanger to Aberdeen. The campsite by Loch Morlich was a favourite, although we weren't often winter tourists.'

'I wondered when you spoke of Loch A'an whether you knew it personally?'

'We walked there once. Quite magical and so beautifully remote.'

'Do you still climb?'

He shook his head abruptly and Rhona wondered if she'd hit a nerve. 'I'm no longer fit enough,' he said as he refilled her glass. 'The conditions on the mountain yesterday must have been difficult.'

'They were, but I was well taken care of.'

It had seemed churlish not to accept Olsen's request that they share a meal, after Chrissy's departure. It was either that or head home to order a takeaway. It had been a long day, and Rhona would have preferred to shower and change before eating, but the wine she'd drunk had served to remind her how hungry she was.

Ashton Lane offered numerous eating places, although

many were full. By luck, there had been a cancellation in the upstairs bar in the Ubiquitous Chip, which is where they now sat, Olsen's tall figure dominating the confined corner space.

The meal complete, Olsen had finally revealed his real reason for the dinner date over coffee, when he'd asked Rhona how aware she was of child trafficking in Europe.

'Only from the news,' she answered honestly.

'Until recently, we suspected that refugee children were being brought into Norway via our northern border with Russia. A group of Sami people discovered the frozen remains of two children, neither of whom could be identified, although evidence pointed to them coming originally from Syria.' He paused. 'Since then, we believe the trade has shifted.'

'This is connected to your interest in the crashed plane and its occupants?' Rhona asked.

He indicated it was. 'Like much police work, assembling sufficient data to be *sure* of anything is difficult. The web of an organized crime syndicate is complex and intricate and for the most part well hidden. Cocaine smuggling is core business, cybercrime increasing dramatically, and the current wars bordering the Mediterranean have offered more opportunities in trafficking, in particular unaccompanied minors.'

'Have you spoken to McNab about the young Syrian girl from the Delta Club?' Rhona said.

'I have.' He appeared to hesitate. 'I understand Detective Sergeant McNab was recently demoted from inspector. May I ask why?'

Rhona had been wondering where all this had been leading. The earlier joking with Chrissy about McNab had seemed harmless enough, but not now.

'Why are you asking me this?' she said.

Olsen sat back in the chair, perhaps reading her antagonism. 'I can't ask him directly,' he said.

'McNab would tell you straight out if you did,' Rhona told him.

Olsen contemplated her reply for a moment, then said, 'At a guess, I'd say he doesn't like authority.'

'And I'd say authority doesn't like him,' Rhona countered.

'But, like Chrissy, you trust him?'

'With my life,' Rhona said firmly.

Olsen gave a half-smile as though she'd confirmed some unasked question and left it at that.

Dumping her case in the hall, Rhona registered how chilly the flat was, suggesting she'd forgotten to set the central heating timer before she'd left for the north. Which was probably why the flat was also glaringly empty. Her cat, Tom, was nowhere to be found, which meant her neighbour had taken pity on his lonely frozen presence and rather than just feed and water him, had obviously taken him in with her over Hogmanay.

I make a shite parent, Rhona thought, *even for a cat.*

Hanging up her jacket, she sat to pull off her boots, only now spotting the postcard that lay on the floor near the front door. Picking it up, she registered the location, somewhere in Thailand, and knew before she turned it over who it was from. The message was short. Just a 'Hi' from her son's latest stopover on his wander round the world. At the sight of his scrawled signature, Rhona felt a pang of – what?

Loss, guilt or relief that he was okay, and still keeping in touch, although always from a distance.

Now, under the shower, she turned the nozzle to a beat and positioned her head under it.

My son, she thought, *is like my own birth mother*, who had been a gypsy at heart, and also a non-parent, having left Rhona in the more than capable hands of her sister and her husband. *Who were wonderful parents*. Being adopted had never concerned Rhona. Her childhood had been happy. She believed Liam felt the same about his adoptive parents. And yet, he'd felt the need to seek her out, the pull to blood stronger than the fear of meeting the missing parent. The one who had given him away.

And I didn't deal well with it.

It had been Sean who'd become the intermediary between mother and teenage son, using his Irish charm and humour to ease the awkwardness of their meetings. Back then, Sean had been staying here in the flat with her. An arrangement that hadn't lasted long.

Her time as a prospective teenage mother had been short-lived too. Edward Stuart, her older lover at the time, hadn't wanted them tied down by a child, with Rhona mid-degree and he on the cusp of a promising law career. He'd tried at first to persuade her to have an abortion. Rhona had reacted angrily at that, so he'd backed off. Although, in the end, she'd succumbed to his entreaties to consider adoption.

I was the same age then as Liam is now. Too young to be a parent.

Although there had been a moment as they'd taken her baby boy away when she would have screamingly held on to him. It was that memory which haunted her. Not constantly, but on occasions, such as tonight.

Guilt has a long shelf life, as does regret.

At this point, she suddenly recalled Olsen's expression when she'd quizzed him on whether he still enjoyed climbing.

He'd spoken abruptly to shut down that topic of conversation, but his face had registered an emotion much like the one that played with her now. A haunting regret. Maybe even guilt.

Everyone had their secrets.

173

38

His room looked out over Great Western Road. Sealed windows prevented the infiltration of traffic noise, but the constant stream of headlights told of a Glasgow not yet, if ever, destined for sleep. Much like himself.

Sleep had never been his friend, but with Marita beside him, it had grown easier to embrace. When she was away from him, his old habits had returned. *With a vengeance.* Winter nights and their extended darkness wakened his brain, setting in motion numerous trains of thought which met, collided or repelled one another.

The long bright nights of summer in Norway were no better, merely suggesting there was no requirement to sleep. Shutting down then had been even harder. No matter how thick the blinds or curtains, northern daylight was avid in its search for a chink. A way to penetrate the fragile darkness and find its prey.

As a child, Olsen hadn't suffered from his own lack of sleep, *although I'm sure my mother and father did.* Being on duty with a child twenty-four hours a day, when you were dropping from exhaustion yourself, must have been a nightmare. Especially when his father, a fisherman, had been away at sea.

Although, I was not, my mother told me, a fractious child because of it.

When Marita and he had been trying for a baby, he'd warned her what his genes might produce. She'd smiled and informed him, since he didn't require any sleep, that she would put him in charge of their offspring at night.

Something I would have welcomed.

Olsen turned his mind to why he was here, although in essence the two were linked. The trip he'd made to the north of Norway to view the small frozen bodies that had lain on their northernmost border had begun this investigation.

And had landed him here in Scotland.

It seemed inevitable that he would have come back to the country of his wife's birth, but he'd systematically avoided it until now. The proper plan for return had been to visit one of her favourite spots like Loch Lomond, the closest stretch of water to her birthplace, or the wildness of Cairngorm, a place close to her heart.

He'd managed to persuade himself that that was only possible during the summer months when there was no snow on the ground. That excuse had succeeded in keeping him away up to now, but then fate had intervened.

And brought me here, at the wrong time, and to the wrong location.

Leaving the thick, lined curtains open, Olsen lay down on the bed, his body weary, his mind active, processing the day's events and the personnel he'd met. Detective Inspector Wilson he'd liked immediately. He recalled the officer's open manner, his thoughtful responses, his interest in what Olsen had to say. In contrast, DI Wilson's superior officer, DCI Sutherland, hadn't made a good impression. Olsen had met high-ranking officers like him before, in Norway, Sweden and Denmark. Often outwardly efficient, but definitely self-serving. Everything was about them and the status they'd achieved in the force. In contrast, he suspected DI Wilson wouldn't seek to climb any higher, because the job he did now was the one he liked and did best.

Olsen's mind now went to the third of the trio. He'd messed up with Detective Sergeant McNab at first. He recalled their initial confrontation occasioned by his visit to the detective's flat. DS Michael McNab had been on his radar before he'd set foot in Scotland. The Delta case had flagged him up and what little Olsen had known then had suggested that the detective might be the ally he needed here, if he could recruit him as such.

And he is the only one I've told of my suspicions.

That in itself had been a revelation, especially after their initial meeting. *But I was right to.* He'd almost done the same with Dr MacLeod, but had held back. Why, he wasn't sure. Perhaps to test McNab's agreement that he wouldn't reveal it to anyone else?

Everyone had a button to press, and he suspected Dr MacLeod was DS McNab's button.

His mind lost in thought, he didn't initially register the drone of his mobile. Glancing at the screen and recognizing the caller, he answered.

Hjerngaard's voice sounded hoarse, as though he'd been rudely woken from sleep. Checking his watch, Olsen registered it was an hour later than this in Stavanger. A time most people would be in their beds.

'Harald,' Olsen said. 'You're up late.'

'So are you,' Harald's voice crackled across the line. 'But then that's normal.' The line went silent for a moment, and Olsen thought he'd lost the connection. Then it returned, this time more clearly. 'We have what you asked for.'

'Good.'

'Who should I send it to, apart from yourself?'

Olsen gave him the email address.

Ringing off, he wondered how late DS McNab stayed up of a night and how often he checked his email.

She was asleep now, only the top of her head showing above the duvet. McNab eased the cover back enough for him to slip out, and padded towards his clothes. Lifting the pile, he exited the bedroom before putting them on. His intention hadn't been to spend the night, but then he rarely managed to match any good intentions he had.

Lying awake after their encounter, he'd heard her drift into sleep, curled as she was in the crook of his arm. Once her breathing changed, he'd slipped free, then waited until she adjusted herself into what he thought was her normal sleeping position before extracting himself from the bed.

In minutes, he was outside in the cold night air, the warmth and comfort of her bed fast fading from memory. Beginning his walk back to the car, he checked his phone to find an email ostensibly from Olsen, via someone called Hjerngaard. McNab halted in his walk to read it. *So, Olsen had done what he said he would.* McNab allowed himself a moment's grudging appreciation of the detective's thoroughness. Maybe they would get on after all.

A car swept by in the sleeting snow, kicking up a mess of slush from the kerb to soak his trousers. Swearing in a distinctly audible fashion, he gave the finger to the disappearing vehicle, hoping it would be seen in the driving mirror. As he did so, he noted a female figure across the road, huddled in a doorway, and it wasn't hard to guess what she was about. Ellie's flat, being close to the Ink Parlour, was not in the most salubrious part of town. When he'd pointed this out to her, she'd given him a look that would have floored larger men than him.

Despite the weather, the woman was wearing an outfit more suited to going clubbing, although that definitely wasn't her intention.

She signalled across to him in a manner that displayed the wealth of her wares.

If a prostitute (whether male or female) who for the purposes of prostitution loiters in a public place, solicits in a public place or in any other place so as to be seen from a public place, or importunes any person in a public place, they shall be guilty of an offence.

But who the hell would make life worse for a woman doing just that in such weather? As he dismissed the possibility of doling out a warning, a big four-by-four swept past on his side of the road. Spotting the woman, it did an abrupt U-turn. She immediately stepped towards the car, and now McNab saw her face clearly, and recognized it.

He shouted her name as he sprang across the road, but Ursula Gorecki didn't respond to his call. Barely waiting for her to climb inside, the vehicle took off again. This time McNab saw the driver, who made a decided attempt to mow him down in his getaway. Springing for the pavement, McNab found himself on his knees in the slush, his brush with death less annoying than the soaking that had followed it.

Expressing a litany of curses that would have made Billy Connolly blush, he slithered to his feet and immediately sought the tailgate of the fast-retreating SUV.

It seemed they'd been wrong. If Brodie had made the trip to Aberdeen with Amena, he was no longer in the Granite

City. As the rear of the vehicle swept out of sight behind a curtain of sleet, McNab made an effort to read the number plate, wishing he had a fraction of Ollie's ability to recall numbers as well as faces.

39

Cairngorm, a little earlier

He'd tailed the van down the hill. Luckily for him there was only one route as far as the roundabout at the entrance to Aviemore, and with the hill verging on empty, little traffic on the road.

His anger at being thwarted in the car park was played out by his white-knuckled grip on the steering wheel, and the rapid beat of the pulse at his forehead. A guy he recognized from the TV reports as Annieska's boyfriend had arrived in the distinctive Cairngorm Mountain Rescue Land Rover, and was obviously who the girl had been waiting for. As he'd followed her out of the cafe, the Land Rover had appeared from nowhere and drawn alongside her.

That's who she was on the phone to, he'd decided. *No doubt tearfully asking for help.*

Realizing what was about to happen, he'd backed off and immediately headed for the hired car, as the boyfriend, who he was beginning to hate with the same degree as the girl, parked the Land Rover and helped her into the van.

So, here he was, back in Aviemore, outside Macdui's, trying to figure out his next move. The van had turned into the car park at the Cairngorm Hotel, and it looked like that was where she planned to stay the night. The crowds that had filled Aviemore for Hogmanay had dwindled, many visitors heading back south once the road had opened again. Music still drifted out of Macdui's, and was matched from the bar of the Cairngorm Hotel. The celebrations for the New Year had depleted, but weren't yet entirely over.

Irritated by his own indecision, he got out and, locking the car, headed into Macdui's. If Annieska was on duty, he might, through her, discover what the girl planned to do.

Once inside, he took up residence in his usual place, scanning the room for the familiar blonde head. Locating her behind the bar, he gave her a friendly wave.

'I thought you'd gone?' she said as she approached.

'I decided to stay a bit longer and enjoy Aviemore without the tourists.'

She'd smiled at that. 'Yes, it has been hectic, what with the rescues and the crashed plane.'

'What's happened about that?' he said.

'Well . . .' she said. 'Folk are saying the plane came from Stavanger, and there's a detective come over from there to investigate.'

He felt his spine go rigid, and forced himself to relax before he responded. 'So it's a Norwegian plane?'

'Seems to be.'

He waited for her to continue, but it looked like she'd run out of news, so he prompted her.

'And the girl who was hurt?'

Annieska nodded in the direction of the hotel. 'She thought she could drive her van back, but there's no way that would happen, although I'd give her points for determination.'

'So how will she get home?'

'Train or bus, I expect. Kyle brought her down the mountain and she's staying the night across the road.' Her face assumed a sad expression. 'That's where they were supposed to stay on Hogmanay.'

'So what happens with the van?'

'Kyle's looking for someone going back to Glasgow to drive it down for her.' She had a sudden thought. 'You're not headed that way?'

He attempted a 'sorry' look, even as his heart pounded with the thought of such an opportunity. 'Sadly, no.' Then discarding the menu she was offering, he said, 'I'll have the same as last night.'

She repeated last night's order verbatim, including what he'd had to drink.

'You've a good memory,' he remarked cautiously.

'Yes. And I never forget a face.'

40

'So she was lying?' Chrissy said as she poured them both a morning coffee.

'Possibly. Or she was genuinely confused about that night. Not everyone with hypothermia recalls what happened during their delirium state,' Rhona said.

'But she did scratch someone other than the boyfriend?'

'The blood and DNA from under her nails came from the same person and it wasn't Gavin, her boyfriend.'

'What about the results on the pilot?'

'The hair and blood from the instrument panel are a match for the body we found. So he did hit his forehead on landing . . .'

'But?' Chrissy demanded.

'It wasn't a serious injury. The initial blood-splattering suggests—'

'When he exited the plane he still had a blood pressure, which meant he was very much alive,' Chrissy took over. 'Then, coagulation kicked in, which accounts for the lack of a blood trail afterwards.'

Rhona nodded. 'However, the wound we examined in the postmortem wasn't that injury. It was in the same location, but the newer wound was occasioned by a sharp instrument, not the blunt-force trauma from the instrument panel.'

It wasn't unknown for someone to be able to walk into a Casualty Department with brain substance oozing from a single hammer blow to the head, Rhona reminded Chrissy. 'But if you're moving onto the weapon, the combined speed can prove fatal.'

'So you think the blow came as he went towards his assailant?'

Rhona nodded. 'And Sissons recorded the injury as potentially fatal.'

Chrissy lapsed into a brief silence. Not something that happened often. Rhona waited for what she suspected would come next.

'The forensic evidence you collected from the pilot,' Chrissy said. 'Is there any chance there's a match in there with Isla's assailant?'

'That's what we have to establish,' Rhona confirmed.

The number Isla had given Rhona rang out unanswered, making her wonder if there was a chance she'd entered the number incorrectly, or if Isla in her injured state had made a mistake when giving it. They'd exchanged mobile numbers as soon as they got Isla on board the helicopter. Isla had appeared lucid at the time, and insistent they keep in contact, because, she'd said, *you saved my life.*

'Any luck?' Chrissy said.

'No, but if she's still up north, she may not have a signal.'

'I thought she'd been discharged from Raigmore?'

'A little earlier than I thought she should be, and probably determined by her.'

'You can't climb places like Hell's Lum and be a wimp,' Chrissy told her.

'How would you know about Hell's Lum?' Rhona said, surprised.

Chrissy assumed an offended air. 'Patrick's climbed it.'

Chrissy's one sensible older brother, Patrick, was her pride and joy. The other men in her family, including her father, were best forgotten about, according to her forensic assistant.

'These results are important.' Chrissy voiced exactly what Rhona had been thinking, something that tended to happen on a regular basis. 'Shouldn't you let Alvis know?'

Rhona already had Inspector Olsen's number on the screen. Hesitating, she wondered if she should give McNab the heads-up first.

Chrissy was reading her mind again. 'McNab will throw a wobbler if he's not first in the queue.'

Despite insisting to Chrissy that she had no intention of asking if he had a tattoo, Rhona found herself watching McNab closely as he took his seat opposite her in the canteen. And she didn't detect any discomfort as described by Olsen in their conversation at the jazz club.

When he looked over, catching her studied gaze, his expression suggested he believed she was 'up to something'.

'What's Chrissy been saying?' he demanded.

'That you have a new *lurve* interest.' Rhona attempted Chrissy's rendition of the word.

McNab smiled at that. 'How does she do it?'

'So it's true, then?'

'I'll talk about my love life *if*, or *when*, you talk about yours,' McNab offered.

It was his smug look that drove her to it. 'Chrissy says

you've got a tattoo on your back. She thinks it's a Viking,' Rhona said swiftly, before she could change her mind.

'It is not!' a surprised McNab immediately retorted.

'Ah. You did get inked,' Rhona pounced. 'So, if it isn't a Viking, what did you get?'

'You really want to know?' he challenged her.

Rhona should have known by McNab's expression that she was on dangerous ground, but she still said *yes*.

'I didn't have my back inked.' He caught Rhona's eye at this point and declared, 'I had "I'm nuts about you" tattooed on my balls.' His look confirmed exactly who the 'you' referred to was.

Touché.

That interchange over, Rhona quickly changed to the subject she'd really come to discuss, which resulted in McNab's thoughtful study of his coffee cup.

'If she's been discharged . . .' he began.

'She has,' Rhona interrupted. 'I spoke to Charlie. Apparently she's due to come south from Aviemore by train today.'

'And we have her Glasgow address?'

Rhona quoted the one Charlie had given her.

'Olsen and I will interview her, but it might be better if you approach her first.'

'I called the Cairngorm Hotel,' Rhona said. 'They think she was going for the 9.30 train. If she caught it, she's due at Glasgow Queen Street at 12.17.'

'You'd recognize her?' McNab asked.

Rhona was pretty sure she would.

'So, can you meet her at the station?'

41

'He's waiting for you in interview room four,' Janice told McNab, with a stare that resembled a warning.

McNab gave her a wide-eyed innocent look in return.

Olsen stood unsure which direction to head in, obviously trying to recall where McNab had taken him when they'd had their private discussion. McNab wasn't about to make it easy for the Norwegian inspector. Olsen was on his turf and should therefore be at a disadvantage. If he was ever to go to Stavanger, he had no doubt the same rules would apply.

And they'd all talk in Norwegian.

Gesturing to Olsen, McNab pushed open the door and headed down the corridor, taking a circular route in a concerted attempt to confuse. His plan backfired.

'I think room four's along this way,' Olsen said, his gaze steady.

McNab smiled. 'Of course it is.'

Olsen was regarding him with an amused air. The fact he hadn't irritated Olsen served to irritate McNab instead.

He threw open the door with a flourish, causing it to bang back against the wall. The sudden noise startled the occupant and he looked up at them with an annoyed expression.

'My solicitor isn't here yet,' Petter Lund said.

Olsen responded with something in Norwegian which brought a flush of colour to Lund's cheeks, after which

Olsen exited, indicating McNab should follow. Now outside in the corridor, McNab asked him what he'd said.

'You don't want to know, Detective Sergeant. Suffice to say it wasn't pleasant.' He paused. 'Do you know who Lund's lawyer is?' When McNab indicated he didn't, Olsen said, 'I believe he will have contacted his father in Oslo, requesting a Norwegian lawyer, or at least someone who can speak the language.'

'But he speaks perfect English.'

'He will use Norwegian, if only to annoy you.'

The detailed information on Lund and his influential family connections sent to McNab in the middle of the night had indicated how difficult it would be to deal with Petter Lund. When McNab had suggested they go after the other two Norwegians first, Olsen had shaken his head. 'We'll get them too, but it's Lund who is the direct connection.'

McNab had been party to numerous interviews involving mainly Eastern Europeans, where a translator had to be present, often when he suspected the interviewee understood English perfectly. He'd chosen that moment to remind Olsen of that fact.

'Nevertheless, I suggest I conduct the interview as we discussed.'

McNab had surprised himself by agreeing and now had to concede that Olsen had been right about how the meeting would pan out, although there had been moments up to now where he'd wished for the days when, under Scots Law, he had been able to question someone without a lawyer present. He and the boss, DI Wilson, had been an excellent double act back then.

But not any more.

Lund's lawyer, having been helicoptered down from Aberdeen, was spending most of his well-paid time advising his client to say nothing. Even McNab could work out what *Min klient ønsker å forbli taus* meant when he heard it as often as this.

As far as McNab could follow, via intermittent translations by Olsen, Lund denied purchasing sex. According to him, the party at the Delta Club had been a private affair among consenting adults. No money had changed hands. And even if it had, his lawyer reminded them, 'Unlike Norway, in Scotland, the exchange of sexual services for money is legal. Only associated activities such as public solicitation, operating a brothel or other forms of pimping are criminal offences.'

McNab had desperately wanted to come in at this point, but Olsen reminded him with a shake of his head that that hadn't been the plan. Instead he produced the iPad and slipped it across the desk to Lund. McNab watched Lund's face change colour as he saw himself in penetrating action against the thin young body that was Amena Tamar.

'The child in the video is thirteen years old,' Olsen said in English, 'and I don't have to remind you that having sex with a minor *is* a criminal offence, whether in Norway or Scotland.'

As he said this he played the short clip again, this time with the sound turned up full volume. Amena's painful pleading for Lund to stop could be clearly heard, despite the surrounding grunts, proving that Brodie had been keen to provide vivid video memories for those involved in the orgy, or offer an enticing advertisement for those who might like to participate in the future.

The lawyer reached over and stopped it.

'You are able to confirm the age of the young woman in the video?' he replied in English, glancing at McNab.

'The *underage girl* in the video,' Olsen corrected him. 'And yes, we can.'

McNab knew this wasn't true, but he admired the surety with which Olsen said it.

'I understand the young woman has disappeared,' the lawyer said. He didn't add *and therefore her age can't be proved, and neither can she give testimony against my client.*

Olsen gave a half-smile. 'And how would you know that, since Amena's disappearance wasn't released to the press?'

The lawyer, realizing his error of judgement, adopted a stony silence, motioning his client to do likewise.

Olsen, seemingly unperturbed by this, said, 'Amena is clearly distressed in the video and begging Mr Lund to stop raping her. I'd say that was proof enough of an offence having been committed, without her testimony.'

McNab watched the self-assured look slide from Lund's face, and allowed himself a smile.

'Now,' Olsen said. 'Let us discuss Mr Lund's Norwegian activities.'

42

Rhona checked the arrivals board to find the Inverness train was running late. The announcer stated that this was due to snow on the tracks between Inverness and Aviemore. The estimated arrival currently stood at 12.40, which gave her time for a coffee before she tried to intercept Isla. Rhona bought one from an open stand and found a seat with a view of the ticket barriers.

The station was busy, mostly, she suspected, with folk returning from their Hogmanay break, judging by the number of suitcases being trundled past her. Checking her mobile again, she found no response to her attempts to contact Isla by text. It looked as though she did have a wrong number. If so, whoever was receiving her messages couldn't be bothered letting her know she was trying to contact the wrong person.

As the board displayed the imminent arrival of the Inverness train at Platform 4, she dumped her coffee cup in a nearby bin and took up a stance whereby she could watch the approaching train disgorge its passengers. What she hadn't anticipated was just how many there would be. With only four carriages, the occupants must have been standing two deep in the aisles. God knows where they'd stacked their considerable luggage. By the expressions on the faces coming towards her, they were mightily glad to escape the confines of the over-packed coaches, despite the freezing air of Glasgow which greeted them.

Knowing Isla had an injured ankle, Rhona assumed she might have been given help to exit the train, maybe even collected by wheelchair. But although there was one wheel-chair user heading for the barrier, it was an elderly man and not Isla.

There was a moment when Rhona thought she'd been wrong to assume she would recognize the young woman she'd ministered to that night in the snow cave, but that frightened face was indelibly etched in her memory, even if the circumstances were different. And surely, with her injury, Isla couldn't be one of the mass of people striding purposefully towards the exit?

As the crowd gradually began to thin, Rhona thought she'd spotted Isla, at the rear of the platform. But her certainty was short-lived. It *was* a young woman and she *was* walking with the aid of a stick, but the young man who supported her in such a caring manner made it obvious they were a couple.

Isla had been part of a couple, but was no longer.

Maybe she'd been told to wait for assistance and that was why she hadn't yet emerged from the train? The guard now stepped off and, slinging his bag over his shoulder, came towards the barrier.

Rhona intercepted him. 'Excuse me. I was supposed to meet a young woman here. She had a sprained ankle and got on at Aviemore?'

The guard looked puzzled for a moment, then shook his head. 'We were late into Aviemore and sat there for ten minutes at least. I didn't see anyone like that get on. Did she ask for assistance?' he added, concerned.

'I don't know,' Rhona admitted.

'Maybe she waited for the next train?' he offered. 'This one was busy, if you had mobility problems.'

'When is that?' she said.

'An hour's time if there isn't a hold-up. Check online,' and he was off.

Rhona's unease at Isla's non-appearance was tangible, yet common sense told her that there had been no certainty she would have caught that train. She brought up the number of the Cairngorm Hotel again. It rang out half a dozen times, then a slightly harassed male voice answered. By his accent he was one of the many Poles working in the Spey Valley.

Rhona asked again about Isla's departure.

'Miss Crawford settled her bill last night,' he said.

'The last person I spoke to said Isla was catching the 9.30 train this morning to Glasgow?'

'I don't know about that,' he replied in a slightly defensive tone. 'Didn't she have a vehicle?' he added, as though just remembering. 'A blue van with a climbing logo on the side?' He sounded pleased at his recall. 'Shall I check the car park?'

Rhona murmured an affirmative and the line went silent. He was back two minutes later.

'It's gone.'

'But she couldn't drive,' Rhona said.

'Then someone must have driven her.' He was clearly growing exasperated by her questions.

Realizing she would get no further, Rhona thanked him and rang off.

Her final try was to Kyle Dunn, her fellow rescuer.

'Hey, Doc, how are you? Back in the city?'

As Rhona began her answer, Kyle, picking up on her

unease, interrupted to ask what was wrong. She explained about Isla, the train and the van.

'No way could she drive, although she clearly wanted to.' Kyle explained about picking Isla up on the mountain and taking her to the hotel. 'I brought the van down the hill and told her I would try and find someone from the team willing to take it south for her. She said she'd leave the keys at reception.'

'Did you find anyone?' Rhona said.

'Not yet, no.' When she didn't respond to this, he asked outright. 'Something's happened, hasn't it?'

Rhona couldn't tell Kyle the full details of her discovery, but she could alert him. 'We have reason to believe her original story of an assailant to be true,' she said.

Kyle's outburst was a replay of his curses in the ice cave when he'd been trying to hack a way out for Isla's stretcher.

'So there was a bastard on the loose up there . . .' He halted. 'Did he have anything to do with the body from the plane?'

'Nothing's certain as yet—'

Kyle interrupted her. 'Except that Isla saw the bastard and could probably ID him.'

43

'Does McNab know?' Chrissy said.

'He's in an interview with Olsen, so I left a message with Janice.' Rhona discarded her outer garments and began to kit up.

'She could be on a later train,' Chrissy suggested.

'She could be,' Rhona agreed. 'But if the van's no longer there, it seems more likely that she managed to find a driver to bring both her and the van south.'

'But wouldn't she have told Kyle that?'

Rhona was playing devil's advocate, knowing Chrissy would pick holes in all her suggestions, which was a good way to examine the possibilities.

'And,' Chrissy went on, 'if someone did try to kill her and found out they hadn't succeeded, wouldn't they try again?'

Rhona's conversation with Kyle had resulted in just that line of thought. She'd indicated as much to DS Clark, who'd promise to contact Aviemore police and have them look for both Isla and the van's current whereabouts.

Kitted up, Rhona entered the lab. Her prime concern now was to complete her examination of the evidence she'd taken at both deposition sites. The postmortem on the pilot had established that he had been attacked. On the other hand, the PMs on the three climbers hadn't proved with any certainty exactly how they'd died. Something which concerned her. As Sissons had confirmed, both hypothermia and suffocation were subtle, and it was often the circumstances surrounding the death from either that led to a conclusion.

And she had been the one to examine the victims in situ.

Rhona replayed the video she'd taken in the Shelter Stone. The suffocating darkness, only lessened by her head torch, had felt like being in a grave. *And it was a grave.*

Three young people, who, having had both the courage and the ability to scale Hell's Lum, had found themselves not anticipating the turn of the year below on the valley floor as planned, but stuck in the Arctic wilderness that was Cairngorm.

But they hadn't minded. They'd played games, drunk whisky. Then they'd climbed into their sleeping bags. Both couples had had sex. That had been obvious by the evidence she'd collected. They'd anticipated the New Year in extremis by celebrating life.

But life had changed in a moment, just as it always did. Isla had wakened and gone outside. That need, that action, had sealed the fate of everyone in the cave.

Of that Rhona was sure. Not through forensic science – yet – but through intuition, something a scientist wasn't allowed to rely on.

But that didn't mean she couldn't prove it through science.

Evidential sources of DNA were variable. Blood was good, because the white cells were a rich source of DNA. Sweat stains, something all humans produced no matter how they tried to avoid it with deodorants, provided skin cells which were also rich sources of DNA. The nose and its secretions – not just sneezes, but mucus that dripped from the nostrils for a variety of reasons – were another rich source of DNA. One of which had happened in that cave.

Cocaine.

Chrissy's careful examination of the top Gavin had worn had found both mucus and traces of cocaine. A powerful combination – but who had snorted and who had dripped?

An image of what might have happened had played over in Rhona's mind as she'd surveyed the results of her tests.

No one who'd been present when Isla had gone out to relieve herself had sprayed mucus on her boyfriend, Gavin. The pattern of who we are and what we leave behind, Locard's principle of 'every contact leaves a trace', had played out in that cave, in the middle of a blizzard, on a remote mountaintop, despite the freezing temperatures.

But that wasn't all.

The first thing Rhona had noticed on entering the cave had been the scent of urine. She hadn't been surprised by this. Some bodily functions continued when the heart had stopped. Because of the slacking of the sphincter muscles, urination was one of them.

But the source of the smell hadn't only been the climbers' bodies. Someone had urinated copiously near the rear of the cave, over the brick. It had struck her at the time that it was an odd place to relieve yourself unless you were dousing a fire. Sampling the fire brick had led her to sample the urine too.

Later, when they'd rescued Isla from her ice prison, the injured girl had rambled on about how she'd gone outside to pee in the middle of a blizzard, because 'No one does it in the shelter'.

So no one in the climbers' party of four would have urinated in the shelter.

Which meant someone else had been in the cave.

Rhona admired the manner in which death acquired the body. This wasn't a ghoulish feeling, but more a celebration of life. Breath had gone from the victims in that dark space under a fallen rock, but yet the detritus of life lived within, on and around them, revealing the story about how and why those hearts had stopped beating.

As Rhona exited the lab and lowered her mask, Chrissy indicated that the analysis had arrived. Rhona skimmed the printout, aware that the conclusion would be one she'd reached already.

The blood and skin deposits under Isla's nails had proved to be a match for the mucus found on Gavin. That in itself placed her attacker inside the Shelter Stone; the urine test and the cocaine analysis, she suspected, would only add to the picture.

The tall white figure that had appeared to Isla like Am Fear Liath Mòr out of the blizzard had most likely taken the lives of the three climbers, probably by suffocation.

The ditched plane, destined for somewhere other than the frozen Loch A'an, had visited a kind of hell on the mountain, worse than any blizzard or spectre.

44

McNab had emerged from the Lund interview with a cracking headache and a belligerent air, which wasn't helped by the news from Rhona, via DS Clark, that Isla Crawford hadn't got off the train at Queen Street station.

The headache, he decided, could be rectified by a double dose of caffeine. Hence his swift walk in the direction of the coffee machine. The bad mood might also be a sign of his caffeine addiction, but had more likely been caused by the interview with Petter Lund and his insufferable wee prick of a lawyer.

'You have an addictive personality,' Janice informed him en route.

'Tell me something I don't know,' McNab shot back at her.

'Caffeine's more addictive than nicotine.'

Jesus, she was on her high horse today.

'So, I was better off on the whisky?' he challenged her.

Janice's withering look in response was one McNab would have been proud of himself.

'Okay, what do we know?' he said as he waited for his coffee cup to fill.

'The van was spotted exiting Aviemore around midnight in a northerly direction. One witness, unconfirmed. There have been no subsequent sightings on the A9 north or south. If it was in a hurry, the average speed cameras would have clocked it somewhere on that route.'

'Any idea who was driving?'

'Our witness thought a male, with no one in the passenger seat.'

'Jesus.' McNab pressed for another coffee. 'And the girl definitely slept at the hotel last night?'

'They couldn't confirm that, but her bag was found in the room by cleaning staff this morning around eleven. It didn't contain her mobile. We had them check.'

McNab ran his hand through his hair. He'd never met this climber girl, though judging from what Rhona had said, she was resourceful.

But you can't be resourceful if you're dead.

Janice came back in. 'DS Abernethy says if the van didn't take the A9, the other major route out of the valley would be to Aberdeen via Grantown and Aberlour.'

'Those roads were open?'

'The majority of the snow fell on the Central Highlands and the west, so yes.'

'Any traffic cameras?'

'It's not the A90,' she told him bluntly.

It seemed all roads led to Aberdeen. He was beginning to hate that city and he'd never even been there. Something that looked about to be rectified by Inspector Olsen, his new best pal. Still, he was doing what the boss had ordered, cooperating with Ragnar Lodbrok. The thought of the boss made McNab pull out his phone. Rhona had said the DI wanted to be kept informed.

Should I call him?

According to Janice, DI Wilson was camped out at the hospital, which didn't bode well for the prospect of getting

Margaret home. McNab's thoughts went to the boss's kids, both teenagers. How would they cope with their mother gone?

Same as I did.

He dragged his mind back to a problem he *could* try to solve. If Isla's mobile wasn't in her bag, then it might be with her. He didn't allow himself to think the words, *whether she's dead or alive*. It wouldn't be the first time they'd run a mobile literally to ground with its deceased owner.

Ollie was circumspect. He never promised anything, yet always seemed to come up with the goods if given time. The last occasion they'd focused on Aberdeenshire together had been during the Stonewarrior case. Then it had been a Neolithic stone circle that had drawn them there. Ollie had been his right-hand man on that case, something McNab wouldn't forget.

'The number you gave me is registered to Isla Crawford. She pays fifteen a month for it but often runs the bill to twenty. The mobile's been rarely used over Hogmanay, remembering that the signal for Tesco mobile and others is pretty rubbish up there. Go outside Aviemore and there's nothing.'

That sorry story, McNab acknowledged, seemed to apply to the whole of the north of Scotland, including during his recent sojourn on the Orkney island of Sanday.

'However, she made a call from the Day Lodge on Cairngorm yesterday afternoon to . . .' Ollie quoted a number.

'That's the bloke from Cairngorm Mountain Rescue. He brought her and the van down the hill,' McNab said. 'So nothing after that?'

Ollie shook his head. 'Not from her mobile, but –' he hesitated – 'I took the liberty of calling the hotel. I wanted to check if they had CCTV footage of the car park. They don't. But the guy on reception said that a man professing to be from CMR had asked to be put through to her room around ten last night. A few minutes later she went outside. He was off-duty after that, so couldn't tell me when or if she came back in.'

'Fuck's sake, could the Aviemore police not tell us that?'

'Apparently the guy wasn't on duty when they came by asking questions.'

Ollie interrupted McNab's few choice words about the inadequacies of rural policing.

'There's no CCTV at the hotel,' he said, 'but there are webcams dotted about the area. Mostly for observing the scenery and the wildlife.' At McNab's thunderous look, he swiftly added, 'That's how I found this.'

McNab eased his seat nearer the screen.

'It's a recording of the Coire Cas car park next to the Day Lodge and the cafe.'

'That's her van.' McNab pointed at the image. 'But we know she left there with the CMR bloke.'

'Wait,' Ollie instructed him. 'There's a little tableau acted out here that's worth watching.'

McNab tried to quench his impatience and concentrate, but figures walking about a car park in the snow wasn't riveting TV.

'Note,' said Ollie, 'most people are dressed for skiing and are wearing ski boots. That makes them walk in a particular fashion. There are very few without that gait going in and out of the cafe. I've isolated them.'

McNab watched Isla's figure get out of a taxi and limp towards what was definitely the blue van. She opened the door and with an enormous effort pulled herself inside. A few minutes later she was sliding back out.

'She couldn't do it,' McNab said, only wishing she had, then she would have been back in Glasgow by now, and safe.

In the next section she was limping towards the cafe and soon disappeared from view. Disappointment flooded McNab. 'Is that it?'

'No,' Ollie told him. 'Let's go back a bit.'

The figure this time was male and tall. He wasn't dressed for skiing either and didn't sport the required gait, although his walk was distinctive. He approached the blue van in the first instance, then after a few moments walked towards the cafe, which he entered.

McNab felt his hackles rise. *Was that the bastard? The Iceman who'd thrown her from the hill?*

'Wait,' Ollie, ever the patient one, urged him.

Moving forward in time, he saw Isla re-emerge, to limp towards a Cairngorm Mountain Rescue Land Rover as it drew up. Out climbed the man McNab took to be the Kyle Rhona had spoken about. He helped the girl to the blue van and supported her into the passenger seat. As the van reversed, a figure came into view. The same man as before. He moved swiftly towards a car with a hire sign on the side and drove quickly off.

'He's following them,' McNab said.

'I contacted the hire firm and gave them the number plate. They sent me this.' Ollie handed McNab a copy of the hire agreement, with a name and address.

'Let me guess, it doesn't exist?' McNab said.

'The Aberdeen address is a pub near the docks.'

'What?'

'The CCTV footage I found Lund in? It was taken just round the corner from there.'

45

Sergeant McNab is pursuing his own agenda . . . off the record.

Olsen smiled at this thought, because it was exactly what he wanted. It had been difficult to keep McNab on the leash during the Lund interview, but he had succeeded, just. And it had played out as he'd suspected.

Of course the finale had been the attempt to exempt Lund from any charges based on the fact that his father, an occasional diplomatic visitor to Scotland, had immunity. That had nearly caused McNab to have apoplexy. The detective might be very useful in a showdown, Olsen decided, when your life was on the line, but he definitely didn't do diplomacy.

After their exchange with Lund and his lawyer, McNab had disappeared. Going somewhere he didn't want to divulge to Olsen. Fair enough. He hadn't told the sergeant everything either. It was, Olsen thought, something to do with the girl rescued from the ice cave, close to the downed plane. The only one to survive that night.

And the plane was his department, now that it had been established where it had originated from. So he'd questioned DS Clark and discovered that the girl had been discharged from hospital, and had been expected back in Glasgow at midday, but hadn't arrived.

Olsen had taken himself outside then to think. He missed

his morning walk between Kirkegata and the Commissariat de Polis on Lagårdsveien, but most of all he missed his visits to Lagård Gravlund.

Despite the fact that he and Marita had visited Scotland on numerous occasions, they'd come to Glasgow only occasionally and briefly, mainly because Marita's Highland family had had to move here for work, and there were some surviving relatives whom they'd dutifully visited. Those stays in the city had been short, eager as they had always been to get to the real object of their desire, the Highlands.

Outside, the snowy downfalls had retreated, and the weather was now delivering what Glasgow, like Stavanger, knew best . . . rain. Olsen didn't mind the *smirr*, as Marita had called this version of it – a damp cold droplet mist like a blanket that softly cocooned you, while penetrating all outer layers of clothing. Norway, experiencing the same version of rain, had its own name for it, *yr*.

Scottish weather was for the most part a replica of Norway's. In fact the weather in Aberdeen was usually the same as Stavanger's. Taking off from one airport you arrived at your destination under exactly, it seemed, the same sky, which wasn't surprising, considering the shared latitude and the short distance between the two countries.

Had the earth's continents moved in another way, we may have had a land border.

As it was, Norway, despite the reservations of its inhabitants, was connected physically to Europe. And Scotland, despite its desire, would always be part of an island that merely lingered off Europe's shores.

You're thinking too much, Marita's sudden clear tones reminded him. And not about what's important. *Where are the children?* she demanded.

As if on cue, a young woman, wearing a headscarf, exited a cafe, struggling with a pram that held a toddler. Olsen helped her negotiate the step down to the pavement by guiding the pram's wheels. When he looked up, he discovered an older child who studied him with intense dark eyes.

The woman thanked him in a language he recognized as Arabic. His answer in the same tongue caused the woman a start of surprise, and the older child's liquid eyes to open wide in astonishment. Believing they deserved an explanation, Olsen said he was from Stavanger in Norway. He knew a little of their language, because he was a chess partner of a Syrian refugee translator, who now lived in his home town. To say that the woman was pleased by this was an understatement.

Olsen finally withdrew from her profuse thanks and entered the cafe. No one else in there sported refugee status, of that he was certain, judging by the voices he heard and the clothes that they wore.

The cafe was filled with the smell of fry-ups, brewed tea and strong coffee. Olsen liked it immediately. Approaching the counter, he ordered a mug of tea, and pointing to a selection of iced buns, asked for one.

Settling himself at a table, he considered his next move. DI Wilson's current absence with his terminally ill wife had seemed a blow at first, particularly after he'd met the man and liked him. But since those further up hadn't yet chosen to fill DI Wilson's shoes with a replacement, it had left Olsen free to make his own arrangements, which included Detective Sergeant McNab.

As he sampled the strong dark brew and sweet bun, he felt the vibration of his mobile in his inside pocket.

'Where are you?' McNab's voice asked in a somewhat indignant manner.

'A hundred yards down the street in a cafe called—' Olsen didn't get a chance to finish.

'Stay there,' and having issued this order, the sergeant rang off.

Olsen took another bite of his bun and a mouthful of tea. So McNab's visit wherever it was had been fruitful.

'Do you know who he is?' McNab said again.

Olsen wasn't about to be rushed and therefore didn't respond, merely replaying the clip yet another time. The male figure captured on CCTV was tall by Scottish standards, but not by Norwegian. The winter jacket disguised his build, although Olsen sensed by the swaying manner of his walk that he was fit. The face was more problematic, concealed as it was firstly by the collar of the jacket, secondly by the ski hat pulled down low on his forehead.

When he ran the clip again, he heard an exasperated sound behind him, which he ignored, concentrating only on the screen. Finally he managed to halt the clip at exactly the point he wanted.

'There,' he said in satisfaction.

'What?' McNab demanded, glaring at the screen as though it was a drunk defying him on a Friday night.

'Look closely,' Olsen said.

'I've fucking seen this a million times.'

'Which makes it too familiar,' Olsen stated. 'Look at the face.'

'There is no fucking face or at least there's only half of one.'

'It's enough,' Olsen said, satisfied now he was right.

McNab peered like a man hoping to discover his lottery ticket number was the winner.

Olsen didn't recognize the words uttered, the idiom and accent defeating him this time, but there was no doubt the detective had spotted the scratch.

McNab turned to him. 'It's the fucker that pushed her off the hill, isn't it?'

'I think it's a distinct possibility,' Olsen said.

'The address he gave the hire-car company was an Aberdeen pub,' McNab conceded. 'And our resident super-recognizer spotted Lund on a nearby camera.'

'So we head for Aberdeen.'

46

McNab was happy. It was a strange and unfamiliar feeling which he seldom experienced. It happened briefly during sex, and it had happened on his recent motorbike ride with Ellie, the adrenaline rush of which he hoped to revisit . . . tonight in fact.

Standing in the shower, he even found himself humming a tune. As the hot water hit his back, he registered no tingling or discomfort. So no more cling film. He'd not yet had the other shoulder inked, but found himself looking forward to a second session with something almost approaching pleasure.

Would getting inked be his next obsession?

McNab stepped out of the shower, not wishing to contemplate this line of thought any further. The reason for his buoyant mood was a mixture of anticipation for tonight's event, plus the minor success he'd had with Olsen. The Norwegian inspector was proving more to his liking than he'd thought possible.

Up to now McNab's knowledge of Norway had been scanty, little more than images of fjords, and bizarrely something about a king penguin at Edinburgh Zoo, plus the fact that every Norwegian citizen was now a millionaire, because that small country had harnessed its oil reserves, unlike his one.

But Olsen had proved valuable. They hadn't got the van yet or its possible driver, but they suspected they knew where he was headed.

Dressed now, he checked his mobile. Ellie, having accepted his invitation, had indicated she would pick him up shortly. McNab smiled at the thought of their arrival at Davey's place. Davey, like McNab, had had a hankering after a Harley in his teens. McNab had gloated a bit when he'd run with the motorbike cops, but by then, Davey had made enough money to fund the real thing.

Then during a boozy session after Davey and Mary had got it together (which had pissed McNab off big time), Davey had revealed that Mary had put her foot down about his bike riding, some motorbike death in her family on a Highland road having poisoned her against them.

And wasn't I the sad bastard who was pleased about that.

So who was he trying to impress tonight, with both his mode of transport and his date?

When he'd invited Ellie to dinner with 'his old school pal', Davey Stevenson and his wife, Ellie had immediately recognized the name. It seemed Nurse Debby wasn't the only one who used Davey's gym for a workout.

'You've met Davey?' McNab had asked, somewhat taken aback at this, although Ellie's reply of, 'No, not in person,' had dispelled his unease somewhat.

Hearing the roar of the Harley's approach, McNab headed out and down the stairs.

'So why the bike?' Ellie asked as he donned his helmet. 'It sort of restricted my choice of outfit for a dinner party and stops me drinking.'

McNab pulled a *sorry* face. 'Davey and I had a thing about Harleys back in the day.'

LIN ANDERSON

The look Ellie bestowed on him spoke volumes. *She knows that's not the reason*, he thought, *but what the hell?*

If Ellie's flat wasn't in the most salubrious district of Glasgow, his was only marginally better. So a trip to the leafy stone villa district of the city was an eye-opener. Though for McNab all this open space, parks, trees and big expensive houses was the opposite of desirable.

Turning into Davey's impressive drive, he had a moment's disquiet. What the hell was he doing here, and dragging Ellie with him? Then he remembered how long it had been since he'd seen Mary, and felt the desire to know what she looked like now.

Her Highland accent, when she'd arrived at school in Glasgow, had been the butt of numerous jokes, usually featuring the term *teuchter*. Her reaction to this hadn't been to alter her voice to fit in, but to maintain it, out of defiance. McNab had liked that about her . . . *among many other things.*

He now registered that Ellie had produced a bag. 'My outfit for tonight,' she said, glancing up at the pillared entrance as the door opened to produce a smiling Davey.

McNab adopted what he hoped was a matching smile, and led Ellie up the steps.

The dining room was impressive too, McNab had to admit that. The room *and* the house, at least what they'd seen of it. And he'd been dismayed (or pleased) to discover that the Mary he recalled had only improved with time. It seemed a Glaswegian's requirement for places to bet, drink and have their hair and nails done had paid off for Davey.

And Mary.

She'd greeted him warmly in that familiar voice, planting a scented kiss on his cheek. Then she'd taken Ellie off to the

212

ladies' room, as requested, to let her change into her party outfit.

If McNab had thought Ellie arriving in her biker's leather gear was to be a talking point, her transformation from biker to chic was a revelation. The dress revealed much of the inking on her upper body, which, under the candlelight, resembled to McNab's mind a work of art.

More beautiful than any painting that hung on Davey's walls.

McNab felt a mixture of admiration for Ellie for rising to the occasion and irritation at himself for using her as a pawn in the continuing competitive game he and Davey were wont to indulge in. Then again, how could he stop if Davey didn't? And why else had he been invited here *with a date*?

Ellie and Davey were now deep in conversation about Harleys. If Davey had stopped riding them, he obviously hadn't stopped loving them.

McNab felt a hand on his arm.

'Fancy helping me with the coffee?' Mary asked.

McNab nodded and followed her into the kitchen, which was as sumptuous as all the other rooms he'd been party to.

'The meal was delicious,' he offered. 'Davey boasted you were a good cook . . .'

He tailed off as she regarded him critically.

'What?' he said.

'Don't give me that innocent look,' Mary demanded. 'I know it too well.'

'Okay.' McNab tried to oblige. 'But what's wrong?'

'You've got Davey involved in something, and it's not bikes.'

McNab remembered that stance, those flashing eyes and that voice, sweetly musical when happy, and like this, when not.

'We talked about a couple of people he knew, that's all,' he defended himself. 'And it was Davey suggested we meet, not the other way round.'

Mary had a way of examining him which was more of a brain scan than a look.

'And he's in trouble because of it.'

Her head went down, but not before he saw fear flit through her eyes. McNab came swiftly to her side.

'Mary, who was it?' he demanded, lifting her face to his.

It was an unlucky moment for Ellie to enter. Or maybe she'd been in the doorway a while, watching the interchange. McNab dropped his hand, and they both turned to look at Ellie.

Mary mustered herself more quickly than he did, saying, 'I bet Davey's out admiring your bike.'

Ellie gave a half-smile and nodded. 'He is.'

'Allow him five minutes. No more,' Mary told McNab. 'I'll manage the coffee. You get the wannabe biker back inside.'

Avoiding meeting Ellie's eye, McNab headed out, where he found Davey astride the bike, a keen look of hunger on his face.

'Fucking hell. I have to get one of these, even if I keep it in the garage and creep out at night and pretend to ride it.'

'What's going on, Davey?' McNab demanded.

There was a moment's silence as Davey attempted to interpret McNab's voice and expression. 'I wondered why Mary had cornered you with the coffee request.' He got off the bike. 'I assumed she still had the hots for you.'

His attempt at a joke failing, he shrugged dismissively. 'I've had some threats. Not for the first time, of course. You don't run businesses like mine in the locations I'm in without meeting with some aggro.'

'These threats have anything to do with our meeting?'

'Hard to say.'

'Brodie or McVitie?'

'They frequent the same cesspool,' Davey said non-committally.

'Fuck's sake, Davey. If Mary's worried enough to speak to me . . .' When Davey didn't respond, McNab added, 'At least tell me how the threats were delivered.'

'Someone daubed the walls of the gym, and one of Mary's salons. And a wee lassie, one of her trainees, was cornered.'

'They tried to abduct her?'

'They stuck a hand up her skirt. Said things.'

'This needs to be reported.'

'I just did, to Detective Sergeant Michael McNab. Now can we go have our coffee?'

The end of the meal had been strained. Had he consumed alcohol, McNab might have weathered it better, but having asked Ellie to drive them there, it had seemed wrong to have a drink when she couldn't. Catching her expression as he climbed on the bike for their earlier than anticipated homeward journey suggested that his concession hadn't been enough to countermand whatever suspicions she was nursing about Mary.

This was proved true when she made for his place rather than hers, confirming that he'd blown it in some fashion. He made an attempt at reconciliation as he removed his helmet.

'We both had the hots for Mary as teenagers. I had my chance and blew it. Davey did much better. They married. That's it.'

'That's it,' she said in disbelief. 'That was what was going on in the kitchen?'

McNab, seeing her expression, came to the swift decision that the truth, or at least a portion of it, was his best option now. 'No. What was going on in the kitchen was her telling me that Davey's getting threatened, because of some information he gave me.'

'About what?' she said cautiously.

'A guy who runs drugs and sells refugee kids for sex.'

'Here, in Glasgow?' she said, open-eyed.

'Here, there, everywhere.' McNab didn't want to pursue this topic of conversation any further. 'Do you want to come up?'

Give Ellie her due, she thought about it for about three seconds.

'No. Give me a ring tomorrow.'

Then she was gone, the roar of the bike reverberating off the stone walls of the tenement building.

Inside the flat, McNab went straight to the kitchen cupboard, took down the bottle and poured a nip. He contemplated it briefly, before reminding himself that if he had yet another cup of coffee, he would be sick. The whisky, he set about convincing himself, was by far the better choice and might also lead to a good night's sleep. McNab added a second shot to the glass, but decided to forgo adding water.

He wanted it straight.

47

'Are you alone?'

'Are you?' McNab challenged her.

'Yes,' Rhona lied, glancing down at Sean who lay asleep beside her.

'Me too.'

Rhona thought his laugh sounded hollow and a little morose.

'Have you been drinking?' she said.

McNab ignored her question and asked one of his own. 'Why are you calling me this early?'

'I've had a text,' Rhona said, 'about five minutes ago. It's from Isla, or from her mobile at least.'

Rhona heard the swift movement as McNab drew himself upright.

'Do I answer it?' she said.

'What does it say?'

'It's just an empty space.'

'Have you tried calling her?'

She had, but the number had gone to voicemail.

'Okay, we need to locate that mobile,' McNab said. 'I'll see if I can find it, then ring you back.'

Rhona rose, carefully extracting herself from under the duvet, although Sean, having arrived late after he'd finished at the jazz club, wasn't likely to wake until mid-morning.

She wondered as she made for the kitchen whether McNab had also been lying about being alone and suspected he had been.

Chrissy seemed to believe that McNab's relationship with his new-found biker chick was pretty intense. Intense enough for him to have had a tattoo done. Or maybe being inked was McNab's new obsession.

Rhona tested herself to see if it mattered whether McNab was with a woman when she'd called, and decided it didn't.

So why lie to McNab about Sean?

Because he's an insufferable arse.

She'd once asked McNab if anyone had ever told him that, and he'd looked seriously at her and replied, 'Yes.'

Having set up the coffee machine, she sat down at the table and studied the text again. The best-case scenario was that Isla was okay, just laying low in her grief. The worst-case scenario was . . . what? That she'd been abducted and her abductor was playing with them?

There was another explanation of course. If she was somewhere off the beaten track, then the message could've been sent hours ago, and only achieved transmission when she reached a mobile hotspot.

Rhona took her cup of coffee to the window, where dawn was just touching the sky. Below, the grounds of the nearby convent were in darkness, the statue of the Madonna that stood in the centre of the lawn lost in shadow, although the lighted windows of the chapel behind indicated that the nuns were already up and at prayers.

Rhona didn't pray herself, but there had been times when she'd hoped the nuns might include a mention of someone she was worried about.

McNab had figured in that list, more than once. Now it was Isla Crawford.

The buzzer was insistent, so much so that she heard it despite the noise of the shower. There were few people who tended to abuse her buzzer like that. Chrissy was one of them, the other was McNab.

Rhona went to press the release button to let him in, grabbing her dressing gown on the way. McNab came up the stairs at what sounded like a gallop. Rhona, refusing to rise to whatever panic he was in, went back to the kitchen and refreshed her coffee.

McNab found her there.

'Olsen was wrong about Aberdeen,' he said. 'They've found the van, parked up, not far from Aviemore.' Noting her worried face, he quickly added, 'The girl's not inside. But there's blood in the back, and it looks like there's been a struggle.'

'How far from Aviemore?' Rhona prompted, imagining herself back in the Spey Valley, and the roads she'd driven with Sean.

'Does it matter?'

The arrival of a figure at the door caused them both to turn. Sean appeared half asleep and, by the look on his face, had been disturbed by their raised voices. He was also naked, which didn't appear to concern him, nor did it Rhona. Registering McNab's presence with a nod of recognition, he made for the coffee pot. Rhona smothered a smile at McNab's stunned silence as Sean poured himself a cup and exited.

'You fucking lied,' McNab said indignantly.

Rhona ignored his accusation, merely asking, 'Has a forensic team been dispatched from Inverness?'

McNab gave a belligerent shrug. 'Probably.'

Rhona made up her mind. 'I'll go up there.'

'Why? We haven't found a body,' he countered.

'Not yet,' she said.

48

It was as though the blizzard had never happened. Cairn-gorm was still topped by snow, but on the lower slopes and in the valley a rapid thaw had taken place, creating a patchworked landscape and swollen rivers. There were scattered flood-warning signs, including one on the exit to Pitlochry, and the hill which was home to the old stone Ruthven barracks near Newtonmore, built to quell the Highlands, had become an island surrounded by flood water from the Spey.

Her companion had for the most part maintained his silence. Olsen had regarded the passing scenery with interest, and familiarity, now and again making a comment about the hills he'd climbed with his wife, Marita.

Rhona had initially wondered whether his desire to accompany her to the crime scene was more about revisiting old haunts than about the current investigation. Then he'd indicated that the Norwegian Accident Investigation Board, AIBN, had sent a team over to assist their British counter-parts in the AAIB and he wanted to speak with them in Inverness, after which his intention was still to head for Aberdeen and meet DS McNab there.

'McNab's heading for Aberdeen?' Rhona had said, surprised.

After Sean's appearance, McNab had moved into truculent

mode, signalling that he had things to do in Glasgow regarding the Delta case, which he thought held more chance of discovering the whereabouts of Amena Tamar than heading for the Granite City with Ragnar Lodbrok, or 'the fucking Highlands' with her. Then he'd departed, but not before bestowing a final accusatory look, indicating Rhona had yet to be forgiven for her fib about being in bed alone.

'We're to make for the police station on the main street,' Rhona told Olsen as she indicated her intention to leave the A9 just south of Aviemore. 'Someone will take us from there to the locus.'

Aviemore was hardly recognizable from that morning when she'd trudged through the drifts outside the Cairngorm Hotel and climbed into Kyle's Land Rover to head for the hill. Devoid of both snow and New Year revellers, it seemed the village had returned to normal.

Rhona realized that the police officer who greeted them on entry had been a member of the CMR team who'd been spearheading the search for the missing climbers. Ruaridh greeted her with a friendly handshake, and after she'd introduced Inspector Olsen, directed them out to the police car.

'The SOCOs from Inverness should already be there, and I recruited some of the CMR team to search the surrounding area and nearby woods.'

'Where is the van exactly?' Rhona said as they took the road southwards again.

'Towards Feshiebridge,' Ruaridh told her. 'Well off the beaten track. A local farmer out checking his stock after the big thaw spotted it parked up, and luckily called it in.'

After ten minutes of negotiating narrow winding roads, they now emerged from the shadow of planted pines to sweep into a bright wide glen, bordered on one side by the river, on the other by a high-rise escarpment, which, Rhona suspected, was the western edge of Cairngorm.

Directly in line with the escarpment was a long strip of levelled land, obviously tended and definitely free of sheep.

'Is that an airstrip?' Rhona said, surprised.

'Yes, for the Feshie club. The clubhouse and hangars are over there.'

As Ruaridh gestured to a distant group of buildings, Olsen exchanged a questioning glance with Rhona.

'You're saying a flying club operates from here?' he double-checked.

'Just gliding, although they launch the gliders via a Robin light aircraft,' Ruaridh told them. 'According to my brother-in-law, it's one of the best locations in the UK for ridge, wave and thermal flying, because of that escarpment. Something about updrafts—'

Olsen interrupted him. 'Can we get into the hangars?'

'Why?' Ruaridh looked puzzled.

'Whoever drove the van here had to leave somehow.' Rhona watched as light dawned in his eyes.

'Shit. I never thought of that,' he admitted, shamefaced.

A line of cars including a CMR Land Rover stood just outside the club's perimeter fence. Beyond that an incident tent had been erected to shelter the van.

Rhona stopped at the crime scene tape and began the process of kitting up. 'If you want a closer look,' she told Olsen, 'you'll have to do the same.'

'I should call this in to Stavanger first.'

'You won't get a mobile signal here,' Ruaridh told him. 'You could use the car radio and have the station contact Stavanger?'

Olsen nodded his agreement. 'I'll catch you up,' he told Rhona.

Rhona had only seen the climbers' van via the brief footage McNab had shown her that morning. Now in close proximity, the poignancy of the mountain motif, with the names Isla, Gavin, Lucy and Malcolm emblazoned on it, was a cruel reminder of what had happened on Cairngorm summit and its tragic aftermath.

Ensconced now in the tent, Rhona was grateful for this time alone. After the introductions, the two SOCOs sent from Inverness had indicated they'd already covered the outside of the vehicle, and would now comb the immediate area, while she examined the inside, 'as suggested by DI Abernethy.'

Rhona said a silent thank you to Ruth. It wasn't that she didn't trust the SOCOs to do their job, it was just that, for her, first impressions were as vital as the evidence she collected.

The smell of blood and urine met her as she eased open the sliding door on the driver's side, but also the fusty scent of damp clothing. The back seats had been folded up to make use of the floor below. In this space lay a bundled sleeping bag, the top of which was darkened by blood stains, with individual blonde hairs adhering to the sticky mess.

Alongside were two pairs of walking boots – his and hers by the sizes – and a bag which at a quick glance looked to contain bits of climbing equipment.

The similarity to the Shelter Stone scene in both smell and claustrophobic darkness brought back the image of three young people who'd lain dead inside their sleeping bags. Nor could Rhona ignore the feeling that the fourth member of that party might have been here, and perhaps dead too.

Suffocated as before?

Trying to detach her thoughts from the result, she focused on context. Everything was about the environment, and the circumstances of a crime scene. Stepping back, she viewed that scene through the frame of the door, and spotted it. Her breath catching in her throat, Rhona registered what she was looking at, the presence of which was a pointer to what could have happened here.

The frame of the open door served as a window on the interior, like the screen of a television set. And it told its own story. A smear of what she instinctively knew was blood, but which was easily checked as such, marked the frame on the right-hand side. A moving image immediately presented itself of an injured girl's head meeting the frame as she was being pushed in, or pulled out of the vehicle.

Rhona went to speak to a SOCO, a young woman with a distinctive Inverness accent and a professional air.

'Have you found any evidence of someone walking away from the van?'

The SOCO nodded. 'Footprints in the snow patches heading in that direction.' She pointed up the track that led into the woods. 'Only one size, though. Large, a twelve at least.'

'How deep were the impressions?'

'Pretty deep.'

'So whoever it was could have been carrying something?' Rhona asked.

She nodded. 'It's possible. We've taken both images and a cast of the print.'

Rhona looked to the wood where a sprinkling of high-vis jackets were spread out among the pines. If Isla had been picked up in Aviemore and brought here, then her captor had had plenty of time to dispose of her body among the trees, and the rapid thaw would have made that easier.

'What about tyre tracks?' she said.

'The place was pretty churned up when we arrived. The farmer's truck had been across it, and the Land Rover.'

'What about in that direction?' Rhona indicated the hangars.

'You think he may have made for the river?'

That wasn't what Rhona had been thinking, but immediately the SOCO said it, she realized its significance. The river was in spate and disposing of a body there would be an easier task than hiding or burying it in the woods. And who knew where or when it would turn up downstream, if it wasn't deposited in the North Sea?

49

There was no sign of Ursula in the spot he'd last seen her. Mid-afternoon wasn't the normal time for her to be on the job, the punters preferring to pursue their pleasures after dark.

His telephone conversation with Cheryl Lafferty had been short and unproductive. She'd basically told him that none of the women removed from the Delta Club that night were with her any more. McNab's irritation at this had brought a fiery response. A safe house wasn't a prison, Cheryl had insisted, and she couldn't make the women stay, or prevent them from going back to their handlers.

'It's your job to find the bastards that threaten them and their families,' she'd told him sharply.

McNab's plea of, 'That's what I'm trying to do', had fallen on deaf ears.

So, if he wasn't to locate Brodie via Ursula . . .

Unsure now of his next move, and still harbouring a small hope that she might yet turn up, McNab looked for some place to hang about. Being not too far from the Ink Parlour, he contemplated dropping in on Ellie. That thought dissolved in seconds as he remembered her frosty parting glance of the previous night.

But she did say phone me, he consoled himself.

The street was home to a couple of drinking dens, one of

227

which promised girls dancing, although the advertising board had been around a while. Neither establishment looked like a place you could openly order a coffee or a bottle of water.

McNab made his decision and chose one. He could order alcohol for appearance's sake, but that didn't mean he had to drink it.

Who was he trying to kid?

The tiredness of the exterior was replicated inside with a scattering of customers as bored-looking as the barman. A big screen flickered silent news, the announcements running along the bottom, all ignored by the clientele, who appeared to prefer staring into their pints like crystal balls. There were no women, although a couple of strategically placed poles suggested dancing of some description might be available, if not in the present, then in the past. The only light in the dismal darkness was a large poster advertising the nearby Ink Parlour, which, at a closer look, surprisingly included a picture of Ellie.

His heart lifting a little at this, McNab defiantly ordered a pint of lager shandy, ignoring the raised eyebrow and the 'Whit?' response. Carrying it to the alcove nearest the poster, he pulled out his mobile. Now, he decided, with such a backdrop, would be an appropriate time to call Ellie and apologize for last night.

That was the one thing he *had* learned about relationships . . . there was always a lot of apologizing required – on his side anyway. A text from an unknown number pinged in as he set about the task. The message was signed 'Mary', and asked McNab to call her as soon as possible. Which he did.

'Davey didn't come home last night,' were her first words to him.

McNab tried to process this. 'But I was at yours last night?'

'He went out after you and Ellie left . . .' She hesitated. 'We had an argument about that business. He swore he'd reported what happened to you and that you would do something about it.' She paused as though awaiting confirmation that McNab had.

'Davey did speak to me. I will do something about it—'

She cut him off. 'Looks like you're too late.'

The desperation in her voice upped McNab's pulse. Mary hadn't given him details of the threats, though she'd obviously been spooked by them. As for Davey, it appeared he may have downplayed them.

'Where are you?' McNab said.

'At the salon.'

'I'm coming over.'

There was no one in Ursula's spot when McNab emerged from the bar, his pint abandoned and unconsumed. He'd parked the car round the corner from the Ink Parlour, and headed there now.

Davey, together with Mary, had built a business from nothing, starting it in the more challenging parts of Glasgow. Neither of them scared easily, and although they'd risen high, they hadn't forgotten their roots, something that had stood them in good stead with their unreliable or occasionally insolvent clientele. Plus they hadn't had any trouble with the less friendly elements of the world they inhabited, at least as far as McNab was aware.

All of which, McNab told himself as he walked briskly to the car, led him to believe that Davey had both a good lawyer and probably someone watching his back.

It just wasn't me.

Their meet-ups had grown fewer, the more Davey's businesses multiplied. Pressure of work, or just the fact that their lives had taken such different directions? Better for Davey to mix with his own kind, businessmen and entrepreneurs, than a police pal who hadn't yet reached, and probably never would, the upper echelons of the force or society.

That was why they'd stopped meeting up and, McNab suspected, Mary had been behind that decision. *And who could blame her?* So, Davey's recent text had been a surprise, and even more so when the subject had turned out to be Neil Brodie.

Could Brodie have found out about that meeting?

McNab recalled his most recent brush with Brodie in the four-by-four. If Brodie wasn't averse to mowing down a police officer in public, then it was likely any threats he'd made to Davey would be carried through. If only to get his revenge for McNab's raid on the Delta Club and the confiscation of his cocaine.

No wonder Mary was frightened.

His mobile, which lay on the passenger seat, lit up on his route through the city centre, but there was nothing he could do but let it ring, despite the name on the screen. McNab eventually pulled in at a bus stop, much to the annoyance of a bus driver also headed that way, and snatched at the phone, a second too late. Drawing out again into traffic, he determined he would call back, once he'd spoken to Mary. Ellie knew he was working, he reasoned. If she was in the middle of inking someone, the same would apply to a call from him, was how the argument went.

It was easy to find the salon. After all, he'd walked past it dozens of times; even thought of going in once or twice, just to check on Mary, like an old friend. Those possible visits had been linked to his drinking habits, or when he got shot, or when he got dumped. Mary had always seemed like the pot of gold at the end of the rainbow – unlikely, unreal, but always desirable.

We wouldn't have lasted six months. We didn't last six months. But if?

If he had been better. At everything. Then maybe?

He pushed open the door and was greeted by a wave of perfume. The contrast with the establishment he'd just departed wasn't lost on McNab. In here women reigned supreme and he was definitely the intruder, albeit a welcome one.

It was like being cocooned in colour, scent and the sound of female voices, interspersed with laughter. McNab stood for a moment breathing it all in, before a red-haired beauty asked his name. After which he was swept from the general throng and ushered into the inner sanctuary.

Mary sat behind an impressive desk, staring at her mobile as though willing it to ring. By her expression there was no point in asking if there had been any word from Davey, although she looked composed, the make-up perfect. She was dressed in dark red. All of this McNab noticed, but most of all he read the anger in her eyes when she registered his entry.

'What time did Davey go out?' McNab began.

'Midnight.'

'He took the car?'

'Stupidly, yes. If he'd had a Harley, no doubt you'd have scraped him off the road by now,' she said accusingly.

'Have you checked all his usual hang-outs?'

'You should know about those,' Mary said coldly.

'Me and Davey have met up once in the past eighteen months,' McNab said, mystified by her anger. 'And that was a couple of days ago.'

Her face was crumpling, the sight of which made McNab's insides turn over.

'What did you or Davey *not* tell me last night?' he asked quietly.

'I told him you couldn't fix it, even if you did catch Brodie.'

'Fix what?' McNab said, growing more worried by the minute.

Mary went to a cabinet on which sat a filled decanter and two glasses. She poured herself a measure of what he assumed was whisky, then looked at him for confirmation that he would join her.

McNab hesitated. He had the car. He was on duty.

'No,' he finally said.

'If you don't take it now, you'll need it once I've told you,' Mary said, lifting the glass to her mouth.

'Told me what?' McNab said, already dreading her answer.

50

'They've found something,' Olsen told her.

Emerging from the van, her examination complete, Rhona had been contemplating her next move when the tent flap had been pulled back.

'Where?' she said.

'To the right of the track into the wood. Disturbed earth and branches, they think might indicate something's been buried there.'

'Any sign of a shovel?'

He shook his head.

If the perpetrator had planned to rid himself of a body in the vicinity, then the river, although further away, would have been the easier choice, in particular if it was in spate by the time he got here. But a quick search of the bank behind the hangars had revealed nothing. Not surprising, since everything was currently being swept downstream, including uprooted trees and fallen branches. The soil samples taken from the wheels and the pedals might indicate he'd been close to the water's edge, but that would take time and forensic testing.

The hangars had proved to be a further disappointment. When they'd finally got a key via the club secretary and gained entry, he'd declared the contents intact, including the plane and the tow truck.

So how had the perpetrator left here?

He'd descended Cairngorm on foot in difficult conditions, so he could have walked out of the valley, but Rhona didn't think he had. She believed this choice of location wasn't random, but part of his plan.

Why an airfield, if you don't plan to use it?

'I'll come,' Rhona told Olsen's questioning eyes above the mask.

Darkness was descending and swiftly, the light from their powerful torches insufficient to analyse what she was now observing. Occasionally aided by moonlight on the remaining snow, she'd done her best to survey the area of disturbed earth. To excavate it would take time and patience, and could only be done during the hours of daylight, otherwise the different soil layers wouldn't be distinguishable. Plus she would need to rig up a time-lapse camera to record the slow and often laborious forensic excavation.

The earth had been disturbed. There was no doubt about that. *But for what purpose?*

Rhona made her decision.

'We'll tent it, and take a proper look tomorrow . . . unless we find evidence that Isla is elsewhere.' She didn't say Isla's body, because nothing she'd found in the van had convinced her that Isla had died inside it.

'What about Inverness and Aberdeen?' she asked Olsen as they made their way back to the car.

'Tomorrow,' he said. 'They've booked us both rooms at the Cairngorm Hotel for tonight. It seemed sensible.'

Rhona felt relief wash over her. Up to that point she hadn't even thought about what might happen next, concentrating only on the here and now. There had always been the possibility that she might not get back to Glasgow tonight. Sean, realizing this, had offered to stay and look after the cat, 'to give your neighbour a rest', he'd said.

Seeing as it had been Sean who'd brought her Tom in the first place, *against my better judgement*, that had seemed fair.

It appeared that Olsen had been busy while she'd been in the tent. He'd alerted Stavanger to what had been found here. Like her, he suspected abandoning the van near the only airfield for a considerable number of miles wasn't a coincidence. Sitting in the car, heading back to Aviemore, he revealed his thoughts on the matter.

'Maybe he was always headed for the Feshie airstrip, and the blizzard and the crash merely made him late?'

Rhona now voiced the mystery she'd been wrestling with ever since that fateful night on the Cairngorm plateau. 'If we assume the man we're looking for killed four people and attempted to kill a fifth merely to shield his identity, the question is why? Super-recognizers can pick out partial faces from poor CCTV footage. But is it likely that a young woman would be able to recognize someone she met in a blizzard on a mountain in the dark?'

Olsen remained silent at this, and Rhona gained the impression there was something he was considering revealing, but wasn't quite prepared to . . . yet.

He's like McNab, she thought. *Older, probably wiser, but in many ways just as inscrutable.*

'Let's talk later. How about some food,' Olsen said as they drew up outside the hotel. 'Say in an hour's time?'

Back among the rosy lights and checked tablecloths of La Taverna, Olsen told Rhona that they'd been lucky to get a table.

'It might be the live music, or they're here to celebrate getting their village back from the Hogmanay hoards,' he said.

Rhona suspected it was a bit of both. There was certainly a party atmosphere in the place. The solo guitarist on stage she recognized from the jamming session with Sean at Hogmanay in Macdui's. Gilly, Irish, but living locally for many years, was obviously well known and had already captivated the audience.

Rhona relaxed. Tonight would be okay. Glancing over at Olsen, she realized that he felt the same. They were in the midst of an investigation with the adrenaline running, but tonight they could do nothing more than they'd done today. And standing back often resulted in a perspective that wasn't possible close up.

'Do you need to phone home?' Olsen offered as they were ushered to their seats.

'The cat's been fed and watered,' she told him.

'Cats are pretty self-sufficient,' he said. 'Oh to be like them,' he added with a smile.

Presented with the menu, Rhona immediately ordered the calamari to start, followed by a Sicilian pizza, both of which she'd enjoyed on her previous visit.

'You've eaten here before?' Olsen said.

'Yes,' Rhona said, choosing not to elaborate.

Olsen gave his order, then checking with Rhona as to whether she preferred red or white wine, ordered them a bottle of Fiorile Pinot Grigio delle Venezie.

As she ate her meal, Rhona began to suspect from the glances coming their way that some of the other diners were aware of who they were, and why they were here. The guitarist, Gilly, had already noted her presence, no doubt recognizing her as Sean's partner from the Hogmanay party. She realized that, by now, word would have got out that the missing climbers' van had been found at Feshie airfield and a couple of forensic tents had been set up there. She didn't need to be a native of Skye to be aware just how quickly news travelled in a rural community and how big a story could become. Particularly one with a mystery at its heart.

And local interest and knowledge might prove invaluable. The perpetrator had more than likely spent time in Aviemore. He would have eaten, perhaps even here in La Taverna. Spoken to folk, probably asked questions about the injured climber plucked from an ice cave on Cairngorm. His turning up at Coire Cas car park to watch for Isla suggested as much.

Olsen regarded her quizzically as the coffee was served.

'Better?' he said.

'Much,' Rhona answered honestly.

He sat back, taking an affectionate look around him. 'Marita loved this place. We always came here when climbing in the area. For the food and the atmosphere.'

At this point Rhona could have mentioned that she'd been here with Sean just a few days before, but she didn't, and wasn't sure why.

'Where are you from originally?' Olsen asked.

'I was brought up on Skye.'

Olsen nodded. 'I wondered where,' he said. 'I knew it wasn't a city.'

'And you?'

'My father had a fishing boat, and we lived on a small coastal farm, like many of my countrymen. Rural Norwegians used to have three names,' he explained, 'the first being their given name, the second a patronymic, like Olsen meaning son of Ole. The third was really where to find them, usually the name of their family's farm. I am really Alvis Olsen Bakken. If a family moved to a different farm, then the name changed. A nightmare for folk trying to trace their ancestors.'

'In Scotland the Mac means son of, so not that different, and on Skye we often refer to folk by their house or farm to be clear which MacLeod we're talking about. There are a lot of us,' Rhona added with a smile.

A moment's silence followed in which Rhona decided it was time to pose her question.

'What is it that you haven't told me about this case?' she said.

Olsen hesitated. 'I'd rather we discuss it back at the hotel, in private. Your room or mine.'

Rhona didn't imagine for a moment that this was a come-on, more secrecy or reticence on the Norwegian's part.

'It's fucked up,' he said quietly, perhaps reading her thoughts. 'And better not voiced in company. Especially since every table surrounding us will be listening.' He gave a half-smile. 'This isn't the city after all.'

Arriving at the hotel, Olsen went to the bar and, asking for a bottle of whisky, brought it with him. Rhona had already indicated she'd prefer Olsen's room for their discussion. It would be, she'd thought, easier to retreat from there, although she'd discerned no indication that he planned anything other than a talk about work.

Olsen was an intriguing character, as reticent as herself. Definitely not Sean, and not McNab either, neither of whose advances could be described as oblique.

Once inside he poured them each a dram, using the tumblers from the bathroom which were thankfully glass.

'Water?'

'Just a little,' she said.

He produced a bottle and asked, 'How much?' Rhona nodded at the appropriate moment.

Adding a similar amount to his own glass, he joined Rhona at the small table near the window.

Rhona sampled the whisky, wondering why it always tasted better when she was in the Highlands, or better still on Skye.

'Okay,' she said, 'tell me.'

Olsen seemed to let go of his studied look, dropping it like a veil, and Rhona knew that whatever followed was likely to be the truth, or at least a portion of it.

It had started to snow again. Soft flakes drifting past the window. They hadn't shut the curtains, probably because, unlike in the city, there was no one outside to look in.

She rose and, padding to the end of the bed, began to dress. She felt no regret, no wish that it hadn't happened. Neither alcohol nor frantic desire had fashioned what had taken place between herself and Alvis Olsen.

Then why had she let it happen, or even encouraged it?

It had been his revelation about the children, she acknowledged. His distress at voicing this out loud had made her want to console him. They'd sat together then on the bed, talking, drinking whisky. She'd felt a strong attraction to this man who carried such a burden.

It had been the same with McNab, she recalled, when he'd 'risen from the dead' after the almost fatal shooting.

Then their coupling had been at her instigation, inflamed by a desire to make him live again.

And then as now, sex – for a short time at least – made us both forget the horrors we'd faced, or had yet to face

Rhona closed the door quietly behind her. *Let him sleep.* It seemed that sleep had been a companion he'd seldom encountered, and one that had grown even more of a stranger since Marita's death.

He'd said that name even as he'd made love to her. Rhona wondered if he would remember and hoped that he wouldn't, because she hadn't been offended. Olsen had been loving and gentle and somehow in those few moments it had seemed to Rhona that he'd crossed a boundary back into life.

They hadn't talked of his wife or how she'd died, but Rhona sensed he carried a weight of guilt and regret about it. It was something she and Olsen had in common. Guilt, not at what they'd done, but regret at what they hadn't.

As she'd left the room, he'd stirred, and when his eyes flickered open and he registered her departure, she thought that the looks they'd exchanged indicated they understood one another very well, and that whatever had happened tonight between them wouldn't be discussed or referred to again.

Rhona now sat on her own bed, unable to contemplate sleep. What Olsen had told her about the circumstances surrounding this case had horrified her. No other word described it. If it were true, then what he and McNab had shared had no doubt helped fashion the version of McNab she'd encountered recently.

Now there are three of us who share this knowledge.

A triumvirate who were aware of what they were dealing

with, and why it mustn't become common knowledge. Not yet anyway. Rhona thought of Bill Wilson and what he was facing. She longed to discuss what Olsen had told her with her old friend and mentor, but that wasn't possible. Not because Bill couldn't be trusted, but because of what he must deal with himself in the coming days.

How to face the imminent loss of your partner of thirty years, your lover and your best friend? The person you could turn to. The person you most trusted.

Margaret had been, in Bill's words, the light of his life. *I can only do this job because of her and the kids*. That was why Bill had spent so much time encouraging Rhona to make something good with Sean. Something permanent. Something you could depend on.

But that is as unlikely for Sean as it is for me. As indicated by tonight's proceedings.

Rhona briefly contemplated calling the flat. Sean would probably be back there by now and she could enquire after Tom. Her call would be welcome, but definitely unexpected. Sean would think it odd, maybe even ask her what was wrong.

And I can't discuss the case with Sean.

The only person, other than Olsen, that she could discuss it with was McNab.

51

'I'll need time,' Ollie told him, eyeing the laptop and mobile that McNab handed over.

'I'll make us coffee,' McNab said. 'Where's the kitchen?'

Ollie pointed to a door on the left. 'It's a mess in there,' he offered.

'Then I'll feel at home,' McNab said.

It wasn't the first time he'd visited Ollie at his flat. During the Stonewarrior case, he'd enlisted his favourite techie in a clandestine operation. *And put the guy's job on the line.* But this was different, McNab told himself. This was just a favour for a friend that had got locked out of his laptop and his mobile.

Indebtedness. It all boiled down to that in the end. Davey had got a bit too ambitious, or maybe it was Mary. No matter whose fault it was now, McNab thought, as he spooned large helpings of instant coffee into two mugs and added boiling water.

Davey was in the shit via McVitie, or Brodie, because they were intertwined, although Mary had claimed he didn't know that at the time.

Davey's story of the boxing bouts had proved true, except he had let them happen in his gym, apparently as a way to pay off a debt to Brodie, but for what exactly?

But whatever hold Brodie had on Davey hadn't been paid

off through the boxing bouts. So cocaine became part of the game, quietly and efficiently disseminated via the clubs and probably the betting shops.

'He started coming home drunk. I thought he was meeting you. He never denied it,' Mary had said.

'You should have called me.'

Mary had shaken her head in a manner he remembered. '*Should have* covers a lot of things I didn't do.'

And they were back there again, the night she'd told him that his pal Davey Stevenson was the one for her.

You fucking idiot, McNab admonished himself silently. *This isn't about you and Mary. This is about Davey.*

'Where's his laptop?'

'Here,' she'd indicated a desk drawer. 'There's a mobile too.'

'You told me he took his with him,' McNab had countered.

'His personal one. Not this one.' She'd opened the drawer and taken out both items.

'He conducted his business on this?' McNab said.

'He conducted the *other* business on it.'

Her face had been white and strained beneath the make-up, making McNab think of a painted doll.

McNab had told her to continue as normal. Any contact that featured Davey, via phone or person, he wanted to know about immediately. He'd taken her hand then, finding it cold to the touch. Mary Grant was a tough operator. McNab had never doubted that. But in that moment fear had overtaken her.

McNab carried the two mugs through to the sitting room which looked nothing like a place for sitting and relaxing.

In fact it looked more like the *Starship Enterprise* than Ollie's official workplace.

Both the phone and the laptop were already wired into his system, and on two adjacent screens things were happening. What, McNab had no idea.

Ollie accepted the coffee and took a sup, immediately grimacing. 'How many spoonfuls are in there?'

'Enough to warrant you buying another jar tomorrow,' McNab told him. 'Any luck?'

'I told you I needed time,' Ollie stated. 'And you staring over my shoulder won't make it go any faster. Drink your coffee or go for a kip.' Ollie gestured to a decrepit-looking couch.

'I've slept on worse,' McNab informed him and, taking his caffeine with him, settled down on the sofa. Noting the time, he was suddenly reminded that he should have been on his way to the Granite City by now. He checked his mobile, expecting a message from Olsen, and found one. He contemplated leaving it unopened, but not knowing the result of his non-show seemed worse than knowing.

The text was short. They'd located the van near Aviemore, with evidence Isla may have been inside, and Ragnar Lodbrok was staying there with Dr MacLeod tonight and travelling to Aberdeen tomorrow.

Fucking hell. Maybe he should have gone north with Rhona after all.

He was awakened by the buzz of his phone. McNab imagined it was his morning alarm at first, until he registered he was on a couch and not a bed. The time at the top of the screen indicated he'd barely been asleep for twenty minutes, which was probably why he felt so groggy.

'Ellie.' He tried to sound awake.

'Where are you?'

McNab glanced around, because in truth when he'd opened his eyes he wasn't sure. Then his brain went into action as he recognized the back of Ollie's head.

'I'm working,' he said.

'Were you working in the pub across the road earlier?'

Fuck. She'd spotted him emerging from the pole-dancing club. McNab jumped in with his explanation. 'That's when I tried to ring you. I was back in the car when you called back and I couldn't pick up—'

He halted as she interrupted him. 'Are you near a TV? There's something on the news you should see.'

'What?' he said, his heart suddenly upping its pace.

There was a catch in Ellie's voice as she answered. 'It's Mary Stevenson. She's been in an accident.'

'Mary?' McNab dropped the phone. 'Switch on the telly,' he screamed at Ollie. 'Ellie?' he said as he retrieved his mobile. 'Tell me what happened.'

'The news said she was knocked down coming out of her salon tonight. A hit-and-run, the police think.' When McNab didn't immediately respond, she said, 'Will I come over to yours?'

McNab marshalled himself. 'No. Don't do that. I'll call you.'

Stunned, McNab laid the phone down to concentrate on the TV. The broadcast currently playing made no mention of the accident, but below, the news McNab feared was running along the bottom of the screen.

Wife of eminent Glasgow businessman seriously injured in possible hit-and-run.

52

Rhona listened in silence to McNab's angry voice.

'I thought they had Davey. I thought he was the one in danger, but the fuckers obviously knew they could get to me via Mary.' He gave a hollow laugh. 'We're fucked, and everyone close to us is fucked too.'

Traumatized by McNab's tone, Rhona told him to stop, and asked if there had been any word from Davey.

'No,' McNab said sharply. 'Ollie's working on his second mobile and laptop, looking for a link to Brodie, McVitie or any of the bastards.'

McNab's call had arrived just as Rhona had finally drifted off to sleep, her dreams plagued by images conjured up by her conversation with Olsen. It now appeared that McNab had been keeping more than one secret from her.

Rhona had known nothing of McNab's friendship with the Stevensons, a couple she'd heard of. *Who hadn't in Glasgow?* But she'd never met them personally. Now it appeared that McNab's raid on Brodie's club had resulted in more than just McNab's skirmish with a bullet.

'If what you say is true, might Davey just have gone somewhere on his own to cool off after the row?'

The silence that followed suggested McNab was contemplating that as a possibility. Then he came back in. 'If he's watching TV and sees the news—'

'He'll make contact,' Rhona finished for him. 'Go to the hospital. Stay with Mary until Davey shows up.'

This suggestion was followed by another silence, and Rhona guessed that that hadn't been in McNab's plan.

'Don't do anything about Brodie on your own,' she tried to warn him. 'This is official now.'

'I'd say it was personal,' had been McNab's final remark.

Rhona decided that what little sleep she'd enjoyed was to be her ration. Dispensing with the idea of returning to bed, she headed for the shower, flipping on the kettle for coffee as she went. It would be dawn soon, and before that, she could study the recordings she'd taken in and around the van, and later in the woods.

Standing under the spray, she acknowledged her concern for McNab's state of mind, and considered what to do about it. If Ollie didn't produce any leads that might direct McNab to Brodie's whereabouts, then he couldn't pursue them.

Then again, getting to Brodie and hopefully finding out what had happened to Amena Tamar was vital, not just for McNab's sense of justice over the attack on Mary, but because of what Olsen had told Rhona last night.

Her other option was to call Bill. He'd asked to be kept informed. His main reason for that was invariably his detective sergeant. Rhona had said she would, yet found herself reluctant to do so without knowing the current situation with Margaret. Eventually, Rhona emerged from the shower, her decision made.

Olsen was seated in the hotel dining room. They'd asked for an early breakfast, and he was already tucking into his. Rhona helped herself to the hot buffet and joined him.

Having given Rhona some basic Norwegian the previous

evening, Olsen now tried it out on her. *'God morgen,'* he offered as she sat down. *'Hvordan sov du?'*

Rather than tell the truth, which was that she hadn't slept much at all, Rhona answered in the affirmative.

'Og du?' she tried.

Olsen's twitch of a smile suggested she may have got the words right, but not the delivery.

'I'm going to head for Inverness, then Aberdeen,' he told her. 'I texted McNab to let him know that we stayed here last night.'

'He called me early this morning,' Rhona said. 'There have been some developments.'

Olsen listened as she gave him the whole story, his expression growing grim at the news of the hit-and-run.

'Brodie's directly linked to this operation. If we can find him, Petter Lund might be persuaded to give us a location.' He studied her expression. 'You think McNab's working off the record?'

'He did it in the Stonewarrior case, with help from the same tech guy, Ollie.'

'That's how he lost his promotion?'

'And nearly his life,' Rhona said truthfully. 'The perpetrator decided killing McNab was his ultimate goal and he almost achieved it.'

'Because he went out on his own,' Olsen said thoughtfully.

'Don't let him go that way again,' Rhona said.

53

He'd intimated to Rhona that he wouldn't go to the hospital, but McNab found himself headed that way anyway. The traffic across the Kingston Bridge had him swearing even at this hour of the morning. He'd done nothing yet about Ellie, and couldn't bring himself to call her and let her know where he was and what he was doing. She and Mary had made friends, despite the fact that he had set Ellie up as his biker chick. Ellie would be worried about Mary, maybe even asking herself why the hit-and-run had happened.

She'll find out soon enough, McNab thought, *that choosing to hang out with a police officer needs a health warning.* One that he should have handed out before getting together with her. Which was probably the reason most relationships in the force were in-house. Then nothing had to be said or explained about the job or the baggage that came with it. Reaching the new Queen Elizabeth hospital, locally known as the Death Star, he entered the giant car park again to look for a space, noting that the coming and going of ambulances hadn't dwindled despite the early hour.

After the abrupt termination of his conversation with Rhona, McNab had considered his next move. There had been no result as yet from Ollie, but it would come soon, or so he'd been promised. NcNab had briefly wondered if Ollie was stalling, and whether he already had contact details for

Brodie but was intent on preventing McNab from charging in, without proper authority or back-up.

After all, Ollie nearly lost his job the last time I did that.

Despite this, McNab had decided to take Ollie at face value, and had left him to it, and come to see Mary . . . for two reasons. First, to make sure she was alive and would stay that way, and second, to stoke his anger and determination by viewing what the bastards had done to her.

Accident and Emergency was brightly lit and though certain indicators suggested it had been very busy, there were now only about a dozen people still waiting to be seen. McNab assumed these were the ones deemed not serious.

At least she's not in the mortuary, McNab consoled himself as he was directed towards the acute receiving unit.

It wasn't possible to visit Accident and Emergency at any time of the day or night and not find at least one pair of police officers hanging about, having delivered a casualty who'd been involved in some nefarious activity. There were four of them tonight; two he discovered were there because of Mary's accident. Recognizing McNab, they were quick to tell him what they thought had happened.

According to statements from nearby pedestrians and her staff, a black four-by-four had come out of nowhere just as Mary had emerged from the salon. Having mounted the pavement and mowed her down, the vehicle had regained the road and driven off.

'There's someone with her.'

'Who?' McNab asked.

McNab hesitated at the door, his heart quickening at the sight of the monitors and tubes attached to the still figure propped up against the pillows. Mary's head and face in particular had taken a heavy punishment on impact, like a boxer whose opponent had far outclassed her, giving her little opportunity to fight back. The eyes were blackened, the cheeks a mass of bruising. A gash on the forehead had been sewn shut, as had one on the chin. McNab imagined what she would think when she saw herself in the mirror.

But she's alive, thank God.

Her saviour sat alongside, her hand held in his. McNab couldn't see Davey's face, but it was obviously him. Rhona had been right. Davey had reappeared. And just as the attack had happened. So how come he'd been there at that moment? And where the hell had he been up to that point?

McNab made a concentrated attempt to control his anger. The way he felt towards Davey at this moment, he could have let fly. They had physically fought plenty of times as teenagers, a habit which had endured well into their twenties. These physical jousts had eventually become a war of words, and attempts at one-upmanship, as exhibited by McNab turning up at Davey's posh house on the back of a Harley-Davidson, driven by a biker chick.

Had Davey's disappearance been just another of his moves in the endless game they played?

Gathering himself, McNab opened the door. Davey didn't turn immediately, so intent was he in his study of Mary. When he finally did, McNab could see that he'd been crying. The realization of that brought him up short and stifled the harsh words ready and waiting in his throat.

'How is she?' McNab said instead.

'Until she comes round, they won't know for certain. Her head . . .' Davey tailed off in distress.

That news changed everything for McNab. His decision to suppress his anger gone, he said what he really thought.

'Where the fuck were you? Mary's been frantic.' McNab clenched his fists as he waited for an answer. When he got none, he said, 'Fucking tell me, Davey, or I'll arrest you here and now for dealing cocaine out of the clubs.'

'What?' Davey's head jerked round in disbelief.

'Mary told me everything. She thought Brodie had you. She thought you might be dead.'

Davey looked at him in puzzlement, like a drunk man suddenly presented with reality.

'Mary knew where I was,' he said. 'I texted her. I was at the cabin at Loch Lomond. I needed time to think.'

McNab wasn't buying that. 'Mary called me at work and asked me to come to the salon. She said you hadn't come home and that you were in debt to Brodie. Why would Mary lie about that?'

Davey attempted a shrug. 'I have no idea,' he said, his face shutting down.

The bastard's hiding something. McNab felt his anger bubble up again. How he would like to put a fist in that stupid stubborn face.

'She gave me your laptop and the other mobile,' McNab told him.

Davey's expression moved through surprise to fury, suggesting to McNab that Davey hadn't realized his wife knew about the existence of either item.

Davey rose to his feet, Mary's hand dropping from his, to lie small and white and abandoned on the cover. 'She shouldn't have done that,' he said coldly.

'Why?' McNab said.

A multitude of conflicting emotions crossed Davey's face, none of which McNab liked.

'It's time we had a talk, Davey, a real one this time,' he said sharply.

Davey's laugh sent a shiver down McNab's spine.

'Fuck you, Michael Joseph McNab. You have fuck all to do with Mary. She chose me, or don't you remember?'

As though cued by his outburst, an alarm when off, shattering the anger between them. In moments the room was besieged by hospital personnel and they were both ordered to leave.

Once in the corridor, Davey gripped McNab's arm. 'It'll be your fault if Mary dies,' he told him. 'Your fucking fault.'

54

McNab had come straight to Ollie's from the hospital, hoping that Ollie had managed to extract information from Davey's laptop or mobile that would lead him to Brodie. During the journey, McNab had tried to analyse Davey's behaviour.

Davey had been terrified as well as angry, but it was the terror that had triumphed. That's why he'd been accused of being responsible for the attack on Mary.

But maybe it was my fault? If Brodie or one of his minions was watching the salon, then me turning up there would have been bad news for Mary.

But other things Davey had said just didn't add up. The cabin story for one. McNab was pretty sure that Mary hadn't known where Davey was. Her fear when she'd called McNab and then later in her office had been real enough. McNab could still conjure up the image of her alarm, but now Mary's battered face replaced the wide-eyed horror as she'd looked to him for help.

But Mary can lie, and lie convincingly, McNab reminded himself. She'd lied to him about seeing Davey when she was still going out with him. She and Davey both had. He'd been a fool to believe them back then. So what was different now?

McNab had eventually come to the conclusion that both Mary and Davey had been reluctant to reveal the true nature of their involvement with Brodie. *And Davey's been keeping something back from Mary too.* Hence the laptop and mobile.

Whatever was on those devices might be the reason for Davey's behaviour.

And here it was. The truth in all its ugliness.

Ollie was regarding McNab with sympathy. 'That's what's on the laptop,' he repeated.

As McNab stared at him in disbelief, Ollie set the show in motion. A bewildering array of images began to pass McNab's eyes. Images he didn't want to see, let alone absorb or remember. Eventually he slammed down the lid to end the agony.

Ollie's shrug suggested he'd seen and heard it all before. The instant denial that you might have a friend, a partner, a relative with a double life. A sexual existence that you couldn't conceive of. It happened with politicians and celebrities, and businessmen just like Davey Stevenson.

'There's something not right about this . . .' McNab said, trying to get his head round it.

'I'll have to hand the laptop and phone in,' Ollie told him, grim-faced.

McNab pulled himself together. 'First, I need to know if you found anything on there relating to Brodie. Brodie's *my* investigation,' he stressed.

Ollie looked uncomfortable.

'You found something?'

When Ollie didn't answer, McNab exploded: 'For fuck's sake. That's why I brought you the laptop in the first place. The guy who owns it has connections with Brodie.'

'That's not what you told me. You said it was a friend . . .'

'He is – *was* a friend. He said he was being threatened by Brodie. I wanted to know why.'

'Well now you do.'

McNab sat in the shadows of his kitchen. Through the window, the city's continuing sound and movement suggested all was normal, but it wasn't, and would never be again. The bottle of whisky he'd kept as a reminder of his sobriety stood empty on the table.

The sickness and distaste he'd felt at Ollie's revelation about Davey had brought him back here, with a desperate need to drown the images he'd viewed. His horror at these had been partially numbed by the alcohol, but McNab knew it would soon be back in force, and probably threefold.

He wanted to know the truth, was desperate to ask Davey outright, but he'd have to move quickly before Ollie reported the material he'd found, after which Davey would be off-limits to him at least.

Draining the last drop from his glass, McNab decided it was a relief to let go. For the first time since he'd embarked on his caffeine crusade, he felt . . . what? *Human* wasn't right. It was more like being free again. Free to be a piss-head. Free to make mistakes. Free to fail.

And he'd definitely done that. He'd forgotten that the first rule of a detective was that everyone was a suspect. Everyone was guilty until proved innocent. Instead, he'd assumed that Davey was his pal. That Mary still had a soft spot for him. That Davey was the Davey he'd known. That he wasn't a fucking paedophile wanker that snorted cocaine while fucking wee lassies who'd run away from war and other bastards like him.

McNab's stomach, unused to processing alcohol in such

speed and quantity, was threatening to rebel. As he bent over the sink, he contemplated the irony of it all, even as the walls of certainty that surrounded him, his professional and personal life crumbled to dust.

The only brick left to shatter was the one he'd allotted to Dr Rhona MacLeod. Surely she wouldn't let him down?

55

The meandering river had crested its banks in places, adding to the already sodden nature of the neighbouring fields. Twice on her journey from Aviemore they'd met flooding where the ditches that lined the narrow road had disgorged their load. A combination of fast-melting snow from the higher reaches of Cairngorm, plus heavy overnight rain had transformed the landscape.

Inspector Olsen had departed for Inverness, then Aberdeen, his intention to meet McNab there seemingly in place. Rhona hadn't quizzed Olsen about what was planned, although it appeared to involve Petter Lund and the Statoil connection with Stavanger. She only hoped McNab was in a better frame of mind by the time he got there.

As the Land Rover eased its way along the track to the airfield, Rhona glanced up to the escarpment, now virtually free of its snow cover. The light wind that brushed the trees would no doubt provide the required updraft for any glider who wished to take advantage of the lull in the wintry weather.

Even as she thought this, she spied a car parked outside the hangar, the doors of which stood open.

Ruaridh seemed to be sharing her thoughts. 'Looks like someone's planning a flight.'

'Can you drop me here?' Rhona said. 'I'd like a word with

them.' She didn't respond to Ruaridh's puzzled expression, unsure whether the question she planned to ask of the possible flier was even sensible. 'I'll be with you shortly.'

As she approached the hangar, the tow truck appeared, trundling the Robin light aircraft out. Rhona waited until it was clear of the building before approaching the driver and introducing herself. The man got out and shook hands with her.

'Ben Cruikshank. The Robin pilot.'

'You're taking her up?'

He nodded. 'Weather's ideal for a flight.' He glanced at the distant forensic tents. 'I was sorry to hear about the missing girl. I hope she's okay.' He waited then, sensing Rhona wanted to ask him something.

'Would you be able to tell if an aircraft other than this one had used the runway recently?'

Her question had surprised him. Rhona watched as he processed it. 'This one hasn't been out for a week, so probably yes.'

As they walked together towards the exposed runway, he elaborated. 'You're thinking of the night the melt started?'

That was exactly what she was thinking. If a plane had landed and taken off from here as the thaw set in, then there might be evidence of that in the now-softened ground surface.

They had to walk half the length of the runway before they found it. Ben halted suddenly then crouched. 'Here,' he said, pointing at the bruised and muddy grass. 'That's not our tracks. If you can take a print you might be able to identify the make of the tyre and possibly the aircraft.'

Rhona thanked him and placed a marker at the spot. 'Can you delay your flight until I lift the evidence?'

'Sure thing. I'll be in the clubhouse if you need me.'

The two SOCOs from Inverness were already on site. Rhona sent them to do the necessary on the runway, including taking soil samples from the tyre track. If they did locate the plane there was a chance it would still have soil evidence in its tyres that would prove it had landed and taken off from this exact location.

Buoyed up by possible confirmation that she and Olsen had been right about the suspect's escape from the valley, Rhona made for the blue tent just inside the wood, hoping that if he had taken flight from here, Isla, alive, had been with him.

Rhona contemplated stepping outside briefly for some fresh air. A winter sun shining on the tent, plus her own multiple layers under the forensic suit, were combining to raise her temperature. That was the problem with this outfit. You were never sure just how much you needed to wear underneath it.

Had Chrissy been here, they would have worked swiftly and in tandem. Chrissy had recovered human remains with Rhona on numerous occasions. Her forensic assistant knew what was required and when, without instruction. As it was, Rhona had thought it easier to tackle the ground cover herself, without the aid of the other SOCOs. Hence her slower and warmer progress.

Once begun, it had become obvious that the heap of branches wasn't the result of managed woodland, where off-cuts tended to be fresh on top, with successively decomposing layers beneath. In this case, the pile Rhona was carefully working her way through appeared to have been drawn together, and to be all of the same vintage.

Picking away the last of it, Rhona studied the now fully exposed rectangular area of moist, disturbed earth. Breathing in, she picked up, without a doubt, the telltale scent of decomposition. Faint but present.

Something's buried here. Something in the process of decay.

Rhona realized in that moment how much she wanted that not to be the case. With every twig she'd removed, every photograph she'd taken, she'd hoped to find nothing of any consequence below.

Immediately her brain moved into analysis. If it was Isla, how long had she lain here? How decomposed could her body be when the weather had been so cold? Then came the realization that the disturbed area appeared too small to accommodate even the slight figure of the girl she'd strapped to the stretcher in the ice cave.

Unless of course the body had been dismembered.

Rhona began to remove the first layer of topsoil.

56

He'd forsaken his plan to head for Inverness when the preliminary report from AAIB on the downed plane had arrived via email. Its initial findings had indicated that the pilot had been flying by Visual Flight Rules and had been in receipt of Flight Information Service from Air Traffic Control. The Robin light aircraft had been on a non-commercial flight from Stavanger to Inverness, and had encountered severe weather conditions over the Cairngorm plateau which had resulted in icing. The outcome had been an emergency landing on Loch A'an.

The dead pilot had yet to be identified, but he'd brought the plane down safely when he could just as likely have flown into a mountainside in the blizzard conditions.

And for that he'd been rewarded with death.

Olsen had his own theories about that non-commercial trip and its reasons, but they were only theories. As for why the pilot had been murdered, he suspected that he'd become a liability. Why, he didn't know.

He flipped on the windscreen wipers in response to the latest deluge. The heavy rain that had dispersed the snow from Cairngorm had seemingly moved east, in tandem with his journey. Here the open fields were dotted with flood water, the sheep huddled on higher ground. It was obvious the blizzard that had swept Cairngorm hadn't hit Aberdeenshire with the same ferocity, but the following rain had.

Having headed eastward via Grantown and Aberlour, the journey was proving to be much shorter. He'd done it before with Marita, but in summer, although like Norway, that hadn't guaranteed an absence of rain. Olsen found himself noting various familiar landmarks and remembering incidents they'd encountered, in particular Marita's desire not to hit the large number of pheasants that had had a habit of dashing out in front of their vehicle.

On one occasion they'd thought they'd avoided one such bird only to be honked at by various cars once they'd entered Aberdeen. Further puzzled by the aghast stares of pedestrians at traffic lights, the truth had finally been revealed by a bus driver, who, rolling down his window, had informed them that they had a chicken stuck to their radiator grille. The chicken had turned out to be a pheasant displayed like a trophy on a wall. Olsen had been the one to prise it out and dispose of it in the nearest bin. Not an easy job. Marita's expression, Olsen remembered, had been a mix of horror and intense amusement.

With a startling rush of emotion, Olsen realized just how much he missed the sound of his wife's laughter.

That painful thought was interrupted by his mobile ringing. On the last stretch before his entry to the city, he found himself sandwiched in a line of lorries, with no chance to park. The mobile rang impatiently a few more times, then stopped. Reaching to the seat where it lay, he expected to discover Dr MacLeod's name, but instead found an unknown landline number.

The juxtaposition of Marita and Rhona in his thoughts

LIN ANDERSON

had an unsettling effect on Olsen, the result of which was a sudden stab of guilt suggesting he had cheated on his wife.

Marita's dead.

This internal reminder only served to increase his self-reproach. And Olsen instinctively knew why . . . last night when he'd been with Rhona, he'd briefly forgotten to mourn Marita.

A kerb minus a double yellow line eventually presented itself and Olsen pulled in. The unknown number rang a few times before being answered by a male voice that said, 'Feshie Flying Club?'

Taken off guard by this unexpected response, Olsen explained who he was and why he'd called the number.

'Dr MacLeod asked to use this phone,' the man explained. 'There wasn't a signal for her mobile.'

'Is she still on site?' Olsen asked.

'I don't think so. The police cars have all left.'

'Have you any idea why she called?' he tried.

'I'm sorry, I don't.'

As Olsen thanked the man and proceeded to ring off, he was offered one piece of important news regarding a study Dr MacLeod had made of the landing strip, which brought the semblance of a smile to his lips.

'Well done, Rhona.'

Aberdeen and Stavanger, separated by some 300 miles of harsh North Sea, had much in common, although the centre of the grey Granite City bore little resemblance to the eighteenth-century wooden structures of old Stavanger.

The two cities, however, did owe their twentieth-century rapid growth to the same thing – petroleum harvested from the neighbouring sea which they shared. The flow of money, and influx of foreign as well as local personnel, had helped encourage the usual problems encountered by any city whose inhabitants had cash to burn.

The company Olsen was about to visit had been set up by former police officers as a forensic service, developing state-of-the-art software to process and record crime scenes. The versatility of their product had seen them move into other areas – including the oil business, and counterterrorism, all of which had spread their work internationally. He and one of the founders, Roy Hunter, went way back.

Olsen smiled as he pressed the entry button. Despite the circumstances, he was looking forward to seeing Roy again.

The small conference room Olsen was shown into at R2S reminded him of the room in the Commissariat de Polis where he'd shared his tentative findings with his fellow officers. On this occasion coffee was also provided, but without the *pannekaken*. The other difference being that the two men and one woman who sat round the table weren't police officers, or at least not any longer, although they arguably pursued the same goals – the collection and processing of forensic evidence pertinent to major crimes.

The general discussion that had followed Olsen's presentation had centred on the downed plane, the likely route it had taken and its possible cargo. Roy's team had reacted with studied interest to the video, photographs and forensic evidence taken by Dr MacLeod at the crash scene and later at the deposition site.

The story of the young climbing party's demise at the Shelter Stone and the attack on Isla Crawford had followed, to which Olsen had added the ambiguous result of the subsequent postmortems.

'You don't know if they were murdered?' Roy had said.

Olsen had acknowledged this. 'However, we do know that someone attacked the fourth member of the party, Isla Crawford, who was lucky to survive that attempt on her life. She fell down the mountain, landing in a snow cave over a stream from which she was rescued by Dr MacLeod and a member of the local rescue team.

'After discharge from the hospital in Inverness, Isla and the van used by her party disappeared from Aviemore only to turn up here.' Olsen now brought up an image of the van in situ near the airstrip, followed by the recordings Rhona had taken internally.

'Evidence suggests the young woman had been forcibly taken from Aviemore and transported here in an injured state, but we have as yet found no human remains in the vicinity, and we believe there's a possibility she may have been removed alive from there by plane.'

'That's the Feshie airstrip?' Roy said, staring at the screen.

'You know it?' Olsen asked.

'I've used it on occasion.' Roy thought for a moment. 'If the perpetrator was eliminating witnesses to his presence on Cairngorm, then went to the bother of kidnapping Isla Crawford, why would he keep her alive?'

It was a question Olsen had been asking himself. He gave the only answer he could.

'Something happened that changed his mind.'

The Glasgow end of the investigation had proved to be the missing link. McNab had neither turned up nor been in contact to say why. Olsen's annoyance at this had been tempered by concern, particularly after his conversation with Rhona about McNab earlier in the day. The detective, he knew, had a history of going off-grid and doing his own thing. That wasn't what worried Olsen.

It was why McNab was missing that concerned him.

In McNab's absence, Olsen had done his best to outline the suspected connections of his own investigation with the Glasgow drugs raid on the Delta Club and the subsequent disappearance of the Syrian refugee Amena Tamar. Neil Brodie's name in particular had sparked a reaction, which had surprised Olsen, having been given the impression from McNab that Brodie was in no way attached to Aberdeen.

He said as much.

'Brodie's name cropped up in a recent dockland investigation we're working on,' Roy had explained. 'A face appeared on CCTV which one of our observers maintained was a Glasgow-based criminal called Neil Brodie, whom he knew from previous work in the city.'

'And Petter Lund?'

'Someone we're looking into as requested.'

Roy indicated that the others in the team should now leave, seemingly intent on speaking to Olsen alone.

'So, old friend,' Roy said, when the door clicked shut, 'what's the bit you haven't told me?'

Coming to R2S had been a decision he'd taken on the flight from Stavanger. It was necessary to involve Police Scotland, but some aspects of the investigation were better kept off the table both at home and here. R2S could work independently if required, which meant what he had planned was under the radar for now, at least. The image on the Coire Cas CCTV had been the trigger for their involvement. Viewing it had rung the alarm bells even louder, because Olsen suspected he knew who Isla's abductor might be.

If he was proved right, then the link he'd suspected between the drug barons, the traffickers and the establishment on both sides of the North Sea was no longer tenuous, but a certainty. Exposure would be dangerous without sufficient proof, and even with, if it wasn't handled properly. Petter Lund's involvement at McNab's raid on the Delta Club and Amena's presence had signalled that the up-to-now shaky connections Olsen had sought to establish were probably true.

Roy listened to Olsen's sorry tale and his reason for approaching an independent forensic company. His response was, 'If this is exposed, it puts *you* in the firing line.'

'And if you help, *you* could be in it too,' Olsen reminded him.

Roy's expression didn't alter. 'I know DS McNab, and of course Dr MacLeod. We've worked on many cases together before Police Scotland moved to make the most of their scene capture in-house.' He paused. 'McNab's a brilliant detective . . .' He halted again. 'The establishment don't like him. DI Wilson, his boss, has saved him on more than one occasion.' Roy eyed Olsen. 'He trusts Rhona.'

Olsen gave a half-smile. 'So I've chosen wisely?'

'McNab's coming?'

Olsen nodded. 'He should have been here by now.'

Roy paused. 'And Dr MacLeod?'

'We're out of contact at the moment, but yes. When we make the move, I want her with us.'

57

The girl was nervous, her hands trembling a little, her voice cracking as she spoke. Kyle had his hand on her back, encouraging her.

'Can you describe this man?' Rhona said.

'He was tall, with blond hair, spoke good English, with little to no accent.' She hesitated as though remembering something that frightened her. 'I never forget a face.' She swore in Polish and looked at Kyle. 'That's what I said to him. *I never forget a face.*' She turned to Rhona. 'Does that mean he'll be looking for me too?'

Kyle urged her into a seat, realizing her legs were unlikely to hold her up any longer.

'He's gone,' he said, then turning to Rhona looked for confirmation of that fact. 'He has, hasn't he?'

'We believe that's likely, yes,' Rhona assured him.

'I told him everything he asked.' Annieska shook her head worriedly. 'Even where the girl was staying. And the van.' She looked to Kyle. 'I told him you were looking for someone to drive it south for her.'

'So he may have pretended to be that someone,' Kyle said to Rhona.

Rhona couldn't deny the likelihood of that.

It went some way to explaining the phone call to Isla's room, then her exiting the hotel, which at least one employee had thought he'd witnessed. It would have been so easy for a man such as Annieska had described to force Isla into the van, the blood on the door frame and the sleeping bag testament to the force he'd used.

'If she's dead, it's my fault,' Annieska said, her face growing even paler.

Kyle put his arm round her shoulders. 'No, it's not. Who says you were the only person he was talking to about what happened? The whole village was alive with the story, either true or imagined.'

Rhona agreed with him. 'But what you've told us is important. And the fact that you can recall him in detail even more so.'

Annieska looked mollified by her words, but not less frightened.

'I need you to speak directly to Inspector Olsen,' Rhona continued. 'Tell him exactly what you've told me.'

She considered how that might be possible. Ruaridh could perhaps set something up via Aviemore police station or she could bring Olsen back this way to talk to Annieska in person.

Another possibility came to mind. One that might ease the young woman's fear. Olsen had said he planned to meet McNab at the R2S headquarters in Aberdeen. Apparently the leader there, Roy Hunter, was an old friend of Olsen's. Roy's forensic team had worked with Rhona many times and their facilities were extensive.

'Would you be able to come to Aberdeen with me? Be interviewed direct by Inspector Olsen?'

Rhona watched as the idea took root.

Annieska glanced at Kyle, who nodded his encouragement. 'Okay,' she said. Her decision to go on the offensive brought her to her feet.

'Will I need an overnight bag?'

'I could drive you both through,' Kyle offered. 'That way Dr MacLeod doesn't need to come back.'

His suggestion pleased Annieska, and made the logistics easier for Rhona too. She shot him a grateful glance.

'There was something, apart from his accent,' Annieska said, as though just remembering. 'His left hand. He had a tattoo on his wrist like a band. It said . . .' She grabbed her notebook and, writing something down, handed it to Rhona.

'*Uten Frykt*,' Rhona repeated. 'It's Norwegian for "without fear".'

Annieska's alarmed eyes met hers.

'That's the man you're looking for, isn't it?'

The meeting with Kyle and Annieska had taken place on Rhona's return from the deposition site. Rhona hadn't been able to identify the three large bird carcasses she'd exposed in the shallow grave, but birds of prey they'd undoubtedly been. How they'd died wouldn't be for her to determine, but by their burial, it did appear their deaths had been orchestrated.

Her relief at discovering that the disturbed earth had nothing to do with the missing Isla had been considerable. She'd tried to call McNab late morning from the flying club to tell him the result, but had encountered only an incoherent and obvious drunk at the other end of the phone. Her anger at this had resulted in a slammed-down receiver. A subsequent attempt to then update Olsen had proved less dramatic, but equally unsatisfactory.

On the return journey to Aviemore, Ruaridh had been apologetic for wasting her time with the burial site.

'It had to be done,' Rhona had told him. 'I'm just glad it didn't prove to be a human grave.'

'It'll cause a stooshie in the valley, none the less,' he'd said, knowing he didn't have to explain why.

On the way back to the hotel, Rhona had tried to plan her next move. She couldn't leave until she'd heard from Olsen at least. *As for McNab*. He'd been drunk on the midday phone call. Her worry hadn't been caused by his open admission that he wanted her, but by the fact that he was drinking to excess again. Something had triggered his fall off the wagon, and the longer Rhona had considered it, the more she'd thought it had to be about Mary.

McNab had been really cut up about the hit-and-run. She'd urged him to go to the hospital although he'd seemed reluctant to do so. *What if he had gone there, and his meltdown had been the result?*

Checking her mobile as they'd approached Aviemore, she'd watched the signal strength increase, finally reaching 4G as they encountered the roundabout outside La Taverna. Seconds later, Rhona had heard the ping as her emails were delivered to the inbox.

Glancing swiftly down the list, she'd spotted one from Olsen, but nothing from McNab. Unhappy about that, she'd made a call.

After Rhona had explained about Annieska, she'd asked Olsen about McNab.

'He never turned up at R2S as requested,' Olsen had said. 'And I can't reach him anywhere.'

'There's one more thing we could try.' Olsen had waited

as Rhona had explained. 'McNab always went to Bill when things got really bad, and he's at the same hospital as Mary.'

'You'll call DI Wilson?'

Rhona had said she would.

'After which I need you and Annieska here,' Olsen had stressed. 'As soon as possible.'

When the mobile had rung out, Rhona had pictured its insistent tone cutting through the silence of that hospital room. Eventually, she'd killed the unanswered call. The reason Bill hadn't chosen to respond, Rhona had hardly dared imagine.

Knowing the hospital was unlikely to give an update on either Mary or Margaret's condition over the phone, Rhona had considered another possibility, which she hadn't mentioned to Olsen.

Not being in Glasgow, she couldn't turn up in person, but Chrissy could.

God bless Chrissy, Rhona had muttered as her forensic assistant had answered immediately. Allaying Chrissy's fears with a brief résumé of the morning's excavation, she'd then switched to the real reason she'd called.

'McNab's on a bender?' Chrissy's voice had been tinged with concern. 'Shit. He was in a good place, what with the new girlfriend and all. I'll find out what's going on, don't worry.' There'd been a moment's silence. 'Want to tell me why you're headed for Aberdeen?'

'Olsen asked for me.'

'To do what?'

'I don't know as yet,' Rhona had told her honestly.

58

It was a replay of the pizza scene. Him dripping wet with the towel round his waist. The female with the wide-eyed look in the doorway. Only this time it wasn't the new delivery girl, Sandi, but a pissed-off-looking Ellie standing before him.

'I've been pressing your buzzer for five minutes.'

And don't I fucking know it.

McNab fought to control his inner thoughts and the tone of his reply. 'I'm sorry. I was in the shower.' He stood aside to let her enter.

'You didn't answer your mobile.' Ellie glanced around the room, her gaze coming to a halt on the empty whisky bottle and glass on the table. 'Been having a party?'

'A one-man occasion,' McNab said. Keen to be free of her penetrating look, he indicated he was going to get dressed.

Once behind the door, he told himself to get a grip. Ellie wasn't the one at fault here. Dressing swiftly, he exited to face the music.

This time he went to her and kissed her lightly on the lips, hoping his breath didn't smell or taste of alcohol. 'You okay?' he asked, now noting her look of distress.

'When I couldn't get hold of you, I went to the hospital.' Seeing his expression, she quickly added, 'I thought you'd be there.'

'I was for a while,' he admitted.

'I said I was her sister . . . and they told me Mary was in a critical condition. A subdural haematoma. They may have to operate to relieve the pressure on the brain.'

McNab tried to assimilate this. He'd known it was bad when they'd been ejected from the room. Then he and Davey had had the bust-up and Davey had insisted he get the fuck out of there.

'Is Davey with her?' he asked.

'I didn't see him.'

'The bastard,' McNab hissed through his teeth.

Ellie took a step back from him, and McNab caught the wary look in her eye.

'What's going on between you two, Michael?'

'You don't want to know,' McNab said with a coldness he felt in his bones.

'Can I help?'

She looked so vulnerable at that moment, McNab drew her into his arms. 'It's police shit. My job.' She felt slight and fragile against him, although he knew Ellie was anything but that.

She let him hold her briefly, then pulled away.

'The vehicle that took Mary down,' she said. 'I think I know where you can find it.'

He should have called it in, but hadn't. His excuse was that it might be nothing. The truth was, McNab hoped the opposite.

Eyewitnesses to the hit-and-run had provided a description of the vehicle involved, but like him, recalling number plates hadn't been anyone's strong point. Besides, McNab had no doubt that those number plates wouldn't see the light of day again.

They had more hope via the CCTV cameras that had caught the vehicle in its escape. Although if it went off-road and into hiding, or was altered to disguise it, things would get much more difficult.

A normal run-of-the-mill idiot who bolted in terror after they'd hit a pedestrian didn't have the mates, the tools or the know-how to disappear the car and the driver. In most cases a hit-and-run happened through drink, drugs, dare-devil driving or even a temporary blackout. Not this time. Attempted murder more than fitted the bill.

McNab's head was pounding, although he suspected insufficient caffeine was exacerbating the after-effects of his whisky binge. Ellie's story had had an urgency that meant they left the flat immediately on the back of her bike, with no recourse to coffee first. McNab hadn't argued with the chosen mode of transport, aware that the level of alcohol still in his bloodstream would be above the legal limit, and likely make him a danger on the road.

It had been impossible to talk on the journey and Ellie hadn't been clear about their final destination when they'd set off. How she'd located the vehicle had also been sketchy and McNab had the impression Ellie wasn't giving him the full story, which appeared to involve a couple of bikers who'd come into the shop.

But if she was right and it was the car they'd seen?

He wasn't geared up to ride pillion, apart from the helmet supplied by Ellie, and the accompanying drizzle felt more like pelting rain when travelling at thirty miles an hour, which quickly soaked McNab through. His mobile tucked next to his heart had sent up a vibration on more than one occasion during the journey, but McNab had made no attempt to check who the caller was, even during their brief traffic-light stops.

This being his third journey on a backie with Ellie, McNab tried to convince himself that it would be a lucky ride. He would locate the bastard that had mowed Mary down, and find out where Amena Tamar had been taken, although he knew that was more a hope than a likelihood.

Eventually Ellie drew to a halt and cut the engine. A quick glance around indicated the setting wasn't what McNab had expected. The row of modern bungalows with adjacent garages and neat gardens didn't seem like Neil Brodie territory to him, although in truth, most drug-gang masters preferred their abodes to be outwith the areas they were intent on exploiting.

'Here?' he said, indicating the house opposite.

'No,' Ellie shook her head. 'The garage at the end of the road.'

McNab tried to get his bearings. The poor weather conditions and restricted view riding pillion had seen him give up on mapping the route, yet it seemed by Ellie's expression that she was assuming he knew where exactly in Glasgow he was.

When the realization came that he did, it arrived like a thunderclap.

'This is Davey's old street, before he moved up to the mansion,' he said, as much to himself as to Ellie.

'He still owns the garage,' she told him. 'They repair motorbikes, as well as cars.'

McNab was beginning to put two and two together to make more than just four.

'And you think the hit-and-run vehicle's in there?'

LIN ANDERSON

'At the back, covered and out of sight,' she explained. 'The biker who got curious was visiting the garage for a reason other than motorcycle repair,' she said bluntly.

Fuck. So Davey was allowing folk to deal in his workplaces.

McNab felt anger flood his face. He caught Ellie's glance and knew that was why she hadn't elaborated before bringing him here, and probably why she hadn't urged him to call it in.

A silence hung between them, before he said, 'I want you out of here, now.'

'You've no transport . . . I can wait.'

'I want you to go,' he ordered. 'And let me do my job.'

When she didn't immediately respond, McNab added a *please, Ellie.*

Her look softened. 'You'll call me?'

McNab quickly promised, impatient now for her to be gone.

Waiting until the throb of the bike melted into the distance, McNab set off towards the garage.

59

The forecourt was busy with cars, either emerging from the main building or waiting to go in for repairs. Noticeably, all the vehicles in view were towards the top of the range. It seemed Davey's customers weren't short of cash.

A quick reconnoitre gave McNab an idea of the layout of the buildings. According to Ellie, the vehicle he sought was somewhere at the rear and under cover. An area where the dealing might also be taking place.

McNab headed round the back, attempting to look as though he should be in the vicinity. If he was stopped, he decided he would simply brass-neck it and say he was there to see Mr Brodie on business. He'd even give his name minus the police tag. That way, if Brodie was about, the bastard's curiosity would be whet at least.

As he circled the buildings a series of lights clicked on, puncturing the late-afternoon gloom and indicating the presence of security cameras. If dealing was happening here, then the buyers were being recorded big time. All the better to blackmail them if required.

Like Davey, was the thought that entered his head.

McNab decided not to go down the how-did-it-happen path, but to stay focused on the here and now. As far as he was concerned, Davey was fucked whatever way he looked at it, and by being fucked, he'd endangered Mary.

As he approached a rear shed that aligned with a high wire fence, a door in the metal opened and light streamed out. Beyond the guy exiting, McNab spotted another set of overalls seemingly at work on a vehicle in the privacy of the shed.

Slipping into shadow, McNab watched as the guy outside lit up a cigarette, then walked in the general direction McNab had come from. Once he was out of sight, McNab approached the open door and stepped in as a high-powered drill whined into action.

Goggled up and wearing ear protectors for whatever he was doing to the tail of the big black gas guzzler, McNab's entry apparently went unobserved. Circling the vehicle, he noted that the front bumper had been dented and a head-light damaged. The number plate had also been removed.

As he backed towards the door, it swung open. McNab's swift attempt to get out of sight appeared at first to have worked. He watched a pair of overalls walk past, then a voice barked an order for the mechanic to finish up. After a few minutes both men exited, the door was slammed shut and McNab found himself alone. Something he wouldn't have been averse to, if he hadn't heard the lock being turned behind them.

At this point McNab began to suspect the second man at least had been aware of his presence, hence the swift shut-down.

If so, what happened now?

While he waited to see if anyone would come back, McNab took a closer look at the vehicle. The mechanic had succeeded in removing the back number plate, which lay nearby. McNab brought up the CCTV footage Ollie had sent to his phone and set it in motion again. If there was the slightest image of a partial that matched this plate he wanted to see it.

It had been over in seconds. Mary's brief appearance at the door of the salon. No sound, but every time he'd watched the muzzed footage McNab could hear in his head the screech as the vehicle took off from somewhere just off screen, then the thump as it had hit her. Its presence masked Mary, but McNab's imagination had run wild with what her face had looked like on impact.

Realizing he'd been too caught up in his imaginings and not focused on the micro moment the back plate had been in view, he ran it again. But it was no clearer now than any of the times he'd viewed it previously. The first couple of letters might be the same but only a forensic study of the actual vehicle could prove that this was the one.

He was two-thirds round the car with his camera phone when he heard the click of the door being unlocked. McNab slipped his mobile in his pocket and moved in behind a set of shelves laden with parts.

A silent figure stood for a moment in the open doorway, then stepped inside. By the manner of the entrance, McNab decided that his visitor was aware someone was in the shed. The door clanged shut and a voice called out his name.

The tone, the inflection in the way it was said, told McNab what he wanted to know. He didn't move, afraid that anger would propel him forward to hit the bastard who'd said it. Had it been Brodie, McNab wouldn't have felt any angrier than he did at that moment.

'You bastard,' he hissed into the space between them.

There was nothing for a moment, then he heard it. The sound of a man weeping.

The noise, loud enough to echo against the metal walls of

the shed, fell on him like splinters of glass. McNab hated the man that was making those sounds, yet found something akin to pity stirring in his heart.

Which is what the bastard wants.

Davey was sitting on a stool, or had collapsed onto it, such was the curled shape of his body. McNab registered the T-shirt stretched by an upper body developed in one of Davey's gyms or through bouts in the boxing ring. The muscled forearms, the big hands that cupped his friend's face in despair as he fought to suck in a breath between the sobs.

'Shut up!' McNab told him. 'You have no fucking right to cry.'

His words seemed to hit home. Davey dropped his hands and drew himself upright on the stool.

'I've dug me a big one, Mikey. And I've no fucking idea how to get out of it.'

McNab gritted his teeth, which he'd had to do more than once while listening to Davey's sorry tale, most of which he had no wish to recall. Davey had flat out denied that he'd accessed the material that was on the laptop. He'd been set up, was the excuse, planting child pornography being one of the methods used to keep him in line.

'Brodie knew no one would believe me if I went to the police.' Davey had glanced sadly at him at that moment. 'Not even my old friend, DS Michael McNab.'

'Was it Brodie who got you to meet me?' McNab said, suspecting that had to be the case.

Davey admitted it had been. 'After the raid on the Delta Club. He was way pissed off about that. He wanted to pay you back. Draw you in. Screw with you.'

'And the girl he took from the hospital?'

'I told you the truth. He did take her to Aberdeen. She's probably out of the country by now. And for telling you that, I paid a price.' Davey shrugged. 'Brodie's got guys everywhere, including among your lot. You way underestimated the size of his empire and the influence he has when you sprung that raid.'

'Does Brodie know I'm here?' McNab demanded.

Davey shook his head. 'No, definitely not.'

McNab's brain was racing through all the possible scenarios that had resulted in him being brought here and they all pointed the same way.

'It was you that told Ellie about the car.'

Realizing he was right, McNab launched himself at Davey, who made no effort to get out of the way. His hand round Davey's throat, McNab strangled the reply he didn't need to hear.

'You fucking involved Ellie in this, you stupid moron,' he shouted into his face. 'You want *her* killed too?'

McNab released him in disgust, fear at the outcome of all this already formulating in his mind. Amena Tamar, Isla Crawford, then Mary. Who was next on the list of innocents to pay the price for all of this – Ellie?

I should never have taken her to Davey's house that night. It had all been a set-up.

'I didn't talk to Ellie direct,' Davey was saying. 'I got a biker who comes here to tell her the story.'

'A biker who comes here for drugs? That Brodie sells? Like he's going to keep schtum.'

McNab observed his erstwhile mate, wondering how the fuck he had become so rich yet was so stupid. No wonder Brodie was able to play him like a concertina.

'I'm calling in the vehicle.'

As McNab reached for his mobile, Davey grabbed his arm.
'Don't do that. Not yet. Please.'

McNab threw him a look of disgust. 'And this is how you plan to climb out of that hole?'

Davey was struggling with what he wanted to say. Eventually it came out.

'I don't care about me any more. It's Mary I need to keep safe.' His voice caught in his throat. 'If Brodie finds out I've talked to you . . .' He stuttered to a halt.

They were the first truly honest words that had emerged from his mouth.

'So, what do we do?' McNab said quietly.

'We get him together.'

60

The journey through to Aberdeen had proved useful.

With Kyle driving, Annieska had visibly relaxed once she'd departed Aviemore, and had seemed happy to relay to Rhona every detail she could remember of her meetings with Isla's possible kidnapper.

As the full story had unfolded, Rhona had made notes linking the sightings of the man in Aviemore with her own timings on the hill with CMR and in the valley. Kyle had chimed in at this point, in particular suggesting that it was likely by the timeline that the Iceman, as he'd chosen to call him, may have been hiding out in one of the same snow holes he'd recommended to Rhona on the night they'd found Isla.

'Which suggests, not only is he skilled at survival, he's probably familiar enough with Cairngorm to know about both the Shelter Stone refuge, and the snow holes along Feith Buidhe.'

Watching now as the girl engaged with the forensic professionals regarding an identikit image of the man they were looking for, Rhona decided that bringing Annieska with her had been a smart move and by Olsen's expression he agreed with her.

His silent yet intense manner as he'd listened to Annieska

give detailed descriptions of her encounters with their suspect had led Rhona to suspect that Olsen knew or thought he knew who the girl was describing.

After she'd settled on a photofit, Olsen asked if Annieska would be willing to view some CCTV footage. Rhona, unaware of what was to come, was surprised to see the car park at the Day Lodge come on the large screen at the end of the table. The images were grainy with an occasional snow flurry making things even more difficult. To Rhona it just looked like a mass of indistinguishable figures in ski gear.

But not, apparently, to Annieska.

'Wait, there,' she suddenly announced. 'Behind that car.'

Rhona had no inkling how Annieska could tell one suited figure from another, let alone know that this was the man who'd engaged her in conversation in Macdui's. With his head and face only partially in sight and further obscured by a snow flurry, it didn't seem possible. But when asked by Olsen if she was sure, Annieska declared she was.

Olsen nodded his support. 'Now, I'd like you to take a look at some photographs I have and see if you can recognize anyone in them as possibly being the same man.'

When Olsen gave the go-ahead, the first image appeared. This wasn't CCTV footage but what looked like a press photograph. Two men stood on a set of steps of perhaps a public building or set of offices, their faces towards the camera, shaking hands. Rhona didn't recognize either of them or the setting.

Annieska shook her head, almost apologetically.

The next photo appeared. In this the taller of the two men appeared again, this time with an attractive well-dressed woman on his arm, outside what Rhona took to be a luxury hotel. Judging by the sunshine and nearby palm tree, it looked more Mediterranean than Nordic.

Annieska shook her head again in disappointment, then a light seemed to go on and she shouted 'wait' just as Olsen made a move to change it.

'There's someone else in the picture,' she said. 'Look, there.' She pointed at the far right of the screen.

Rhona couldn't see who she referred to at first, then Annieska said, 'The reflection in the glass door.'

Despite her best efforts, Rhona still wouldn't have noted this if it hadn't been pointed out to her.

'He's looking the other way, so I can't see his face,' Annieska said, obviously irritated by this.

Olsen moved to the next image.

'There,' Annieska's voice rose in her excitement. 'He's off to the right again, on the edge of the picture.'

The same male stood in his handshake pose, this time with a third man. Hovering on his right was the figure Annieska referred to.

She sat back in the chair. 'That's him,' she said. 'That's the man in Macdui's.'

Rhona looked to Olsen for his reaction, to find a half-smile playing his lips.

'You're certain?' he asked.

Annieska seemed puzzled by the question. 'One hundred per cent sure. I never forget a face.'

She, Roy and Olsen sat in the conference room together. Someone had delivered coffee and, Rhona was glad to see, some chocolate biscuits. She helped herself to one.

'So,' Roy asked the question both he and Rhona wanted answered. 'Who is he?'

'The man in all the photographs is Tor Hagen, a Norwegian oil businessman and shipping magnate. The man Annieska identified is I think part of his entourage, in what capacity I don't know, although he does appear to be camera shy.'

'A bodyguard?' Rhona suggested.

'Could be.'

'And he's the guy you believe was on that plane?'

'We've yet to prove it forensically or otherwise, but yes, I think it is,' Olsen said.

'So the plane that came down on Loch A'an, plus the killer, are linked in some way with this businessman Hagen?'

'I don't know, and believe me, if we make the slightest move towards linking them publically we'll never get to the truth,' Olsen said with conviction. 'Hagen is one of Stavanger's foremost sons. A favourite with police, politicians and the people. Unblemished. Untouchable.'

'Jesus Christ!' Roy said.

'Not quite, but close enough,' Olsen said with a small laugh.

'Have you told Roy about what we discussed?' Rhona said.

Olsen glanced at Roy Hunter. 'I've shared what's necessary and expedient for his part in all of this.'

'So what happens next?' Rhona said.

61

McNab felt the mobile vibrate against his chest again. This time he decided it was better to answer. Expecting Ellie, he found Chrissy instead.

He only managed her name and a 'Hi' before Chrissy interrupted him with a deluge of Glasgow vernacular which established how seriously pissed off she was at him.

Join the club, McNab thought, but didn't say.

When she demanded to know where he was, McNab told her home, although that wasn't strictly true. He was currently awaiting the arrival of a taxi, which he'd called to take him there.

'I'm coming over,' Chrissy informed him. 'There's things we have to talk about.'

There seemed little point in arguing. Chrissy rarely changed her mind when on a crusade, especially one that involved him.

McNab rang off as the taxi approached, aware it would be a good idea if he got there before she did, dumped the dead whisky bottle and opened a window or two.

Chrissy McInsh had a face perfect for poker. McNab knew that well, having played against her on a number of occasions. Inscrutable, unreadable, impenetrable when required.

LIN ANDERSON

In this instance, none of those qualities were what she chose to exhibit.

This was no game, poker or otherwise, her expression said.

She'd found the empty whisky bottle with ease. Much like the dumb killer who deposits the murder weapon in the bin nearest to the scene of crime, McNab, although a detective who should know better, had simply hidden his bottle in plain sight . . . in the kitchen bin.

'How much of this?' she'd demanded, waving the empty litre bottle in his face.

'Enough to feel pretty good,' he admitted.

In his former drinking days, he would have berated Chrissy for what he would have called 'nebbing' at him. This time McNab didn't. The pleasure of being drunk hadn't lasted as long as the sick aftermath.

'I've ordered pizza,' she told him. 'One each. You can pay when it arrives.'

She now proceeded to set up the coffee machine. For a brief moment, McNab decided he quite liked being bossed around by a woman, but only if it involved food, drink and sex . . . although the latter with Chrissy had never been an issue.

Unlike just about every other female he'd worked alongside.

McNab pondered briefly why that had been the case, then realized he knew. Chrissy had always treated him like one of her wayward brothers (when she was pissed off at him), or like her favourite sibling, the older Patrick (when she thought McNab was doing the right thing).

And Patrick, McNab remembered, was gay.

*

They were seated on the couch, pizzas consumed, and McNab had had a few refills of coffee, so was now equipped to face Chrissy's interrogation, which he knew by the look she threw him was about to begin.

'I went to the hospital,' she said. 'Mary Stevenson's out of surgery. She's critical, but stable.'

McNab nodded.

'You knew?' She sounded surprised.

'I've seen Davey.' McNab didn't elaborate.

Chrissy appeared about to tell him something else, but in this instance, was having difficulty. Eventually she said, 'The news on Margaret isn't so good. It could happen any time within the next twenty-four hours.'

So that was it. Shit. McNab felt a stab of guilt. In the midst of everything that was going on, he'd completely forgotten the boss.

'What do we do?' he said.

Chrissy shook her head. 'Our jobs. That's what Bill would say, anyway.' She paused. 'He asked after you.'

I might forget the boss, but the boss never forgets me, he thought, conscience-stricken.

'And you told him, what?'

'That you were on the case, as usual.' Chrissy eyed him. 'Why aren't you in Aberdeen?'

'I had stuff to do here.'

'Like getting pissed?'

McNab side-swerved that cutting remark. 'Following a lead to Brodie.' He decided that was all he was prepared to say.

'Rhona's in Aberdeen with Inspector Olsen,' Chrissy told him. 'A girl working at Macdui's in Aviemore ID'd Isla Crawford's possible abductor. He's Norwegian.'

A faint memory of his drunken phone call with Rhona came surging back. McNab decided it best to come clean about what he didn't know, or at least couldn't remember about that call.

From Chrissy's reaction, he'd made the right choice. She filled in the rest for him. 'The grave Rhona excavated turned out to be for illegally killed birds of prey, not Isla.' She then added a story of an aircraft taking off from an airstrip close to where the climbers' van had been dumped, which may have taken both Isla and her abductor away.

'There's an airfield next to Cairngorm?' McNab said, bemused.

The Cairngorm crime scenes had been Rhona's responsibility. Despite what Chrissy was saying, McNab couldn't forge a link between what had gone down on that mountaintop and what he was focused on here.

Chrissy was watching him and probably, McNab suspected, reading his thoughts.

'Bill told you to help Inspector Olsen,' she reminded him. 'And Olsen wants you in Aberdeen.'

62

Olsen longed for the familiarity of his own space, both at the Commissariat and in his flat.

He also yearned for his morning walk via Lagård Gravlund and his conversations with his dead wife. His sudden and unexpected reference to Marita as dead, even internally, brought him up short. Until now, the words 'Marita' and 'dead' had rarely shared the same space in his brain.

He could almost hear his wife's chuckle in response.

I knew you would get there eventually, Alvis.

'If that were true,' he answered the imagined comment, 'I wouldn't be hearing you now, would I?'

This time, as though to prove her point, his wife didn't respond and the sudden emptiness of the hotel bedroom drove Olsen to locate the remote and switch on the television. As the newsreader filled the silence, Olsen went to shower.

He found standing under the gushing water a good place in which to think. For some reason things seemed clearer, and sudden insights more frequent.

And, he believed, despite drawbacks, the bits of this particular puzzle were gradually coming together. Although for some time it *had* felt like one of those giant jigsaws that boasted a thousand pieces, all of which looked exactly the same colour.

A pictorial representation of this investigation, Olsen realized, would be either a blanket of snow or, alternatively, the monotone surface of a grey North Sea.

But all snow isn't the same.

Norwegians had many different words to describe snow, though not as many as the Scots, who, Marita had informed him, had over four hundred words for snow logged in the *Scots Thesaurus*. As for the expanse that was the North Sea, fishermen and ships' captains wouldn't agree to its uniformity either.

All you required was a landmark to give it perspective.

And Olsen believed he now had that perspective.

Dressed again, he checked his laptop, but there was no word from Harald as yet. From the fourth-floor window Olsen watched as a Scandinavian Airlines plane took off from the nearby Dyce airport runway and wished he was on it and heading for home.

Soon.

He poured a whisky from the bottle he'd purchased before heading for the hotel. The prices in the Scottish shops always surprised him, used as he was to Norway's higher cost of living. The Scots themselves complained bitterly that they could buy their national drink cheaper anywhere in the world than at home.

Except of course in Norway.

The shock price of alcohol for itinerant North Sea oil workers and visitors to Norway was alleviated by the airport shops offering special cut-price deals on arrival. Norwegian nationals also took advantage of this, using what they bought for *forspil*, the Norwegian equivalent of a pre-drinks party before a night on the town where the bigger prices had to be paid.

He recalled that the last time he'd brought a bottle to his hotel room, Dr MacLeod had been with him. Olsen stopped himself from wandering down that particular memory lane and tried to focus instead on what was likely to happen next.

Depending on the word from Harald, the investigation might shift to Stavanger. Should that happen, his plan had been to ask DS McNab to accompany him together with Dr MacLeod, who would then work with Harald on the forensic side, as she'd done before.

The ship they sought, the *Solstice*, was registered under the Norwegian flag. Which is what Harald had revealed in his phone call. That made their move on it so much easier. Had it been registered under the flag of a different country, then getting permission from that country to board could have proved both difficult and time-consuming. What they believed went on there involved the physical and sexual exploitation of refugee children.

It appeared that the Tor Hagen parent company had been so confident of their owner's prestige and position that he, and they, at no time considered the company or its ultimate owner would be challenged. After all, should what was happening on that ship be revealed, how many more people in positions of power might be exposed? The safety net offered to those who were partaking in the ship's offerings seemed impregnable.

Alvis recalled Marita's reaction when he'd initially revealed his suspicions that just such a ship existed, and its purpose. He had no idea then that she was in the first weeks of an insecure pregnancy, or of what that would cost her. What he did register was that his suspicions were enough for her backing. She believed in him. If his dogged determination to expose this resulted in the end of his career, then so be it.

'So be it!' Alvis repeated out loud this time.

Up to this point, he'd been careful not to challenge the order of things, keeping everything under the radar. The interview with Petter Lund on Scottish soil had changed all of that. Lund's father wasn't at the top of the tree, but he had connections there and the diplomatic immunity being claimed for his son's actions was already causing a stir.

Once word got out regarding the true focus of Olsen's investigation, then the powerful would move, if not to close the investigation down, then at least to neutralize it.

But if we're right about the ship?

It was a gamble, but one he and his fellow officers were prepared to take.

With this thought, Olsen's mind shifted to DS McNab. According to a recent conversation with Rhona, he'd learned that Chrissy had made contact with the detective in Glasgow and had reminded him that he was wanted in Aberdeen.

Yet he's neither turned up here, nor been in touch, with either Rhona or myself. A fact that was beginning to give Olsen some cause for concern. He and the Scottish detective had got off to a shaky start, but they both had the same objective. That had been clear in the interview with Lund, although it hadn't been easy for McNab to take the back seat in what he considered his own investigation.

Olsen recalled McNab's struggle to keep his mouth shut at various moments in the proceedings. In particular during the replaying of the video of Lund and Amena, when McNab had had an obvious desire to punch the supercilious and despicable Lund in the face.

McNab, Olsen decided, reminded him of a younger version of himself.

The Scottish detective could be seduced by drink and self-doubt, but the brain that wrestled with those problems was also capable of powerful leaps of intuition, as Olsen's study of McNab's most recent cases had shown. The detective's tendency to play the maverick, according to the evidence, apparently got results. Something his superiors, apart from DI Wilson, found threatening.

The difference between McNab and myself . . . by his age I'd met Marita and she'd become the humanity that anchored me.

Olsen revisited the conversation in the jazz club on Ashton Lane where both Rhona and Chrissy had been strong in their championing of McNab. As far as Olsen was aware, neither women were romantically connected to the detective, although it seemed to him that McNab was strongly drawn to Rhona.

Yet both women had spoken highly of him, despite his faults.

In that, Olsen decided, *McNab was a lucky man.*

Dressing after his shower, Olsen studiously avoided looking at his back, although Chrissy's desire to discover whether McNab had got himself a tattoo had reminded Olsen of his own sortie into the world of inking. Seventeen years old, with a love of motorbikes that had been all-consuming, and fired by more than just speed, he'd had his own back inked.

Olsen could still picture the youth that he'd been back then, especially when he viewed the skull and crossbones tattoo. What he couldn't remember, or even imagine, was what had been going on in his head at that age.

Many years later when he'd met Marita, he'd considered

having the tattoo removed. She'd encouraged him to leave it there.

We are what we are, because of our past. 'Besides,' she used to say with a smile, 'I like it. It makes you look like a bad-ass.'

The chance of a woman other than Marita viewing the tattoo hadn't occurred until the previous night in Aviemore, although Olsen had chosen to keep his top half covered. He now considered why he'd done that, and came to the conclusion that exposing the tattoo to Rhona would have compounded his betrayal of his wife.

Foolish man, came Marita's response. *Or is her imagined inner voice just my way of assuaging my guilt?*

He'd turned up the sound on his laptop to be sure he would hear the arrival of any communication from Harald. The ping that now resounded brought Olsen out of his remorseful reverie to read the message, which was simple.

We've found the *Solstice*. Call me.

63

McNab lay on the bed in the darkness, his mobile alongside. Davey had indicated the message would come before midnight and it was already past that now.

He decided he would give *pal* Davey fifteen more minutes, then make his move regardless, relying on the information Ollie had retrieved from the laptop.

Either way, I'll reach my prey.

In the end it was the landline that rang out. Something McNab hadn't expected, and he hesitated before going for the receiver. When he did pick up, he was met by silence, then a click as the connection was cut.

At the same time, his mobile rang out briefly with Davey's name on the screen. The signal they'd agreed on.

McNab went swiftly to the window and, keeping out of sight, checked the street below, looking for Davey's vehicle. The guy was so shit-scared that whatever plan they'd hatched together could likely go belly up.

Both sides of the street were lined with parked cars, but there was no sign of Davey, frightened or otherwise.

Then another idea occurred, one that was worse than Davey simply getting the jitters.

If the landline call wasn't the usual robot communication, then maybe someone was checking whether he was at home. Which might mean that his shit-scared mate could well have sold him out. McNab had a fleeting image of Davey with Brodie's gun pointed at his head and acknowledged he would cave in, especially if the threat involved Mary.

Even as his mind raced with these thoughts, McNab's body was also on the move. If he was wrong then it didn't matter. If he was right . . .

Opening the door on to the landing, he listened. No one had pressed the buzzer, but that didn't mean someone hadn't entered the close. His fellow occupants had a habit of leaving the latch off, so that their late-night pizza deliveries didn't piss off the sleeping neighbours.

McNab eased himself out and clicked his own door shut behind him. Now came decision time. Did he go up or down? A sound from below of feet being placed carefully on the stone stairs made up his mind for him.

He was one level from the top of the building, and that's where he now headed. Reaching the upper landing, he grabbed the hook that released the access door to the flat roof of the tenement block, and pulled down the short set of metal steps that would take him up there.

Once above, he would be exposed, but able to use the roof like a highway to the adjacent building, and descend that way.

If I'm wrong about this, then I've taken a stroll along the rooftops. If I'm right, then I might live a little longer.

That was the positive way of looking at it. The negative was that once up there he was completely exposed to whoever should choose to follow.

McNab began to make his way gingerly along the dark rooftop, the only light coming from the cupolas that marked the top of the internal lighted stairways. Reaching the second of these, he disturbed a resident seagull that rose with a shriek, shitting its fear, or annoyance, in a splattered trail that just missed him.

Two blocks on, McNab decided enough was enough. He lay flat on the roof and edged his way towards the short balustrade that formed the edge. Below was the street. Not his street but the cul de sac that ran alongside. Brodie was known to make use of cars that were built like tanks. No self-respecting drug dealer would have it otherwise.

There had been nothing like that parked on his street. What about here?

And there you are.

Sitting under a street lamp, the engine turning over, was the vehicle he recognized from Davey's garage, its changed plates in place.

The sight of it made McNab's skin crawl. There was no way Davey, on his own, would have chosen to turn up here in that vehicle, which suggested McNab's worst-case scenario was probably the right one. Even as he thought this, McNab heard the undeniable creak as a trapdoor to the roof was opened, then a torch spread its wide beam like a lighthouse across the roof.

Nowhere to run. Nowhere to hide.

If whoever was looking for him was armed, which he had to assume they would be, then *I'm not the disturbed seagull that could quickly fly away, but a fucking sitting duck.*

Keeping low, McNab went for the next cupola and hopefully the next set of stairs. As he did so, he heard a thump and accompanying curse as the flashlight departed his follower's hands and met the deck. The rolling light came to an abrupt halt, with the beam shining right at McNab as he attacked the neighbouring trapdoor.

If it was bolted below, he was fucked.

McNab put all his weight on it and felt it give. He was waiting for the pop of a gun as the open door now framed him in light, but nothing came. With no extended ladder, he had no choice but to dreep down, a skill he'd learned in the back courts as a boy.

McNab hit the stone landing with a thump that knocked the breath from him. Dragging himself up by the banister, he made his way shakily down the stairs.

At the bottom, he found the front door latched shut. There was no way he could discover what awaited him outside without opening it. As he reached for the handle, he heard his pursuer hit the upper landing, sounding as winded as he'd been.

Which means I have a chance. Albeit a small one.

McNab flung open the door and was faced by the black four-by-four awaiting his arrival, Davey's face at the driver's window.

'Quick, get in,' he shouted, revving the engine.

McNab, glancing up the street to see two more blokes headed his way, decided to chance it. As he moved towards the vehicle, the passenger door was thrown back, slamming his chest, as something even harder met his skull.

Then it was all over.

64

The knock was soft but audible, especially since Rhona had been anticipating it. She rose and went to answer. Olsen's expression when she opened the door suggested that they were to be on the move and soon.

'The Norwegian Coastguard have identified what they believe may be the ship we're looking for. We'll catch the early flight to Stavanger scheduled to leave shortly, meet up with my team there and take a helicopter ride out to the ship.'

'How long do we have?'

'Can you be ready in ten minutes?'

'Of course. Have you heard anything from McNab?' Rhona said, hoping that he had at least got in touch with Olsen.

Olsen shook his head, confirming that despite Chrissy's best efforts, McNab was likely still in Glasgow. Rhona fought back a desire to express how annoyed she was by that and instead told Olsen she'd meet him shortly in the lobby.

Now that she knew she was definitely on the move, Rhona sent a quick text to Sean and told him to take Tom to his flat as she wasn't sure when she'd be back in Glasgow. Reading the message, Rhona wondered if her choice of words sounded a bit churlish, but sent it anyway. There would be time enough to explain to Sean when this was all over.

'The ship is flying a Norwegian flag so we don't have to seek the authority to board, which saves time. If the owners have sufficient warning then I suspect whatever's happening on that ship will be well hidden by the time we get there. A bit like the 3.2 tons of pure cocaine your border force found in the Turkish tug a hundred miles off Aberdeen, buried so deep in the hold it took a forensic team two days to unearth it.'

Rhona was aware of the incident Olsen referred to. 'But they can't hide people like that?' she said.

Olsen looked at her candidly. 'What would you do with such a cargo, if you learned in advance that you were likely to be boarded?'

Olsen's response chilled Rhona to the bone.

'That's why our move on the ship has to be kept as low-key as possible,' he said, seeing her distress. 'Once she's under our control,' Olsen continued, 'we'll take her into Stavanger harbour and examine her properly.'

Reaching the car, Olsen put their bags in the boot and held open the passenger door for Rhona to get in, just as they felt the first drops of rain promised by a heavy grey sky.

'The weather won't be on our side out there,' Olsen admitted as he started up the engine.

'It wasn't on Cairngorm either,' she reminded him.

The rain came on in earnest as they exited the car park and Olsen flipped the wipers to fast mode. Rhona found herself relieved that it wasn't snow, although just as on Cairngorm, it would be the strength of the wind that would likely cause the most difficulty.

The lights of Aberdeen were visible in the near distance and, beyond the city to the east, Rhona registered the vast grey expanse that was the North Sea. Those who worked out there were used to being shuttled back and forth to the numerous rigs and attendant oil vessels by helicopter in all weathers. So she and Olsen weren't the only ones headed out from the cluster of hotels next to the airport, which supplied overnight accommodation for itinerant oil personnel. A couple of minibuses packed with men accompanied them en route, peeling off on entry to the airport, bound for the area where the resident helicopter companies operated from.

'Stavanger's about 300 miles east from Aberdeen harbour. A bit far for a standard chopper,' Olsen explained. 'The plane'll have us there in forty-five minutes.'

The aircraft having already boarded, they were swiftly ushered through ticket control, down the metal staircase and, buffeted by a rising wind, led across the tarmac to board the small plane. Their entrance caused some interest from the twenty or so passengers, wondering no doubt the reason for their late arrival and the special dispensation they seemed to have been given. Swiftly seated by the air steward and belted in, minutes later they were airborne.

Rhona watched as the lights that signified land were left behind, and the dark choppy mass of water began to dominate the view from the small window.

Here we go, she said silently, *but where the hell's McNab?*

65

His eyes, although clenched shut, were struggling to cope with the glaring spotlight that beat down on his face. To open them, he knew, would subject him to more pain.

Instead, McNab attempted to turn his head from the unremitting glare, which proved to be impossible. Whatever had been used to anchor his head in this position merely tightened its grip across his forehead.

Eyes still closed, he tried to take stock. He was seated, albeit on the floor. He could feel his outstretched legs, but couldn't move his feet, which were obviously tied together. His hands, twisted behind him, were attached to a pipe, which was hot. Any movement which took his bare skin closer resulted in what felt like a surface burn.

The surrounding temperature too was stifling, and his face dripped sweat as his body tried to regulate itself. Preparing himself, he slowly opened his eyes a crack. The light was red and hot and positioned to play on his face, but in between blinks, McNab saw enough to suggest that he was in what looked like a cellar.

His memory of what had happened to land him here was sketchy and McNab had no idea how long he'd been unconscious. One thing he *was* certain about: he hadn't been shot this time. There was no scent of fresh blood and no pain

radiating from anywhere other than his bonds, his eyes and
. . . the back of his head.

So that's where they got me.

McNab remembered it all with sudden clarity. The four-
by-four had been there right in front of him with Davey
behind the wheel. Davey had shouted that he'd tried to call
and warn him and that he should get in and quick.

And I believed the bastard.

The hot light that played over his face suddenly went out,
plunging wherever he was into darkness. The relief that he
was no longer being cooked morphed into trepidation about
what that change in his surroundings might mean.

He didn't have long to wait.

With a deep rumbling sound, an engine in his vicinity
fired into life and his prison began to vibrate, then move.

He wasn't in a cellar, McNab acknowledged with a mix of
anxiety and horror. He was, he suspected, in the bowels of
a boat.

How the fuck had he got here?

McNab wasn't a fan of travelling by boat. Miles of open
water was as uncomfortable for him as open countryside,
only made worse by what might lie beneath the surface.
Who knew what lurked down there in the depths?

He licked his dehydrated lips, and subliminally recalled a
few words of poetry forced on him at school – 'Water, water,
everywhere, nor any drop to drink' – which didn't help with
his desire for exactly that, a drink.

McNab drew his mind away from the thought of cold
clear fresh water, past the even more attractive image of a
full whisky bottle, and tried to plan his bid for freedom,
from the bloody hot pipe at least.

*

In the darkened interlude since the engine had started up, he'd succeeded in freeing his head from the rope binding by a constant turning motion, although his brow now smarted like hell to match the burns his hands were registering every time he tried a similar manoeuvre near the hot pipe. As for his feet. No chance.

He wet his lips again with what little saliva he had left, and almost longed for the return of the streams of sweat which had earlier run down his face, some of which had trickled into his parched mouth.

It was important that he stay alert – and angry, he acknowledged. Anger had kept him alive in more difficult circumstances than this, but he preferred to have his opponent in front of him so that he might direct his hate in looks and verbal abuse.

Muttering obscenities about Davey wasn't doing the trick, and he had a poor recall of Brodie's face and had never heard his voice, so not much mileage there.

As though on cue, a metal door clanged open and someone stepped into the room. The smell until then had consisted of his own sweating body coupled with diesel and salty dampness. All that changed as a strong whiff of men's cologne invaded the darkness.

The light from the corridor merely outlined the figure in the doorway, so McNab couldn't see the face, but the height and build didn't suggest Davey. Nor did the cologne. He waited for a voice, but got none.

The figure stepped forward, and McNab knew he was being studied intently, although how much of him was clearly visible he wasn't sure. His visitor, of course, had the advantage of the light behind him. Then there was a click, which made McNab jump, imagining as he did that a gun was being cocked in his direction. But the sound was only accompanied by a beam of light. The torch beam swept over his face, then ran down his body, descending his legs to his feet.

McNab decided that he'd kept silent for long enough.

'I'm a detective with a Police Scotland Major Investigation Team. Assaulting and kidnapping a police officer is a very serious offence,' he offered.

When there was no response to this, McNab continued, 'I'm looking for Neil Brodie on charges of cocaine and people smuggling.'

A small, dry and pitying laugh greeted his announcement.

McNab, pissed off now with the official approach, shouted, 'Whoever the fuck you are, untie me.'

There was a moment's silence, then the man turned on his heel and exited, pulling the door closed with a bang behind him.

'Fuck off, then!' McNab shouted to the restored darkness.

So they weren't interested in anything he had to say. Why then had they plucked him from the streets of Glasgow and deposited him on a boat? McNab took a moment to wonder where exactly he'd joined this boat. The nearest water to where they'd picked him up was of course the Firth of Clyde, Britain's largest and deepest stretch of coastal water. But judging by the pitch and yaw his stomach was currently enduring, he was no longer in sheltered water but on an open sea.

If he was right about Brodie's cocaine supply coming in somewhere on the west coast of Scotland, then they could be heading up there now. *But if Olsen's right, then I'm more likely somewhere off Aberdeen.*

McNab found he didn't like either scenario. Added to the fact that he had no idea why they would snatch him at all, and increase the heat on themselves, if not as pay-back. Brodie, he knew, was a vindictive bastard, and McNab had taken his cocaine and, for a short time at least, some of his women.

He tried to recall the description of the man who'd brought Amena to the clusterfuck in the Delta Club. Could cologne guy have been him? Maybe he'd chosen not to speak because his accent would have given him away.

Or maybe he just came to gloat in silence?

Another thought occurred. Could Amena be here on the boat as well? And if so, then where were they taking her, and him?

At that moment, the bow of the boat, which had been rising and falling with ever greater rapidity, suddenly lurched upwards, as though climbing an oncoming wave. This resulted in McNab being pulled abruptly downhill away from the pipe, before being thrust back towards it as the bow suddenly dropped.

McNab smothered a cry as he met the metal again, its heat searing through the back of his jacket.

The shock this created made him even more determined to get free, even if it did mean scalding his hands further in the process.

As the boat started to climb a second time, McNab began to tug desperately at his right hand, sensing it was the looser of the two.

66

'Politiinspektør Jonas Silvertsen, Organized Crime, Oskar Gerhard, Child Sexual Abuse, and of course Harald Hjerngaard, Forensics, who you already know.'

Rhona shook hands with all three police inspectors in turn, after which Harald asked what had happened to Detective Sergeant McNab, who they'd also expected. Rhona realized at this point that Olsen had indeed held out a hope that McNab would eventually show himself and that the empty seat next to her on the plane had been for him.

'Sergeant McNab seems to be missing in action,' Olsen said, his tone registering concern rather than annoyance at this. 'However, we've been promised full cooperation from Police Scotland, should we need to venture into Scottish waters.'

They were in a private room at Sola airport awaiting the departure of their chopper. The picture window overlooked a rain-soaked and windy runway. The landing of their standard SAS flight earlier had been a little shaky. Winds on the flight over had seen them strapped in for the entire journey, plus the abandonment of the service trolley, although the captain had assured those new to the Aberdeen–Stavanger flight that this wasn't an unusual occurrence when crossing the North Sea in January.

A sleety shower had accompanied their take-off from

Aberdeen, and the same conditions had met them on landing at Sola, reinforcing Olsen's declaration that despite a distance of 300 miles, the two cities shared the same weather.

Once seated, there had been little chat between them on the way across, with Olsen apparently deep in thought. Rhona had registered no noticeable change in their relationship since the night they'd slept together, although he had intimated that when the investigation was over he would like to tell her about the circumstances that surrounded his wife's death, should she wish to know.

Rhona had accepted this, suspecting that by talking to someone about it, Olsen might begin to forgive himself for whatever part he thought he'd played.

After the introductions and a rundown on what was planned, Harald had encouraged her to eat something from the display of open sandwiches and coffee.

'It might be all you get for some time.'

Noting her reticence, he checked whether she might be inclined to sea sickness. 'If so –' he produced a strip of tablets from his pocket – 'I have a fast-acting solution to a helicopter ride.'

Rhona thanked him. 'I was okay hovering over Cairngorm in a blizzard. I'm not so sure about bobbing around in a boat on the North Sea, though.'

He nodded. 'Well, don't hesitate to ask.'

They helped themselves to a breakfast plate and took a table near the window.

'How much has Alvis told you?' Harald said as they settled down to eat.

'Not the whole story, I'm sure.'

'Did he mention the refugee kids he found lying frozen on the Russian border?'

Rhona indicated he hadn't.

'Just one of the horrors he's been unearthing. It's been a long, slow, laborious business and we went down a lot of blind alleys before we got this far.' Harald met her eye. 'Of course we could be wrong. There might be nothing when we get out to the *Solstice*, especially if they've got wind of our interest.'

That had been Rhona's concern as well.

'We had hoped DS McNab's pursuit of the Glasgow connection would have confirmed our suspicions of the link between the *Solstice* and the people smuggling.' He waited for Rhona's response.

'McNab tends to go his own way.' She hesitated.

Harald was reading her expression. 'You're worried he might be in trouble?'

'McNab has a reputation for going AWOL. He worked undercover for a while. He still has the habit.'

They were interrupted by a call from Olsen indicating that they'd been given permission to board.

'We're in the hands of the Norwegian Coastguard now,' Harald told her.

Rhona found his declaration strangely comforting.

Climbing aboard, she experienced a similar sensation to that morning in Aviemore when she'd joined CMR at the converted church to look for the downed aircraft on Loch A'an, which they'd later discovered had originated from this airport.

The circle's closing. Let's hope we have those we want inside.

The lift from the tarmac was smooth and only indicated by noise and the image that swept by the window. Rhona checked on Olsen, whose handsome face exhibited everything she felt herself at that moment. Anticipation, excitement, determination and trepidation. If Olsen was right, and a vessel owned and operated by one of Norway's most respected citizens was implicated in what was an international crime, then the fallout would be considerable. If Olsen was wrong, the other officers involved might survive, but surely the kickback from the investigation would harm or even end his career.

She glanced over at Olsen again. Sensing her gaze, he returned it, giving her a small, almost apologetic smile.

He's a brave man, Rhona thought as her eyes roamed around the assembled team. *And he's brought them with him. Into hell or damnation.*

67

Isla woke as the boat began to pitch. Grabbing the side of the bunk to stop herself falling out, she waited for the rise to end and the fall to follow.

She was comfortable at sea even in poor weather, having sailed since an early age. Gavin on the other hand could never be persuaded to go out on the water with her. Mountains hadn't fazed him, but this . . .

You wouldn't like this, would you?

She imagined she could hear Gavin's exaggerated groan as the vessel hit a wall of water with a thud, followed by a shudder as the hull attempted to absorb the wave's energy. Isla could feel the vibration travel from the side of the bunk through her hands.

Most of the time she'd sailed on the west coast of Scotland where you could always find shelter from a storm in one of the myriad sea lochs and inlets. This was no sailing boat, and she wasn't in sheltered waters, which suggested they were in the wildness of the North Sea.

The first time she'd opened her eyes, she'd had no idea where she was, nor how she'd got there. Then gradually bits of what had happened had come surging back. A man waiting by the van in the hotel car park, telling her Kyle had sent him. He would be happy to drive the vehicle south for her. He'd been courteous and kind, asking after her injured ankle. She'd been delighted that he wanted to help, even suggesting if he could manage to go the following day, then she'd come with him as a passenger.

Then I saw it.

A long half-healed scratch mark on his cheek, which made Isla think of another scratch on another face. Another similar pair of ice-blue eyes caught in the light from her head torch.

'It's you,' she'd stupidly said.

His retribution had been swift, doing no doubt what he'd planned all along.

Her hand moved instinctively to her head, feeling the bloody scab where he'd hit her with something metal from the climbing box. With the back doors of the van already open, locating a weapon had been easy, the attack over in seconds, and she'd been unable to do anything about it.

He must have got me inside the van and away from Aviemore in minutes.

Only snatches of the journey that had followed remained with her, suggesting he may have drugged her in some way. Anything she did recall was in slow motion or kaleidoscopic, much like she'd experienced in her hypothermic delusion in the ice cave on Cairngorm.

Though she did recall a woman's face inhabiting her strange dreams. It was the face of the woman who'd rescued her from the cave, who'd eased her pain and kept her alive. Who'd cajoled her into talking when she wanted to sleep. The woman, Rhona, who'd sat by her side in Raigmore Hospital.

Where I was safe.

Tears filled her eyes and Isla brushed them away in annoyance. Crying would get her nowhere.

Better to understand why the Iceman had gone to the

trouble of bringing her this far, when it would have been so much simpler to kill her and dispose of her back at the airfield.

He could have thrown me in the river. Or buried me in the woods.

But he'd chosen not to, because, Isla suspected, he wanted to punish her for not dying that night on the mountain. *And maybe alive, I'm worth something. Here at least.*

She'd studiously avoided facing the cameras Isla knew were watching her. Her initial horror that she was being spied on was compounded by her nakedness. Even asleep she wasn't awarded any privacy. She was certain at least one night had passed, although darkness had never descended in the cabin or in the tiny shower and toilet room that adjoined it. She suspected her hobbling visits there were also being recorded, but couldn't avoid going.

Then there were the visitors.

Isla squashed that memory and focused on her anger. Anger was keeping her functioning in spite of everything that had happened. Anger and the desire to kill the man who'd brought her here. Isla had never thought herself capable of such rage or a thirst for revenge. Her persecutor, she now accepted, had killed Gavin and her friends. Blotted out their existence without a second thought, just as he'd pushed her off that mountainside.

He made a mistake in not killing me when he got another chance, she told herself. *A big mistake.*

Isla lay back down. She'd fought a mountain and survived. She would survive this, and have her revenge. She told Gavin what she planned to do, and listened as he praised and encouraged her. *You get him. For Lucy and Malcolm. And for me.*

ANDERSON

The red light peered down and the camera whirred, capturing her every movement for whatever sad bastard sought pleasure from viewing the incarceration and subjugation of a woman.

Isla gave the watchful eye the finger of defiance.

318

68

As she'd crossed the tarmac, Rhona had felt her mobile vibrate beneath her suit, heralding the arrival of a text. There had been no time to view it before boarding the helicopter and getting buckled in. The noise on take-off had been deafening, the rush of adrenaline to her heart and brain just as powerful, as the big rotating blades, seemingly defying gravity, pulled them up and into the sky. Her immediate thought then had been of their mission as she and Olsen had exchanged looks. Now Rhona reached for her mobile to check the origins of the incoming text, although her hopes that McNab's name might be on the screen were quickly dashed. Still, the text – which she noted had come from Ollie, McNab's declared IT genius collaborator – might just contain some knowledge of McNab's whereabouts.

Rhona scanned the message, which began with Ollie's concern that McNab might be 'off the radar' and that it could have something to do with a laptop and mobile he'd given to Ollie to examine.

Rhona immediately sensed that Ollie was a lot more worried about McNab than his cautious words suggested. And if Ollie was worried, so was she.

She read on.

I retrieved a mobile number which McNab was certain would lead him to Neil Brodie. I haven't seen DS McNab since.

Then followed the worry that if Ollie told the station about the laptop, which had contained illegal images involving child pornography, McNab would be in trouble.

Suddenly a bigger story around McNab's recent return to the world of his pal Davey Stevenson was emerging. If, as well as Mary's hit-and-run, McNab thought Davey was involved in child pornography via Brodie, *no wonder he'd gone into meltdown.*

'Is something wrong?' Harald said.

It wasn't the time or place to try to explain. 'Later,' Rhona promised.

Sola airport being situated on the coast, south-west of the Stavanger inlet Gandsfjorden, the NH-90 had already departed the landmass. According to Harald's briefing, the NH-90 was set to replace the British-built Sea King for SAR operations.

'They normally operate out of Bardufoss *flystasjon*, further north, in Tromsø county,' Harald explained. 'But since we might be required to land on a moving ship in high seas, the 90's the better vehicle to travel in.'

Harald showed her a palmtop on which their position was recorded with the backdrop of the coastline marked by coloured dots. 'The Automatic Identification System on ships exchanges data with other nearby ships, AIS base stations and satellites,' he explained. 'The dots near the coast are Norwegian trawlers or fishing boats. The ship we're heading for is here.'

He drew the screen image in, so Rhona could see further west. 'The *Solstice* is perfectly legit. One of the smaller RAS, replenishment at sea, vessels, she's a station for diesel oil, aviation fuel and fresh water. It's what's been docking with her that raised Alvis' suspicions.' He continued, 'Smaller craft, from northern Norway, close to our border with Russia, from Aberdeen and surrounding ports, and even more significantly, North Africa and Turkey.'

'They're bringing refugee children?'

'And drugs. We know there's a big market in both. Porn and drugs tend to go hand in hand. And then there's the other lucrative use for the refugees who can't pay their way with the traffickers . . .'

He tailed off, although Rhona knew what he referred to.

'As a support vessel, the *Solstice* has a hospital with around twenty beds, an operating theatre and a helicopter pad for a quick exit.'

Lapsing into silence, Rhona looked down on what was now a seething white-topped mass. Up here, the chopper was dealing with some turbulence, but nothing to what it must be like in a small vessel trying to make its way through such high seas.

Rhona registered Olsen's worried look. If a ship in the vicinity required help, then the coastguard helicopter would have to provide it, whatever its current status.

Rhona said a silent prayer that that wouldn't happen.

69

Now that he was free of restraint, it was hard to stay either upright, or in one place. The boat was tossing about, dipping from side to side like some daft fairground ride. The shouts, bangs and general clamour suggested things weren't going too well aloft either, which probably accounted for the fact that no one had ventured near him after the earlier visit by cologne man.

It had taken a while to free himself completely from his bonds and attachment to the metal pipe, the pitching boat having hampered his attempts, but he'd eventually done it, only to be thrown across the room for his efforts.

McNab didn't like to admit that his insides were also doing somersaults. He'd never been in a position to check whether he might suffer from seasickness, having avoided anything bigger than a Clyde ferry. Now, it seemed the truth was about to come out, both physically and metaphorically.

Up to this point he'd been blaming his desire to retch on lingering concussion, dehydration and the angry burns on his hands and back. Now he decided to go with the flow and bring up what little there was in his stomach.

Having done that, McNab steadied himself as well as he could and made his swaying way to the door. Although his visitor had slammed it shut, McNab hadn't detected a key turning. And why bother locking him in, when they'd thought he was securely tied up? Now that the crew were fully engaged in keeping the boat afloat, they wouldn't have time to worry about a prisoner. After all, how the hell could he escape, unless he dived into the North Sea?

Something McNab had no intention of doing.

Clasping the handle, he pushed the door away from the metal doorstep. It was heavy, obviously designed to close tightly, sealing the compartment from any water which might find its way below decks. Checking there was no one in the corridor, McNab stepped out into the thin film that was already sloshing across the floor in miniature waves.

In that moment, as the boat pitched crazily again, McNab registered that maybe ships did still go down in storms. And this was one helluva storm. The noise was much louder out here: the creak and groan as the hull coped with the next deluge, the muted howl of the wind and a constant chime of metal hitting metal with a loud clang.

Holding on to the railing to stay upright, McNab made for the stairs without any real plan except to get away from his underwater prison. Emerging onto the next level, McNab found himself in another corridor, but this time it was lined with doors which he assumed led to cabins or other living quarters. Still no one appeared, although he could hear shouting from the level above, none of which he could make out.

If he went any higher, he was bound to meet crew, or maybe even Brodie himself, and McNab wasn't ready for that . . . yet. He needed a weapon and a plan. He also needed to stop stumbling about like a mad man. If he could find somewhere better than the bilge to hang out until the storm ended . . .

McNab made his decision.

He rested his ear against the first door, but the general noise made it impossible to confirm if there was anyone inside so he tried the handle.

The door opened on a small cabin, with a single bed. An opening led into a toilet. On the opposite wall, a further door led, he assumed, to a neighbouring cabin. McNab took advantage of the toilet first, then held his scalded hands under cold running water. Examining his beaten face in the mirror, he registered the rope mark on his forehead, which reminded him of an image of Rambo, minus the headband. His hair, auburn in its own right, had been darkened a deeper red by the blood from his head wound. McNab touched the matted mess gingerly, wondering if the skull beneath remained intact.

After his minimal ablutions, he considered what to do next. Rumpled bedding on the bunk plus some clothing on the shelf above suggested the cabin had an occupant. If that was the case then he couldn't wait the storm out here, collect his wits and make plans.

What fucking plans? an inner voice questioned. Until this boat made land, he wasn't going anywhere. *Unless they decide to throw me overboard.*

Just then an abrupt movement of the boat saw him land against the internal door with a thump. In that moment McNab heard a smothered cry from the adjacent room. A cry that sounded like a woman.

McNab pressed his ear to the door. Whoever had been momentarily shaken by the pitching boat had now gone quiet, but McNab was convinced the voice he'd heard had been female. He checked the intervening door and found the lock on the handle had been turned, on his side at least.

He made a decision and released it, then knocked quietly.

'Hello, anyone in there?'

A pregnant silence followed and McNab had a strong sense that someone had indeed heard him and was considering whether they should respond.

Then it came. 'Who are you?' The voice was young and female and frightened.

'Michael McNab.' He repeated his earlier mantra. 'I'm a detective sergeant with Police Scotland.'

There was a sound very like a sob of relief.

McNab now asked her the same question in return.

Her answer, when it came, didn't totally surprise him. It seemed that Olsen had been right all along, and the incident on Cairngorm, which Rhona had been involved in, and which he'd chosen to ignore, had been as important as his own lead on Brodie.

'Can I come through?' McNab said.

'No, you mustn't,' she blurted out. 'They have cameras in here and they watch everything I do.' There was a moment's silence. 'I'm sitting down by the door pretending to talk to myself. They know I do that, although they may be listening, as well as watching.'

McNab could hear her enervated breathing, her excitement and relief at being found.

'Do they know you're on board?' she asked.

'The man I was chasing caught me first,' McNab told her. 'I was tied up down below, but got free when the storm hit.'

As though reminding them of its continued presence, the swell suddenly tipped the boat abruptly to the right, thrusting McNab away to thump against the outer wall. Crawling back, he took up residence like her on the floor, his back to the intersecting door.

'Are you all right?' she asked anxiously.

'Yes. What about you?'

'The man who abducted me hit me over the head with my own crampon.' She sounded really pissed off about that.

McNab knew by the hesitation that followed, there was something she wasn't telling him.

'What is it?' he demanded. 'What have they done to you?'

'I'm naked,' she said, as though that was all he needed to know.

70

The boat in trouble below had apparently lost the windows on its bridge, blown in by the power of the wind. Having radioed for help from the coastguard to guide it ashore, it was at present at the mercy of the sizeable waves that appeared to be coming at it from all directions.

Their own helicopter pilot was currently in conversation with the captain of the fishing vessel in Norwegian, which was ironically called the *Herr Olsen*, the translation of their conversation being fed to Rhona via Harald.

'The captain wants us to stay with them until the coastguard vessel arrives,' he told her. 'In case his crew needs to be winched off.'

'Is that likely?' Rhona asked.

'In these seas, yes, but they won't want to do that. They won't abandon their boat unless it's going down. The ship's their livelihood.'

'How long before help comes?'

'There are forty-three rescue craft ranged along the Norwegian coastline, and the coordinating rescue centre's at Stavanger, so the captain thinks it won't be long.'

Harald was putting on a brave face, but it was obvious he was worried both for the crew exposed below, and of course for their own mission, so long in the planning. Rhona couldn't

327

see Olsen's face, but didn't have to, to know how concerned he would be too.

Catching the *Solstice* unawares, they perhaps had a chance of success. If there was time for someone to warn the ship of their arrival, they were probably lost. Whatever was happening on that vessel could be dispensed with, and cleaned up. Rhona had no doubt they were talking about professionals here. Folk like herself and Harald, who knew what they were about. Who were aware how to destroy forensic evidence, as well as find it.

If they know we're coming, there'll be nothing to find. Cocaine they might hide or drop into the sea to collect later. Human beings, the other cargo . . .

Harald seemed to be reading her mind.

'Alive, they're worth a great deal,' he told her. 'If they become a threat to the continuing operation . . .'

It was growing dark. The sheeting rain and heavy cloud cover weren't helping but they weren't the real problem. She and Olsen had arrived at Sola airport this morning in the dark. By the time they left Stavanger just after 10.30 a.m., the sun was up. But at this latitude, daytime was short, about six and a half hours short according to Harald.

Already the fishing vessel below could only be spotted among the seething grey waves by its lights and any spotlight the pilot chose to focus on it. They had been hovering above the stricken vessel for fifteen minutes, every moment of which had seemed at least twice as long.

Like the Bristow helicopter used by CMR, the NH-90 was well-equipped for night-time rescues, but to her at this moment, the dwindling light just reminded her of the swift passage of time and how long they still had before they reached the *Solstice*.

Her thoughts were interrupted by a shout from Olsen and a blast from the *Herr Olsen* as they spied their rescuers on the horizon. Not one, but two vessels bearing down on her at as high a speed as the sea would allow.

Their own pilot waited until the two vessels drew a little closer, then Rhona heard a flurry of Norwegian as he spoke to the rescue ships.

'We'll be on our way now,' Harald told her, with a relieved smile.

The fishing boat blew its horn in thanks as their chopper rose above the scene, and turning north, headed towards its goal.

Darkness had all but descended, its arrival heralded by a sunset that had broken through the cloud cover to stain the sky blood red. The sea still seethed below them, but they'd encountered no more shipping, distressed or otherwise, since the fishing boat. Only the bright lights of the intricate metal structures of oil rigs, which made Rhona think of strange fairy-tale castles, their surrounding moats being the open ocean.

Harald was following their progress on the palmtop, and he showed her it now. 'The *Herr Olsen*'s almost at port, you'll be glad to know.' He indicated the small blue dot charting its progress.

Pleased, Rhona asked how long before they reached the *Solstice*.

'Unfortunately, it's on the move,' Harald told her. 'Probably has been, since we first spotted the fishing boat.'

'Where?' Rhona said.

'South-west.'

'What does that mean for us?' she asked.

'A longer journey, and perhaps a need to refuel.'

'Where can we do that?'

'Another replenishment boat, a coastguard vessel or an oil rig.'

'But that'll take time,' Rhona said.

'Exactly.'

'Do you think they know we're coming and that's why they're moving?'

Harald shrugged. 'It depends who they have on the inside. And they've had someone, otherwise we would have pinpointed their activities earlier.'

It was a depressing thought. One that met Rhona's other niggling concern, which was undoubtedly McNab.

71

Isla's declaration that she was naked, and what that meant for her staying in that room, had decided McNab.

'Come through, now,' he told her.

'But they'll know I've gone,' she said anxiously.

'We'll find somewhere to hide. They're too busy keeping afloat at the moment to think about either of us.' McNab hoped that was true.

She made an exasperated, yet determined sound that suddenly reminded him of Ellie.

'Keep as low as you can,' McNab told her as he held the door open enough to let her crawl through.

She was trembling and he could smell the fear emanating from her bare skin as she pulled herself over the intervening step. He'd already found a pair of jeans and a sweater from the shelf above the bunk. Both were way too big for her, but with the help of his belt, the trousers would stay up. The one thing he couldn't supply was shoes.

Isla dismissed his concern. 'I'm fine barefoot,' she told him.

He'd averted his gaze as she'd dressed. Isla now touched his arm to signal that she was decent.

'Do you know anything about the layout of the boat?' he asked.

She shook her head. 'He injected me with something

when we got on the plane. After that it was just wild dreams until I surfaced next door.'

McNab had experienced something similar himself. 'He didn't mention where he was taking you?'

'No. Although he took great delight in informing me that I'd wish I *was* dead when I got there.'

'Did you see a man who looked like . . .' McNab gave a brief description of Neil Brodie.

Isla almost recoiled at his words, then regarded him defiantly. 'A man like that came to the cabin, plus a man who smelt strongly of male cologne.'

'I'm sorry,' he said quietly, thinking how inadequate that word was.

When Isla dismissed his concern again, McNab asked his next question. 'There was a girl, Amena Tamar. Young, Syrian, thirteen years of age. Those men took her from her hospital bed—'

He stopped, as Isla shook her head. 'I've only seen the men,' she said.

'They didn't talk about any other females aboard?'

'No. I'm sorry,' she added, seeing his disappointment. 'But that doesn't mean there aren't any.'

McNab had already shut and refastened the intervening door. Now, as the sound of multiple running footsteps echoed in the corridor, he quickly turned the lock in the main door and ordered Isla into the toilet. She briefly looked as though she might refuse, so McNab reinforced his command with, 'And stay there, whatever happens.'

His initial search of the cabin hadn't turned up a weapon. McNab had hoped for a knife at least. Had the bunk been occupied by one of Brodie's gang, a gun might even have been a possibility, but if it was the quarters of a crew member, that was unlikely.

In its place, McNab had smashed the small mirror above the sink and fashioned himself a chib. As a Glasgow boy, he'd carried one in his youth, for protection. He wasn't averse to using the makeshift knife if required, although it might be for persuasion this time.

McNab had no illusions as he contemplated the outcome of their present situation. He'd worked undercover long enough to know that once they have you, your clock is ticking. It seemed Davey, for all his ability to make money, was an innocent in that respect.

Or was he?

Tethered in the bilge, McNab had had plenty of time to consider how all of this had come about. How Davey had been propositioned. How he'd sold out. How that had led to the hit-and-run. How much Mary had known. How much had been kept secret from her.

Secrets and lies. Like a spider's web that needed constant spinning.

And that had ended up with him being kidnapped and brought here . . . but why? To be punished like Isla for annoying them, for thwarting their plans, for simply staying alive?

And Davey. What had been his reward for offering up his childhood mate? Maybe Mary's continued existence?

McNab took a moment to consider that should he die, Mary might live. There was a time when such a trade-off would have convinced him. *But that was when I was young and stupid.* A noble death rarely solved anything. If he died out here in the North Sea, Davey would still be in the thrall of the Brodie cartel. Drugs and kids without countries would still be exchanged and abused for his weakness.

McNab remembered as a child his mother telling him that the only way to deal with bullies was to smack them in the face. Ignoring them didn't work. Trying to appease them had even less traction.

McNab thought of the girl now hiding, despite her protestations, in that toilet. Isla was a fighter. She'd defied a mountain, an attempt on her life, and the ice cave. He could at least match up to that.

Whatever he did now, McNab told himself . . . could change everything.

The footsteps had passed them by, the corridor quiet again. Realizing he'd been holding his breath, McNab released it. They couldn't stay here, that was a certainty, but in this boat there had to be somewhere they could hide, and perhaps delay the inevitable. Not for the first time did McNab curse the fact that he no longer had his mobile.

If only I could've got a message to Ollie . . .

That thought sprang the memory of Ollie avidly showing him the mapping locations of all the shipping traffic currently in the North Sea. All vessels use the Automatic Identification System, he'd said. Then if they get into trouble, they can be rescued.

Two thoughts hit McNab at once. And he liked both of them.

McNab called to Isla and gave her the all-clear. 'Let's go,' he said.

72

'We're landing to take on fuel,' Harald told her.

Rhona looked down. An oil rig stood below her. Like an island in the icy waves, its twin platforms were brightly lit, as was the walkway between them. The larger of the two structures sat on four fat legs, against which the seas raged. Like a dragon, it spouted fire from a tall crane that towered above.

She spotted the yellow circle and large H on the smaller, rectangular structure, denoting their landing place. Alongside it, a small supply boat was braving the waves. As they began their descent, the wind fought the blades, whipping the chopper from side to side as though attempting to throw out its occupants.

'Be grateful we're not trying to land on a barge or a supply vessel, or even a floating rig,' Harald told her. 'At least our landing place is fixed.'

Rhona watched, her heart pounding, as the pilot attempted to manoeuvre them into position above the yellow circle, and after what seemed like an eternity, eventually their feet met the solid surface and they were down.

'They've got some food and hot drinks for us below,' Harald said.

'Any chance I can pick up mobile messages or make a call while I'm here?' Rhona asked.

Harald assured her she could. 'Planning to locate your detective sergeant?'

'Hoping to.'

From worrying about the delay involved in a fuel stop, Rhona was now glad of it, as they were marshalled through the driving sleet and wind that whipped at the deck, and down below into the sudden warmth and relative silence.

Rhona headed for the toilets first, passing some men on the way, who were surprised to find a woman wandering about. Rhona didn't take the time to enlighten them as to why she was there, but left them with their puzzle.

Her mobile, obviously logging a signal, was busy downloading. Rhona ran an eye over the texts first, but found nothing more from Ollie. There was one from Chrissy expressing an equal concern as to McNab's whereabouts, and a request to be contacted as soon as possible.

When she did so, Rhona found herself extraordinarily glad to hear Chrissy's voice, although it was anything but crystal clear.

'On an oil rig,' she answered Chrissy's demand to know where the hell she was. 'The SAR helicopter's refuelling.'

Chrissy sprang into action with her own news. 'Ellie went by McNab's place last night,' she told Rhona, 'worried he wasn't answering his phone. She found the door of his flat lying open, but no sign of McNab, although the ladder to the roof was pulled down.' Chrissy rushed on, 'His neighbours reported noise in the close after midnight.'

None of this was what Rhona wanted to hear.

'Bill's instigated a full-scale search for him.' Chrissy's voice cut out briefly at this point.

'You still there?' Rhona asked. The tone of the return 'yes', indicated just how worried her assistant was. 'You know McNab,' Rhona said, as much for her own benefit as Chrissy's. 'It's not the first time he's made off like this.'

'Nothing's gone right since that raid on the Delta Club.'

Rhona couldn't argue with that statement. 'Does Bill know about the Stevenson connection with Brodie?' she said.

'Yes, but it doesn't help,' Chrissy told her. 'They can't find Davey either.'

'And Mary?'

'Still in intensive care.'

God, it was a mess, and getting messier. Rhona was in the corridor now, and Harald, obviously looking for her, waved her towards an open doorway.

'Food's here, although we'll have to be quick. We're heading off in fifteen.' Once settled at a table with a filled roll and a strong cup of coffee, he asked about McNab.

Rhona told him what little she knew, and he had some news for her. 'The *Solstice*'s only an hour away.'

'And they still don't know we're planning a visit?'

'We'll use a story of a distress call nearby, and ask to land with a casualty and make use of their hospital facilities. In this weather, they can't refuse.'

As they made their way towards the helicopter, it was clear that the giant swell which surrounded the fixed installation was only increasing. Cresting waves broke against its legs, the resultant spray almost obscuring the rig, bar the burning flare. The small supply boat was having an even worse time, bobbing about like a cork.

'How could anyone survive on a wee boat like that?' Rhona said.

'The crew will have already evacuated to the rig,' Harald told her.

Once back in the chopper, Harald reminded Rhona that if the wind speed got too high, even the NH-90 would be grounded. 'It doesn't happen often,' he said.

'And if it does?'

'We abandon the mission and find a place, any place, to land and ride out the storm.'

Rhona didn't ask *how high is too high*, suspecting from her earlier experience on Cairngorm that the wind might be fast approaching that speed now.

73

They'd successfully negotiated the corridor outside the cabin without incident. Had they encountered anyone, Isla might well have passed unremarked, or be taken for a young male crew member, if there were any on board.

McNab was more concerned about his own appearance. The beaten, bruised face shouted 'problem' and there was no concealing that. He had no idea who knew about his imprisonment below, and wasn't keen to find out. His main concern at the moment was to find a place for Isla to hide, so that he might execute his plan.

For he now had a plan.

This time as they'd moved through the boat, McNab had taken more interest in his surroundings. By his estimation, this was a sizeable tug, not unlike the one used to smuggle cocaine from Turkey to Scotland, via a trip across the Atlantic to South America. It was battling the North Sea, and having some difficulty, but it was still making progress and heading somewhere. At a guess, he decided, there could probably be six crew members, plus cologne guy, Brodie and maybe Isla's Iceman.

And one of me.

Not great odds, McNab had to admit, but all he needed to do was get a message out to Ollie, to anyone, that they were on this boat. That was the first idea.

The other was more risky. If the ship got into trouble in these high seas, then the captain would call for help. Of course in the interim between the call and help arriving, they could quietly dispose of any unwanted baggage. Like himself, and Isla.

And, McNab thought, they would have no scruples in doing so.

But if they couldn't find their passengers . . .

McNab's stomach was considering a second revolt. The pitching of the boat had become more extreme, listing heavily from side to side. Any movie he'd ever watched that involved a computer-generated storm at sea had definitely not prepared him for this. A glance at Isla showed she was faring better. No green tinges, no drawn expression that suggested she was concentrating really hard on not being sick.

'Okay?' he checked.

'I don't get seasick, if that's what you mean?' She gave him a faint smile.

'It shows then?' McNab mustered himself. If Isla could even attempt a smile after what she'd just been through . . . 'Right. You stay here. I'm going to vomit somewhere else.'

He'd located a hiding place to the rear of the tug. It was a tiny store of some sort, but empty at present, with just enough room for the two of them, although McNab hadn't been planning to stay long. He'd a feeling that once the tug reached its destination, their chances of escape would only diminish. The storm offered some kind of cover for his attempt to alert the authorities to their position, which he planned to take.

When he'd told Isla what he had in mind, she'd looked dubious.

'I could come with you and distract them.'

McNab had seen by her expression that it was a genuine offer. And a courageous one, after what she'd had to submit to with the men she might have to face.

'You stay here. I'll be back and we'll sit it out until we're rescued.'

It sounded so simple when he'd said it like that.

She'd seemed to acquiesce then, slipping back into the darkness, drawing her knees up, hugging them with her hands.

McNab had left her there, hoping that even if he didn't return, help might come for Isla at least.

Once the detective had gone, Isla checked her pocket. She'd removed the fragment from the broken mirror when he'd ordered her into the toilet. An ice axe or a crampon would have been more her weapon of choice, but since neither was available, she'd extracted a sizeable piece of glass, wrapped it in toilet paper and slipped it in the pocket of the trousers.

She'd spent a great deal of time during her incarceration imagining just what punishment the spikes on a crampon might do to the Iceman's face, or even better, his prick and balls. She was now altering those images to incorporate the slither of glass and focusing more on an artery.

Both her work as a mountaineering instructor and her own recreational pursuits in the hills involved survival techniques, and a knowledge of first aid. Isla knew how to try to save a life, and how to take one. She'd already decided that she was unlikely to be set free, despite the detective's good intentions. What she could do was take revenge for her friends.

Abandoning the hiding place the detective had so carefully chosen for her, Isla now retraced her steps towards her prison. Through the small portholes, it was obvious that the seas were still enormous, whipped to a frenzy by the storm. She thought of McNab's hope that rescuers might reach them – a coastguard vessel or a Search and Rescue helicopter. It was obvious he wasn't aware that when winds reached this strength, helicopters were grounded. As for a boat reaching them in these seas, even if McNab did manage to raise the alarm . . .

As the boat suddenly encountered a deep trough, Isla was thrown to the floor, the breath knocked out of her. Trying to rise again, she spotted a figure at the end of the corridor. The young man, holding on to the walls for traction against the swell, regarded her with a wild expression.

Isla had no idea if he was crew, or whether he'd been aware that she was aboard. His current expression could suggest he was regarding her as an escaped prisoner, or else he'd discovered a stowaway. The garbled shout that followed didn't help because it wasn't in English.

As he came quickly towards her, the boat gave the most violent pitch to date. The size and power of the wave they'd encountered sent water rushing into the corridor to take the feet from under her. Trying to rise again on her injured ankle, as she slammed down again Isla realized that her plan might come to nought. That she wouldn't kill the Iceman. That in all likelihood she would drown on this boat.

The boy was now beside her. She registered his youth, the dark good looks and the concern in his eyes. He was attempting to lift her. Isla resisted at first, her body heavy, then she found herself helping him. No longer a dead weight, she was drawn to her feet, her arm placed over his shoulder.

'Who are you?' she said.

'Tarik, a prisoner like you.'

74

'There she is,' Harald said, 'the *Solstice*.'

The replenishment at sea vessel was lit up like a landing strip. Although bigger than Rhona had envisaged, even she was taking a pounding by the waves, whipped up by a wind Harald estimated as ten on the Beaufort scale. There was always a lag between an increasing wind and subsequent high seas. Judging by the giant seas below, it seemed that lag was over.

There had been much discussion in the cockpit over the last fifteen minutes, all in Norwegian. The four-man crew consisting of captain and co-pilot, winchman and radar operator were conversing calmly, but there was no doubt, as Harald explained, that the high wind speeds were demanding that they set the chopper down and soon.

This part of the North Sea wasn't as crowded with rigs and accompanying vessels as other sections, so catching up with the *Solstice* had become a priority.

And they'd done it, although Rhona couldn't imagine how they might set down on that pitching deck. At least when she'd landed on the tiny airstrip on the Orkney island of Sanday, the field hadn't been lurching about like the surface below them now.

The call had already been put through to the *Solstice* requesting to land. Olsen threw Rhona an encouraging look as they waited for a response. It was inconceivable that they wouldn't be permitted to set down, but in conditions like these, they would need all the help they could get to do so safely.

A voice replied now, and after a rapid exchange of instructions, the chopper began its move towards a hover position above the rolling ship. Rhona could barely make out the deck below as the constant waves breaking against the *Solstice* threw up a continuous wall of white spray. It was, she thought, like being back in the blizzard.

As the pilot battled to keep the chopper in position, the winchman began to lower a cable.

'They'll attach the messenger cable to a tethering cable which will help guide us down,' Harald explained. 'Once we're on board, they'll secure the chopper and move it into the hangar.'

'You've done this before?' Rhona said in awe.

'A few times,' Harald assured her. 'Seas weren't quite so wild though.'

Rhona kept her gaze fixed on the pilot. Despite the tension in the chopper, it was obvious that those in charge knew exactly what they were doing and she could only hope the ground crew had the same level of expertise.

She barely felt the feet touch the surface before they were flung left as the wind caught the chopper side on. Buckled in, Rhona was briefly crushed against the reassuring bulk of Harald, who steadied her as the chopper was secured. The noise of the rotor blades and engine now quenched, the scream of the wind had become even more pronounced.

'You're liable to be blown away, so stay between Alvis and me when we get out,' Harald ordered.

He was right. Emerging head down, Rhona felt the wind

try to take her feet from under her, before Harald and Alvis each grabbed an arm and began hustling her across the waterlogged deck towards the light of an open door. Even as a gust tried to pull her upwards, the crest of a wave topped the deck, sending swirling water to drag her towards the railing. As the wash threatened to upend her, Rhona found herself lifted by the men and carried to safety.

Once inside, the door was clanged shut by a crew member and secured behind them, and they stood in the sudden but welcome internal silence of the ship.

'What about our forensic equipment?' Rhona said.

'Once the helicopter's been secured in the hangar, we'll fetch it out,' Alvis told her.

The crew member indicated they should follow him, which proved, if not quite as difficult as their walk from the chopper, not easy either, as the ship continued to pitch and roll. The man never spoke to them, despite Olsen trying to engage him in conversation in English, then Norwegian, and a couple of other languages. None worked until the final one, which Rhona thought might be Arabic. The man started at that and turned to stare at Olsen, but whatever it was Olsen had said, there was still no response.

The ship they gradually moved through wasn't luxurious, but it was definitely lived in and by quite a few people. Rhona was conscious of activity going on, figures moving about and voices, male and definitely not speaking English.

Harald said nothing en route. The helicopter crew they'd left behind to secure their aircraft and retrieve their luggage, so it was only the investigating team of herself, Olsen and Harald who were being escorted, Rhona assumed, to meet the ship's captain.

The crew member eventually halted and, opening a door,

ushered them inside, saying 'Wait here, please' in Norwegian, as translated by Harald.

Once they were all three inside the room, which was furnished with some tables and chairs, the crew member left. Olsen waited until the door swung shut behind them, then checked that it hadn't been secured. It hadn't.

'They don't know why we're here?' Harald immediately said.

'They think the weather forced us down.'

'So, they have no idea we're police officers?'

'Not yet,' Olsen said. 'The coastguard know where we are. If we can find anything to raise our suspicions, we'll make this official.'

75

McNab's stomach hadn't given up on its revolt. Only once before had he endured such a level of nausea. On that occasion, it'd been caused by a morphine drip after he'd been shot. Gradually the relief from the pain of his injury had been replaced by a need to vomit, frequently, which had only been relieved by the administration of an anti-nausea drug given intravenously.

On this ship, under these conditions, there was no morphine for his beaten and sore body, nor anything to end the nausea.

Mind over matter, McNab told himself as he sat in a dark corner, his back against the wall, his stomach in turmoil.

I will never set foot on a boat again, he vowed. *Not even a bloody rowing boat in Victoria Park*. As for now, maybe if he was sick over the enemy, that might distract them enough for him to put the knife in . . . literally.

That thought, once visited, began to entice McNab.

If he could vomit to order.

McNab held grimly on to the step handrail as the tug rose to meet the latest wave, then waited as it plunged into the trough that followed. It was, he decided, like being on the big dipper, without the fun or the excited screams. A briefly overheard conversation from a couple of passing crew members had steered him in this direction. Not far from Isla's cabin, although up one level, he suspected the bastard he sought might be in one of the rooms in this corridor.

From the sarcastic comments uttered in what he took to be Aberdonian voices, it appeared the bold Brodie was laid out in his bunk, suffering from seasickness. And he apparently wasn't the only one, which was probably why the alarm hadn't been raised over the missing Isla, or himself.

Thus he was now within spitting distance of the man who'd shot him, crushed Mary's skull with his four-by-four, and been happy to video a child like Amena being raped.

At the orgy and the subsequent chase, he and Brodie hadn't met eye to eye. Whatever happened now, they would do that at least. McNab allowed himself a smile. If Isla stayed put, this might all work out. Eliminate the top player and the gang might fall apart.

Assuming Brodie was the top player.

Perhaps the Iceman Isla talked about was the pinnacle, or even his visitor who'd smelled of cologne. McNab decided not to argue with himself over the relative value of his enemies. For him, Brodie was the man. It was personal, just as the Iceman was personal to Isla.

Then again, justice might only be served if all three met their end.

Justice is for the courts to decide.

At this thought a wave slammed against the porthole, reminding McNab that out here there was no justice, because humans, their failings, wishes, loves and hates, counted for nothing. The weather decided all.

Thinking about Amena had reminded McNab that he'd failed to find her, let alone rescue her. He would have to accept that the little Syrian girl was more than likely dead. Brodie would have snatched her from the hospital to make sure she told the police nothing. After that, why keep her alive?

Because there were a lot of sick bastards that liked fucking kids, and on camera.

McNab turned and retched quietly in the corner. That would be the last for a while, he decided. He would save it all now and use it to his advantage. He checked the corridor, then rose, holding on to the wall. The tug was still battling the waves, but built like a tank with an engine that could pull and push ships many times its size, it would, McNab thought, survive, despite the high seas.

The question was, would he?

76

There were perhaps six or seven of them sitting squashed together in the cramped damp space. A dim overhead light revealed only the mixed shadows of their upturned faces. The pervading smell was of body odour and fear. Isla recognized the scent, because it reminded her of herself in the ice cave.

Tarik had led her down below, further towards the stern. He'd seemed able to steady himself regardless of the motion, whereas Isla had stumbled along, longing for firm ground beneath her feet. When she'd asked how he'd got free, Tarik revealed that since the storm began they'd been left unguarded. She'd still wondered how they would pass through the tug unchallenged, but it had become obvious that Tarik had devised a route which, although tortuous in parts, appeared to avoid human contact, especially in such high seas.

At one point, however, their chosen path had required them to go on deck, albeit briefly. The few seconds they were exposed to the storm were more terrifying than any mountain Isla had ever climbed. Up to that point she'd only imagined the waves and the wind. The reality of both was much more frightening, despite the fact that Tarik had gripped her hand throughout.

As her eyes grew accustomed to the light, Isla did a quick

head count. It looked like five girls and two boys. Ages, at a guess, somewhere between ten and fifteen.

Children.

Isla now understood what Tarik had tried to tell her. There were other prisoners on this boat besides herself. And she was looking at them now. Shocked by the discovery, she tried to compose herself as tears sprang into her eyes. The group, having established her presence, now talked excitedly, until a worried-looking Tarik put his finger to his lips to indicate they must quieten down.

'Do any of them speak English?' Isla said.

'Some have a little,' Tarik told her.

'Where have you come from?'

'Fari from Nigeria, Mohammed from Sudan, Amena and myself from Syria.' He stopped as Isla interrupted him.

'One of the girls is called Amena?' she said, recalling McNab's earlier enquiry.

The exchange of the name caused a ripple of interest to run through the group, and they all turned to one dark-eyed, pretty girl, who sat at the back. The girl's expression was one of bewilderment that she'd been singled out.

'Yes, why?' Tarik asked.

'A policeman, DS McNab, is looking for her,' Isla said.

When Tarik translated this, the girl gave a small excited gasp. 'Michael?' she said in surprise.

Isla couldn't recall if that was the policeman's first name, but the expression on the girl's face suggested that it might be.

'Where is this policeman?' Tarik asked.

'Here,' Isla told him, 'on the boat. He was a prisoner too, but he got free.'

Tarik's quick translation of her explanation caused

another excited explosion of talking, until his quick order for silence.

'He's trying to get a message out,' Isla explained.

Tarik looked concerned. 'By radio?'

'I'm not sure,' Isla said, realizing she hadn't been party to the exact plan, even though she'd offered to accompany McNab.

'I'll find him,' Tarik said.

McNab had checked two cabins before this one. Both had displayed evidence of an occupant, but were empty. This one, he decided, would be his final try before he went looking for the radio room. He was conscious that Isla would be worried about him and the longer he stayed away the worse it would be.

In truth his plan to enact revenge was fading a little, as common sense told him that getting word out of their position would be a better way to use his time before they caught him. As they would.

The storm couldn't occupy them forever. Never having paid any heed to shipping forecasts, McNab had no idea how long conditions like these might last in the North Sea. He'd caught a weather forecast on the radio prior to his capture that had promised high winds and possible power lines down in the north of Scotland, but since Glasgow hadn't been mentioned, he'd barely registered the warning.

There was one thing he was sure of. Once the storm was over, they'd be back looking for him, and Isla. Should they already know they'd escaped from their separate prisons, they also knew that neither of them could get off the ship until they reached their destination.

Despite the wild conditions, the tug seemed to be moving

doggedly onward, heading somewhere in as big a hurry as was possible. Where, McNab had no idea. Although Isla's captor had insisted she would wish she was dead when the tug reached its final destination.

McNab pressed his ear to the door and heard what he thought might be a muffled snore.

Third time lucky.

A wall of stale vomit met him on entry. Whoever was lying in the bunk was as bad a sailor as himself, so it was unlikely to be a member of the crew. Cologne guy hadn't seemed perturbed by the swell when he'd visited McNab in the bilge, so it probably wasn't him. And by the length of the body in the bunk, it wasn't the tall Iceman.

McNab crept close enough to view the face properly, registering that the sour smell was emanating from the waste bin by the bed. A dusting of white powder on a nearby shelf suggested the patient, who was definitely Brodie, had been self-medicating. McNab ran his finger along it, sniffed, then realizing what it was, chose to rub some on his gums in the hope it might quieten his own heaving stomach.

Brodie's next snore was loud enough to disturb his slumber, and he shifted to turn his face to the wall. McNab had instinctively stepped back, his heart moving up a pace, no doubt aided by the coke. He waited for Brodie to settle, and eventually the snores became steady once again.

Now McNab saw what his hand had been resting on as the muzzle of a gun peeked out at him from below the pillow. A desire to vomit over Brodie evaporated as McNab's immediate wish moved to possessing the gun.

Men like Neil Brodie understood the power of guns. For persuasion and retribution. That's why any self-respecting drug dealer carried one, and was willing to use it. Were the gun in his hands, McNab decided, it could serve the same purpose.

But he would need a steady hand to extract it.

The beating, followed by constant nausea, had rendered McNab's hands shaky, but the small amount of cocaine he'd already ingested seemed to be helping. Wetting his finger, he hoovered up all that remained on the shelf and applied it as before, waiting for a repeat of the cocaine rush.

Now he was ready.

77

The fixed rig they'd set down on earlier had been battered by waves, but still had the solidity of a small island. The *Solstice* was another matter. Rhona was used to sailing in the waters off the west coast of Scotland. Her adoptive father had been keen on boats and had taught her the rudiments. She'd never been seasick then, or even on the notorious Irish Sea crossings as a child, but she had no idea how her normally steady stomach would cope with the obvious and sickening swell they were dealing with now.

'You okay?' Harald checked.

'So far,' Rhona said, gripping the rail to steady herself as the boat gave another lurch.

Olsen had waited for their escort to leave, then proposed that they should take a look round the *Solstice* for themselves.

'If they have nothing to hide . . .'

They'd split up then, with Rhona and Harald looking for the infirmary. Where Olsen had planned to go, he hadn't shared, but Rhona didn't think he was headed for the bridge, not right away. There'd been no sign of the chopper crew since they'd landed, something that bothered Rhona, because it meant she and Harald had no forensic kit, bar what was in the small backpack she carried.

'It's not easy hangaring a large chopper on a pitching

deck,' Harald had told her. 'It'll take time. Alvis is right. Better that we take a look around while the storm is keeping everybody occupied.'

Their first stop had been at a wall panel, detailing the layout of the *Solstice*, including its muster stations, plus what they sought, an area called *Sykehus* on the next level up.

'The hospital,' Harald confirmed.

At that moment, a couple of men appeared at the end of the corridor and, spotting their presence, looked interested enough to begin heading their way.

Harald, stepping in front of Rhona, told her to make for the hospital. 'I'll meet you there,' he promised.

Quickly doubling back, Rhona hurried along the corridor until she found a set of steps leading upwards. At the top, a wider space declared itself as an area to meet should an emergency occur aboard, something Rhona fervently hoped wouldn't happen.

She hesitated there, trying to recall the map below and the position of the hospital relative to where she now stood. Three corridors led off from here and she eventually settled on one, after checking the sign above which mentioned the word *Sykehus*.

If what Olsen believed was true, there should be some evidence to support it in the infirmary or operating theatre. Men took ill offshore, just as they did on land, and could require urgent treatment as near to their rig as possible.

A glance at the map Harald had shown her back in Stavanger of the Norwegian sector of the North Sea had given Rhona the impression of an area the size of another country lying just off the coast. With a quarter of a million people working in the oil industry, the majority of them on rigs and supply vessels, plus the ever-present possibility of a major disaster, the oil business – just like the Royal Navy – needed support and hospital vessels like this one.

But operating theatres could be used for more than just saving lives.

'Dr Rhona MacLeod.' Rhona offered her hand to the young male auxiliary who was stationed just inside the main door to the infirmary. 'I arrived on the SAR chopper that's just landed.'

He looked startled both by her arrival and her announcement. 'Did you bring a casualty aboard?' he asked anxiously.

Rhona reassured him that that wasn't the case. 'We attended a call, then the weather hit us and we needed a place to sit out the storm.'

His worried expression faded and he visibly relaxed, giving the impression that he wouldn't have liked it if she had brought him a patient, which made Rhona wonder why.

'Yes. It is a bad one,' he agreed about the storm. 'If you're not here about a casualty . . .' he began.

'I heard the *Solstice* had a hospital and an operating theatre aboard, and I thought I'd come and take a look.'

The perturbed look was back.

'We don't have any patients at the moment. And nothing scheduled for surgery. In fact there's no one here but me.'

Rhona wasn't, according to Chrissy, a very good liar. Hence her ineptitude at poker. She might not be an expert at telling a lie, but she could spot one.

'I thought you'd be filled with seasickness cases,' she joked.

He gave a half-smile. 'Sailors don't get seasick. Otherwise they're in the wrong job.'

'True,' Rhona said. 'So since I'm not disturbing anyone, may I take a quick look at your facilities?'

'Dr Toppe's off-duty at the moment, and I'm not supposed to leave the desk unattended, just in case we do get an emergency,' he told her.

Rhona adopted a conspiratorial look. 'The truth is,' she began, 'I'm considering a job offer from Mr Hagen to work on one of his hospital ships.'

As that appeared to sway him, Rhona vowed to learn to play poker properly and confound Chrissy into the bargain.

'Okay,' he finally conceded. 'Go on in.'

Rhona felt his eyes follow her as she opened the inner door, and knew that it was more than likely he would check up on her once she was out of sight.

Which meant she should work fast.

The door led into a corridor lined with individual rooms on one side, much like the layout of a modern hospital, where traditional larger wards had been replaced by private ones. The auxiliary had intimated they had no patients in the infirmary at present. Certainly the rooms Rhona passed were all empty, although a portion of the beds had been made up, as though in preparation for possible arrivals.

Having no idea what the Norwegian word for operating theatre was, she took a guess at *Operasjonssal* and found it to be right. Not being a medical doctor, let alone a surgeon, an operating theatre wasn't a familiar place, but what Rhona found looked state of the art, to her at least. And, she thought, ready for use.

The only things missing in the suite of rooms were patients and staff.

Emerging from the theatre, Rhona did a quick check on the other doors in the corridor, finding all of them locked.

Not surprising, if they contained equipment or medicines. Aware that if she didn't reappear soon, the auxiliary might come looking for her, Rhona decided to retreat and try to locate Harald.

As she made her way back down the corridor, something caught her eye. The object lay near the back wall under one of the made-up beds, barely in view through the glass partition. Opening the door, Rhona dropped to her knees and, stretching beneath the bed, retrieved it.

Bedraggled, dirty, with most of its stuffing missing, it was undoubtedly a child's soft toy. Something completely incongruous in such a setting.

But not, if what Olsen suspected about the *Solstice* was true.

Rhona retrieved an evidence bag from her backpack and dropped the toy inside, just as footsteps came down the corridor. Rising, she decided rather than exit the room, she would just stand there, as though admiring it. After all, she was 'taking a look around', and with permission.

The figure who now regarded Rhona was female, possibly mid-fifties, dressed in standard hospital scrubs.

Rhona, smiling, introduced herself as she'd done earlier to the auxiliary. 'I assume you're Dr Toppe?'

The woman's face didn't change from what Rhona read as blank anger. 'Why are you in here?' she said in English, with the slightest tinge of an accent.

'I wanted to see the ship's hospital.'

'Did you enter the operating theatre?' she demanded.

'No. I merely glanced in,' Rhona said.

'The facility has been prepared in case it's required. Wandering about, introducing germs . . . I thought as a doctor yourself, you would understand that.'

Rhona didn't dispute the accusation, even though it was over the top. It was obvious she was unwelcome here, and the best thing would be to leave, but she had something she wanted to ask first.

'Do you ever treat children on board the *Solstice*?'

The question startled Dr Toppe. 'This facility is for oil workers,' the woman said, her tone sharply dismissive. 'There are no children out here in the North Sea.'

'Of course not,' Rhona said.

As she was ushered out of the room, then the facility, Rhona contemplated whether the toy may have belonged to an oil worker's child, kept with them as a reminder of home. But, were that the case, it was unlikely to have been left behind.

Dr Toppe, Rhona thought, *is lying*.

A child had been here, and more, if Olsen's suspicions proved to be true, were expected.

Harald examined the contents of the evidence bag without handling the toy.

'Where did you find this?'

'In one of the side wards.'

'Did Dr Toppe see it?'

'No.'

'Nothing else?'

'The place is set up to receive patients.'

'How many beds?'

'Six made up,' Rhona said.

'Alvis believed a shipment was expected, which is why we made our move. I think the weather has delayed that.'

After their brief interchange, Dr Toppe had delivered Rhona into the hands of the two men she'd seen in the corridor, who in turn had escorted her back to the original waiting room, and Harald.

At that point, Harald had attempted to extract information from the reluctant crewmen regarding the storm's status. Their response in rapid Norwegian was that it was expected to reach its peak within the next two hours, and everyone was required at their stations, including the captain, who'd requested that they follow orders and remain here, for their own safety. This was said with such a degree of concern that it made Rhona think it might be true.

She caught enough of what followed to realize Harald was asking about the whereabouts of the SAR crew, but didn't understand anything in the reply.

'They're lying,' Harald said, when the men had gone. 'I think it's unlikely the SAR crew have stayed with the chopper. The hangar's hardly the place to be in a storm like this. They're keeping us apart on purpose, and, I think, away from the helicopter.'

'Why away from the chopper?' Rhona asked.

'To cut our lines of communication.'

78

For a moment McNab was paralysed by indecision. The sliver of glass was in his hand. The neck it might slice inches away. It would be so easy to finish Brodie here and now. Noiseless. Swift. Were their places reversed, he knew that Brodie wouldn't hesitate. The jugular vein was both discernible and easily accessed. It would be over in minutes. Brodie would feel no pain, which was a shame, but the world would be rid of a scumbag, and Mary would be revenged.

Or would she?

If he ended Brodie now, what would happen to Davey, wherever he was? And Mary? Not forgetting that Davey may have implicated Ellie in all of this. A flicker of horror began to form at that thought. Might they not all be punished for Brodie's death at his hands? Brodie was like an octopus, tentacles waving, suckers spreading in all directions.

In this job we're fucked, and everyone around us is fucked too.

Even as he breathed his hesitation, the door began to open, forcing him to act. McNab dropped the glass fragment and grabbed for the gun instead. The sudden movement next to his head roused Brodie, and like a dog he barked into action.

In moments there were three of them in the room and

McNab was outnumbered. He fired wildly and his shot met the roof and embedded itself there, but the noise and reverberation were enough to make both his opponents fall silent, and still.

Brodie, a groggy, spaced-out look on his face, was trying to work out what had just happened. The male who'd entered now thought better of the move and promptly exited, suggesting he wasn't armed, and didn't feel like taking a bullet.

The likelihood, McNab knew, was that he would return and soon, with backup.

McNab ordered Brodie to his feet. With the gun pointed at him, Brodie decided to do as commanded, although the continuing violent motion of the ship quickly drained any colour sleep had returned to his face.

It seemed both pathetic and ironic seeing a hardman like Brodie reduced to a wreck by something as simple as seasickness. It almost made McNab's own struggle with it bearable.

'Turn round,' McNab said. 'And face the door.'

'Fuck off!' Brodie made a sound in his throat that suggested he was about to puke, causing McNab to take a quick sidestep, at which Brodie laughed.

'You won't kill me, pig.'

'But I might blow your balls off,' McNab offered. 'Stop you fucking kids.'

'Like your pal, Davey, you mean?' Brodie sneered.

'Bad answer.'

Brodie's eyes widened as McNab swung the gun to point directly at his crotch. Then it was Brodie's turn to do a sidestep. But not quick enough. As McNab's knee met Brodie's balls, the gun butt met his head. Brodie didn't know which to cradle first.

As he crumpled, moaning, McNab repeated both moves, this time with his feet.

'That's for Mary, and that's for Amena.'

Minutes later he'd tied an unconscious Brodie's hands and feet together. Looking down on the punk, he almost wished he wasn't a police officer, because then he would have finished the bastard off.

McNab rose and spat his distaste on the inert body.

Now all he had to do was find a radio and send out a message.

And he knew who his contact would be.

McNab expected the guy he'd shot at in the room to rouse the troops and quickly, and yet it didn't appear that he had. He realized why at the next corner. Turning it, gun at the ready, he was met by the same guy, who now stood in the middle of the corridor, hands held up.

'Is your name Michael?' he said. 'Amena sent me to look for you.'

It was like some sort of weird nightmare that he used to have when on a drinking spree. Fixate on an idea prior to falling asleep, then try to follow it through in your dream.

'Amena's here on the boat. She's with Isla,' the young man told him.

McNab thought he might be hallucinating, verbally at least, which meant he was hearing what he wanted to hear, while other words were being spoken, like *you're fucked, arsehole*.

'Amena?' he finally managed.

'My name's Tarik,' the young guy told him. 'There are eight of us on this boat, and one of them is Amena Tamar.'

His words were like a firework display in McNab's head,

complete with the bangs at Hogmanay. Something he hadn't experienced this particular New Year.

The young guy was watching him, and eyeing up the gun at the same time.

McNab kept the gun pointed at him. 'If you're lying . . .'

'I'm not lying. Come with me.'

She was huddled amongst the others, yet McNab's eyes were drawn to her straight away. The facial bruising had faded and she looked younger now than in the Delta Club and the hospital, as though, in the interim, she'd become a child again.

Seeing his entry, she stood up, wonder on her face. 'Michael?'

Her voice speared him like an emotional knife.

'I've been looking for you,' McNab said, in an attempted jocular fashion. 'And here you are.'

'They know we're all here together,' Tarik said. 'But they don't care. They know we can't get off the boat. And there's the storm.'

'Where are they taking you?'

'Rumour is there's a ship.' Tarik glanced at the others. 'Things happen there.'

McNab felt Isla's touch on his arm and interpreted the silent message that he shouldn't ask what those things were.

'Okay,' he said. 'Now we get that message out.'

The wind was abating, the difference audible. Shouting, necessary before to rise above the rattling of the boat and the crash of the sea, was no longer required. The tug too, as though in relief at the end of a fight, was springing forward.

'They'll come to check on us soon,' Tarik told McNab.

'Which means we go now,' McNab responded.

Isla had remained silent as they discussed their plan, before informing them that they might be wrong on the subject of shortwave frequency radio.

'If the tug's only working the North Sea and not over long distances,' she said, 'it'll probably have MF on board and possibly VHF on the bridge. Maybe also multiple satellite comms.'

'I don't care what fucking comms it has, will we be able to use them?' McNab said.

'There's normally a guide posted next to the set,' Isla told him. 'For dummies,' she added, with a smile.

'Which of course you're not?' McNab said.

'Neither are you, if you've used a police radio.'

79

Olsen steadied himself as the *Solstice* took the brunt of the next wave. According to the forecasts before they'd left Sola, the wind should pass its peak soon. That wouldn't mean an immediate improvement in the state of the sea, or the size of the swell. It did mean, however, that the SAR helicopter could take off, and would be expected to, since they'd claimed their sojourn here had been caused by the weather.

He noted that there were no neighbouring lights, which meant the ship was staying in open water, well away from both rigs and other vessels. Which could be for one of two reasons. For safety's sake, since a collision between boat and rig was a distinct possibility in seas as high as these. Or it might be that, whatever the *Solstice* crew had planned for the next few hours – such as a delivery – they preferred it go unobserved.

Up to this point, Olsen had succeeded in moving through the ship without being challenged, mainly because he'd acquired a crew jacket. But that couldn't last much longer. Nothing he had viewed so far he'd deemed suspicious, although there were a number of areas he'd not yet investigated, in particular the lower decks.

If, as he suspected, the *Solstice* was being used not only for the storage and transport of the children, but possibly also for the filming and transmission of material involving them, then that's where the centre of operations was likely to be located.

The discovery of the children's bodies on Norway's border with Russia had started him on a path that had eventually led to the middle of the North Sea. The initial trickle of unaccompanied minors into Europe had become a flood as the conflicts in Northern Africa and the Middle East had developed. Both as easy prey and a highly sought-after commodity, they offered an international business opportunity, which appeared to have an ever-expanding customer base.

According to recent statistics, there simply wouldn't be enough jails to incarcerate all the men who, the police believed, were regularly viewing child pornography online. The dossier of images collected by the Norwegian team had indicated just how widespread and international that business had become, and how much money could be made from it.

It had been Marita who'd drawn Olsen's attention to the added possibility that the children were being harvested for more than just sexual abuse and exploitation. A journalist herself, she'd been writing a piece on the transportation of refugees into Europe, and she'd got a lead. One of the traffickers she'd spoken to had discovered he had a conscience, revealing that some of those he'd trafficked had been sold on for their organs, with young people being the most profitable shipment.

And a ship such as the *Solstice* was equipped to retrieve and supply such a commodity.

Olsen emerged from his hiding place, knowing there was a decision to be made. Nothing he'd seen as yet had given him the green light to seize the *Solstice* and bring her into harbour, with all the furore and fallout that would instigate. So, he could seek out Harald and Rhona to check whether they'd found anything at the hospital which would warrant him commandeering the ship. Or he could take his search onto the lower decks, before the wind dropped.

Now deep in the bowels of the ship, Olsen halted, hearing the ringing sound of following footsteps on the metal walkway. Glancing round, he established that there was nowhere here to hide, so if he were challenged by a crew member, he'd have to brazen it out.

From his foray up to now, he'd established that the crew were mostly foreign, with a strong preference for using Arabic, so he assumed they might well have been recruited on the *Solstice*'s not infrequent visits to Sousse in Tunisia, where Marita's whistle-blower had hailed from.

His own knowledge of that language was limited, although he'd been working on it with Mohammad during their chess matches – hence his ability to talk to the woman in Glasgow. Still, he could recognize the language of anger when he heard it. The two men were disagreeing about something, one of them obviously dismissing the other's arguments. Olsen decided to take his fate into his own hands, and ask what it was about.

Stepping out in front of them he demanded, in Norwegian, to know where they were going.

The effect of this was for them to stop in surprise, then regard him with some consternation. When no response came, Olsen repeated his question, but in Arabic.

This resulted in a torrent of a reply, mainly from the older of the two, next to nothing of which Olsen could understand, apart from one expression which he thought might mean 'emergency'. Standing aside, he waved them on, then followed.

Down a further flight of metal steps, Olsen caught the strong scent of diesel, and a glimpse of an area of large metal containers which he presumed housed the goods the RAS vessel would deliver offshore. The two men peeled off here, taking a stepladder down into the hold.

Olsen followed.

At the foot was a further walkway, leading to a container. As he approached, Olsen caught the smell of human. Not an everyday scent, but something primeval, tormented and terrible. Olsen almost ground to a halt, but knowing that in itself would arouse suspicion, he walked on . . . and into hell.

In the dim interior light sat or lay the humans whose scent had so distressed him. All were chained together, and by their young eyes, either desperate or else resigned to their fate. Olsen was reminded of drawn images of the interiors of slave ships that had horrified him as a child. Ships that had ploughed between the old world and the new, two centuries ago.

Nothing really changes, he thought. *Humans were a commodity then, and are again now.*

Aware his distress must be evident on his face, he mustered himself and said briskly in Arabic, 'Where are you taking them?'

His question had perplexed the older man, as though he expected Olsen to already know the answer. Olsen registered suspicion in his eyes, before he responded dismissively in Arabic.

As the two men began to lead the group out, Olsen's brain attempted to translate their gaoler's response. He'd heard the expression before, but when, and in what context?

Then it came.

It had been a day last summer. He'd persuaded a nervous Mohammad to go on a boat trip to Flor & Fjære, the garden island near Stavanger. During the journey, his friend had revealed how he'd escaped Syria. He'd chosen, he explained, to take his family overland, rather than subject them to a possible death at sea.

I didn't want them to become food for the fishes.

Olsen stood back, allowing the chained group to pass. Every nerve in his body urged him to intervene and stop them being marshalled to their probable death. But if he interceded now, his chance of preventing that might be over.

The older crew member had his suspicions, which he hadn't yet acted on. The moment Olsen showed concern for the prisoners, or interfered with what were obviously the man's orders, Olsen's cover, however superficial, would be blown.

As the tail end of the sorry procession went by, the final pair of female eyes fastened briefly on Olsen. In that look was fear, despair and, worst of all, the question *Why don't you help us?* That look changed everything.

'Stop,' Olsen shouted in Arabic. 'I'll take them up.'

The older guy had swung round at his command and Olsen knew by the look on his face that it wasn't going to work. The younger guy picked up on the other's rapidly fired order and came towards Olsen, a knife in his hand, the children cowering back against the guard rail as he pushed past.

Olsen had the fleeting thought that he may have put the children in even more imminent danger by his challenge.

Some of them barely reached past the guard rail of the narrow walkway, and if they slipped below, they'd take the others with them, to free-fall to their death in the hold.

Olsen stepped back a little, making a space between the fight that was about to happen and the children. The older guy was watching, a gleam of anticipation in his eyes.

Olsen raised his hands and said in halting Arabic that he was a police officer and that they were about to be boarded by the Norwegian navy, then watched as the two men sought to understand his words. A flicker of concern crossed the younger one's face, but the older guy wasn't backing down. His command sent the younger one forward.

Olsen, rather than moving away from the brandished knife, now went towards his attacker. When the knife swung, Olsen turned swiftly side-on and, angling his forearm, tried to anticipate the moment to strike. He judged it well. There was a satisfying grunt of anguish as the solid bone of his elbow met the guy's trachea. When the guy doubled over in an effort to breathe, Olsen grabbed the knife hand and bent it back until he heard the wrist bone snap.

But his next move wasn't quick enough. The knife dropped free, and missed his catch to clang on the walkway and sail into the void that lay below. The young guy, nursing his wrist, was struggling to get back on his feet. Olsen had no desire to continue their fight. He was tempted to push the guy off the walkway, but did the next best thing. The scream when it came resounded off the metal walls, but the guy wasn't walking anywhere, not on a knee shattered by an Alt-Berg heavy-duty police boot.

Olsen, free now of the fight, suddenly realized that the children had been mustered and were being quickly herded up the walkway by their other captor, who held a knife to the throat of the girl who'd silently begged Olsen's help.

There was no doubting what would happen if he made any attempt to follow.

He waited impatiently as the clanging sound of their feet faded. Once he was certain they'd progressed a level, Olsen headed upwards, intent now on making his way across the ship and heading for the comms aboard the helicopter. As he attempted to run on the still-pitching ship, he questioned why the removal of the children from the hold had happened and came up with only one answer. *Somehow they know that we're onto them. Or at least they suspect it.* And once the kids' captor reached the upper levels, they would know it for certain.

Despite all the plans, the carefully kept secrets, the dedication, the determination, it might all come to nought. Olsen allowed himself a brief moment to consider failure before Marita's voice resounded in his head. *Hurry.*

80

Tarik led the way, McNab and the gun following, Isla bringing up the rear. McNab had attempted to leave her behind, but she was having none of it, highlighting the fact that she was the only one who'd been on the bridge of a boat, any boat.

By Tarik's expression, he agreed with her, and to be truthful, McNab was impressed by Isla's determination and resilience. Plus he didn't want to reach his goal and not know what to do when he got there.

There had been no uproar since he'd whacked Brodie, so McNab was assuming he still lay tied up on the floor of his cabin.

As they staggered along, matching the rise and fall of the waves, McNab was conscious that although the swell continued, the strength and screech of the wind had definitely abated. He was initially pleased by that, until he remembered that the weather had succeeded in slowing down the tug's progress towards the bigger ship.

And that gave more time for them to be rescued. If anyone had any idea where they were.

McNab's thoughts were drawn to the others in this investigation. Had they figured out yet what had happened to him? Did they even care? It wasn't the first time he'd done his own thing, and Rhona was well aware that he'd fallen off the wagon, otherwise Chrissy wouldn't have shown up when she did. That in itself would suggest he was out of the picture.

But Chrissy would worry. Surely Chrissy would look for him?

But how the hell would she think to look on a boat in the middle of the North Sea? *When I refused even to go to Aberdeen in the first place.*

One person who might know where Brodie had taken him would be Davey. Since Davey had already given him up to Brodie, McNab couldn't imagine he would even approach the police, let alone volunteer any information about his association with the drug baron.

Unless of course Ollie has defied me and handed over the laptop and mobile.

McNab found himself wishing, even praying, that that was exactly what Ollie *had* done.

Tarik had gone ahead to check if the coast was clear, instructing them to wait here. When McNab had reminded him that he was the one with the gun, Isla had informed him that since Tarik had been moving about the tug unobserved for some time, if anyone could get them safely to the bridge, it would be him.

Huddled together awaiting the boy's return, Isla had revealed what she had planned.

'I don't want you to do that,' McNab had swiftly said.

'It's the best way to distract whoever is on the bridge. And they'll assume that I'm alone.'

What she said was true, but that didn't make it right.

Seeing his discomfort, Isla added, 'We have to get those kids off the boat before it reaches its destination.'

McNab ran the plan over in his mind. They must know

that both he and Isla had escaped their prisons by now, but there had been no active search for them. The storm had occupied the crew and laid Brodie out, and there was nowhere for them to go anyway, except overboard.

He could barge in with the gun, take his chance, but it wouldn't be the smartest move.

'You should join the police force,' he said, only half joking.

'I may yet do that,' she threatened.

They fell silent, hearing footsteps approach their hiding place. Then a low whistle told them it was Tarik.

'There are two men on the bridge. One is the captain. The other is the one from the cabin.'

So Brodie was free.

She must be frozen, was all McNab could think as Isla walked away from them. Tarik averted his eyes and McNab knew that the young man was deeply uncomfortable with what was about to happen.

'She'll distract them. Possibly enough for us to enter unannounced,' McNab said.

'What if they hurt her?'

McNab couldn't answer that one.

They'd gone over the plan with Tarik before approaching the bridge, then Isla had stripped. The oversized male clothes gone, she seemed to McNab as frail and vulnerable as when she'd crawled through to him. But her reaction had been just the opposite. Being naked had appeared to give her strength.

And her plan just might work, he thought.

81

The interior door that led into the hangar was guarded, although the two men who sat outside appeared relaxed.

Hoping they spoke English, she reminded them that she'd come in with the SAR team and wondered where they were.

'Not in there,' came the reply.

When Rhona looked puzzled by this, the same man responded, 'They're below, getting some food and sleep.'

'That's good,' Rhona said. 'Where exactly?'

That threw him a bit, but Rhona still had the impression that his response might be genuine. 'B deck. That's where the cafeteria and bunks are.'

Rhona swore lightly under her breath for effect. 'I left my bag on the chopper, and I really need it.'

The two men exchanged further words in Norwegian, before the English speaker said, 'It's not safe out there.'

'I can cope,' Rhona insisted.

They reluctantly opened the door for her. Even as Rhona stepped inside the hangar, she registered something odd about the interchange. Just like everything else about their time aboard the *Solstice*. Their separation from the SAR crew. The reaction when she'd visited the hospital.

All of which might have an innocent explanation. They'd taken refuge on a commercial ship. They'd been treated okay, if not in a friendly fashion, but everyone had been fastened on the storm, only now abating. Yet, she still didn't buy it. None of it. And neither did Harald.

The wind was tailing off, as evidenced by the level of noise in the hangar. They would be expected to leave soon, unless Olsen decided to alert the authorities. And Rhona was convinced that he should. They had nothing tangible from their search, apart from a child's toy. And yet . . .

Only when the *Solstice* was brought into Stavanger and forensically examined could they be sure that they were right, or wrong. If they were wrong, then they would have to face the consequences. But if they were right, and had done nothing to prove it?

The hangar was in darkness. Rhona checked for a light switch as the door clanged shut behind her, with the thought that having persuaded them to let her in here, they might not let her back out.

Rhona turned, expecting to view the large bulk of the NH-90, and found something quite different. There was a helicopter in the hangar, but it wasn't the one they'd arrived on. Slightly smaller in size, but sleek and obviously powerful, it was the only resident of the hangar apart from a variety of equipment.

No wonder the men had been puzzled by her desire to enter, and what was it they'd said? *It's not safe out there.* They hadn't been referring to the hangar, Rhona realized, but the deck. The NH-90 had never entered the hangar, as Harald had suggested it would, possibly because the conditions were too difficult at the time, or because there was insufficient room inside for both choppers.

Rhona made her way round the helicopter, noting the symbol and name of the Hagen Corporation emblazoned on the side. The thought occurred that someone from the corporation might well be aboard the *Solstice* at this very moment, and like them, unable to leave because of the weather.

Rhona located the door that led on to the deck and tried it. The wind was coming from the north, sweeping across the front of the hangar and still strong enough to take the door from her hands as it was opened. Crossing the deck wouldn't be easy, and, assuming she could reach the chopper and get inside, Rhona wasn't sure she would be able to follow Harald's instructions on using the comms.

But she had to try.

If the wind's too high, you get on your hands and knees. That had been Kyle's advice on Cairngorm, and Rhona decided she would take it now. She let the door go with the wind and it slammed back, metal against metal, with a resultant bang.

The deck she looked out on was in darkness, apart from the light that streamed from inside the hangar, and the fainter light from the upper regions of the ship. But Rhona was able to distinguish the large dark bulk of the NH-90, presumably anchored to the helicopter grid via the harpoon line they'd drawn up to help them land on the ducking ship.

Rhona dropped to her knees. Without Harald and Olsen to shield her, crawling was the only way she was likely to reach the aircraft. In the initial part of her journey she must have been in the lee of a deck structure, because when she emerged from behind it, she had to drop lower to avoid being rolled by the wind.

As she got closer, a light came on in the chopper. Startled by this, Rhona attempted to quicken her approach. Then she

saw various figures moving about and around the helicopter, beginning to disengage it from the grid.

The engine started up, and the blades began to turn.

All Rhona could think about was that the team was leaving and without her. She got onto her knees, and waved her
hands above her, screaming in a voice that was immediately
swept away in the wind.

82

McNab glanced at the young man crouched beside him. Slightly built, barely into his mid-teens, he had ingenuity, but McNab couldn't see him survive a fight unless he had some sort of weapon.

'How did you defend yourself before this happened?'

'My father was a university professor. He said words were our weapon.'

And that had worked out well.

McNab produced the mirror knife from his pocket and showed it to Tarik. 'Could you use this if you had to?'

'Yes,' he said without hesitation, reaching for the glass.

Isla's naked figure had halted at the foot of the set of steep steps that led up to the bridge. Above her the 360-degree windows gave the helmsman an uncontested view of the still-restless North Sea. The wind had mercifully dropped and dawn was about to break, judging by the line of fire on the horizon. Framed against it, a distant giant oil rig roared a dragon-like flame.

As Isla began her cold climb, McNab got a clear view of the second figure behind the glass and saw that it was definitely Brodie.

When he'd discovered Isla in the cabin, McNab's conviction that the Iceman too would be on board had lessened.

Isla had declared her tormentor had never come to the cabin and the last she'd seen of him had been in the plane.

So maybe they only had to deal with cologne man now, who, McNab suspected, had been Amena's handler, Stefan, at the Delta Club.

The tug bridge was isolated. Two levels above the main deck, surrounded by a walkway, and only accessible by the ladder Isla now climbed. If they managed to secure it, there was a chance, albeit small, that they might hold it until help arrived.

But – and here was the big problem in the plan – if they sent out a message, how soon could help arrive? It had taken a two-hour chase across the North Sea before the UK Border Agency and coastguard vessels had caught up with the cocaine-smuggling *Hamal*; how long before the authorities, either UK or Norwegian, managed to catch up with this tug?

Then the worst thought of all. In the interim, what would happen to the children below deck?

'They've spotted her,' McNab told Tarik as Isla halted in her climb.

They watched as the door to the bridge opened and Brodie appeared on the walkway.

'He mustn't hurt her,' Tarik said, his voice sharpened by fear.

'He won't,' McNab assured him.

Brodie was out and descending the stepladder even as Isla retreated downwards. She reached the bottom and waited. Until that point, McNab hadn't registered that she had something in her hand that caught the dawn's light reflection.

'Glass,' he realized. 'She took a piece of the fucking mirror.'

LIN ANDERSON

Brodie was taking his time in his descent. Why worry when you have a naked female waiting below. That was his mistake. Isla delayed until he was almost level with her, then struck. McNab couldn't see the mirror splinter, but he knew she'd wielded it and where.

Brodie gave a cry of anguish at its entry, sliding down the remaining steps of the ladder to land on the lower walkway. The shard had pierced him somewhere in the groin. McNab flinched at the thought of where, even as he rejoiced that Isla had gone one better than him.

'Go,' McNab said to Tarik.

Reaching Isla, McNab urged her to follow him up the ladder. What had just occurred below would have been difficult for the helmsman to see, tucked as they were at the foot of the stepladder, but it wouldn't be long before he came out to check.

The door above lay open, warning McNab the helmsman might already be aware of the skirmish below. The question was whether there was a weapon ready and available in that cockpit, and whether he would use it.

McNab eased himself into view, indicating that Isla should wait. He was aware her body temperature must be dropping, and swiftly, but hypothermia was preferable at this stage to death. And, he reminded himself, she'd faced extreme exposure before and survived.

The helmsman stood observing McNab's entry, his expression astounded. When he finally spoke, his voice was Aberdonian, his surprise, even irritation at the shenanigans he was witnessing, personified by his indignation.

He went into a babble about being hired to carry a container to a supply vessel. That was his job, nothing more.

McNab waved Isla into the room. She made no attempt

to cover her nakedness, but stood there, McNab thought, magnificent in it.

'That was your cargo,' McNab said. 'Her and eight children.'

The man's expression faltered as he tried to figure out his next move, or next denial.

'I want to make a call,' McNab said.

'If I cooperate?'

'Then I don't make a hole in your balls, which is what just happened to your running mate downstairs.'

Ollie's number was written indelibly on his brain. His voice even more so. McNab could see the owl eyes. Anticipate his voice. Oh, how he would welcome that voice.

'Ollie?'

There was a pause as Ollie registered who was speaking.

'What the fuck, McNab—'

'Shut up, Ollie, and listen.'

Isla had been right. The satellite comms system had allowed him to call an onshore mobile number, and that call had been direct to Ollie, the man who'd shown him a picture of the North Sea and all the ships currently on it. The man who'd explained that he couldn't locate a particular ship unless he knew its name. The man who might save them now.

Much to McNab's surprise, Ollie interrupted him.

'Your pal Davey handed himself in. Told us they'd taken you to Aberdeen, and the name of the boat they were leaving on. UK Border Agency and the coastguard are already on their way.'

'How long?' McNab said.

'It depends. The weather—'

'I know all about the fucking weather.'

Tarik, dispatched to the hold, had brought them here. Bedraggled, excited, traumatized, the children were ushered into the cockpit, the door locked.

'Any problems?' McNab said.

Tarik shook his head. 'Seems like the crew are lying low.'

McNab nodded, pleased at least for a lull in the proceedings.

They might yet be challenged, if the injured Brodie managed to muster Stefan and the rest of his forces. They were in a glass enclosure, with frightened children on an open sea, and a helmsman who seriously didn't want to be caught. According to Ollie, in constant touch, help would arrive within the hour.

It would, McNab accepted, be the longest hour of his life.

83

'Rhona. Come.' It was Olsen's voice, and his hand that dragged her up. 'We have to get you on board.'

She felt his arm round her shoulders, his attempt at steering her towards the helicopter, primed and ready to go. There was no room for a question or an answer during the process of boarding, as to why they were abandoning the *Solstice*. The noise of the prospective take-off drowned any prospect of that.

Once inside, Harald urged her to buckle in as before beside him. 'I'll explain later,' he mouthed.

Voices conversed in rapid Norwegian; the crew, wherever they had been, were back now in charge of their aircraft. The sky was still dark, although a promise of dawn streaked the horizon. *This has been the darkest, longest day*, Rhona thought, as the aircraft rose from the moving deck, the blades still fighting the wind, but no longer requiring the same degree of determination as when they'd landed.

'The *Solstice*'s leaving,' Rhona said worriedly, seeing the ship's lights move swiftly southwards.

The *Solstice* might be leaving, but the helicopter wasn't following its path, hovering instead above the area the RAS ship had just departed.

'What's happening?' Rhona asked.

'Alvis discovered children in a container in the hold,'

Harald told her. 'He thinks the crew are definitely on to us, and may have dumped their cargo already.'

'My God,' Rhona said. 'They threw them overboard?' She looked out at the seething surface of the sea. 'They'll never last without life jackets.'

'Fishermen don't wear them, and we've picked up a few of them.' Harald was trying to offer Rhona hope, or maybe the hope was meant for himself.

The chopper, she knew, had FLIR cameras. Night-vision technology for sea rescues in the dark. 'And,' Harald said, 'Alvis made the call. The *Solstice* will be boarded and escorted into Stavanger by the Norwegian navy.'

'There's a Hagen Corporation helicopter in the hangar,' Rhona said.

At that, Harald moved forward to where Olsen stood by the opening, looking down. Their rapid interchange sent Harald forward to give the pilot whatever orders Alvis had just issued.

The Hagen helicopter was a perfect escape vehicle for whoever on the *Solstice* was deemed important enough to be saved, and a helicopter like that might set down anywhere along Norway's coastline, or even further afield.

A small flotilla of Norwegian Sea Rescue Society speed boats dotted the surface below. In the rear of the chopper, in its emergency medical berths, were two of the children they'd pulled alive from the waves, and one, a young boy of perhaps ten, who hadn't survived.

Olsen sat with them, his face only occasionally lit by the flash of lights from the cockpit.

'He counted eight in that container, although there may have been more on the ship,' Harald told her.

'Someone wanted them to live.' Rhona indicated the oversized life jackets that had been hastily pulled about the rescued children.

'They didn't want it hard enough.'

Olsen looks like a dead man himself, Rhona thought, as a blinking red light illuminated his face.

Olsen came through then and spoke to the pilot. There was no doubt in Rhona's mind that they were about to abandon their search. That those bodies they had pulled from the water might be the only ones they ever found. The Norwegian Sea Rescue Society would continue the search alone, and the NH-90 would take its live and deceased casualties back to Stavanger.

84

Olsen finished his coffee, and rinsing the cup, placed it upside down next to the sink. Through the window, he could make out the lighted glass roof of the cultural centre rising above the neighbouring buildings. Although officially day, it was still dark enough to require the lights on. He hadn't slept on his return from Sola airport, although he had closed his eyes, in between checking his mobile for updates on the *Solstice*, and from further afield.

The news that had arrived had been both good and bad. More bodies had been pulled from the sea, ten in total, which suggested that there had been other children hidden on the *Solstice*. Ones he hadn't discovered. The ship itself had now been boarded and was currently being escorted towards the harbour at Stavanger. As suspected, the Hagen helicopter had gone from the hangar. Where it was now, they didn't know. Neither did they know who had been on the aircraft when it had departed the ship.

They'd also learned on landing at Sola that a tug from Aberdeen had been intercepted by the UK Border Agency with the assistance of the Norwegian Coastguard as it had crossed into Norwegian waters. On it eight children had been found, one of whom was the Syrian girl Amena Tamar who Detective Sergeant McNab had saved, then lost, then apparently found again.

A smile played on Olsen's lips at the tenacity and success of his Scottish counterpart, something which didn't altogether surprise him.

The jigsaw, the uniform grey and white pieces so difficult to distinguish and to align, seemed closer to completion. Although the picture was far from clear yet.

Hearing the shower in the guest bedroom, he guessed Rhona must also have risen. She'd accepted his offer of somewhere to wash and change, and maybe even sleep a little before the arrival of the *Solstice*. Her distress at the outcome of their own investigation had been tempered a little by the news that McNab had been located, and further enhanced by word that both Isla Crawford, the girl she'd helped on the mountain, and Amena Tamar had also survived. It seemed too that Brodie and Stefan, Amena's handler, had been on the tug.

Olsen wished the Norwegian side of the investigation had proved so successful.

He refilled the coffee filter and switched the machine back on. He had nothing here for Rhona to eat, but they could go out for that. The team would have to be debriefed, of course, but that could wait until after they got a forensic team onto the *Solstice*. He realized with a jolt that they were back with the practicalities of life, rather than the state of war they'd been in for the last twelve hours.

Rhona came through then, looking brighter than Olsen felt.

'Did you sleep?' he asked.

'A little. Is the *Solstice* here yet?'

'Soon,' he promised. 'They're just coming into Byfjorden. We could go down to the harbour and get some breakfast. Once we know which dock they're tying up at, we'll meet

Harald and the rest of the team there.' He handed her a freshly brewed coffee. 'Have you made contact with home yet?'

'With my forensic assistant. I wanted to let her know I was still breathing.' Immediately the words were out, she looked ill at ease at having said them.

'The two children we picked up are well,' he said, then realized she probably didn't know about the other bodies the SAR teams had pulled from the water. There was no point in keeping that back from her.

'There were that many on the ship?' She looked shocked.

'That was my mistake,' Olsen said. 'I should have instigated an official boarding sooner. I gave them time to dispose of their cargo, and they took it.' Now that he'd said it out loud, he was even more convinced that it was true.

'If they'd had advance word, they would have done the same thing,' she said. 'A raid, any raid, has consequences. Ask McNab.'

She sipped at her coffee. Then made a face.

'Too strong,' he offered.

'McNab would like it very much,' she assured him.

It had been raining and the cobbles shone underfoot as they walked down towards the guest harbour. Sørensens, Olsen thought, would be open for breakfast. If not, one of the other cafes that lined the quay. They walked together in silence. He liked that, the quiet of their togetherness. It was why Olsen felt comfortable in her presence. What had to be said, was said. Anything else was simply inferred.

It feels like being with Marita.

That thought brought an immediate feeling of guilt, answered almost as swiftly by Marita's internal voice.

She's a Scot, like me. What she says, she means. What she says she'll do, she does. Stop fussing.

He turned to find Rhona's eyes on him as though those inner words had fashioned themselves into sound.

'Talking to myself again,' he apologized.

'A habit I also have, usually while in the shower,' she told him with a smile.

The moment passed but Olsen was fairly sure he'd spoken some of the words out loud, and Dr MacLeod was merely covering for him.

They took a table inside and ordered standard breakfast fare. When the flatbread, cheese and smoked fish arrived they both seemed to register at the same moment how hungry they were.

'You're a fan of Norwegian food?' he said.

'Brown cheese not so much,' she admitted, 'but the fish, yes.'

They were just finishing up when the call came through. Harald's tone had been subdued; his mood, Olsen read, was much as their own.

'They're tying up at Strandkaien, across on the west bank,' Olsen told Rhona when Harald had rung off.

The *Solstice* was already in place on the opposite side of the harbour from where they now stood. The location, one of those normally used for cruise liners, had been commandeered by the police, and access restricted.

Lying in flat calm water, its sleek red and white lines proudly announcing it as part of the Hagen line, it was hard to believe it was the battered vessel they'd landed on, approaching the height of the storm. Looking up at the *Solstice*, Rhona relived the early hours of that morning, recalling the high seas, and wondering from where on the ship the children might have been thrown to their deaths.

As the car pulled up alongside, Olsen told her that he would leave her here with Harald.

'You're not coming aboard?' Rhona asked, obviously surprised.

'I want to interview the two men I saw with the children,' he explained. 'If they realize the man they met was really a police officer, we might get them to talk. The other crew members are likely to clam up and deny everything.'

'What about Hagen?'

'He's already been in touch offering his full cooperation "in this startling and horrific find on board one of his Tunisian-staffed ships".'

'So a full denial?'

'The only direct connection we have between Hagen and this trade is your mountain killer. The elusive Iceman. And we've yet to locate him.'

'You believe he may have been aboard the *Solstice*?' Rhona asked.

'According to your detective sergeant, he wasn't on the tug and the last Isla saw of him was in the plane. He may have made directly for the *Solstice* in advance of the delivery, perhaps via the helicopter you saw in the hangar. I don't think there's any doubt that the tug was heading there too.'

'So we try and find forensic evidence that he was on the *Solstice*, and if he had contact with the children held there.'

'That would be a start,' Olsen agreed, then added, 'Call Detective Sergeant McNab. Talk things through with him. There might be something that happened to him which could help direct your search here.'

*

McNab sounded hoarse. 'I spent most of the time honking up, which fucked my throat,' he explained.

'So not a sailor then?' Rhona said.

'Let's say I'm better off in the police than the navy.'

Their light interchange over, McNab gave her a brief but succinct overview regarding his time on the tug.

'And Brodie?' she asked.

'In hospital, under guard.' Before Rhona could ask why the hospital, McNab said, 'I speared him in the groin with a broken mirror.' Then he swiftly moved on. 'A forensic team's aboard the tug at the moment, searching for cocaine. They suspect there's a load somewhere in the ballast, like the previous shipment on the Turkish tug, but if so, it's well hidden.'

'And Isla?' Rhona said.

'She's okay. They checked her out, then allowed her home.'

Her final question was about Amena. Here, McNab's tone changed. 'It turns out she's pregnant,' he said sharply.

Rhona swore under her breath. 'They didn't check that the first time she was in hospital?'

'The test was negative back then.'

It wasn't unusual to have a negative pregnancy test followed later by a positive, but a positive was rarely wrong.

'One of the bastards at the Delta Club, probably,' McNab said.

'Maybe.' Rhona chose not to confirm something that might spike McNab's anger further.

'When are you back?' he demanded.

'When we finish with the *Solstice*.'

85

McNab fingered the empty coffee cup. Now back at the police station, he hadn't been fully honest with Rhona. At least not regarding Brodie. The groin wound had, of course, been inflicted by Isla. He'd told the girl that he had to take ownership of it, otherwise she could face an assault charge.

'I was aiming for the artery,' she'd told him on the bridge as they'd waited for help to appear on the horizon. 'I wanted him dead.'

Dressed in a selection of items borrowed from the others, she'd stopped shivering, although the nerve at the side of her mouth had still twitched from either adrenaline or fury.

'It's better if I own up to it,' McNab had insisted.

'Brodie will like that,' she'd offered.

Brodie might dispute McNab's version of events, but McNab thought he would probably go along with it *in the hope of inflicting damage of some sort on me.*

He threw the empty espresso cup in the bin and pressed the button for another. His next move should be to speak to Davey, which he'd been warned against doing by Ollie.

'I had to hand in the mobile and laptop.' Ollie had sounded apologetic. 'I told them you'd asked me to check it out for a friend who thought they'd been hacked. Then Davey came to the station of his own volition.'

That had been the big surprise.

McNab, however, wasn't sold on its sincerity. To his mind, Davey had known or suspected that the police would be on to him, *even with me disappeared*, because of the laptop, and he decided to come to them before they came *for* him. Davey, the businessman, understood the nature of a deal.

In view of Brodie's capture, Davey's twelve-hour standard stint in custody had been extended to twenty-four, on the decision of a senior officer, so he was still in the building. McNab made up his mind. As he drank down the second espresso, he said a silent apology to Ollie.

They had him in a holding cell, not quite as plush as Davey's usual surroundings. Back in school, they'd had bets on who would be the first one to get lifted by the police. It'd turned out to be McNab, although he hadn't been lifted, merely given a warning. They'd been with a group messing about in a cemetery with a couple of girls, drinking vodka they'd got an older guy to buy for them. At fourteen, it had been innocent in comparison to what others were up to.

It seems someone had spotted them and told the police of their underage drinking den. McNab had been the one to get caught, actively slugging from the bottle. After giving his address as demanded by the officer, a pissed McNab had found himself being driven home in a squad car, and delivered to his mother, in full view of their neighbours. Her reaction had scared him more than his first brush with the law.

The bold Davey had of course got away with it, having hidden among the stones until the police had left.

He was always good at getting what he wanted, McNab thought, *including Mary*.

Davey was pale under the tan, which he topped up, McNab knew, during frequent visits to the Spanish villa they owned in Marbella. Recalling the existence of the villa, McNab wondered why Davey hadn't just escaped there rather than walk into the police station and give himself up.

Davey, spotting his entry, quickly rose from the bed, the expression on his face one that McNab realized could only be interpreted as joy.

'Mikey, you're okay.'

McNab stepped back, perturbed at both the echo of his youthful name and the tenor of the voice that had just said it.

Davey, seeing his reaction, halted, the joy in his face being replaced by – what? Sadness, disappointment? Or simply guilt?

McNab stood in silence, for once unsure how to play this. It wasn't and couldn't be an official interrogation. Someone would interview him about Davey. Then someone would interview Davey concerning him. And so much would be lost in between, in particular, the truth.

At least, if I questioned him, we might get close to it.

'I didn't put that stuff on the laptop,' Davey was saying. 'Brodie framed me to keep me under control.'

McNab snorted his derision. 'Really. That wasn't your face I saw? Your arse? Your prick?' McNab took a breath to try to control his anger. 'You were at the Delta Club. You took part in one of Brodie's sessions.'

Davey opened his mouth and shut it again. 'Okay, I had sex with probably a prostitute, and he filmed it. That's how he caught me.'

McNab could feel his teeth grinding together, taste the sick, much like on the tug, after he'd just vomited for the zillionth fucking time. 'Not a prostitute. A thirteen-year-old trafficked refugee by the name of Amena Tamar.'

It had taken time for the images to distil and come together. His memory of the video he'd watched with Ollie of that fateful night at the Delta Club, the clips on Davey's machine. But then Ollie as a super-recognizer had confirmed what McNab couldn't bear to acknowledge. Davey, on some earlier occasion, had been one of the men using Amena.

Davey was staring at him, horror in his eyes.

'I swear I didn't know. They fed me cocaine. They—'

'Shut the fuck up,' McNab said.

But he didn't; Davey just kept on going.

'I didn't betray you, Mikey. I tried to tell you they were on their way to your place. I called your mobile. Remember? I was driving the vehicle that lifted you, but then I came here to the station and told them about the boat. That you might be on it. That's why you're alive, Mikey. I'm the reason you're alive.'

McNab turned and banged on the door.

He wanted out and fast, so that he might vomit up all those weasel words he'd just swallowed in that room.

86

A small shoe. A torn notebook containing drawings and words in Arabic and English. A hairband Rhona had extracted from a corner, the tangled dark strands bound tight to the elastic like a rope. But it was the smell of the place that told the story. Of incarceration, lingering fear and outright terror.

From here, Olsen had watched the children led out, tied together. He'd tried to stop it happening and had failed, something that would probably haunt him to the end of his days.

It wasn't difficult to image that scene as, on hands and knees, Rhona went over every square inch of their prison. There might not have been visible evidence other than the small collection of objects they'd left behind, but there was plenty of other evidence of the children who'd been imprisoned here, and probably of the men who had guarded them.

The number involved in the cull last night, judging by the live casualties and bodies retrieved from the water, numbered thirteen in total, and only two of those remained alive. Olsen had been able to identify a girl the helicopter winchman had plucked from the waves as being part of the group he'd watched being taken from this container.

Startled by recognition as she'd been hoisted semi-conscious into the aircraft, he'd told Rhona that the same girl had silently begged him for help, even as she'd passed him by.

Rhona looked up from her work to find Harald watching her. Fully suited like herself, the only way he was recognizable from the army of Norwegian SOCOs that had invaded the ship was by his bulk and his eyes.

'How are you doing?' he said through the mask.

'Fine,' she acknowledged.

'Want to take a look at what we've found?'

The suite of rooms lay to the rear of the cargo hold, although discovering them without prior knowledge of their existence would, Rhona suspected, have been difficult. According to Harald, sometime between the discovery that the police were on board and the time the NH-90 had taken off again, a team had been dispatched down here to wall up the evidence.

'They did a good job,' Harald said. 'If it hadn't been for the noise of the storm we might have heard them.'

Rhona stepped through the door that had been cut in the recently constructed metal bulwark to find a short corridor with open doors on either side. In each of the cabins, a SOCO was at work.

Rhona watched as one swabbed blood from a wall. Above him, a camera eye lay dormant.

'All the cameras are linked to a central source at the end of this corridor. The equipment's state of the art. The desire for the commodity they were exploiting, international. The money being made from it . . .' Harald ground to a halt, shaking his head in disbelief.

'How long do you think the *Solstice* was being used like this?' Rhona said.

'Alvis picked up on rumours maybe three years ago. His wife was an investigative journalist following stories about trafficking of refugees, predominantly from North Africa. Then one of Marita's Tunisian contacts prompted him to look into the Hagen Corporation, who recruit their crews mainly in Sousse. Nobody believed him at first, especially me,' Harald admitted.

'They've taken the computer equipment off the boat now,' he went on. 'I'm glad I'm not going to be one of the people who has to view that stuff.' He threw Rhona a look of horror. 'Makes our job seem like a piece of cake, doesn't it?'

Olsen scooped the scrambled eggs onto two plates and added the smoked salmon on top.

'I apologize. This is more like a Norwegian breakfast than dinner. Except for the wine, of course.' He topped up Rhona's glass.

Leaving the *Solstice* earlier, she'd discovered Olsen waiting for her on the quayside.

'Harald told me he was calling it a day. I thought you might appreciate some food, and a shower,' he'd said.

An offer which Rhona had gratefully accepted.

'We could eat out, or . . .'

Rhona had indicated the 'or' would be better. All she'd wanted to do at that point was stand under a hot shower and wash away the terrible smell of that container.

As they'd made their way back to his flat, Olsen had asked how the forensic search had gone.

'My part's done. Harald's team will be there for a while yet. I'll head home tomorrow and we'll keep in touch about the results from both sides of the investigation.' She'd looked round at Olsen then. 'Did you interview the two men?'

'I did. They decided not to recognize me and denied there had ever been children on the *Solstice*, even though the younger one had a dislocated kneecap and broken wrist from our encounter. I expect that to be the same for everyone employed on the ship.'

'How do they explain the bodies in their wake then?'

'I suspect the story will be refugees trying to reach Norway by sea, rather than land. Their boat went down in a terrible storm and they drowned. The press and public are more likely to go for that explanation, because it's easier to believe than one that might implicate someone like Hagen. He's the image of an internationally respected Norwegian company, which employs a great many people.' Olsen paused, a pained look on his face. 'And the truth is no country really wants refugees arriving uninvited on their shores, even if they are children.'

Olsen, she knew, was right. A single child washed up dead on a beach provided a worldwide photo opportunity that generated sympathy. The threat of boatloads, not so much.

'We'll produce DNA evidence that proves those children were aboard the *Solstice*,' Rhona told him. 'And the two survivors from the *Solstice* will tell the true story.'

'I'm counting on you, and them, to do that.' Olsen gave her a half-smile. 'Although I fear the children's voices are likely to be less effective than the scientific proof.'

As they moved to the sitting room with their coffee, Rhona judged there was more on Olsen's mind than he'd already mentioned during the meal.

'We're getting some kickback from Hagen's lawyers,' he

admitted when questioned. 'The move of course is designed
to separate him and the company from what may have happened on the *Solstice*. And in that they could succeed.' He
paused. 'So we need a direct link between Hagen and someone close to him, who we know was involved.'

And that had to be Isla Crawford's attacker.

87

The boss looks like shit, was McNab's only thought at that moment. And the reason for that had to be that Margaret had gone. Why else would he be here and not at the hospital?

McNab desperately wanted to ask but couldn't bring himself to. He thought of Chrissy. Why hadn't she told him? Then he recalled the undelivered calls while he was on the tug boat, and acknowledged that since he'd arrived back in Glasgow, he'd avoided answering or checking his mobile, determined above everything to speak to Davey first.

Because I knew anyone I spoke to would tell me not to do that. Including the boss, by the expression on his face.

'Sit down, Sergeant.'

McNab wasn't sure he wanted to, but did anyway. Then he waited, trying not to meet the boss's eye, yet attempting to read his manner.

'Davey Stevenson . . .' the boss began.

McNab controlled his desire to spout forth his anger about Davey. 'Yes, sir,' he managed.

'I understand you were childhood friends?'

McNab answered in the affirmative, while wondering how the boss might know that, except perhaps via Chrissy.

'We were, sir.'

405

'And that you discovered material on his laptop regarding Neil Brodie?'

Fuck's sake.

'I asked Ollie in IT to take a look after his wife was knocked down in the hit-and-run.'

'Why exactly?'

'Mary – Mrs Stevenson,' he quickly corrected himself, 'said Davey was being threatened by Neil Brodie. I thought Mrs Stevenson may have been attacked because of that, sir.'

'And this somehow led to your incarceration on that tug?'

'Yes, sir.'

The boss was regarding him with some consternation. 'Okay, Sergeant. This is where you and I both come clean on what's happened to us in the last forty-eight hours.'

McNab side-swerved the coffee machine. Caffeine couldn't deal with or dull what he felt at that moment. He doubted alcohol could either. Emerging from the station after his debrief, although he'd promised the boss that he would finally go home and get some sleep, he made a call instead.

'You're alive.' Ellie's voice sounded hoarse and worried.

'Half alive,' he admitted.

There was a moment's silence. 'Are you going home?'

'I am.'

'Shall I meet you there?'

'That would be good.'

McNab hadn't slept for what felt like an eternity, and he wasn't ready to sleep yet. At this moment he didn't want to shut his eyes ever again, for fear of what his dreams would bring. If he just kept going, perhaps none of what had happened would be true. Not Mary. Not Davey. Not the tug and what had happened out there on that mad frothing sea. And not Margaret.

Keep moving. Keep awake.

Opening his front door, he registered the familiar scent of home. In past days it had often smelt bad, of stale whisky and unwashed dishes. No longer. All he caught was a place that hadn't been occupied for a while.

The place I left in a hurry.

Like a zombie, McNab walked to the shower and stripped off. As he did so, he registered that his body was a map of what had been thrown at him in the time between leaving here via the roof, and now.

I'm a fucking sight for sore eyes. He grinned manically at his reflection. Who needs a skull on their back when they look like this?

It was a replay of an earlier evening. The buzzer, him exiting the shower to answer. Opening the door, draped in a towel. Only this time it was Ellie who carried the pizza box.

McNab felt tears squeeze from his eyes as, seeing him, she deposited the box and gathered him in her arms.

They ate the pizza together, the box sitting on the bed between them. Conscious that he wasn't in a position to tell her everything that had happened since they'd last met, McNab had given her a brief résumé.

'And Davey's in custody?'

'Until tomorrow.'

She was sitting, her knees pulled up, the duvet across her middle. Wintry light played on her upper body and its swirls of colour. McNab thought she looked beautiful.

'You should sleep,' she said, throwing back the cover and stepping out of bed. 'I have a man to ink.'

'Not his balls, I hope?'

She smiled at him then began pulling on her clothes. McNab was sorry to see that happen.

'I could manage one more time,' he offered, in an attempt to keep her there.

'Sleep would be the better option.' She scooped up her hair and knotted it at the back. As she did so, he caught sight of a vertical tatt that ran up the deep inside of her left arm.

'What's that one say?' He raised his own arm to indicate where he meant.

'*Uten Frykt*. It's Norwegian for "without fear".'

A bell rang in McNab's head. 'Why do you have that?' he demanded.

Ellie looked slightly taken aback at both the question and the way it had been asked. She shrugged in answer. 'It's a motorbike thing.'

'A gang slogan?' McNab tried to even his tone, but, by the look on her face, he wasn't managing to.

'Why are you so interested in it?' Ellie fired back at him.

'Is it a gang mark?' McNab insisted.

'It's a motorbike thing,' she repeated.

When it was obvious she wasn't planning on volunteering any more than that, McNab said, 'The dead pilot on Cairngorm had that tatt, as did the man who killed him.'

Ellie digested his outburst and came out fighting. 'As will scores of other people. You've got a skull on your back, for fuck's sake. It's a gang thing too.'

Realizing he was making a mess of things, McNab rose naked to try to make amends.

'I'm sorry. It's just we have to find that guy and if the tatt helped us do that . . .' He tailed off as Ellie turned her back on him and headed for the door.

The tatt had reminded him of something he'd been trying to forget. The Iceman, as Isla still referred to him, hadn't been on the tug, and had, Rhona suspected, departed the *Solstice* before it had been officially boarded. It was the Iceman she thought who'd ordered the death of the children. It was the Iceman in the photographs with Hager. The invisible man who just kept slipping through their fingers.

88

Rhona could hear Olsen moving about in the kitchen. He'd gone out earlier, she assumed for something for their breakfast. On his return, his mobile had rung a couple of times, and she'd heard him in rapid conversation in Norwegian.

Something's up, she thought as she listened to the controlled excitement in his voice. Ten minutes later, she learned what it was.

'Hagen's yacht, the *Mariusud*, is back in the harbour.' Olsen offered her some more coffee as he spoke. 'We're going to meet him there in an hour's time.'

'Meet Hagen?' Rhona set her cup back down in amazement.

'Tor is keen to help, he says, but wants our meeting low-key. I suggested the yacht.'

His use of the chief suspect's first name had confused Rhona. 'You know this man personally?'

Olsen regarded her as though he was about to make a revelation, which in fact it turned out to be.

'Tor and I were teenagers together. We both helped out on our families' fishing boats. We were big rivals in how much fish was caught.' Olsen's look darkened a little. 'His father moved into supplying the oil business. Tor got rich. I became a police inspector.' Seeing her expression, Olsen added, 'Like Scotland, Norway is a very small place. If we're not related to you, then we know someone who is.'

Rhona tried to absorb this news, thinking all the time that nothing Olsen had said before now, or even hinted at, had suggested that he knew the owner of the Hagen Corporation in person. She thought of Harald and the other inspectors, all of whom surely knew of this connection.

'Was Harald aware of your relationship with Hagen?'

'Past relationship,' he corrected her. 'Yes, as were the others. In fact Harald's grandfather's farm is adjacent to Tor's mother's family's farm.'

'That's why it all had to be so secret?'

'That and the fact that he's Norway's blue-eyed boy,' Olsen said. 'No one would believe it without definitive truth, and even then . . .' He shook his head. 'Harald gave me a hard time about my suspicions at first, as did the others. We all believe what we want to believe.' He paused. 'Marita, on the other hand, questioned everything. As an outsider she had a different perspective on all things Norwegian.'

'Was the boy you knew back then capable of what you think he's involved in now?' Rhona asked.

'Who knows?' Olsen admitted. 'I suspect most of us are capable of almost anything, given the circumstances.' He regarded Rhona. 'Maybe the Tor I knew wasn't aware of what was happening on the *Solstice*, but the man with him in those photographs has been close to Tor for years. And that man did know.'

'Are you sure you want me to come with you?' Rhona said. 'I'm not a police officer.'

'You're a forensic scientist, which is what I require.'

*

Hagen had the smile of a successful man. He'd bestowed it on Rhona on their arrival, and graciously accepted her presence, although it was clear from the onset that he had no wish for her to be party to his talk with Olsen.

Having been introduced by Olsen as a relative of Marita's, currently visiting Stavanger, Rhona was then encouraged to take a look round the yacht, while the two men talked. Rhona thanked her host, and without glancing at Olsen, was escorted away by the young crew member who'd welcomed them both on board.

Dressed in smart deck gear, like an image in a fancy yachting magazine, the young man's English was perfect *and* he was swift to exhibit a knowledge of Scotland and its differentiation from England. He was, Rhona thought, the perfect tour guide. No doubt had she been from London, Wales or Yorkshire, she suspected his knowledge of that location, its habits and eccentricities, would have been equally evident.

Rhona followed him round like the usual gawking spectator on the lives of the rich and famous, making appropriate noises in all the right places. Aware that she had no idea how long the talk between Olsen and Hagen would last, she eventually managed to break away, asking in a manner which she wasn't used to if she could have a few minutes to walk alone and admire this stunning yacht.

He agreed fairly swiftly, and Rhona suspected, being the only apparent member still working, he really wanted to be off-duty. Once he'd left her, Rhona began to retrace her steps. As they'd moved through the yacht, she'd tried to commit to memory the areas he had purposely not shown her, the private cabins in particular.

Olsen suspected the man they sought had been on board and recently. The yacht, which they'd had under surveillance as it cruised the Norwegian shoreline, had seemingly crossed paths with one of the corporation's helicopters. Possibly the one which had departed the *Solstice*.

If they had connected, then whoever had deserted the ship prior to their official boarding may well have spent time on board the *Mariusud*.

The main cabins were situated one level down from the staterooms. Rhona halted when she reached the main room and listened at the closed doors. The two men were deep in conversation; the words she couldn't understand, but the interchange was obviously tetchy. Hagen's voice sounded as though he was trying to convince Olsen of something. Olsen's short replies and longer silences suggested he wasn't persuaded.

Leaving them to it, Rhona headed downstairs to the sleeping quarters.

There were six cabins, one of which, by its double-door entry, implied it was the master bedroom. A swift look inside confirmed it was currently being used by Hagen. Rhona began checking the others, only one of which looked as though it had recently had an occupant.

If Olsen's intelligence sources were correct, then that occupant may well have been the man they sought.

Conscious of the time, Rhona quickly unpacked her forensic equipment and headed for the toilet. Just as in the bedroom, no personal items had been left behind, but that didn't mean the recent occupant hadn't left evidence of themselves. Rhona worked the raised toilet seat in particular, then any other surface he may have engaged with. Had the room been cleaned, much would have been lost, but it hadn't yet, which suggested the occupant had only recently departed.

Exiting the guest room, she hesitated. They would emerge soon, and she would have to vacate this area of the yacht before that happened, but before she did . . .

Rhona stepped back inside the master bedroom.

She was climbing the stairs when she heard the stateroom door open. Olsen emerged first, followed by Hagen. Olsen's anger was evident. Hagen, seeing Rhona waiting for them, tried to muster his previous manner and almost succeeded.

To cover the obviously uncomfortable moment, Rhona stepped in and, still playing the role of tourist, delivered a gushing appreciation of the yacht. Olsen, catching Rhona's eye, offered her a silent thank you.

Hagen rallied. 'I understand you're leaving later today or I would have offered to take you for a sail in her.' He gave her his signature smile. 'Perhaps next time you visit Stavanger?'

'That would be excellent,' Rhona said.

'What happened in there?' Rhona asked as soon as they were in the car.

'Tor gave the guy up. His name's Einer Nilsen. He was hired as a bodyguard five years ago. Ex-special forces. Tor says he was alerted recently to the fact that Nilsen might be working at something under the radar, involving cocaine shipments via the *Solstice*. He sacked him.'

'What about the children?'

Olsen muttered something, which Rhona took to be a Norwegian curse. 'He was horrified. Or so he said. Promised to do everything in his power, and he has plenty at all levels of Norwegian society, "to right these wrongs",' Olsen quoted.

'Where's Nilsen now? Has he any idea?'

'He says not. He maintains Nilsen left his employment over a month ago.'

'That's convenient,' Rhona said. 'And he hasn't seen him since?'

'No.'

'Someone was staying on the *Mariusud* recently,' Rhona told him. 'I have a sample of their DNA. If it's a match for our Iceman . . .'

Olsen's face lit up. This time he chose to swear in English, accompanied by the hint of a smile.

89

McNab pushed open the ward door and, showing his badge at the reception desk, indicated that he'd come to see Neil Brodie.

The young nurse bestowed a knowing look on him, then led McNab to a door at the very end of the corridor, outside which a uniform had been placed. The officer, recognizing McNab, opened the door for him.

'Fuck off,' Brodie said as soon as he saw who his visitor was.

McNab let the spit-laden words pass him by and observed Brodie without responding. Eventually Brodie was the one to break eye contact, turning determinedly to view the silent TV overhead.

'Your Norwegian contact,' McNab said. 'Where is he?'

Brodie drew his eyes from the screen and gave him a withering look. 'Who?'

'The one who delivered Isla Crawford to the tug.'

Brodie was calculating whether he should respond or not. What he needed, McNab decided, was an incentive.

'He's wanted for four counts of murder. So if you know where he is and don't say, you become an accessory.' McNab made sure he sounded delighted by such a prospect.

Brodie went back to studying the screen. 'No idea who you're talking about.'

McNab took a moment to review the telephone conversation he'd just had with Police Inspector Olsen regarding an interview he'd conducted with Tor Hagen, the memory of which made him smile.

'Looks like someone higher up has just ratted on Einer Nilsen. Anyone linked to him – like you – will be going down.'

The name McNab had uttered with such relish had brought a sudden colour to Brodie's pasty face.

'Nilsen,' McNab repeated.

Brodie was mumping his gums in time with whatever thought was going through his head.

As McNab turned to go, a stream of invective issued forth, followed by a request to speak to any fucking pig but him.

As he opened the door, McNab's smile grew a little wider.

He decided to go by Mary's room before he departed the hospital, thinking only to confirm that she was still out of danger. The staff nurse, recognizing him from the time of the rammy with Davey, came to check him out.

McNab raised a hand in a peace offering, and showed her his ID.

'Mrs Stevenson's waiting for her husband,' she said as though it might be McNab's fault that Davey hadn't arrived.

McNab made up his mind in that moment. 'I'd like to speak to her,' he said.

She was propped up on pillows, her head still swathed in bandages. Her eyes, which opened on his entry, were surrounded by bruising, but the swelling, he was pleased to see, had subsided.

She registered it was him, and not Davey. An emotion

crossed those eyes, but McNab wasn't sure if it was disappointment or relief.

'Hi, Mary,' he said. 'You look better.'

'I look like shite,' she retorted. 'As do you.'

Her voice, he noted, was strong, the accent he loved still evident.

'Where is he?' Mary demanded.

'At the station, for at least another twelve hours.'

She looked at him askance. 'What . . .' she said, her face clouding over.

'Davey gave himself up. He came clean, Mary,' McNab explained. 'About Brodie, the blackmail.' He decided to omit the child pornography for the moment, something he was sure she didn't know about. 'And he saved my skin,' McNab found himself adding.

Her startled eyes fastened on him, almost in disbelief. McNab pulled up a chair and, taking Mary's hand in his, he told her the whole sorry story, or at least the part he wanted her to know.

90

The strategy meeting had been short, at least the bit Rhona was party to. Conducted in English for her benefit, it had referred primarily to the continuing forensic examination of the *Solstice*, followed by Olsen's report of their visit to the *Mariusud*. The latter being the part that had provoked the biggest reaction.

'Was it wise to speak with Hagen alone?' Harald had immediately responded.

'No, it wasn't,' Olsen had conceded. 'But we now know the name of the man we seek, and something more about him.' Here he'd glanced at Rhona. 'We also have forensic material which might prove Hagen is lying about the last time he saw Nilsen.'

'And which may prove Nilsen's connections to the Cairngorm deaths,' Rhona had added.

'The evidence from the *Mariusud* was obtained without his consent,' Harald had said.

At that point in the proceedings, Olsen had apologized to Rhona and indicated that he would prefer to talk to his officers alone. As Rhona had exited, she'd heard the discussion move into Norwegian.

Accepting Birgitt's offer of coffee, Rhona took a seat in the reception area. She was booked to fly to Aberdeen shortly, and would be back home in Glasgow by tonight. Chrissy she'd already been in touch with. Plus McNab and she'd had a brief conversation when Olsen had contacted him with the news about Nilsen.

McNab had sounded upbeat, although from what little she'd heard, his trauma on the tug boat had been as great as theirs on the *Solstice*.

Except that McNab had prevented the children's deaths.

The one person she hadn't updated was Sean. Something she should rectify, she decided. Rhona listened as the number rang out, aware that Sean wasn't one to cherish his mobile, often leaving it behind or simply ignoring it, if he was practising. Fully expecting it to go to voicemail, Rhona was surprised when he suddenly answered.

'Rhona? Is that you?' he said as a female voice in the background called out his name in what Rhona thought was a friendly manner.

'Sorry, is this a bad time?' Rhona said.

'Not at all.'

In the brief pause that followed, Rhona imagined she could hear that voice again, before Sean said, 'When are you back?'

'Later today, probably,' Rhona found herself saying as though it might not happen.

'Do you want me to bring Tom round?' He sounded tentative, or disinterested.

'Can you keep him another couple of days,' Rhona said as the door to the conference room opened and the team trooped out. 'Just in case?'

His response of 'Sure thing' sounded, Rhona thought, mightily relieved. *Either he doesn't want to lose the cat or he's not keen on seeing me.*

Realizing Rhona was about to leave, each of the men

came across to bid her farewell. By their mood, she judged the meeting had been less than satisfactory, despite their lead on Einer Nilsen.

Olsen signalled that they should make their way to the airport. Rhona said her goodbyes and followed Olsen down the stairs.

'They didn't look too happy,' Rhona offered as Olsen ushered her through the security doors and across the entrance hall.

'He who sups with the devil . . .' Olsen quoted. 'That was the message from the men.'

A blast of cold air met them as they exited. The few flakes of snow that drifted down were melting in the puddles. Rhona pulled up her hood and followed the tall figure of Olsen towards his car.

'They think you'll be influenced by Hagen?'

'They know he has power and will use it against me, and anyone else who crosses him,' Olsen told her.

'That was why Hagen wanted to see you?'

Olsen opened the door for her, and Rhona slipped inside. Before he started the engine, Olsen gave her his answer.

'Tor was very keen to learn what we knew, although he was trying hard to conceal that. I gave him a story, which I think he believed,' Olsen said. 'We'll know soon enough.'

Olsen abandoned his car at the Commissariat, choosing instead to walk home via Lagård Gravlund. It was, he registered, his first visit since that morning when he'd promised Marita to save the children.

And I failed.

As he approached the rear of the graveyard, Olsen caught the stifled sounds of male voices and female laughter. The graveyard, he knew, was a favoured spot for teenagers to drink and smoke together, away from the public eye, and the police.

No one, they figured, would come strolling here in the pitch black, like him.

Olsen was neither angry nor censorious about their presence. He didn't regard their antics as defiling this space. Marita, he knew, would have welcomed them dancing on her grave, *because they're so alive and full of desire*.

He felt a stirring in his own loins, a memory of his continued longing for the woman he'd lost, but still loved.

A sudden silence and a trio of mobile phone lights suggested Olsen's arrival had occasioned the group's departure. Olsen watched as the small entourage of two girls and three boys gave him a wide berth, departing through the gate to run laughing down the main road.

Locating his seat, Olsen settled himself down. Wet snowflakes, drifting down among the cypress trees, stroked his face like soft fingers. It seemed to him that, like the snow, he too was dissolving, his resolve and his reason for being.

Alvis. Her voice was clear and loving. Olsen let it wash over him, wondering why he ever thought he might live without this, without her.

You're nearly there, she said.

Why would she say this when he'd failed so dramatically?

Whoever said it would be easy? Olsen could almost see that look on her face.

'Eleven children died,' he said aloud to the darkness.

And two lived.

It was almost as if he was convincing himself.

You can save more.

'How?' he found himself saying.

By accepting what Tor was back then, and what he is now.

A frost glittered the walkway as Olsen made his way round the lake towards home. The sky, having cleared of snow clouds, now sparkled with icy stars. His communication with Marita had been, he acknowledged, as much about his own thinking process as reconnecting with hers.

91

'I come bearing gifts.' McNab plonked the large coffee and steaming paper bag on Ollie's desk.

Ollie sniffed his appreciation. 'What's in there?'

'A hard-top roll with a double helping of tattie scones and black pudding. The perfect all-day breakfast.'

'Which I can eat now?'

McNab shook his head. 'It's an enticement, not a reward . . . yet.'

It was as though Ollie had suddenly registered the bruised state of McNab's face.

'That looks bad,' he offered with a slight grimace.

'You should see the bits that are not on view, like my balls.'

The grimace strengthened.

'But you're not going to,' McNab promised.

Ollie, with a further wistful glance at his waiting reward, said, 'I found him, although it wasn't easy.'

'It never is,' said McNab with a smile.

McNab left Ollie munching on his crispy roll, and went looking for a replenishment for his own coffee, long since consumed. Ollie was right when he said it hadn't been easy to trail the man currently called Einer Nilsen. If not for

Ollie's super-recognizer status, and his fortitude when asked to watch the unwatchable . . .

'You should join Interpol,' McNab had suggested. 'Or MI5 at least.'

'You want rid of me?'

'No way. I'd never venture in here if you weren't around.' McNab had indicated his distaste for the digital environment in which he stood.

'Anything else I find, I'll call you,' Ollie had promised, turning his attention to his reward.

McNab located the nearest hot drinks machine, and pressed for a double espresso. If Ollie was right and Hagen was aware of Einer Nilsen's history and proclivities when he'd employed him, that suggested Hagen was at least sympathetic to those beliefs.

'The FSK, Forsvarets Spesialkommando, or Armed Forces Special Command,' Ollie had told him, 'is pretty secretive. It was initially formed to protect oil platforms against terrorism. Nilsen left the service abruptly. Not sure why, but I suspect he formed a neo-Nazi subgroup, known as *Uten Frykt*. Their major interest being no more immigrants in Norway, especially from the Syrian conflict.'

McNab had gone a little cold at this point, recalling the stupid argument he'd had with Ellie over the tattoo. He'd even gone as far as questioning Ollie about the *Uten Frykt* tatts.

'A Fearless tatt doesn't mean you're a Nazi sympathizer, just as a skull doesn't mean you're a Son of Anarchy,' Ollie had told him, slightly puzzled by the reference.

McNab pressed for a refill, knowing he should call Ellie, but unable to do so, yet. Swallowing down his second double shot, he dispensed with the cup, then headed out, avoiding meeting any of his colleagues, especially Janice.

When this was all over he would deal with what the boss had told him.

He'd warned Cheryl that he was on his way to the safe house. Her reply to his tentative text had been brief but positive, so it looked as though he may have been granted a reprieve at least.

When he was ushered into the room set aside for visitors, Amena was already there, with someone McNab hadn't expected to see. Ursula watched as Amena ran towards NcNab and hugged him. McNab, not sure what he should do with his own arms, chose to pat the girl lightly on the head.

Now that they'd greeted one another, McNab wasn't sure where to go from here, until Ursula stepped in to help. It seemed she could converse a little with Amena, or at least they'd worked out what Amena wanted to say. McNab listened to the translated 'thank you'. The reassurance that Amena was well, and that the baby was too.

McNab was taken aback at this point. He'd assumed that she would have agreed to have the pregnancy terminated, but this appeared not to be the case. His worried glance at Ursula saw her explain further.

'Amena lost her entire family in Syria. With the baby she doesn't feel alone any more.'

McNab wanted to protest, state that she was only a child herself. Noting the look Ursula gave him, he decided not to.

With a final hug and a 'Thank you, Michael', Amena indicated she would leave them now.

McNab waited for the door to close behind her, then asked Ursula why she'd returned to the safe house herself.

'You made that possible when you arrested Brodie, and Amena's handler. They told me they would kill her if I went.'

'You'll testify then?' McNab asked the million-dollar question.

She gave a little nod. 'About the club and the drugs, and the kids on that ship.'

'You knew about that?' McNab said, surprised.

'We were threatened with the death ship if we gave them any trouble. Only one girl came back from there, with a scar and missing a kidney.'

'Did you ever meet a head guy, name of Einer Nilsen?' McNab gave as good a description as he could manage. 'He had a tattoo on his wrist, maybe elsewhere too. It said *Uten Frykt*.'

A shadow crossed her face. 'He was at one of the Delta Club sessions,' she confirmed. 'A vicious bastard.'

She regarded McNab. 'Brodie nearly killed you that night when he picked me up in the four-by-four.'

'I bet he wishes he had.'

As he departed the safe house, McNab heard someone rap at the window and, looking up, spotted Amena. Returning her wave, McNab pondered why, after what she'd been subjected to, Amena should choose to give birth at all.

The call from Ragnar Lodbrok arrived as he walked to the car. McNab listened in silence to the full story regarding what had happened on Hagen's yacht, including Rhona's clandestine forensic examination, and what now concerned Olsen.

'You were mates with this guy?' McNab said.

'I hear you've experienced a similar childhood relationship?' Olsen's tone was dry but understanding.

The fucking Viking warrior isn't that different from me, McNab reluctantly admitted to himself as he accepted that word of Davey's association with Brodie had crossed the North Sea.

'Okay. What do you need me to do?'

92

The flat felt empty and abandoned. It was cold too, the windows covered by a filigree of frost. She'd remembered to set the timer on the central heating, but had obviously got the required hours wrong. Rhona switched the system on full blast, saying a silent thank you to Sean for removing Tom, otherwise the poor cat may have frozen to death.

Standing under the shower, Rhona reflected on everything that had happened since Hogmanay. McNab, she concluded, had used up another of his nine lives. For someone who disliked cats, it seemed he possessed some feline qualities, in particular the act of falling on his feet.

She'd turned then to Olsen and their conversation in the car on the way to the airport. Enigmatic as ever, Rhona had no idea what Politiinspektør Alvis Olsen's next move might be.

She'd kept the third and worst memory until the end. Chrissy's call had arrived as she'd emerged from the plane in Aberdeen. Of everything that had happened, the news of Margaret's death had hit Rhona the hardest, even though she was aware of its inevitability.

It had been the absence of hope she'd viewed in that hospital room. And nothing she could have done, or said, would have changed that.

*

As she departed the bathroom, she heard her mobile play one of Sean's jazz tunes, and remembered she'd set it up late last night at Olsen's. *In a definite moment of weakness.* Searching for the phone, Rhona vowed to change the ringtone back to normal as soon as possible.

Expecting Chrissy again, or maybe even Sean, she was surprised to find Isla's name on the screen.

Rhona's opening of 'Isla, how are you', was cut short by a breathless, 'I need to see you.'

Perturbed by the edge of fear in the girl's voice, Rhona immediately told her, yes, of course. 'D'you want to come over here?' she offered. 'Or would it be better if I came to you?'

'No, don't do that,' Isla said swiftly. 'What's your address?'

Rhona told her, then suggested Isla take a cab. 'There's a pepperoni pizza on its way, but I can supplement the order, if you're hungry,' she offered, only to discover that the line had gone dead.

Puzzled by this turn of events, Rhona discarded her bathrobe and got dressed again. In truth, the last thing she'd expected, or wanted tonight, was a visitor. Her dream had been to devour the pizza and immediately head for bed.

Yet, whatever was worrying Isla didn't sound as though it could be put off until tomorrow.

The pizza arrived first, promptly followed by her buzzer being played like a nuclear warning, which Rhona knew could only be announcing the arrival of Chrissy or more probably McNab. Unlatching the door, she retreated to the kitchen to begin eating, aware that her share of the said pizza was rapidly diminishing.

Moments later, McNab's vividly bruised face appeared round the door.

'All alone, I see.' He looked, or feigned, surprise at this. 'And with pizza.' McNab extracted a bottle of white wine from his pocket and plonked it on the table. 'It's cold,' he promised.

Rhona observed him go in search of glasses. 'So, not on the whisky?'

'No. Despite the fact that I've just escaped from the fucking tug boat from hell.'

'Your face . . .' she began.

'Bad, but not the most colourful part of my anatomy,' he told her. 'Although I assure you I'm still in perfect working order.'

The joke over, a silence fell between them.

'The boss,' Rhona ventured at last.

'We've talked,' McNab said swiftly. 'The funeral's on Friday.' He cleared his throat. 'Olsen called. There's been a possible sighting of Nilsen in the Spey Valley. He thinks, if it's true, Nilsen may have come back to retrieve any cargo that was on the plane. With the tug in custody, and his place with Hagen gone . . .' He tailed off when he spotted the look on Rhona's face.

'Was it the Polish girl, Annieska, that reported a sighting?' Rhona said.

'I'm not sure who reported it, but the Aviemore police are checking it out.'

'Annieska will need protection. He knows she can recognize him.'

'Why would he go near her? With all the media attention, that would be suicide,' McNab protested.

'I don't need a degree in forensic psychology to know, given half a chance, Nilsen will seek revenge on anyone who's thwarted him. That's why he abducted Isla in the first place.'

Saying Isla's name reminded Rhona how long it had been since the girl had called her. Glancing at the kitchen clock, she registered it had been almost an hour ago. She abandoned the pizza and went in search of her mobile.

'What's up?' McNab called after her.

Locating the phone in her bedroom, Rhona called Isla's number as she walked back through. It rang out half a dozen times then switched to voicemail.

'What wrong?' McNab tried again.

When Rhona quickly told McNab about Isla's call, he admitted he'd encouraged it.

'I called her after Olsen told me about the sighting. She sounded okay about it, but I thought if the press got onto the story, they might turn up on her doorstep. I said to speak to you if it all got too much for her.'

Rhona recalled the girl's voice. Her quick rejection that Rhona might come to her. Then the abrupt ending of the conversation, as though she may have changed her mind.

'It's been an hour since she planned to catch a cab from Byres Road. I think we should check she's okay.'

McNab glanced upwards as they drew alongside the red sandstone building. 'Isla's flat's on the top floor, and there's a light on. I suggest you give her another call. At least warn her we're here.'

Rhona did as asked, listening to the number ring out before switching again to voicemail.

She opened the car door. 'I'm going up,' she said.

Checking for the appropriate button on the entry phone, Rhona realized that the main door wasn't shut to. When pushed, it swung back, the bottom scraping noisily over the concrete floor as though the door had fallen on its hinges, or been recently forced open.

Reaching the upper landing, the first of the two doors indicated a Ms Taylor lived there. Rhona made for the second door. Painted a bright blue, the plaster plaque that stated both their names had the image of a snow-topped mountain as its backdrop.

Rhona pressed the bell a couple of times, hearing it echo noisily beyond the door. If Isla was in there, she couldn't fail to hear that.

When there was no response, Rhona pushed open the vertical brass letter box and shouted Isla's name.

McNab appeared beside her and added a heavy knock to her efforts.

'Could she be asleep?' McNab's expression suggested he was clutching at straws.

'The noise we're making could raise the dead.' Pulling out her mobile, Rhona tried the number again.

There was a moment's silence, then what she dreaded might happen, did.

'Listen,' Rhona said. The ringing is coming from inside.'

93

Isla was frightened, but no more so than when she'd been buried in the ice cave, or worse still, in her prison on the tug boat. She understood why Michael had urged her to go to Rhona's if she needed a place to hide out for a bit, but the thought that *he* could be so close had made her change her mind.

It was all she'd thought about on that boat, all she ever thought about. How she might replay what had happened that night on the mountain. Reverse their positions, so that he was the one to suffer. He was the one to die.

As soon as she was told he was in Scotland (maybe even looking for her), everything changed. That terrible feeling that there was nothing she could do, no way to feel different, to feel clean and whole again . . . all those thoughts were swept away.

That night on the tug boat when she'd sliced Brodie with the mirror glass, she'd known exactly where the point should go, where the artery was. But at the last minute she'd failed and he had lived.

She wouldn't make the same mistake again.

Lying in that bunk, the camera eye watching her, she'd made her plan, never thinking it might, just might, be possible to carry it out.

She smiled as she remembered how surprised Michael

had been by what she was capable of. *What anyone could be capable of given certain circumstances.* He'd insisted that he would take the blame for the attack on Brodie. She hadn't agreed, but she hadn't disagreed either.

He thought I did it because I was in shock, because of what happened on the boat.

But what she'd done to Brodie had been a practice run for what she might do to the Iceman, if given half a chance. Her resolve had begun in the ice cave, even as she'd descended into delirium. It had been there when she'd woken in the hospital, but the need for revenge against the Iceman then had been only for herself.

Then they told her about Lucy and Malcolm and then Gavin, and some part of her knew that the bastard who'd pushed her down the mountain had killed them all.

And she had told him where they were.

At first her fear had been larger than her resolve. She'd been frightened that *he* would come for her too, so she hadn't admitted to what had happened up there, hoping *he* would leave her alone.

I'm sorry, Gavin. So sorry.

But *he* hadn't given up. *He*'d come looking for her in Aviemore, because she'd been a coward the first time, and during that trip in the van she found she was no longer frightened of him. Hate had replaced fear.

The walk-in cupboard in the big old-fashioned kitchen used to be a coal store. That's what Gavin had told her when they'd bought the flat. He'd even pointed out the large hook on the stone wall outside the kitchen window, where, he said, they used to hoist up the bags of coal.

Even as she thought this, the echo of Gavin's voice in her head brought tears to her eyes.

435

The cupboard, he said, would house all their climbing gear, plus the sleeping bags and the tent. He'd arranged everything in there, the crampons, the ice axes, the boots, the copious ropes, all hanging up so that it was possible to walk in, switch on the light and choose what you needed.

The cupboard had been where she'd chosen to stay when she'd returned to the empty flat. She'd rolled out a mat and a sleeping bag on the floor and pulled the door closed. Surrounded by their gear, and with only the light from her head torch, she could imagine herself back in their tent . . .

Or even at the Shelter Stone.

Now, a skein of rope brushed her head and as she reached up to push it aside she realized her hand was wet and sticky. The stickiness was, she remembered, also on her face and hair. She glanced down and in the light from her head torch noted that the same mess covered the front of her sweater.

I should have been naked, like on the boat.

Isla contemplated standing up, but knew that was impossible, unless she could move the heavy weight from her legs.

I'll wait, she thought. *Michael will come and rescue me.*

94

Olsen lay on the bed, not seeking sleep. The last time he remembered sleeping all night had been at the Cairngorm Hotel. The whisky of course had played its part back then, but that hadn't been the real reason for his night's rest. Lying with Rhona, he accepted, had brought him peace that night.

Through the open curtains, the sky was brightened by stars and a full moon. It was strange to see a night sky that appeared better lit than during the daylight hours.

On the way back to the flat, he'd taken a stroll round the harbour, noting that the *Mariusud* had left her moorings. They were, of course, monitoring her route, which appeared to be heading northwards. Tor ran his empire from aboard his yacht, and was, it seemed, always on the move.

Their exchange of words on board the *Mariusud* had been informative. Hopefully more to him than Tor, who'd sought very hard to distance himself from the scandal of his ship, just now hitting the headlines, while promising rewards for the capture of the former employee who had committed such atrocious crimes.

And yet . . .

Olsen recalled the aspects of the now expensively dressed and smooth-talking businessman that weren't so obvious, some of which they shared. Both had been mad on motorbikes as teenagers, both had had tattoos done in defiance of their parents.

As for Tor's father . . . Olsen's own dad hadn't liked 'that man', as he'd called Bjarne Hagen. The distaste had only grown when Tor's father had moved from fishing into supplying the oil industry and got rich in the process, but that hadn't been the prime reason for his father's aversion. Bjarne Hagen had Nazi sympathies, and hadn't been afraid to say so.

The sins of the father . . .

Olsen, his top half bare, placed himself in such a way that he could view his back. The skull and crossbones he'd chosen as a rebellious teenager had been anarchic, a railing against conformity. Tor's, he recalled, had been as openly neo-Nazi as his father.

He watched as his mobile lit up. Seeing the name on the screen, he quickly answered.

They'd used the ringing of the mobile to find her, Rhona eventually following it into the kitchen, which like all the other rooms was freezing cold.

Already unnerved by the emptiness, McNab became even more so, as Rhona had approached a door in the kitchen. Before she opened it, he'd already noticed the thick viscous pool of blood that crept from under it.

Rhona had initially blocked his view, and McNab had hardly dared ask what was in there.

Then he'd registered the beam of the head torch and Isla's blood-splattered face.

Rhona watched as the stretcher bore Isla away.

'She's alive,' she told a silent McNab. 'Confused, maybe delirious, like in the ice cave, but alive.'

The other body lay bunched up where they'd shifted it to allow access to Isla. The cupboard, he could now see, was festooned with climbing equipment.

'She's been living in here since she got back?' McNab said, indicating the roll-out and sleeping bag and the scattered remains of food.

'She said she was waiting for him. She knew he would come,' Rhona said.

Nilsen's face wore a look of surprise, the ice axe deeply embedded between his eyes. That hadn't been the only weapon Isla had used against him, although the other injuries, Rhona said, might be postmortem. A crampon had been used to score his cheeks and eyes, and a razor-shaped ice saw had been used on his neck.

'Jesus,' McNab whispered. 'How do we save her from this?'

Rhona moved into the practical. 'I'll call Chrissy. It's late, but she'll want to be here to help me process the body.'

95

There was an apology to be made. For him, there would always be.

His excuse for not doing it had been the business with Isla, swiftly followed by Margaret's funeral.

McNab shut his eyes at the memory of that day. The boss, the two kids, grown teenagers now, but each with the crushed expression of a small child who'd just been told that Father Christmas was an elaborate lie.

The boss had been stoically calm, but then he'd always been like that, *even when I was throwing shit at him*. Yet anger, McNab suspected, beat under that solid exterior; he just wouldn't show it in front of his kids.

McNab couldn't begin to imagine what it must feel like to lose someone you love that much.

The place had been full, and pretty well everyone there had been a serving officer.

Funny, how even out of uniform, you could still tell.

He'd been to see Isla, he'd managed that at least. She'd seemed calm and less concerned about her predicament than McNab had been comfortable with. *I've evened things up*, she'd told him quietly.

It was a sentiment McNab was familiar with.

Emerging from his reverie, he checked where exactly

440

he'd walked to, knowing full well that he was back where he started.

Mannie threw him an inscrutable look on entry, or maybe it was just the piercings.

'She's here but not sure she'll see you,' he offered.

'I've come to apologize.' McNab gave his opening gambit.

'You're an arse, Detective Sergeant. I know that, you know that, but I'm not sure she does.'

'So there's hope?' McNab tried.

She was seated in a booth, waiting, he assumed, for her next appointment. She didn't register his arrival at first because she was deep in a magazine which, by its cover, contained all things Harley-Davidson.

He took that brief moment before she looked up to remind himself why he should stick with this girl, if she would have him.

Those blue eyes were observing him now. McNab imagined that they were reading his soul and finding it wanting.

'D'you ever have a holiday?'

Her unexpected question flummoxed McNab. 'I get holidays,' he offered. 'I don't always take them.'

'D'you fancy a trip up the A90?'

'To Aberdeen?' McNab groaned internally.

'Not that far. Just Brechin.'

McNab didn't fancy going anywhere on the A90, but wisely didn't say so.

'Netherton Cottage is where Sandy and Margaret Davidson lived before they emigrated to the States. They're the parents of the Harley brothers,' she said. 'The cottage has been restored by enthusiasts, like me.'

A dozen sarcastic put-downs occurred to McNab in that moment, but he fought them all, and tried instead to imagine holding tight to Ellie, for miles and miles and miles.

'I'd be up for that,' he said with a smile.

Some Months Later

Olsen had indicated he would be happy to walk in to Loch A'an on foot. Rhona, on the other hand, thought that a helicopter ride, no matter how she felt about flying, would be preferable. Olsen had conceded, indicating that once they'd examined the deposition site, and what CMR had found there, then he should be left behind. He wanted, he said, to spend some time in the mountains.

With memories of Marita, Rhona thought, glancing across at Olsen. There had been a change in his demeanour since January. Something had happened. Many things had happened.

He feels alive, maybe even content to be so.

The weather was clear, the sky vacant of clouds. As they'd passed over the funicular and the neighbouring ski slopes, Rhona had noted the gradual retreat of the snow. The ski fraternity hoped that the season might last into Easter, Kyle had told her; 'But, in Scotland, no one ever knows what the weather might offer.'

As it was, the vast quantities of snow that she remembered had gone, leaving only the deep gullies and the managed slopes. But that wasn't to say another fall might not happen at any time.

Loch Morlich was as slick and shiny as a mirror, much

443

like the day she'd walked along its shores with Sean. Among the trees, caravans and tents clustered, indicating that those who loved this place would come regardless of the weather, or even because of it.

When she could make herself heard over the noise of the chopper, she'd asked Kyle after Annieska. He'd told her how upset she'd been about Isla, knowing that something similar could well have happened to her. 'Annieska would have fought him off like a tiger,' he said.

Which is what Isla had done.

'What will happen to her?' Kyle had asked.

Rhona could only offer words of encouragement, although the exact outcome of the eventual trial she couldn't foretell. Isla had defended herself. That was all. Hidden in the cupboard, she'd used what was available to prevent being killed. As a result, her attacker had died.

Kyle was gesturing below. This time, they didn't have the luxury of landing on the relatively smooth surface of a frozen loch, but would come down as close as was possible to the shallows where they'd discovered the hidden cargo.

Rhona, this time with the bulk of Olsen beside her and not Harald, closed her eyes as the helicopter began to descend. When the feet finally settled, she felt the familiar rush of relief.

The landscape is so different from the last time I was here, she thought as she descended from the chopper. Then, snow and ice had defined everything, but now the bones of the mountain were exposed, all the softness of snow cover gone.

The loch was a long thin line of open water rather than an ice rink, the edges and beaches defined. Rhona remembered feeling her feet on the ice, the fear that it would not hold her. Now she walked along the loch's banks, across boulder-strewn slopes and coarse sandy stretches.

She recalled how they'd left the loch at its western end to walk to the Shelter Stone that fatal day. How, through the thinner ice, she'd viewed long tendrils of plants waving in the moving waters of the stream as it entered the loch. How they'd talked of the possibility of someone burying the cargo under the ice, how in the strategy meeting she'd disputed the likelihood of that.

She'd been wrong, of course, *because she'd forgotten that the ice wasn't uniformly thick, especially close to constantly moving water.*

'A group of walkers spotted something sticking up from the melting ice near the shore,' Kyle told them. 'At first, they'd thought it was a foot and, horrified, called the Rescue Centre.'

The wrapped bundle didn't require opening in order to make out that its contents consisted of a dozen tightly packed latex-clad kilo packages of what they assumed was cocaine.

The second item, a small white cool box without embellishment, Rhona did open. Inside was a spherical-shaped object.

'What is that?' Kyle said.

'I suspect it's an orb,' Rhona told him, 'a specially designed container for the transfer of human organs for transplant.' She turned to Alvis. 'Look at the name on the handle.'

The blue handgrip that lay embedded in the upper sphere of the white orb wore the name HAGEN CORP in raised lettering.

'Whether there's something inside there or not,' Rhona

said, 'Nilsen wouldn't have wanted to leave this on the plane as evidence of the Hagen connection.'

They'd already talked of how far down the road of prosecution they'd gone with Hagen. Nilsen's death had complicated matters, but Olsen had assured her that they had a case against Hagen. 'And we won't give up.'

Once they'd transferred the evidence to the helicopter, Olsen collected his walking gear and said his goodbyes.

As Rhona watched him trudge off, a flicker of concern must have shown on her face, because Kyle said, 'Don't worry. Alvis knows the hills round here well.'

'You met him when he climbed here before?' she said.

'We rescued him from the hill, when he lost his wife.'

In the walk to the village, Kyle had told Rhona the story of Marita's death. She and Alvis had been climbing on Cairngorm over the Christmas period. There had been an avalanche and Marita had been swept away.

'We were called out to search for her, but we never found her body until the following spring. She was under the ice on Coire an Lochain, carried there by the avalanche.'

Kyle had halted at that point, the emotion the memory brought still strong.

'Alvis never gave up until she was found. Like many of the people who lose a loved one on the mountain, he became a friend of the centre. Although, since her body was recovered, this is the first time he's returned.'

Rhona understood now why Olsen had chosen not to tell her the full details, especially when the investigation had brought him back here. His goodbye had been warm when he'd left her on the mountain.

'I'm in Aviemore for the weekend,' she'd told him. 'Maybe—'

'I won't be down in the valley,' he'd interrupted her, 'but if you're ever back in Stavanger . . . ?'

It was, she realized, one of the things people said when such a thing was unlikely to happen. Although it just might.

'Harald and I could end up at another forensic conference together,' she'd said with a smile.

'If you do, my advice is to avoid the tattoo parlour.'

He'd hugged her tightly then and his quiet words in her ear were heavy with emotion. *'Takk, Rhona . . . for alt.'*

Macdui's was packed, but Annieska had kept a table for them next to the stage. Rhona searched among the faces and saw him, talking animatedly to Gilly, the Irish guitarist he'd jammed with at Hogmanay. As though sensing Rhona's eyes on him, Sean turned and smiled a welcome.

Acknowledgements

Some years ago, I was asked to give a talk at the Edinburgh Film Festival on the similarities and differences between Nordic and Tartan Noir. My research for that talk began my fascination with the close links between Norway and Scotland, which I had first been made aware of when living in Orkney.

Thus the idea for a joint investigation between Police Scotland and the Stavanger HQ Politidistrikt Sør-Vest was born. The research for this book was only made possible with the help and enthusiasm of people on both sides of the North Sea, including:

In Norway

Egil Eriksen, Politiinspektør (Assistant Chief Constable) Joint Operational Unit/Chief of Staff

Ernst Kristian Rossebø, Politiinspektør (Assistant Chief Constable)

Kåre Moen Olsen, Politioverbetjent (Police Superintendent)

Narve Toppe, Politioverbetjent (Police Superintendent) function: Politispesialist Menneskehandel (Police Specialist Human Trafficking)

Bjørn J. Åmlid, Search and Rescue Coordinator at the Joint Rescue Coordination Centre (JRCC) South Norway (Stavanger)

In Scotland

Willie Anderson, Leader, Cairngorm Mountain Rescue (www.cmrt.org.uk)

Dr James H. K. Grieve, Emeritus Professor of Forensic Pathology at the University of Aberdeen

Ian Carruthers, Cairngorm Gliding Club

Michael Allan, Kirkwall, for his tug boat advice

Mona Røhne, Consul, Royal Norwegian Consulate General, Edinburgh

All the characters are fictional except for Gilly, an excellent musician, who does live and play in the valley, and is my neighbour.

Mary Grant, also from my home village of Carrbridge, donated an agreed sum to Cancer Research to have her name used in the latest book. Since she likes McNab, I gave her a chance to get to know him a little better.

Lin Anderson

CAIRNGORM
MOUNTAIN RESCUE TEAM

Cairngorm Mountain Rescue Team is a group of around forty volunteers who are ready to go to the aid of folk who get into difficulty in the mountains. The Cairngorms can be wonderfully exciting and give extremely rewarding days, but can at times be hugely challenging. Cairngorm Mountain Rescue Team is one of the busiest teams in Scotland, responding to around fifty incidents each year. When winter comes CMRT can expect call-outs. We train to an extremely high standard and are confident that we can deliver a world-class rescue service. Team members are on call constantly and freely give up their time to help fellow mountaineers.

It costs around £80,000 per year to run the team. The Scottish government give us around £18,000 per year towards our costs and Police Scotland also assists with funding of around £7,000 per year. The shortfall is made up from donations from folk we rescue.

Mountain Rescue is a police responsibility. However, Police Scotland could not resource mountain rescue in Scotland with its vast mountain ranges and remote locations. We have a great relationship with the police and also with Bristows, who support us with helicopter assistance.

There is a long history of members not even considering taking payment for their endeavours rescuing others, and long may this continue. As an emergency service we take great pride in our work and we are confident that our efforts are truly appreciated by fellow mountaineers.

To find out more, or to donate,
please visit www.cmrt.org.uk or
www.facebook.com/cairngormmrt.

Willie Anderson,
Leader, Cairngorm Mountain Rescue Team